Praise for beloved romance author Betty Neels

"Neels is especially good at painting her scenes with choice words, and this adds to the charm of the story."
—USATODAY.com's *Happy Ever After* blog on *Tulips for Augusta*

"Betty Neels surpasses herself with an excellent storyline, a hearty conflict and pleasing characters."
—*RT Book Reviews* on *The Right Kind of Girl*

"Once again Betty Neels delights readers with a sweet tale in which love conquers all."
—*RT Book Reviews* on *Fate Takes a Hand*

"One of the first Harlequin authors I remember reading. I was completely enthralled by the exotic locales... Her books will always be some of my favorites to re-read."
—*Goodreads* on *A Valentine for Daisy*

"I just love Betty Neels!... If you like a good old-fashioned romance...you can't go wrong with this author."
—*Goodreads* on *Caroline's Waterloo*

Romance readers around the world were sad to note the passing of **Betty Neels** in June 2001. Her career spanned thirty years, and she continued to write into her ninetieth year. To her millions of fans, Betty epitomized the romance writer, and yet she began writing almost by accident. She had retired from nursing, but her inquiring mind still sought stimulation. Her new career was born when she heard a lady in her local library bemoaning the lack of good romance novels. Betty's first book, *Sister Peters in Amsterdam*, was published in 1969, and she eventually completed 134 books. Her novels offer a reassuring warmth that was very much a part of her own personality. She was a wonderful writer, and she is greatly missed. Her spirit and genuine talent live on in all her stories.

BETTY NEELS

A Christmas Wish
& A Winter Love Story

HARLEQUIN® SPECIAL RELEASE

ISBN-13: 978-1-335-00791-9

A Christmas Wish & A Winter Love Story

Copyright © 2019 by Harlequin Books S.A.

A Christmas Wish
First published in 1996. This edition published in 2019.
Copyright © 1996 by Betty Neels

A Winter Love Story
First published in 1998. This edition published in 2019.
Copyright © 1998 by Betty Neels

Recycling programs for this product may not exist in your area.

Printed in U.S.A.

www.Harlequin.com

CONTENTS

A CHRISTMAS WISH

Chapter 1

The dim and dusty Records Office, tucked away in the depths of the hospital, was hardly a cheerful place in which to work, but the girl going back and forth between the long rows of shelves sounded cheerful enough, singing a medley of tunes as she sorted the folders into their right places with the ease of long practice.

She was a tall girl with a splendid shape, a beautiful face and a head of tawny hair which glowed under the neon lights, wearing a blouse and skirt and a cardigan which, although well-fitting, lacked any pretensions to high fashion.

Presently, her arms full, she went to the table against one of the whitewashed walls and laid them down, still singing—quite loudly since there was nobody there but herself, and she was far from the busy wards. 'Oh, what a beautiful morning...' she trilled, very slightly out of tune, and then stopped as the door was opened.

The door was a long way from the table; she had ample time to study the man coming towards her. He came unhurriedly, very tall and large in a beautifully tailored suit, fair hair already silver at the edges and a handsome face with heavy-lidded eyes. She hadn't seen him before, but then she seldom if ever went up to the hospital. When he was near enough she said cheerfully, 'Hello, do you want something?'

His good morning was uttered in a quiet voice. He laid a folder on the table. 'Yes, I asked for Eliza Brown's notes, not Elizabeth Brown's.'

'Oh, so sorry. I'll get them.' She picked up the discarded folder and went down one of the narrow passages between the shelves, found the folder, replaced the discarded one and went back to the table.

'Here it is. I hope it wasn't too inconvenient for you...'

'It was.' His voice was dry, and she went a little pink. 'Do you work here alone?'

'Me? Oh, no. Debbie has got the day off to go to the dentist.'

'And do you always sing as you work?'

'Why not? It's quiet down here, you know, and dim and dusty. If I didn't sing I might start screaming.'

'Then why not look for other employment?' He was leaning against the wall, in no hurry to be gone.

She gave him a tolerant look. 'We—that is, clerks and suchlike—are two a penny. Once we get a job we hang on to it...'

'Until you marry?' he suggested in his quiet voice.

'Well, yes.'

He picked up the folder. 'Thank you, Miss…?'

'Harding.' She smiled at him, for he seemed rather nice—a new member of the medical staff; a surgeon, since Mrs Eliza Brown was on the surgical landing. He nodded pleasantly and she watched him walk away; she wasn't likely to see him again. A pity, she reflected, making a neat pile of her folders ready for someone to fetch them from Outpatients.

The nurse from Outpatients was in a bad temper. Sister, she confided, was in a mood and there was no pleasing her, and the waiting-room was stuffed to the ceiling. 'And I've got a date this evening,' she moaned. 'At the rate we're going we'll be here all night, as well as all afternoon.'

'Perhaps Sister will have a date too,' comforted Miss Harding.

'Her? She's old—almost forty, I should think.'

The nurse flounced away, and was replaced almost at once by a tall, thin girl with a long face.

'Hi, Olivia.' She had a nice grin. 'How's trade? I want Lacey Cutter's notes. They're missing. I bet Debbie got our lot out yesterday—she may look like everyone's dream of a fairy on the Christmas tree, but she's not heart and soul in her job, is she?'

Olivia went across to the nearest shelf and began poking around. 'She's really rather a dear and so young… Here you are…'

'Well, you sound like her granny. She must be all of nineteen or so.'

'Twenty, and I'm twenty-seven—on the verge of twenty-eight.'

'Time you settled down. How's the boyfriend?'

'Very well, thank you. We'll have to wait for a bit, though.'

'That's rotten bad luck. I say, there's a new man on Surgical—a consultant all the way from somewhere or other in Holland—come to reorganise Mrs Brown's insides. It seems he's perfected a way of doing something or other; our Mr Jenks asked him here so that he can pick up some ideas.' She started for the door. 'He's nice.'

Olivia agreed silently. She didn't allow her thoughts to dwell upon him, though. For one thing she had too much to do and for another she had plenty of things— personal things—to think about. Rodney, for instance. She and Rodney had been friends for years, long before her father had died and left her mother poor, so that they had had to leave their home in Dorset and come to London to live with her grandmother in the small flat on the fringe of Islington. That had been four years ago, and Olivia had found herself a job almost at once to augment the two older ladies' income. It wasn't very well paid but, beyond an expensive education, she had no training of any sort and it was well within her scope. Indeed, after a couple of months she had realised that it was work which held no future, and longed to have the chance to train for something which would enable her to use her brain, but that was impossible. Making ends meet, even with her wages added, was a constant worry to her mother, and she couldn't add to that.

If her grandmother had been more amenable it might have been possible, but Mrs Fitzgibbon, having offered them a home, considered that she had done her duty and saw no reason to forgo her glass of sherry, her special tea from Fortnum and Mason, and her weekly visit to the hairdresser, with a taxi to take her there and back. She had sent away her daily cleaner too, saying that her daughter was quite capable of keeping the flat tidy, but graciously allowed a woman to come once a week to do the heavy housework.

It wasn't an ideal situation, but Olivia could see no way out of it. Nor could she see any chance of marrying Rodney, a rising young man on the Stock Exchange, who had reiterated time and again that once he had got his flat exactly as he wanted it, and bought a new car, they would marry. Four years, thought Olivia, sitting at the table eating sandwiches and drinking pale and tepid tea from a flask, and there's always something—and anyway, how can I marry him and leave Mother? She'll be Granny's slave.

The day's work came to an end and she got into her raincoat, tied a scarf over her glorious hair, locked the door and took the key along to the porter's lodge. She stood in the entrance for a moment, breathing in the chill of the evening, and made for the bus-stop.

It was an awkward journey to and from the hospital, and the buses at that time of day were packed. Olivia, her junoesque proportions squeezed between a stout matron carrying a bag full of things with sharp edges and a small, thin man with a sniff, allowed her thoughts to wander to the pleasanter aspects of life. New clothes—it was high time she had something different to wear when she went out with Rodney; a legacy from some unknown person; finding a treasure-trove in the tiny strip of garden behind her grandmother's flat; being taken out to dinner and dancing at one of the best hotels—the Savoy for instance—suitably dressed, of course, to eat delicious food and dance the night away. She realised with something of a shock that it wasn't Rodney's face on her imaginary partner but that of the man who had asked why she sang while she worked. This won't do, she told herself, and frowned so fiercely that the thin man recoiled.

The street where her grandmother had her flat was suited to that old-fashioned word 'genteel'. The tiny front gardens were all alike—laurel bushes, a strip of grass and two steps leading to the front door behind which was another smaller door, leading to the flat above. All the windows had net curtains and, beyond distant good mornings and good evenings, no one who lived there spoke to anyone else.

Olivia hated it; she had spent the first year that they were there planning ways of leaving it, but her mother felt it to be her duty to stay with Granny since she had offered them a home and Olivia, a devoted daughter, found it impossible to leave her mother there though she disliked it, she suspected, just as much as she did.

She got out her key, unlocked the door, and went into the little hall, hung her outdoor things on the old-fashioned oak stand and went through to the sitting-room. Her mother looked up with a smile.

'Hello, love. Have you had a busy day?'

Olivia bent to kiss her cheek. 'Just nicely so,' she said cheerfully, and crossed the small room to greet her grandmother. Mrs Fitzgibbon was sitting very upright in a Regency mahogany open armchair with a leather seat and wooden arms, by no means comfortable but the old lady had inherited it from her mother, who had acquired it from some vague relation who had been married to a baronet, a fact which seemed to ensure its comfort from Mrs Fitzgibbon's point of view. She said severely now, 'Really, Olivia, your hair is badly in need of a brush, and is that plastic bag you're carrying really necessary? When I was a gel...'

Olivia interrupted her quickly. 'I called in at Mr Patel's as I got off the bus—he had some nice lettuces; you like a salad with your supper...'

She made a small comic face at her mother and went to her room—very small, just room for the narrow bed, the old-fashioned wardrobe and a small chest of drawers with an old-fashioned looking-glass on it. Rodney had phoned to say that he would come for her at around seven o'clock so she poked around, deciding what she would wear, and then, undecided, went to the kitchen to start the supper. Lamb chops, mashed potatoes and carrots. There were a couple of tomatoes in the fridge and a rather wizened apple. She contrived a small salad with the lettuce, laid the table in the poky dining-room beside the kitchen, and went to pour her grandmother's sherry. She poured a glass for her mother too, ignoring her grandmother's sharp look.

She went back to the kitchen and the phone rang. It was probably Rodney, to say that he would be earlier than they had arranged. She turned down the gas and went into the hall where the phone was. It *was* Rodney. His faintly pompous, 'Hello, Olivia,' sounded rather more so than usual, but it was one of the things she had decided didn't matter.

Her own 'hello' was cheerful. 'If you're coming earlier than you said, I won't be ready…'

'Well, as a matter of fact, I can't come, Olivia—something's turned up and I can't get away.'

'Oh, bad luck. Let's go out tomorrow instead.'

She felt faintly uneasy at his hesitancy. 'It's a long job,' he said finally, 'I may have to go away…'

She was instantly sympathetic. 'Big business and very hush-hush?' she wanted to know. 'Well, if it's going to give you a leg-up, I won't crumble. You don't know when you're going?'

'No, no, nothing's settled yet. I'll give you a ring. Can't stay any longer now.'

She was disappointed but still cheerful. 'Don't get overworked…' His goodbye interrupted her, and she put the phone down with the feeling that something was wrong. My imagination, she told herself, and went to stretch the supper to allow for another person and then tell her mother that she wouldn't be going out after all.

Her grandmother, listening, observed tartly, 'You can't rely on the young men of today. Rodney's eyes are too close together.'

Which was difficult to refute, for they were.

The week wore on. Debbie enlivened the days with her chatter, confiding with a good deal of giggling the carrying on of her various boyfriends, while Olivia patiently did most of the filing and hurriedly resorted Debbie's careless efforts.

'You ought to go out more often,' declared Debbie as they drank their mid-morning coffee. 'Never mind that Rodney of yours,' she added with an unconscious lack of concern, 'it would do him good. He ought to be taking you out somewhere every blessed moment he's free. Give him a ring and say you want to go out this evening; there's a smashing film on at the Odeon in Leicester Square.'

'He's not here. I mean he's had to go away—something to do with his firm.'

'Don't you know where he is?'

'No idea.'

'Ring wherever he works and ask for his address. He's not MI5 or anything hush-hush is he?'

'No—something in the Stock Exchange.'

Olivia got up and went back to the shelves with a pile of folders just as the door opened.

Here he was again, as elegant as she remembered him and as calm. She left Debbie to ask him if she could help him.

'Indeed you can. Once again I have here Mrs Elizabeth Brown's notes, but it is Mrs Eliza Brown who is my patient.'

Debbie beamed at him. 'Oh, sorry—that's me. I make mistakes all the time—only Olivia puts them right and covers up for me. It's a dull job, you know.'

'I can appreciate that.' He looked past her and wished Olivia a bland good morning. 'Olivia,' he added, and before she could answer that he said, 'And you, young lady, what is your name?'

'Debbie—what's yours? You aren't on the staff, are you? Have you come here to brush up your technique or something?'

'Or something?' He smiled a little. 'And my name is van der Eisler.'

'Foreign,' said Debbie. 'You wouldn't know it except you're on the large side. Got friends here?'

'Er, yes, I have.'

Olivia, feverishly seeking Mrs Eliza Brown's notes, clutched them thankfully and took them to him. He took them from her with a brief nod. 'I mustn't keep you from your work,' he observed. He sounded as though he had already dismissed them from his thoughts.

As he closed the door behind him Debbie said, 'Olivia, why did you hide? Isn't he great? A pity you found the notes just as I was going to suggest that he might like me to show him round the town.'

Olivia said sharply, 'You wouldn't, Debbie—he might be someone fearfully important.'

'Him? If he were, he wouldn't come down to this hole, would he? He'd send a nurse. I think he rather liked me.'

'Why not? You're pretty and amusing, and you can look small and helpless at the drop of a hat…'

'Yes, I know, but you're not just pretty, Olivia, you're beautiful. Even if you are—well, amply curved.'

Olivia laughed then. 'Yes, I know, and as strong as a horse. Even if I were to faint there wouldn't be anyone strong enough to pick me up off the floor.'

'He could—strong enough to carry a grand piano upstairs without a single puff…'

'I'm not a grand piano!' laughed Olivia. 'Look, we'd better get on, it's almost time for our dinner-break.'

They went to the canteen in turn and Debbie, going first, came back with disquieting news. 'You know that girl who works in the secretary's office?'

'Mary Gates,' said Olivia. 'What's happened to her—got engaged?'

'No, no. She told me something she'd overheard. There's not enough money—they are planning to make redundancies—one's going to have to do the work of two. Olivia, supposing it's me who goes? Whatever shall I do? With Dad out of work, Mother's part-time job barely pays the rent.'

Olivia said matter-of-factly, 'Well, we don't know anything yet, do we? They could have been talking about another hospital—and I don't see how they could get rid of one of us.'

'Well, I do. You're too nice, Olivia. Do you suppose these people who sit around talking over super food and drink care a damn if they cut back on jobs, just as long as they can save some money for some pet scheme or other? We aren't people to them, just stat-stat...'

'Statistics,' supplied Olivia. 'Debbie, don't worry. If—and I say it's a big if—one of us is given the sack it will be me; they have to pay me more because I'm older. You're not yet twenty-one so you earn less.'

Debbie looked relieved and then asked, 'But what will you do?'

'Oh, I can turn my hand to anything,' said Olivia airily, and took herself off to the canteen. She shared a table with two clerks from Admissions, older than herself, competent, hard-working ladies both.

'There's a nasty rumour going round,' one of them said to Olivia as she sat down. 'They're cutting down, starting with the domestics and then us.'

'Is it just a rumour or for real?'

'We're to get letters tomorrow, warning us, and at

the end of next week we shall get notes in our pay envelopes if we're to be made redundant.'

Olivia pushed shepherd's pie and two veg around the plate. Something would have to be done about Debbie. Her own wages would be missed at home, but they wouldn't starve and they had a roof over their heads whereas Debbie's family would be in sore straits. She ate prunes and custard, drank the strong tea, and went along to the secretary's office.

He wasn't there, but his PA was—a nice girl, who Olivia knew slightly. 'I want you to help me,' said Olivia in a no-nonsense voice.

She was listened to without interruption, then the PA said, 'I'll do my best—shall I say that you've got another job lined up? The hospital manager will be delighted; he's going to be very unpopular.'

Olivia went back to her work, and spent the rest of the day doing her best to reassure Debbie.

It was pay-day in the morning and, sure enough, everyone had a letter in their pay-packet, setting out the need to retrench, cut costs and improve hospital services.

'How will they do that if there aren't enough of us to go round?' demanded Debbie. 'I shan't dare tell my mum.'

'Not until next week,' cautioned Olivia. 'You haven't got the sack yet.'

The next week crawled to its end and Olivia opened her pay packet to find a note advising her that she had been given a week's notice. Although she had been fairly sure that she would be the one to go, it was still a blow—mitigated to a certain extent by Debbie's relief.

'Though how I'll manage on my own, I don't know,' she told Olivia. 'I'm always filing things wrong.'

'No, you aren't. Besides, you'll be extra careful now.'

'What about you? Have you got a job to go to?'

'Not yet, but we can manage quite well until I find something else. Look, Debbie, we've got next week— let's check the shelves together so that everything is OK before I go.'

She hadn't told her mother yet; that could wait until she had actually left. Thank heaven, she reflected, that it's spring. We can economise on the heating if only we can get Grandmother to co-operate, and not go round the flat turning on lights that aren't needed and switching on the electric fires and then forgetting them. It was, after all, her flat—something of which she reminded them constantly.

They worked like beavers during the next week, and although Olivia was glad that she need no longer work in the dreary underground room she was sorry to leave Debbie. She put a brave face on it, however, assured her that she had her eye on several likely jobs, collected her pay-packet for the last time and went home. The bus was as usual crowded, so she stood, not noticing her feet being trodden on, or the elderly lady with the sharp elbows which kept catching her in the ribs. She was regretting leaving without seeing that nice man who had been so friendly. Doubtless back in Holland by now, she thought, and forgotten all about us.

She waited until they had had their supper before she told her mother and grandmother that she had lost her job. Her mother was instantly sympathetic. 'Of course you'll find something else much nicer,' she said, 'and until you do we can manage quite well...'

Her grandmother wasn't as easy to placate. 'Well, what do you expect?' she wanted to know. 'You're not really trained for anything, and quite right too. No gel should have to go out to work—not people of our background...' Mrs Fitzgibbon, connected by marriage to the elderly baronet and his family who never took any notice of her, was inclined to give herself airs.

'All the same,' she went on, 'of course you must find something else at once. I, for one, have no intention of living in penury; heaven knows I have sacrificed a great deal so that both of you should have a home and comfort.' She stared at her granddaughter with beady eyes. 'Well, Olivia, perhaps that young man of yours will marry you now.'

'Perhaps he will,' said Olivia brightly, thinking to herself that perhaps he wouldn't—she hadn't heard from him for almost three weeks—and anyway, the last time they had been out together he had told her that he had his eye on a new car. The nasty thought that perhaps the new car might receive priority over herself crossed her mind. Rodney had never been over-loving, and she had told herself that it was because they had known each other for some time and his feelings had become a trifle dulled. Perhaps it was a good thing that they hadn't seen each other for a few weeks; he might look at her with new eyes and ask her to marry him. Something he had not as yet done, although there was a kind of unspoken understanding between them. Anyway, now was not the time to worry about that. A job was the first thing she must think about.

She had been given good references but it seemed that her skills as a filing-clerk weren't much in demand. She went out each day, armed with the details of suitable jobs culled from the newspapers, and had no luck at all; she couldn't use a word-processor; she had no idea how to work with a computer, and a cash register was a closed book as far as she was concerned. The week was almost up when Rodney phoned. He sounded—she thought for a word—excited, and she wondered why. Then he said, 'I want to talk to you, Olivia, can we meet somewhere? You know how it is if I come and see you at your grandmother's place…'

'Where do you suggest? I've things to tell you too.'

'Yes?' He didn't sound very interested. 'Meet me at that French place in Essex Road this evening. Seven o'clock.'

He rang off before she could agree.

He had sounded different she reflected as she went to tell her mother that she would be out that evening. Mrs Fitzgibbon, reading the newspaper by the window, put it down. 'And high time too,' she observed. 'Let us hope that he will propose.' She picked up her paper again, 'One less mouth to feed,' she muttered nastily.

Perhaps you get like that when you're old, thought Olivia, and gave her mother a cheerful wink. It was of no use getting annoyed, and she knew that her grandmother's waspish tongue was far kinder to her mother, an only daughter who had married the wrong man—in her grandmother's eyes at least—and it was because Olivia was more like her father than her mother that her grandmother disliked her. If she had been slender and graceful and gentle, like her mother, it might have been a different kettle of fish…

She dressed with care presently, anxious to look her best for Rodney. The jacket and skirt, even though they were four years old, were more or less dateless, as was the silk blouse which went with them. She didn't look too bad, she conceded to herself, studying her person in her wardrobe mirror, only she wished that she were small and dainty. She pulled a face at her lovely reflection, gave her hair a final pat, and bade her mother goodbye.

'Take a key,' ordered her grandmother. 'We don't want to be wakened at all hours.'

Olivia said nothing. She couldn't remember a single evening when Rodney hadn't driven her back well before eleven o'clock.

Perhaps, she mused, sitting in an almost empty bus, she and Rodney had known each other for too long. Although surely when you were in love that wouldn't matter? The thought that perhaps she wasn't in love with him took her breath. Of course she was. She was very fond of him; she liked him, they had enjoyed cosy little dinners in out of the way restaurants and had gone to the theatre together and she had been to his flat. Only once, though. It was by the river in a new block of flats with astronomical rents, and appeared to her to be completely furnished, although Rodney had listed a whole lot of things which he still had to have. Only then, he had told her, would he contemplate settling down to married life.

It was a short walk from the bus-stop and she was punctual but he was already there, sitting at a table for two in the corner of the narrow room. He got up when he saw her and said 'hello' in a hearty way, not at all in his usual manner.

She sat down composedly and smiled at him. 'Hello, Rodney. Was your trip successful?'

'Trip? What…? Oh, yes, very. What would you like to drink?'

Why did she have the feeling that she was going to need something to bolster her up presently? 'Gin and tonic,' she told him. A drink she disliked but Debbie, who knew about these things, had assured her once that there was nothing like it to pull a girl together.

Rodney looked surprised. 'That's not like you, Olivia.'

She didn't reply to that. 'Tell me what you've been doing, and why do you want to talk, Rodney? It's lovely to see you, but you sounded so—so urgent on the phone.'

He had no time to answer because the waiter handed them the menus and they both studied them. At least Olivia appeared to be studying hers, but actually she was wondering about Rodney. She asked for mushrooms in a garlic sauce and a Dover sole with a salad, and took a heartening sip of her drink. It was horrible but she saw what Debbie meant. She took another sip.

Their talk was trivial as they ate. Whatever it was Rodney had to tell her would doubtless be told over their coffee. He was an amusing companion, going from one topic to the next and never once mentioning his own work. Nor did he ask her about her own job or what she had been doing. She would tell him presently, she decided, and suppressed peevish surprise when he waved away the waiter with his trolley of desserts and ordered coffee. She was a girl with a healthy appetite and she had had her eye on the peach pavlova.

She poured the coffee and caught Rodney's eye. 'Well?' she asked pleasantly. 'Out with it, my dear. Have you been made redundant—I...'

'Olivia, we've known each other a long time—we've been good friends—you may even have expected us to marry. I find this very difficult to say...'

'Well, have a go!' she encouraged in a matter-of-fact voice which quite concealed her shock. 'As you say, we've been friends for a long time.'

'Perhaps you've guessed.' Rodney was having difficulty in coming to the point.

'Well, no, I can't say I have.'

'The truth is I haven't been away—I wanted to tell you but it was too difficult. I'm in love. We're going to be married very shortly...'

'Before you get your new car?' asked Olivia. Silly, but what else to say?

'Yes, yes, of course. She's worth a dozen new cars. She's wonderful.'

She looked at him across the table. Her grandmother was quite right: his eyes were too close together.

She smiled her sweetest smile. 'Why, Rodney, how could I possibly have thought such a thing? I'm thinking of getting married myself.'

'You could have told me...'

She gave him a limpid look. He looked awkward and added, 'What's he like? Has he got a good job? When are you getting married?'

'Handsome. He has a profession and we intend to

marry quite soon. Enough about me, Rodney, tell me about the girl you're going to marry. Is she pretty? Dark? Fair?'

'Quite pretty. I suppose you'd call her fair. Her father's chairman of several big companies.'

'Now that is nice—a wife with money-bags.'

He looked astounded. 'Olivia, how can you say such a thing? We're old friends—I can't believe my ears.'

'Old friends can say what they like to each other, Rodney. If I stay here much longer I might say a great deal more, so I'll go.'

He got to his feet as she stood up. 'You can't,' he spluttered. 'I'll drive you back; it's the least I can do.'

'Don't be a pompous ass,' said Olivia pleasantly, and walked out of the bistro and started along the street to the bus-stop.

Sitting in the bus presently, she decided that her heart wasn't broken. Her pride had a nasty dent in it, though, and she felt a sadness which would probably turn into self-pity unless she did something about it. Of course it happened to thousands of girls, and she had to admit that she had thought of him as part of her pleasant life before her father had died, hoping that somehow or other she could turn back the clock by marrying him. She had been fond of him, accepted him as more than a friend, and although she had been in and out of love several times she had never given her whole heart; she had supposed that she would do that when they married.

'How silly can you get?' muttered Olivia, and the severe-looking couple sitting in front of her turned round to stare.

'I counted my chickens before they were hatched,' she told them gravely, and since it was her stop got off the bus.

'It must be the gin and tonic,' she said to herself. 'Or perhaps I'm in shock.' She unlocked the front door and went in. 'I'll make a strong cup of tea.'

The sitting-room door was half open. 'You're home early, darling,' said her mother. 'Is Rodney with you?'

Olivia poked her head round the door. 'I came home by bus. I'm going to make a cup of tea—would you like one?' She glanced across the room to her grandmother. 'And you, Granny?'

'You have refused him,' said Mrs Fitzgibbon accusingly. 'It is time you learnt on which side your bread is buttered, Olivia.'

'You're quite right, Granny, his eyes are too close together, and he's going to marry the daughter of a chairman of several large companies.'

'Do not be flippant, Olivia. What do you intend to do?'

'Put the kettle on and have a cup of tea,' said Olivia.

'You're not upset, darling?' asked her mother anxiously. 'We all thought he wanted to marry you.'

Olivia left the door and went to drop a kiss on her mother's cheek.

'I'm not a bit upset, love.' She spoke with matter-of-fact cheerfulness because her mother did look upset. Unlike her daughter she was a small, frail little woman, who had been cherished all her married life and was still bewildered by the lack of it, despite Olivia's care of her. 'I'll make the tea.'

She sat between the two of them presently, listening to her grandmother complaining about the lack of money, her lack of a job, and now her inability to get herself a husband. 'You're such a big girl,' observed Mrs Fitzgibbon snappily.

Olivia, used to this kind of talk and not listening to it, drank her tea and presently took herself off, washing the tea things in the kitchen, laying her grandmother's breakfast tray and their own breakfast, before she at last closed the door of her room.

Now, at last, she could cry her eyes out in peace.

Chapter 2

Debbie looked up from the piles of folders on the table in the Records Office as the door opened and Mr van der Eisler came in. Her disconsolate face broke into a smile at the sight of him, although she asked with a touch of wariness, 'Oh, hello—have I sent the wrong notes up again? I can't get anything right, and now that Olivia's not here to sort things out for me I seem to be in a muddle the whole time.'

He came unhurriedly to the table and glanced at the untidy piles on it. 'I expect it will get easier once you have got used to being on your own. And I do want some notes, but there's no hurry. Do you have to file these before you go home?'

She nodded. 'It's almost five o'clock and I daren't leave them until the morning; there'll be some bossy old sister coming down and wanting to know where this and that is. Interfering so-and-sos.'

'Ten minutes' work at the most,' declared Mr van der Eisler. 'I'll sort them into alphabetical order, you file them.'

'Cor—you mean you'll give a hand? But no one ever does...'

He was already busy, and after a moment she did as he suggested.

'I expect you miss Olivia,' he observed presently.

'You bet I do.'

'Does she come to see you?' His voice was casual.

'No, worse luck. Doesn't live near here. Her granny's got a flat Islington way; she and her mum have to live with her since her dad died, left them badly off. Not that Olivia told me much—shut up like an oyster when it came to her private life.' She laughed. 'Not like me.'

He handed her another pile of folders. 'You live near the hospital?'

'Five minutes walk. Me dad's out of work, Mum's part-time at the supermarket. Was I scared that I'd get the sack? Olivia didn't tell me, but the girl in the office said as how she had another job to go to. This wasn't her cup of tea. Been to one of those la-di-da schools, I dare say. Always spoke posh, if you see what I mean.'

Mr van der Eisler agreed that he saw. 'Not many jobs going in Islington, I should have thought.'

'Not where her granny lives—one of those dull streets with rows of houses with net curtains. Had a soppy name too—Sylvester Crescent.'

Mr van der Eisler's heavy lids drooped over the gleam in his eyes.

'Very fanciful,' he agreed. He handed over the last pile, waited while Debbie filed the folders away and came back to the table, made his request for the notes he needed, listened with a kind smile to her thanks and, with the folder under his arm, took himself off.

Debbie, bundling herself into her jacket, addressed the tidy shelves. 'Now there's a real gent for you. That was a nice chat too—no one knows how dull it is down here these days.'

Mr van der Eisler, discussing the next day's list with the senior surgical registrar and the theatre sister, wrung from that lady a reluctant assent to begin operating at eight o'clock in the morning instead of an hour later, gave her a smile to set her elderly heart beating a good deal faster, and took his leave.

'That man could wring blood from a stone,' declared Sister. 'I'm sure I don't know why I let him get away with it...'

The registrar laughed. 'Go one with you, you know you'd agree to open theatre at six a.m. He's a splendid man and a first-rate surgeon. He's been here several weeks now, hasn't he? Handed over several new techniques, shared his ideas with Mr Jenks—between them they've perfected them—look at Mrs Eliza Brown.'

'He'll be leaving soon, I suppose.'

'Yes, and Mr Jenks is going back with him for a week or two.' He turned to leave. 'He'll be back, I've no doubt—goes all over the place—got an international reputation already. Not bad for a man of thirty-six.'

He wandered away to look out of a window, in time

to see Mr van der Eisler's grey Bentley edge out of the hospital forecourt.

'I wonder where he goes?' he reflected aloud.

Mr van der Eisler was going to Islington to cast his eye over Sylvester Crescent. He found it eventually, tooling patiently up and down identical streets of identical houses, and drove its length until he came to Mr Patel's shop, still open.

Mr van der Eisler, who never purchased food for his excellently run household, nevertheless purchased a tin of baked beans, and engaged Mr Patel in casual conversation. Naturally enough the talk led to observations about Islington and Sylvester Crescent in particular.

'A quiet area,' observed Mr van der Eisler. 'Flats, I suppose, and elderly people.'

'You are right, sir.' Mr Patel, with no customers in the offing, was glad of a chat. 'Many elderly ladies and gentlemen. It is not a street for the young—and an awkward journey to the day's work. There is Miss Harding, who lives with her grandmother Mrs Fitzgibbon at number twenty-six, but I see her each morning now, and I think she must no longer work.' He sighed. 'Such a beautiful young lady too. It is dull here for the young.'

Mr van der Eisler murmured suitably, remarked that Mr Patel and his shop must be a boon and a blessing to the neighbourhood, professed himself pleased with his purchase, paid for it and got back into his car. Number twenty-six was in the middle of the row of houses and there was a chink of light showing between the heavy curtains pulled across the windows on the ground floor.

He drove back to the quiet, elegant street near Sloane Square and let himself into his ground-floor flat to be met in the hall by his housekeeper.

'You're late, sir. Your dinner's ready and I'll be so bold as to say that it won't keep for more than five minutes.'

'Excellent timing, Becky.' He patted her plump shoulder and added, 'Here's something for you to amuse yourself with.'

He handed her the bag and she looked inside. 'Mr Haso, whatever will you do next? Since when have you eaten baked beans?' She gave him a suspicious glance. 'What did you want to buy it for?'

'Well, I needed to ask for some information and the best place was the local corner shop.'

Miss Rebecca Potts, elderly now, and long since retired as his nanny, was his devoted housekeeper whenever he was in London, and she knew better than to ask him why he wanted to know something. All the same, she gave him a sharp look. 'I'll dish up,' she told him severely. 'You've time for a drink.'

He picked up his bag and went down the hall to his study and sat down in the leather armchair drawn up to the fire. A drink in his hand, he sat quietly, busy with his thoughts, until Becky knocked on the door.

It was two days before he had the opportunity to return to Sylvester Crescent. He had no plan as to what he intended doing, only the vague idea of seeing Olivia going to or from the shops or, failing that, calling at her grandmother's flat with some trumped-up story about Debbie. Perhaps, he thought ruefully, once he had met her again, he would be able to get her off his mind.

He saw her as he turned the car into Sylvester Crescent, coming towards him in her well-worn jacket and skirt, her bright hair a splash of colour in the sober street, a shopping basket over her arm. He slowed the car and stopped as she drew abreast of it.

The quick colour swept over her face when she saw him but she said composedly, 'Why, good morning, Mr van der Eisler. Have you a patient to visit?'

Mr van der Eisler, an upright and godfearing man, could on occasion lie like a trooper when it was necessary, and he considered that this was necessary. 'No, no, I have a few hours with nothing to do. I am looking for a suitable flat for a friend who will be coming to London for a few months.'

He got out of the car and stood beside her. 'A most delightful surprise to meet you again. I was in the Records Office only the other day and Debbie was telling me how much she missed you. She tells me that you have another job—how fortunate...'

'Yes, isn't it?' She caught his eye and something in his look made her add, 'Well, no, I haven't actually. I told her that because she was worried about getting the sack. Is she managing?'

'Tolerably well.' He smiled down at her, looking so kind that she had a sudden urge to tell him about her grandmother, whose nasty little digs about her not getting a job had done nothing to make her fruitless efforts easier to bear. Instead she said briskly, 'It's nice meeting you, but don't let me keep you from your house-hunting.'

Mr van der Eisler, never a man to be deterred from his purpose, stood his ground. 'As to that—' he began, and was interrupted by the sudden appearance of Rodney, who had pulled in behind the Bentley and was grabbing Olivia by the arm.

'Olivia—I had to come and see you...'

Olivia removed her arm. 'Why?' she asked coldly.

'Oh, old friends and all that, you know. Wouldn't like you to think badly of me—you did walk off in a huff...' He glanced at Mr van der Eisler towering over him, a look of only the faintest interest upon his face. 'I say,' Rodney went on, 'is this the lucky man?' He shook hands, beaming. 'Olivia said she was going to get married—described you to a T. Well, everything works out for the best, doesn't it?' He patted Olivia's shoulder. 'You don't know what a relief it is to see you so happy. Can't stop now. My regards to your mother. Bye, old girl.'

He flashed a smile at them both, got back into his car, and drove away without looking back.

Olivia looked at her feet and wished she could stop blushing, and Mr van der Eisler looked at the top of her head and admired her hair.

'I can explain,' said Olivia to her shoes. 'It wasn't you I described; I said he was very large and had a profession and a great deal of money.' She added crossly, 'Well, that's what any girl would say, isn't it?'

Mr van der Eisler, used to unravelling his patients' meanderings, hit the nail on the head accurately. 'Any girl worth her salt,' he agreed gravely. 'Did you actually intend to marry this—this fellow?'

'Well, you see, I've known him for years, long before Father died and we had to move here, and some-

how he seemed part of my life then and I didn't want
to give that up—do you see what I mean?'

She looked at him then. He looked just as a favourite uncle or cousin might have looked: a safe recipi-
ent of her woes, ready to give sound advice. She said
breathlessly, 'I'm sorry, I can't think why I'm boring
you with all this. Please forgive me—he— Rodney
was something of a shock.'

He took her basket from her. 'Get in the car,' he suggested mildly. 'We will have a cup of coffee before you
do your shopping.'

'No, no, thank you. I can't keep you standing around
any longer. I must get the fish…'

As she was speaking she found herself being urged
gently into the Bentley. 'Tell me where we can get coffee—I passed some shops further back.'

'There's the Coffee-Pot, about five minutes' walk
away—so it's close by. Aren't I wasting your time?'
she asked uneasily.

'Certainly not. In fact, while we are having it I shall
pick your brains as to the best way of finding a flat.'

The café was in a side-street. He parked the car,
opened her door for her, and followed her into the half-
empty place. It was small, with half a dozen tables
with pink formica tops, and the chairs looked fragile.
Mr van der Eisler, a man of some seventeen stones in
weight, sat down gingerly. He mistrusted the chairs
and he mistrusted the coffee which, when it came, jus-
tified his doubts, but Olivia, happy to be doing something different in her otherwise rather dull days, drank
hers with every appearance of enjoyment and, while

she did, explained in a matter-of-fact way about living with Granny.

'I dare say you are glad to have a brief holiday,' he suggested, and handed her the plate of Rich Tea biscuits which had come with the coffee.

'Well, no, not really. I mean, I do need a job as soon as possible, only I'm not trained for anything really useful...' She went on in a bright voice, 'Of course I shall find something soon, I'm sure.'

'Undoubtedly,' he agreed, and went on to talk of other things. He had had years of calming timid patients, so he set about putting Olivia at her ease before mentioning casually that he would be going back to Holland very shortly.

'Oh—but will you come back here?'

'Yes. I'm an honorary consultant at Jerome's, so I'm frequently over here. I do have beds in several hospitals in Holland—I divide my time between the two.' He drank the last of the coffee with relief. 'Do you plan to stay with your grandmother for the foreseeable future?'

'Until I can get a job where Mother and I can live together. Only I'm not sure what kind of job. There are lots of advertisements for housekeepers and minders, although I'm not sure what a minder is and I'm not good enough at housekeeping, although I could do domestic work...'

He studied the lovely face opposite him and shook his head. 'I hardly think you're suitable for that.'

Which dampened her spirits, although she didn't let him see that. 'I really have to go. It has been nice meeting you again and I do hope you find a nice flat for your friend.'

He paid the bill and they went outside, and she held out a hand as they stood on the pavement. 'Goodbye, Mr van der Eisler. Please give Debbie my love if ever you should see her. Please don't tell her that I haven't got a job yet.'

She walked away quickly, wishing that she could spend the whole day with him; he had seemed like an old friend and she lacked friends.

By the time she reached the fishmonger's the fillets of plaice that her grandmother had fancied for dinner that evening had been sold and she had to buy a whole large plaice and have it filleted, which cost a good deal more money. Olivia, her head rather too full of Mr van der Eisler, didn't care.

Naturally enough, when she returned to the flat she was asked why she had spent half the morning doing a small amount of shopping. 'Loitering around drinking coffee, I suppose,' said Mrs Fitzgibbon accusingly.

'I met someone I knew at the hospital; we had coffee together,' said Olivia. She didn't mention Rodney.

Mr van der Eisler drove himself back to his home, ate the lunch Becky had ready for him, and went to the hospital to take a ward-round. None of the students trailing him from one patient to the next had the least suspicion that one corner of his brilliant mind was grappling with the problem of Olivia while he posed courteous questions to each of them in turn.

Olivia had let fall the information that her grandmother had once lived in a small village in Wiltshire, and in that county was the school where his small goddaughter was a boarder, since her own grandmother lived near enough to it for her to visit frequently during term-time. In the holidays she went back to Holland to her widowed mother, who had sent her to an English school because her dead husband had wanted that. Might there be a possibility of Mrs Fitzgibbon and Nel's grandmother being acquainted, or at least having mutual friends? It was worth a try…

'Now,' he said in his placid way, 'which of you gentlemen will explain to me the exact reasons which make it necessary for me to operate upon Miss Forbes?'

He smiled down at the woman lying in bed and added, 'And restoring her to normal good health once more?' He sounded so confident that she smiled back at him.

It was several days before Mr van der Eisler was free to drive down to Wiltshire. His small goddaughter's grandmother lived in a village some five or six miles from Bradford-on-Avon and on that particular morning there was more than a hint of spring in the air. The sky was blue—albeit rather pale, the sun shone—as yet without much warmth, and the countryside was tipped with green. Slowing down to turn off the road on to a narrow country lane leading to Earleigh Gilford, he told himself that he was wasting his time: Olivia had probably got herself a job by now and the chance of her grandmother knowing Lady Brennon was so remote as to be hopeless.

He had phoned ahead and they met as old friends, for both of them had been charged with the care of Nel during term-time. Lady Brennon was a youthful sixty, living in a charming little Georgian villa on the edge of the village, busy with her garden and her paint-

ing, her dogs and the various village committees on
which she sat.

'So nice to see you, Haso.' She looked sad for a moment. 'It seems a long time since Rob's wedding and
your coming here as his best man. I miss him still, you
know. Thank heavens we have little Nel.'

They went into the house together and he asked, 'Is
she here for the weekend?'

'Yes, she'll be here on Saturday. There's no chance
of your staying until then?'

'I'm afraid not. I'll try and get down before the Easter holidays. In fact, I might be able to arrange things
so I can drive her over to Holland.'

'That would be splendid.' Lady Brennon poured
their coffee. 'The child's very fond of you. Rita phoned
this week; she said that you had been to see her when
you were in Holland. Was she happy?'

'I believe so. She likes her work and she has her
friends. She misses Nel, but she wants to carry out
Rob's wishes.'

'Of course. Probably she will change her mind and
come to live here later on.'

'Perhaps.' He put down his cup. 'Lady Brennon, did
you know a Mrs Fitzgibbon—oh, it would be some
years ago? I believe she lived somewhere near Bradford-
on-Avon.' He dredged up the bits and pieces of information that Olivia had let drop. 'I believe her daughter
married a man called Harding—rather a grand wedding in Bath Abbey...'

'Fitzgibbon? The name rings a bell. You know her?
She is a friend of yours? Rather an elderly one...'

'No. No. I have never met her.'

'Then I can tell you that she was a most disagreeable woman—I remember her very well—bullied her daughter, a rather sweet little thing. Married against her wishes, I believe. I met her several times. The daughter had a little girl—the husband died, I believe, it was in the *Telegraph* a few years ago. Dear me, it must be almost thirty years since we met.'

She gave Haso an enquiring look. 'May I know why you are interested in her?'

'I have met her granddaughter—she was working at Jerome's as a filing clerk, got made redundant and can't find work. She and her mother live with Mrs Fitzgibbon and I gather are not happy there. Olivia has said very little about herself, and I am barely acquainted with her, but she got herself sacked so that the girl she worked with, who desperately needs the money, could keep her job, and I wondered if you knew of anything...' He smiled then. 'I have no personal interest in her; it is only that I feel that she deserves a better chance.'

'Is she educated?'

'Yes. Intelligent and well-mannered, speaks well, very level-headed, I should imagine. She is lacking in the essentials—typing, shorthand, computers—all that kind of thing. She had no need to work until her father died.'

'Is she very young?'

'I should guess her to be in her late twenties.' He frowned. 'I think she would make a good governess if they still have such people.'

'Not to any extent, I'm afraid. She might get a post in a private school, with the smaller children perhaps, or even taking drama classes for the older girls. What do you want me to do, Haso?'

'I'm presuming on your kindness, Lady Brennon. If you should hear of something which might suit Olivia, could you possibly find a reason to write to Mrs Fitzgibbon, mention the job, and say how you wished you knew of someone suitable to fill it? It is most unlikely, I know, but a kindly fate does occasionally step in. I don't wish her to know that I have had anything to do with it.'

'I will be most discreet. It would certainly be an ideal solution, and since it would appear to Mrs Fitzgibbon that it was through her good offices that Olivia should hear of the job she might present no difficulties. I'll ask around, my dear. There are any number of schools around here, you know.'

They talked about other things then, and Olivia wasn't mentioned again, and later, as he drove himself back to London, Mr van der Eisler's thoughts were of the week ahead of him—Liverpool and then Birmingham, then back to Holland...

It was three weeks before he returned to his London home. It was late at night on the first day of his return before he had the leisure to sit down and read his post. A good deal of it he consigned to the wastepaper basket and then put the rest aside while he read the letter from Lady Brennon. She had telephoned him, she wrote, and Becky had told her that he was away so it seemed best to write. By the greatest good fortune, she went on, Nel had told her on her half-term holiday that Miss Tomkins, who it seemed was a Jill of all trades at the school, had left suddenly and there was

no one to take her place. Lady Brennon had acted with
speed, recommended Olivia to the headmistress on the
strength of his recommendation, and written to Mrs
Fitzgibbon, using the excuse that a friend of hers had
seen Olivia's mother when she was in London and that
that had prompted Lady Brennon to write to her. A lie,
of course, she had put in brackets. The letter continued:

> 'The upshot is, Haso, that your protégée is at
> Nel's school, working out the rest of the term,
> and if she proves satisfactory she is to be taken
> on on a termly basis and allowed to live in a small
> annexe of the school. Very poky, so Nel tells me,
> but there is room for her mother if she cares to
> go and live there. The salary is barely adequate
> but, as it has been pointed out, she has no quali-
> fications. I hope this news will relieve you from
> further feelings of responsibility towards Olivia
> who, from Nel's account, is well-liked and appar-
> ently happy. Do phone when you can spare the
> time, and tell me how Rita is. Still as pretty as
> ever, I'm sure, and such a delightful companion.
> I hope you found time to see something of her.'

He smiled as he put the letter down, aware that it
was Lady Brennon's dearest wish that he should marry
Rita. What could be more suitable? They knew each
other well, her husband had been his closest friend and
he had a strong affection for Nel. It was all so suitable,
and he supposed that it would be a sensible thing to do.
His thoughts strayed to Olivia; when he went to school
to collect Nel he would make a point of seeing her. He

supposed his interest in her had been heightened by the injustice of her dismissal. Now that she was settled he could dismiss her from his mind, where she had been lurking for the past few weeks.

Lady Brennon's letter had reached Mrs Fitzgibbon at an opportune moment; there had been another letter in the post that morning, for Olivia, regretting that the post of assistant in a West End florist's had been filled. Olivia, listening to her grandmother's diatribe on the inability of young women to find suitable employment, allowed most of it to flow over her head—she knew it by heart now. Instead she wondered about Mr van der Eisler. Back in Holland, she supposed, and best forgotten.

A silence from her grandmother made her look up. The old lady was reading the letter in her hand, and when she had finished it she re-read it. She spoke. 'It is a good thing that I have a number of connections with those of a good background.' She put the letter down. 'This is a letter from an old friend who by some remote chance has written to me—you need not concern yourself as to the details.' She waited for Olivia to say something but, since she had no intention of concerning herself, she went on writing a note for the milkman and remained silent. 'There is a position at a girls' school outside Bath—making yourself useful, as far as I can see. The current holder has had to leave for some family reason and the headmistress is anxious to find someone suitable at the earliest possible moment. She suggests that you telephone and make an appointment. The headmistress is coming to London—let me see—tomorrow.'

Olivia felt her grandmother's beady eyes fixed on her. 'Just what kind of a job is it, Granny?'

'How should I know? You must bestir yourself and go and find out for yourself.'

'After I have talked to Mother. She'll be back presently, we can talk about it then.'

Mrs Harding thought it might be quite nice. 'Of course I shall miss you, love, but you'll have the school holidays.'

'Yes, Mother. If it were possible, would you come and live there if I get the job—I dare say we could rent a small house nearby.'

'Oh, darling, that would be lovely, to live in the country again.' They were in the kitchen with the door shut but all the same she lowered her voice. 'I'm sure Granny would like to have the flat to herself again. Do go and see this lady.'

So Olivia went, and since it was a fine day and quite warm she wore her jersey dress—like most of her clothes not the height of fashion but still elegant. She hoped the headmistress would like her, for although she didn't like leaving her mother she would be able to send her money and they might even take a holiday together. Her grandmother, she felt sure, would be only too glad to be rid of them both.

The headmistress, Miss Cross, was middle-aged, plump and good-natured and, when Olivia explained that she had no experience of any sort other than filing documents, waved this aside. 'Come and see how you get on,' she suggested. 'There are still several weeks of this term—almost a month. If you like the work and we like you, then I'll employ you on a termly basis. You'll live in, of course—there's a small annexe you'll have to yourself. I don't know if you have a dependant? I've no objection to a mother or sister living with you. The salary is fair, I consider, and you get your meals while you're on duty. You're not married or anything like that?'

'No, Miss Cross.'

'Then you ought to be, a lovely creature like you! Start on Saturday. Let me know what time your train gets to Bath; I'll have you met.'

Coincidence, good luck, fate—call it what you will, reflected Olivia, now something or someone had allowed her to fall on her feet. She had been at the school for two weeks and she was happy. She wasn't sure just what she could call herself, for no two days were alike, but being a practical girl she took that in her stride. She plaited small heads of hair, inspected fingernails if Matron was busy, played rounders during the games hour, took prep with the older girls, drove Miss Cross into Bath whenever she needed to go, washed the same small heads of hair, comforted those who had grazed knees and in between these tasks filled in for anyone on the staff who happened to be absent for any reason. It was a good thing that she had been good at games at school, for she found herself on several occasions tearing up and down the hockey pitch blowing her whistle. She had enjoyed it too.

The annexe had been a pleasant surprise. It was small, certainly, but there was a living-room with an alcove used as a kitchen, a shower-room and, up the narrow staircase, two bedrooms just large enough to

contain a bed, a chest of drawers and a chair. Whoever
had had the place before her had been clever with orange boxes, disguising them as bedside tables, bookshelves and an extra seat with a cushion neatly nailed
on to it.

If Miss Cross was to keep her on then there was no
reason why her mother shouldn't come and stay with
her, even live with her. The school was in the country, but there was a good bus service into Bath from
the village.

Olivia, on this particular Saturday morning, was
rounding up the smallest of the girls ready for their
weekly swimming lesson in the heated swimming-pool
in the school's basement. The sports mistress would
be in charge but Olivia was expected to give a hand,
something she enjoyed, for she was a good swimmer
and teaching the sometimes unwilling learners was a
challenge. She marched them through the school and
down the stairs to the basement, saw them into their
swimsuits, counted heads, and handed them over to
Miss Ross, a small woman with a powerful voice, before going off to get into her own swimsuit.

While Miss Ross got on with the actual teaching
Olivia patrolled the pool, swimming slowly, making
sure that the children were under her watchful eye,
encouraging the faint-hearted to get their feet off the
bottom of the pool and applauding those who were
splashing their way from one side to the other. Once
they were all out of the water she wrapped herself in
a robe and went round checking that each child had
showered, finding mislaid garments and then collecting
up the sopping wet swimsuits. Only when they were

all once more dressed and handed over to Miss Ross
could she shower and dress herself, before hurrying
back to the school to the recreation room where she was
expected to dispense hot cocoa and biscuits. It should
have been her half-day but the junior housemistress
had gone to a wedding, which meant that Olivia would
have the charge of fifteen little girls until they were in
bed and hopefully asleep. On Sunday it was her turn
to shepherd the whole school, under the guidance of
Miss Cross and two of the senior teachers, to the village church.

Getting ready for bed that night she owned to being
tired but not unhappy. The pleasure of sitting in one's
own small home, drinking a last cup of tea before getting into bed, was by no means overrated. Perhaps she
was a born old maid? She dismissed the idea. 'I shall
be quite honest,' she told herself, since there was no
one else to tell, 'I should like to marry and have a kind
and loving husband and a handful of children. Never
mind if there isn't enough money, just enough to live
on comfortably, and keep a dog or two, and cats of
course, and perhaps a donkey...'

She put down her mug and took herself upstairs
to bed.

There was the opportunity to think quietly the next
morning; the Reverend Bates' sermons were long and
soothing, a fitting background for her thoughts, and
since they were simple and blameless she didn't suppose that God would mind. The end of term was approaching, she reflected, and she would go back to
Granny's flat for almost three weeks. During that time
she would have to see what her mother thought of com-

ing to live with her, always providing Miss Cross decided to keep her. The letters from her mother had been cheerful; Olivia thought that without her her mother and grandmother lived fairly amicably together. All the same, it would be nice if her mother was to pay a visit.

She glanced down the row of childish faces under the school straw hats. Perhaps she had found her niche in life. She sighed and a small hand crept into her lap and caught at her fingers, and she made haste to smile down at the upturned little face. It was Nel, a nice child whose Granny lived not too far away. She had confided in Olivia one day that her daddy had died and Mummy lived in Holland, but she was here at school because her Daddy had wanted her to be educated in England. 'I'm half-Dutch,' she had said proudly, and instantly Mr van der Eisler's handsome features had swum before Olivia's eyes. She had wiped him out at once and suggested a game of Ludo.

With the end of term so near now there was an air of bustle and excitement at the school. Regular lessons gave way to exams, an expedition to the Roman Baths in Bath, while Miss Prosser, who taught history and geography, recited their history, and finally the school play, with its attendant rush and scurry behind the curtains, and then the last morning, with all the little girls—dressed, cases packed, forgotten articles sought for and found—waiting anxiously to be collected.

The first parents arrived soon after breakfast and after them a steady stream of cars. Olivia, finding stray children, tying shoelaces and straightening hats, remembered that she was to drive Miss Cross into Bath that afternoon. When she got back she would be able to pack her own things and by then she would know if she was to return...

Half the children had gone when Nel, standing beside her, gave a squeal of delight. 'There's Mummy and Uncle Haso.' She gave Olivia a poke to make sure that she was listening. 'We're going to Holland...'

'How nice,' said Olivia, and allowed her lovely mouth to drop open. Mr van der Eisler, accompanied by an elegantly dressed woman with fair hair cut in a boyish crop, was coming towards her.

Her surprise was so absolute that she could think of nothing to say, but Mr van der Eisler, whose surprise wasn't surprise at all but actually looked genuine, nodded in a friendly way. 'Olivia—who would have expected to see you here?'

He suffered a hug from Nel and turned to his companion. 'Rita, this is a young lady who worked at Jerome's. Nel's mother, Olivia—Mrs Brennon.'

'How nice,' said Mrs Brennon, which could have meant anything. She didn't shake hands but kissed her daughter and said, 'Shall we go, Haso? Lady Brennon will be expecting us...' She smiled briefly at Olivia. 'Goodbye. I do hope that Nel has been good.'

She didn't wait for an answer but took Nel's hand and went to the car.

Mr van der Eisler paused just long enough to ask if she was happy.

'Oh, very, thank you.' Just in case he hadn't been listening, she added, 'I have never been so happy.'

His, 'Splendid,' was uttered in a detached manner, as was his goodbye.

Chapter 3

'Well, what did you expect?' Olivia asked her face in the looking-glass in her bedroom. 'I dare say he had a job to remember you—she was very attractive, and he's fond of Nel.'

She started to pack in a half-hearted way, filling in time until Miss Cross was ready to go into Bath.

In Bath she was told to park the car and return in two hours' time, which meant that she had the leisure to look at the shops and have a cup of tea. On the way back to the school Miss Cross, who had hardly spoken, said, 'Come to my study before supper this evening, Olivia. You will be returning home tomorrow?'

'Yes, Miss Cross.' It would have been nice if she could ask if she was to be given the sack but she didn't dare. Fate had been tiresome enough without being tempted.

She had almost finished her packing when Miss Cross's maid came to summon her to the study. It was rather worse than a visit to the dentist, thought Olivia, tapping on the door, and when bidden to enter, she entered.

'Sit down Olivia.' Miss Cross looked her usual cosy self, but that was nothing to go by. 'You have been happy here?' she asked.

'Yes, Miss Cross.'

'Good. You have been most satisfactory—fitted in very well, and the children like you. I am prepared to engage you for the following term, Olivia. The same conditions will apply. You play tennis and croquet?'

'Yes, Miss Cross.'

'Good. Please return here two days before the pupils.' She consulted the desk calendar. 'That will be the fifteenth of April. Let us know the time of your arrival and you will be met at the station.' She smiled. 'You are willing to agree to these arrangements?'

'Yes, Miss Cross. I shall be happy to come back for the next term.'

'That is settled, then. I'll say goodbye now, since you will be leaving in the morning and I shall be engaged until lunchtime.'

Olivia took herself back to her room, dancing along the corridors, humming cheerfully. I may be an old maid, she reflected, but at least I'm a happy one.

It was raining when she arrived at Sylvester Crescent and the row of prim houses looked unwelcoming, but her mother was at the window looking out for her so that she forgot the sudden pang of homesickness for the school. They talked and laughed together, happy to see each other again, until Mrs Fitzgibbon came to join them.

She offered a cheek for Olivia's kiss. 'I was resting but of course your voices disturbed me. Are you back for good?'

'No, just for the Easter holidays. You look well, Granny.'

'My looks have never pitied me, I keep my sufferings to myself.'

Olivia winked at her mother and went to get the tea. Granny was only bearable if one treated her as a joke.

Her mother came into the kitchen presently. 'It's only because Granny had her nap disturbed,' she explained, looking worried. 'I'm sure she's very glad to see you, love.'

Olivia warmed the teapot. 'Yes, dear. How do you like the idea of coming to stay with me for a week or two during the term? I won't be free, of course, but there's a good bus service into Bath and I'll be there in the evenings once I'm off-duty.'

'I'd like that, darling. I won't be in the way?'

Olivia gave her parent a hug. 'Never, my dear. The country's lovely and the village is sweet—very close to Bath, of course, but it's still country.'

Life was a little dull after the bustle of school but she had saved a good deal of her salary and took her mother out and about on modest expeditions.

'This is lovely,' said Mrs Harding, perched on top of a sightseeing bus, doing the rounds of the famous landmarks. 'It all looks quite different from up here.' She turned to look at Olivia. 'I think your grandmother is quite pleased to have the flat to herself. She's been on her own for so long now, it must be tiresome for her to have me there all the time.'

Olivia nodded. 'I know, Mother. I hope that after this next term Miss Cross might take me on permanently, then you can come and live with me. The annexe is small but there's room for two. You could join the WI again, and help with the church flowers and do the shopping. It would be like old times.'

There were two days left of her holiday when Mrs Fitzgibbon, answering the phone, said, 'It's for you, Olivia. A man—surely not Rodney? You had better take it.'

She handed over the receiver to Olivia and sat back in her chair, shamelessly eavesdropping.

'Yes?' She spoke sharply.

'Cold steel,' said Mr van der Eisler in her ear. 'Did you think that it was Rodney?'

She turned her back on her grandmother so that that lady wouldn't see the pleased smile on her face. 'No, it's the surprise.'

'I shall be driving Nel back to her school; we'll collect you on the way.'

'Oh, but I…'

'Go back two days earlier, so Nel tells me. She is going to stay with her grandmother before she returns to school.'

'Oh—well.'

'Olivia, I must beg you to stop bleating and listen to what I have to say. We shall call for you in two days' time. Ten o'clock in the morning.'

He rang off without so much as a goodbye and she put down the receiver.

'Who was that?' demanded her grandmother. 'You didn't have much to say for yourself.'

'There was no need,' said Olivia, and went in search of her mother.

Waiting for him to arrive two mornings later, her mother said, 'I've made some coffee, Olivia. Do you suppose he'll drink it?'

'Mother, I have no idea. He sounded so business-like on the phone. Perhaps he's in a tearing hurry to get to Nel's granny.'

'Well, it's ready if he wants it,' said Mrs Harding. 'But I do hope he stops for just a.few minutes—your grandmother is anxious to see him.'

'I was afraid of that,' said Olivia.

He was punctual, standing there at the front door, handsome, self-assured and elegant in his tweeds. Nel was hanging out of the car window and Olivia said at once, 'Oh, do come in. Nel might like a drink and the coffee's ready. Unless you're in a tearing hurry?'

'Coffee would be nice and I'm sure Nel wants to see where you live.'

He opened the car door for the little girl, who skipped up to Olivia and lifted her face for a kiss. 'I'm so glad you're coming back to school,' she declared. 'I hope you stay there forever and ever.'

Olivia stooped her splendid person. 'How very kind of you to say so, Nel. Come in and have a glass of lemonade.'

Her mother came into the hall then, and Mr van der Eisler shook her hand and smiled down at her and said all the right things in his pleasant voice before Nel was introduced too.

'There's coffee,' said Mrs Harding a little breathlessly. This marvellous man—and Olivia knew him. Her thoughts were already wrapped in bridal veils and orange blossom. 'Come in and meet my mother.'

Mrs Fitzgibbon was sitting in her chair, the uncomfortable one, and one glance at her sufficed to cause Mr van der Eisler to adopt his best bedside manner. He became all at once self-assured, deferential, and the epitome of a successful man who knew his own worth without being boastful about it.

Olivia watched her grandmother's starchy manner melt into graciousness while they drank their coffee and Nel roamed round the room, looking at photographs and ornaments. Olivia had got up to show Nel the little musical box on the side-table when she heard her grandmother remark, 'Of course, Olivia is quite unskilled. Never needed to work, and now that it is unfortunately necessary her limitations are evident. But there, I am an old woman now and must bear with life's disappointments.'

Olivia supposed that she herself was one of them and was much heartened by Mr van der Eisler's grave, 'I must beg to differ, Mrs Fitzgibbon. Olivia is fulfilling a much-needed want at Nel's school. It needs patience and kindness and understanding to care for children. I am told by the headmistress that she is worth her weight in gold.'

He turned to Mrs Harding then. 'You must be so relieved to know that Olivia is so successful. The school is a good one and the surroundings are pleasant. Perhaps you will be able to visit her?'

'Well, Olivia has asked me to go and stay with her during the term. I know I shall love it.'

Mrs Fitzgibbon sighed loudly. 'How lucky that you are young enough to go and enjoy yourself. I, alas, must stay here alone.'

Mr van der Eisler said easily, 'I'm sure you would have no difficulty in finding a companion, Mrs Fitzgibbon.' He stood up. 'You must forgive me if we leave now. Nel's grandmother will be waiting for her.'

There was a small delay while Olivia whisked Nel upstairs, but not before the child had said in a clear little voice, 'Just in case I should get caught short before we get to Granny's house. Uncle Haso is in a hurry.'

'The age of modesty is long past,' said Mrs Fitzgibbon faintly.

'The seat's big enough for the pair of you,' said Mr van der Eisler, fastening the seatbelt round the pair of them and casting the luggage into the boot, then getting in beside them and driving away with a wave.

'I don't like your granny,' said Nel, and her godfather turned a laugh into a cough.

'She's old,' said Olivia, and added, 'I expect when you're old you sometimes say things that other people just think to themselves...'

'She said you were one of life's disappointments...'

'Yes, well, I suppose I am from her point of view. You see, she expected me to grow up small and dainty and get married when I was young.'

'Aren't you young?'

'Not very, I'm afraid.'

'Well, you're very pretty. I must see if I can find a husband for you,' said Nel importantly.

Mr van der Eisler spoke in a matter-of-fact manner. 'Most ladies prefer to choose their own husbands.'

Olivia, rather red in the face, said smartly, 'I had always thought that the men did the choosing.'

Mr van der Eisler chuckled. 'Don't you believe it. They may be under the impression that they are doing so but it is after all the lady who decides.'

'I shall marry a prince,' said Nel, a remark which Olivia welcomed with relief since it was a topic which lasted until they were clear of the last of the suburbs and driving smoothly on the motorway.

As they neared Bath she was rather surprised when he turned off the motorway and took the Chippenham road, and still more surprised when he turned off once more into a narrow country road.

He glanced at his watch. 'On time,' he observed. 'Your granny will be waiting.'

'The school—?' began Olivia.

'After lunch. Lady Brennon asked me to bring you to lunch with her first.'

'But I don't know her.'

'Of course you don't; you've never met her,' he uttered, in such a reasonable voice that she couldn't think of an answer.

Meeting Lady Brennon, Olivia wished that she had a granny like her—smiling a welcome, delighted to see them all, hugging her small granddaughter, including Olivia in the talk. They sat down presently, in the rather old-fashioned dining-room, to crown of lamb and new potatoes and vegetables, which Lady Brennon assured her had been grown in her garden.

'You like the country?' she asked.

Olivia said that yes, she did and that she had spent her youth not so very far away from Earleigh Gilford. She offered no further details, though, and her hostess didn't question her further, and presently, after a stroll around the garden, Mr van der Eisler suggested that they should go.

Olivia got ready without any fuss and went out to the car, with Nel hanging on to her arm, after bidding Lady Brennon goodbye and thanking her with her nice manners so that that lady observed to Mr van der Eisler, 'A charming girl. Miss Cross has got herself a gem there. You did well to busy yourself with her welfare, Haso. She has no idea that it was you?'

'No, and I do not wish her to know either. I'm glad that she has found a worthwhile job.'

'You'll come back for tea before you return to town? We haven't had a talk about Rita.'

At the school he took the key to the annexe and opened the door, fetched her luggage and then inspected the small living-room, wandering slowly round, looking at the cheap and cheerful prints on its walls, peering at the bookshelves. Before the mantelpiece he stopped to pick up the card on it.

'Well, well, so Rodney has invited you to his wedding. Surely an unkind thing to do? Turning the knife in the wound, as it were?'

'Don't be absurd,' said Olivia. 'There isn't a wound. I dare say he asked me because we've known each other for a long time.'

Mr van der Eisler flipped the card with a nicely man-
icured fingernail. 'With companion…' He turned the
card over and read aloud, '"I don't know the name of
your fiancé but we hope that he will come with you".'

Olivia was very pink in the face. 'It's really none
of your business…'

'Ah, but it is, Olivia. I may be only a chance acquaintance but I do not wish to see you humiliated.
You intend going?'

She found herself telling him that she did. 'It's half-
term so I'm free, and the wedding is at Bradford-on-
Avon. I suppose she lives there.'

'I shall escort you. You will wear a pretty frock
and one of those hats women wear at weddings, and I
shall do you proud in a morning suit. You will linger
in Rodney's memory in the best possible light—well-
dressed, carefree, and safe in the knowledge that your
future is secured.'

'Are you joking?' asked Olivia.

'Certainly not; marriage is no joking matter.'

She said rudely, 'How would you know, you aren't
married, are you?' She wished the remark unsaid at
once, but it was too late. She muttered, 'Sorry, that
was dreadfully rude.'

He said silkily, 'Yes, it was. None the less, I shall
accompany you to this wedding. It is the least I can do.'
He put the card back and went to the door. 'We seem
fated to meet unexpectedly, do we not?'

She nodded. 'Yes, but you don't need to come to
the wedding, you know. You could be busy in the city
or something.'

'I rather fancy seeing Rodney safely married.'

He opened the door and she held out a hand. 'Thank you very much for bringing me back. I'm most grateful.' She added, 'Nel is fortunate to have such a loving granny.'

'Yes.' He took her hand and smiled very kindly at her. 'Which cannot be said for *you*, Olivia.'

She said gruffly, 'Well, she's old, and I'm not what she hoped for.'

He bent and kissed her lightly. 'Goodbye, Olivia.'

She stood at the door and watched him drive away. The kiss had rather shaken her but she didn't let it linger in her thoughts. She went back into the living-room and picked up the wedding invitation. 'I very much dislike being pitied,' she said savagely. 'For two pins I shan't go to Rodney's wedding.'

She had no chance to brood. She settled into her little home, joined the rest of the staff for a discussion as to the term's objectives, and was detailed to check the dormitories with the matron and then, when the children arrived, to get them unpacked and settled in—several hours of hard work and bustle, followed by a number of tearful sessions with those who wanted to go home again.

The weeks, slow to pass at first, quickened their pace; she enjoyed her job despite the fact that she was at everyone's beck and call. She found herself painting scenery for the next end-of-term play, acting as ballboy when she wasn't showing the smallest of the pupils how to hold their racquets, playing rounders, or organising games when the weather was wet. From time to time in unexpected emergencies she found herself taking a reading lesson. Not the least of her tasks was caring for the children's clothes, also helping Matron with their hair-washing, driving to the doctor or the dentist and once, when Cook was ill, cooking school dinner.

Half-term suddenly loomed, and Rodney's wedding. She hadn't heard from Mr van der Eisler and she stifled disappointment. Still, she would go to the wedding. Miss Cross was generous with the car; she was sure that she would be allowed to borrow it since it would be half-term and there would be very few people remaining at school.

On her next day off she took herself into Bath; a suitable outfit was essential. All her summer dresses she had had for several years, and Rodney would recognise any of them. Something simple and cheap in a silvery-green, which wouldn't clash with her hair and her pansy eyes, would do nicely.

She found what she wanted after a long search. A plain, delicate green sheath with short sleeves and a modest neckline. Its fabric looked like linen although it was nothing of the sort. It was one of dozens on a rail in British Home Stores, but she guessed that the guests at Rodney's wedding would hardly shop there and wouldn't recognise it for what it was. She had her Italian sandals from better days, and a pair of good stone-coloured gloves. It was just a question of a hat.

She saw several that she liked, but their prices were well beyond her purse. Getting tired and cross, she finally found what she wanted in a department store— a perfectly plain wide-brimmed straw which she bore back to the haberdashery department so that she might match up a ribbon with the dress. The ribbon was expensive, but it transformed the hat and matched the dress exactly. She spent the rest of her day off tying it around the hat, leaving a large silky bow at the back. It might not be a model hat but it gave a very good imitation of one.

Half-term came and the school emptied for four days. Olivia, plaiting Nel's hair and making sure that her school hat was at the correct angle, was touched when the child said, 'I wish you were coming to Granny's with me, Olivia.'

'Well, that would be fun, my dear, but you'll have a lovely time with your granny. I expect she's got all kinds of treats waiting for you.'

Nel nodded. 'Do you ever have treats?' she wanted to know.

'I'm going to a wedding the day after tomorrow, and I've got a new hat.'

'Not your wedding?' asked Nel anxiously.

'No, my dear. Now off with you, Miss Cross wants you all to be in the hall by ten o'clock.'

The place was very empty without the children. The rest of the day was spent clearing up after the last of them had gone and putting everything ready for their return. The next day, with time to herself and only a handful of the staff still there, Olivia took herself off for a long walk and then spent plenty of time washing her hair and doing her nails. Miss Cross had given her permission to take the car and everything was arranged. She went into the garden behind the annexe, her hair still damp and hanging down her back, only to be called back indoors because she was wanted on the phone.

Mr van der Eisler's 'Hello, Olivia' was uttered in a voice of casual calm.

'Oh, it's you…'

'Indeed, it is I. Did I not say that I would telephone?'

'Well, yes, you did. Only it's tomorrow—I thought you'd forgotten.'

'Certainly not. Now, let us see. We need to be at the church fifteen minutes or so before the bride, do we not? Fifteen minutes to drive there, half an hour at your place for coffee and a chat. The wedding is at noon, is it not? I'll be with you at eleven o'clock.'

'Very well, I'll have coffee ready. Where are you? It sounds as though someone's washing up.'

'I've been operating; they're clearing Theatre.'

She wished she could think of something clever in answer. All she said was, 'Won't you be too tired? I mean, to drive down here tomorrow. You'll be careful?'

Mr van der Eisler suppressed a laugh. 'I will be careful, Olivia.'

'I expect you're busy. Goodbye, and thank you for ringing.'

She went back to her room and dried her hair, telling herself sternly not to get too excited, he was only doing what he had promised to do. It was kind of him. He had guessed that to go alone to Rodney's wedding would have been humiliating for her and to refuse would have been even worse—she could imagine the wagging tongues…

Mr van der Eisler went home to his dinner and then went back to the hospital again to check on his patient's condition and talk to his registrar. It was very late by

the time he went to his bed and even then he lay for a
time thinking about Olivia.

She was doing the same thing but since she was
sleepy her thoughts were muddled and soon dissolved
in sleep, and in the light of morning she dismissed
them; there was too much to do.

She had her breakfast, tidied the little living-room,
laid a tray for coffee and put everything ready to make
sandwiches before going to dress. She didn't look too
bad, she conceded, peering at her person in the spotty
looking-glass behind the shower-room door. The dress
would pass muster since her shoes and gloves and
clutch bag were expensive, treasured leftovers from
more prosperous days. The hat was a success too. She
left it on the bed and went downstairs to put on the
kettle and cut the sandwiches.

Just in time. The car came to a silent halt before her
narrow front door and Mr van der Eisler, magnificent
in a morning suit, got out.

She flung open the door. 'Hello—how very elegant
you look…'

He took her hand. 'You've stolen my words, Olivia.'
He studied her slowly. 'You look elegant. You also look
beautiful; the bride is going to have difficulty in cap-
turing everyone's attention once you get there.'

She went pink. 'You're joking—I hope so, it's the
bride's day. We'll sit at the back…'

She led the way into the living-room, adding worriedly, 'And I'm not elegant, it's a dress from British
Home Stores.' As she poured the coffee she said, 'We'll

be able to slip away the moment they've left the reception. I expect you will want to get back to the hospital.'

'I have left things in the capable hands of my registrar. You are happy here, Olivia?'

'Oh, yes. Mother is coming to stay in another week or so. Wasn't it extraordinary that an old friend of Granny's should have written?'

'Indeed. Fate isn't always unkind, Olivia.'

'No. Have you been in Holland recently?'

'Yes. I came back a few days ago. I saw Debbie recently; she has become engaged to someone called Fred. Her father has a job as a part-time porter at Jerome's. So fate has been kind to her too.'

'Oh, I'm so glad. If you see her again will you tell her how happy I am? I'll write once school had settled down again.' She saw him glance at his watch. 'Is it time for us to leave? I'll get my hat.'

It took a few minutes to get it perched just so on her bright head and, although she felt fairly satisfied with the result, she felt shy as she went downstairs again.

He was standing at the window but he turned round as she went into the room. 'Charming. A wedding-hat *par excellence*.'

She had been clever, he reflected. The dress was cheap, but elegant, the hat was no milliner's model but it had style, and her gloves and shoes were beyond reproach. Mr van der Eisler, being the man he was, would have escorted her dressed in a sack and a man's cloth cap without a tremor, but he was glad for her sake that she had contrived to look so stunning.

The church, when they reached it, was already almost full and their seats at the back gave them a good view of the congregation without drawing attention to themselves. Although one or two people had turned round to look at them, recognised Olivia, studied Mr van der Eisler with deep interest and whispered to their neighbours.

Rodney was standing with his best man and didn't look round, even when the little flurry at the church door heralded the arrival of the bride.

Olivia, whose heart was as generously large as her person, felt a pang of concern at the sight of her. A rather short girl and dumpy, and decked out most unsuitably in quantities of white lace and satin. She had a long thin nose, too, and although her eyes were large and blue her mouth was discontented. On her wedding-day? thought Olivia. Perhaps her shoes pinch!

She still looked discontented as she and Rodney came down the aisle later, but Rodney looked pleased with himself, smiling and nodding to his friends. At the sight of Olivia his smile faltered for a moment, and then he grinned and winked before leading his bride out into the churchyard for the photographs.

The reception was at the bride's home, with a marquee on the lawn behind the solid redbrick residence. Rodney, decided Olivia, getting out of the car, had done well for himself.

Guests were arriving all the time and as a car drew up to park beside them a woman of Olivia's age poked her head out of its window.

'Olivia, my dear girl—someone said you were in church. Such a surprise, we all thought that you and Rodney—' She broke off as Mr van der Eisler joined Olivia.

Sarah Dowling had never been one of Olivia's friends but an acquaintance merely, living some miles away from her home and encountered only at dances in other people's houses. 'Hello, Sarah,' she smiled, from under the brim of her hat. 'Isn't it a lovely day for a wedding? Of course we had to come to the wedding—Rodney and I are such old friends...'

Sarah had been taking stock of Mr van der Eisler. 'Is this—are you...?'

He smiled charmingly. 'Haso van der Eisler, and yes, we are.'

Olivia went a becoming pink. 'Oughtn't we to go in?' She didn't look at him as they joined the file of guests greeting the bride and groom.

Olivia shook hands with Rodney's father and mother, introduced Mr van der Eisler, and found herself face to face with Rodney.

'Olivia, old girl. So glad you could come and you've brought...?'

'Haso van der Eisler,' said Olivia calmly, and turned to shake hands with the bride. Murmuring the usual compliments, she heard Rodney.

'You'll be the next man to get caught, I suppose. We shall expect to come to the wedding, you know,' he said pompously.

She was rather surprised at the number of people who remembered her—mostly chance acquaintances whom she had met when staying with her grandmother, none of them friends. They all stayed to gossip and eye Mr van der Eisler, who bore their scrutiny with bland politeness. Olivia was sure that he was finding the whole affair tiresome and heaved a sigh of thankfulness when Rodney and his bride went away to change and presently were seen off with rose petals and confetti.

'Now we can go,' said Olivia, and made her adieux with a serenity she didn't feel, listening to Mr van der Eisler echoing her with impeccable manners. It took them some time to get to the car, for they were stopped by several people eager to discover more about her and her companion, but she fobbed them off politely and with laughing vagueness while he stood silently beside her.

She was feeling cross by the time she reached the car, and he settled her into the front seat, got in beside her, and drove off.

'Well, I'm glad that's over,' she said snappily. 'I hope you weren't too bored. I hate weddings…!'

'A nice cup of tea,' he said, in a voice to soothe the most recalcitrant child. 'There is a tea-room in Bradford-on-Avon, but I suspect that other guests will have the same idea as we have. We'll go on to Monkton—there's a cottage tea-room there. What an awkward time to have a wedding—one is scarcely sustained by vol-au-vents and things on biscuits and, one must admit, indifferent champagne.'

'Tea would be nice.' She peeped at him; his face was reassuringly calm. 'Thank you for being so nice—having to listen to all that nonsense.'

'About you and Rodney? Well, now they will have something to ponder over, won't they?'

'I did try not to give the impression that we—you…'

'You dealt with everyone beautifully, and I must own that your hat was easily the most eye-catching there.'

'Really?' She wasn't cross any more. 'I bought it at a department store and tied a bit of ribbon round it.'

He laughed at that and after a moment she laughed with him. 'I don't know why I tell you things.'

'It's easy to talk to some people and not to others,' was all he said, then added, 'Ah, this is where we turn off for Monkton.'

The tea-room was the front room of a small cottage. The ceiling was so low that Mr van der Eisler had to bow his handsome head and the small tables were too close together for a private conversation. But, since he seemed to have no wish to talk about themselves, that didn't matter. They ate scones and jam and cream, sponge cake filled with strawberry jam and generous slabs of fruit cake, and the teapot was vast and filled with a strong brew.

'This is lovely,' said Olivia, kicking off her shoes under the table and biting into a scone. 'Actually the nicest part of the whole day.'

She licked jam off a finger and smiled at him from under the hat.

Only it didn't last long. In no time at all they were back in the car and driving to the school.

'You wouldn't like to come in?' she asked tentatively.

'Yes, I would, but I cannot—I have an engagement this evening in town.'

A remark which instantly put her on the defensive. 'Oh—I didn't know—if you had told me I could have returned straight here.'

He had got out of the car to open her door and stood

with her by the open door. 'A delightful day, Olivia, and now you can consign Rodney to the past.'

'I'd already done that...'

'And have you plans for the future?'

She shook her head. 'I am content with the present.'

He took the hat off her head and bent to kiss her cheek. 'Give my love to Nel when you see her. Good-bye, Olivia.'

She stood there watching him drive away, feeling lonely.

Chapter 4

The loneliness didn't last, of course; there was too much to do before the children came back for the second half of the term, and once they were back life became busier than ever. Olivia threw herself into her daily chores with enthusiasm, and only in the evenings, when she was on her own in the annexe, did she admit to loneliness.

It was fortunate that her mother was coming to stay for a week or ten days and, over and above that, two expeditions were planned for the pupils before the school broke up for the summer holidays. A trip to Cheddar Gorge and a second one to the Roman baths in Bath. Olivia was to go with the children on both occasions, as assistant to Miss Cutts, the history teacher—a stern lady, an excellent instructor, but given to a sharpness of tone which made her unpopular with the children.

She was unpopular with Olivia too, who had been told off on several occasions and hadn't dared to answer back—it might have meant her job...

Her mother arrived on a Sunday evening and since Olivia was free she had been able to have supper ready and her small bedroom bright with flowers.

'Very nice,' pronounced Mrs Harding. 'What a dear little place and just for you too. I don't suppose I shall see much of you, dear?'

'I get a few hours off each day and a free day once a week. I thought we might go up to Bath one day—there's a good bus service—and then if you want to go there on your own you'll know the way.' Olivia arranged the cold supper on a small table under the window. 'I have to have my midday dinner in school with the children, so if you won't mind, would you get your lunch? I'll be over most days after games and we can have tea together, then I'm free again after the children—the smallest ones—are in bed; that's at half-past seven. The evenings are light so we can go for a walk then if you like, and have supper together.' She paused. 'I hope you won't be bored, Mother?'

'My dear, you have no idea how delightful this is going to be—your grandmother has been most generous in giving us a home but I feel that we are outstaying our welcome.'

'In other words, Mother dear, Granny is behaving like an old tyrant.'

'Probably I shall be the same when I'm her age.'

'Mother, you have no idea how to be a tyrant. I do hope that Miss Cross will keep me on. This place is small but we could make it very comfortable, and we'd be on our own during the school holidays.'

Mrs Harding sighed. 'It sounds too good to be true, love, but I intend to enjoy every minute of my stay.'

Later, as they were washing up together, she asked, 'Did you go to Rodney's wedding?'

'Yes. You remember Mr van der Eisler? Well, he drove me over in his car...'

'How very kind. What was he doing here? Visiting Nel?'

'No, he—he saw the card when he brought me back after Easter and thought it would be much nicer if I had a companion to go with.'

She wrung out the dishcloth with a good deal of vigour and her mother studied the back of her head thoughtfully. 'That was indeed most thoughtful of him. So you enjoyed yourself?'

Olivia was uttering her own thoughts aloud. 'He looked quite magnificent in his morning dress; we went and had tea in a village tea-room afterwards. Why is it that wedding breakfasts aren't anything of the kind? Little bits and pieces and not nearly enough to go round.'

Mrs Harding wisely decided not to pursue the interesting subject of Mr van der Eisler. 'Was it an elegant affair? Did the bride look pretty?'

'Lots of lace and satin. I expect Rodney thought that she looked lovely.' She turned round to look at her mother. 'That sounds horrid. I dare say she's a very nice girl and I don't mind him marrying in the least. Funny, isn't it? When I thought I was in love with him.'

'Only because he was part of your life before your father died, love.'

'Yes, I realise that now. In future I shall concentrate on being a career girl.'

Her mother's murmured reply could have been anything.

They had a delightful two weeks together. Mrs Harding, freed from her mother's petty tyrany, became a cheerful housewife again, going to the village to shop, cooking delicious suppers for Olivia and taking herself off to Bath to look at the shops, and on Olivia's day off they went together to explore the delightful city. Waving her mother goodbye, Olivia vowed that, even if Miss Cross decided not to keep her on, she would find a job well away from London, where her mother could live with her. 'A housekeeper or something,' muttered Olivia, eating a solitary supper, 'there must be heaps to choose from, and at least I should get a good reference from Miss Cross.'

In two days' time two coachloads of children were to go to Cheddar Gorge, and Olivia was to go with them. Her task would be to attend to those who felt queasy, restrain the more lively and hand out the lunch packets under the stern eye of Miss Cutts, who would be travelling in the first coach with her; the second coach would contain the matron and Miss Ross—Matron and Miss Cutts didn't get on and had no hesitation in rearranging matters to suit themselves.

Cheddar was a mere twenty miles or so and the journey was largely taken up with Miss Cutts' dry-as-dust lectures about the various ancient buildings they passed. Olivia, listening with half an ear, was aware that the small girls perched on either side of her weren't listening either—and really, why should they? She reflected, I shan't allow my daughters to be bothered with ancient monuments until they are at least ten years old. It would be different with boys, of course, they would want to know everything like that, and they would be brilliantly clever and grow up to be fine men like—well, like Mr van der Eisler. It was a good thing perhaps that Miss Cutts' voice cut through her daydreaming.

'Miss Harding, are you aware that Amelia is feeling sick? Be good enough to attend to her at once.'

Which kept Olivia busy until they reached the gorge and presently Gough's Cave, where the children were to be taken on a guided tour. Olivia found Nel beside her. 'I don't like caves,' she whispered.

Nor did Olivia, but in the face of Miss Cutts' enthusiasm nothing much could be done about that. 'We'll hold hands,' she promised. 'I think it may be rather interesting. Stalactites and stalagmites and flints and things.'

'Are they alive?' Nel wanted to know.

'No, dear—they're rock or something. You'll see...'

The tour seemed to go on forever. Long before they regained the entrance Olivia's hands and arms had been clutched by small nervous fingers, but it was amazing how soon the more timid recovered over their picnic lunch.

An instructive walk followed and Olivia, detailed to walk at the back so that she could keep an eye on the small children, allowed her thoughts to wander once more. It was a pleasant day, warm and sunny with a light breeze, and this, she told herself, was bliss compared with Sylvester Crescent and the hospital. The thought of which reminded her of Mr van der Eisler once again. I wonder what he's doing? she reflected, and started on a series of imagined situations of a highly colourful nature—operating in an atmosphere of high drama, sitting at a magnificent oak desk in a luxurious consulting-room advising some VIP, driving his beautiful motor car at a hundred miles an hour to save someone's life…!

He was doing none of these things; he was sitting behind a desk in a rather poky consulting-room in the outpatients department of a large Amsterdam hospital. He was hot and tired and rather hungry, since he had chosen to miss his lunch and start his clinic early because he had promised Rita to take her out that evening. She had phoned him that morning, saying that she wanted to talk to him about Nel, and he had suggested dinner. Now he wished that she hadn't accepted so eagerly, although he had to admit that anything to do with Nel mustn't be overlooked. He had tried to persuade Rita to make her home in England again, but in this she was adamant, being content to have Nel to live with her during the school holidays.

'After all,' she had reminded him in her gentle voice, 'her grandmother lives near the school and Nel loves her dearly, and if she came here to live with me she would be so lonely. I'm away all day and I love my job; I simply can't give it up.' She had added wistfully, 'Of course if I should meet a man who would understand this and offer me the kind of life I had before Rob died, someone who could love Nel too...' She had allowed her words to fade and then had smiled at him. 'What a good thing that I have you to advise me, Haso.'

The clinic ended, and he got into his car and drove himself to his home—an eighteenth-century gabled town mansion in a short row of similar buildings facing a narrow *gracht* leading from the Prinsengracht. It was very quiet there, a backwater in the bustling city, with trees bordering the water and a street of bricks. He parked his car, mounted the double steps to his front door, and let himself in.

The hall was narrow, with panelled walls and a high plaster ceiling. There were doors on either side and a staircase, its wooden treads worn with age, rose halfway down the hall, curving away to the floor above.

He had crossed the hall and was at a door beside the staircase when a stout man, no longer young, came through the baize door at the end of the hall.

Mr van der Eisler stopped in his stride. 'Ah, Bronger, I'm late.'

The door was pushed open and an Alsatian dog padded silently through.

'I'll take Achilles for a quick run before I go out.' He laid a hand on the dog's great head. 'I could do with some fresh air myself.'

'You'll be late back, Professor?'

'I hope not. Ask Ofke to leave some coffee on the stove for me, will you?'

He left the house again very shortly, the dog loping silently beside him. The streets were quiet in this part of the city and there was a small park nearby where

Achilles raced around for some time while his master
paced along its paths. Presently he whistled to the dog
and they walked briskly back to his home and went,
the pair of them, into the study, before Mr van der
Eisler took himself upstairs to change for the evening.

Achilles was waiting for him in the hall when he
went downstairs again. 'Sorry, boy, I have to go out,'
Mr van der Eisler told the dog gently and gave him a
pat. 'And for some reason I have no wish to go.'

He got into his car once more. He had no wish to
spend the evening with Rita; for a moment he allowed
his thoughts to dwell on Olivia. Unlike Rita, whose
gentle voice concealed a determination to get her own
way, Olivia would speak her mind with a disregard of
female wiles, cheerfully apologising afterwards if need
be. Rita, he reflected, never apologised, because she
never felt herself to be at fault.

He stopped before a block of flats in the more modern part of the city, got out and rang the bell of her flat.

'Haso?' Her voice was charming over the intercom.
'Come on up…'

'We're already a little late. I've a table at de Kersen-
tuin.'

Rita joined him after about five minutes. She looked
charming; she had an excellent clothes-sense, and the
money to spend on a good hairdresser and beauty parlour. Mr van der Eisler helped her into the car and
wondered why she didn't stir his interest in the slight-
est. They had got on well when Rob was alive, but
he had never thought of her as anyone other than his
friend's wife.

They had seen quite a lot of each other when his

friend was alive and Nel was a baby, and since his death, naturally enough, they met frequently since he was one of his trustees. He had been surprised at how quickly she had returned to work as a PA to an executive in a big oil firm and how easily she had agreed to Nel going to boarding-school in England. True, Rob had wanted that, but he had envisaged Rita going to live in England too. After all, there was plenty of money...

He listened to Rita's amusing chatter, making all the right remarks, and presently, as they sat over dinner, he asked her why she had wanted to see him.

She laughed. 'Oh, nothing in particular, Haso. I suppose I was feeling lonely—you know how it is? Don't you ever wish to have a companion? A wife to come home to?'

'I'm poor company when I get home in the evening.' He smiled at her. 'Are you worried about Nel?'

'Nel? Why should I be worried about her? Her grandmother's only a few miles away from the school; she seems very happy. I had a letter from her this morning. They were taken off to Cheddar Gorge—for a treat. She didn't like the caves very much but there was someone there—one of the teachers, I presume—who didn't like them either, and they held hands. Silly child.'

'A dislike of being in an enclosed place is very common. Luckily there was someone with whom she could share her fear.'

That someone would have been Olivia, he was sure of that as though Rita had mentioned her by name. He frowned—he really must stop thinking about the girl, she had nothing to do with his life. He said easily,

'As long as you are quite happy about Nel. She seemed perfectly content when I took her back to school.'

She handed him his coffee-cup and he went on, 'Have you any plans for the summer holidays? I suppose she'll stay for a while with Lady Brennon?'

'For as long as she likes. She can come over here, of course, but I don't want to take too much time off— I've been asked to go down to the South of France for the whole of August with the van Fonders.'

'You don't want to take Nel with you?'

'There won't be any other children there—she would be bored, my dear.' She smiled her charming smile. 'If you're in England perhaps you would collect her from school and take her to Lady Brennon's—I'm sure you want to see her again.'

Mr van der Eisler agreed; he would like to see Olivia too, although he didn't allow himself to examine this wish.

'I think it would be a good thing if Nel were to get to know you really well,' went on Rita. She met his eyes across the table. 'She does need a father.'

He said at his most bland, 'Oh, are you planning to marry again? Do I know him?'

Rita gave a little laugh to hide her annoyance. To marry Haso would settle all her problems—Nel could stay at school and, since Haso was wrapped up in his work and divided his time between the two countries, she would be free to live as she wished. He was a wealthy man, well-known in his profession, and he came from an old and respected family. Besides, he was blessed with good looks. She had set her heart on marrying him and had felt sure of getting her way.

She would have to be more careful. At least she saw him frequently and there was always the excuse that she needed to know something about Nel. Perhaps she should go over to Bath and collect the child at the end of term? But if she suggested that, probably he would assume that he needn't go too.

'No, of course not. I go out a good deal, you know that, but there is no one—I still miss Rob.'

She sounded sincere and Mr van der Eisler said kindly, 'He wouldn't want you to stay on your own for the rest of your life, Rita. He loved you too much for that.'

She had the good sense not to say any more but began to talk about Nel, a subject she knew always interested him.

It wanted a scant three weeks until the end of term, and the whole school was occupied with preparations of importance for the last day—prize-giving, the school choir rendering suitable songs and the most senior of the girls, due to leave and go on to a variety of private schools, performing a play written by themselves. Olivia spent her days hearing lines, helping to make the costumes and taking prep in the evenings, so that the class mistresses could meet to discuss who should have the prizes. She had no time to herself but she didn't mind; life was interesting, the weather was splendid and Miss Cross had told her that she might return for the autumn term.

'Although I must warn you,' she had added, 'that since you have no qualifications the Board of Governors may wish to replace you after Christmas—even a diploma in music or art would be sufficient. It adds tone to the prospectus, and the parents expect highly qualified staff in a school such as this one.' She had sighed. 'It is a pity, Olivia, for you are a very useful member. Perhaps I shall be able to persuade them to accept you when they meet in January.'

Olivia thought it unlikely, but it was of no use worrying about it now. She had a job until Christmas, and only then would she worry. In the meantime, with certain reservations, she was happy.

On top of everything else there was the visit to the Roman baths—purely instructive; Miss Cutts had made that clear. Olivia found herself on the back seat of the school bus once more, listening to Miss Cutts' resonant voice recounting Bath's history. A pity they weren't to be allowed to see the Assembly Rooms and have tea there, reflected Olivia, longing for a cup of tea as they all got out and trooped at a snail's pace from one end to the other of the baths, stopping to admire the statue of the Emperor Hadrian overlooking the largest of the baths and listening to Miss Cutts reeling off the various measurements of the baths, expounding the beauties of the mosaic flooring, explaining how a Roman plumber had planned and fitted the lead conduit which supplied the water to the largest bath. The children listened obediently, but she could see that they had their minds on other things; the excitement of the end of term was too near to be ignored now.

That wasn't the end to the day either. It was Olivia's bedtime duty, which meant that after a hasty cup of tea she had to start collecting the smallest girls and get them bathed and into bed. They chattered like magpies, full of the things that they would do when they got home and speculation as to who would get the prizes. It was Nel who said wistfully to Olivia as she brushed her hair, 'I'm sure Mummy will come this time—I might get a prize and then she'll be proud of me.'

'I'm quite sure she's proud of you whether you get a prize or not,' Olivia assured her. 'And of course she'll come. The last day of the summer term is a very important one, isn't it? Are you looking forward to singing in the choir?'

Whereupon Nel burst into song and had to be shushed, popped into bed and tucked up.

Olivia was up early on the last day. So was everyone else, anxious to make the day a success. The first parents would arrive mid-morning and by noon, when a buffet lunch was to be served, they should all have arrived ready to take their seats in the nearby assembly hall for the entertainments and the prize-giving.

Everyone was drifting towards the dining-room when Olivia, rounding up stragglers, felt an urgent tug on her sleeve. Nel lifted a troubled face to hers. 'My Mummy hasn't come,' she whispered. 'She said she would—she promised she'd come with Granny—Granny isn't here either.'

Olivia put an arm round the small shoulders. 'There's still plenty of time, Nel—perhaps they've got held up in the traffic. I tell you what we'll do, we'll hurry to the door and make sure they aren't there...'

They reached the entrance as the Bentley came to a soundless halt and Mr van der Eisler got out, opened the door and helped Lady Brennon out. 'They've come,' shrieked Nel, and flung herself at her grandmother as Olivia beat a hasty retreat. Not fast enough, however.

'Don't go.' Mr van der Eisler spoke quietly as he turned to receive Nel's onslaught upon his vast person.

'Where's Mummy?' Nel asked suddenly.

Lady Brennon gave him a speaking look, took a few steps towards Olivia and sighed, 'Oh, dear...'

'She sends her dearest love,' said Mr van der Eisler cheerfully, 'but she just couldn't come—she has to work, you know, and she can't take a holiday whenever she wants one.'

Nel banged her small fist against his waistcoat. 'She doesn't have to work and she's got lots of money and she promised. You mustn't break a promise—Olivia told me so.' The child was near to tears. 'And it's not a holiday, it's me!'

'Ah, but I'm going to take you over to Holland in a week or two. Mummy will make sure to have a holiday then, and we'll all go out together, and we'll take Achilles with us—and Ofke's cat has had kittens. I'm sure she won't mind if you have one to keep.'

'Mummy doesn't like cats...'

'In that case, I'll have him, shall I? He'll be company for Achilles.'

He glanced at Olivia, 'Don't you think that's a good idea, Olivia?'

'Quite splendid. What fun you'll have, Nel. Now, would you like to take your grandmother to the dining-room? I'm sure you'd all like lunch.'

'You will come with us, Olivia?' asked Lady Brennon.

Olivia looked shocked. 'Me? Heavens, no! I'm helping with the serving.' She suddenly wanted to get away from Mr van der Eisler's eyes. 'You'll excuse me?'

She made off at a great pace and in the dining-room was accosted by Miss Ross. 'There you are—where have you been? Cook has cut her hand and can't carve and we're running out of beef and ham. Go to the kitchen and slice some more as fast as you can.' She turned away to serve a parent and Olivia slid away kitchenwards. Mr van der Eisler, escorting his companions to a table near the buffet, watched her go.

Unhurriedly he collected food and drink and brought them back to the table. 'I'll be with you in a moment,' he told Lady Brennon, and wandered off to go through the same door as Olivia.

He stood a moment in the kitchen doorway, watching her. Carving was one of the things Olivia didn't know much about; a small pile of uneven slices bore witness to this, but there was no one to give her advice for Cook had retired to her room and the two kitchen-maids had gone too.

'Allow me,' said Mr van der Eisler, took the knife and two-pronged fork from her, and began to carve in a manner worthy of his calling.

'You can't come in here,' said Olivia when she had got back her breath, 'and you can't do that either.'

'But I am here, Olivia, and who but I am capable of carving this ham in the correct manner? After all, I have learned to be handy with a knife.'

'Oh, don't be absurd…'

'Don't work yourself up, dear girl. Take this dish of ham to the dining-room and I'll start on the beef.'

'You can't…'

'Now, now, off with you!'

So she picked up the dish of wafer-thin slices and hurried to the dining-room, where they were snatched from her. 'And do hurry with the beef.'

'Gratitude,' snorted Olivia, speeding back to the kitchen. Mr van der Eisler reduced the beef to a pile of evenly cut slices, took one, and sat down on the table to eat it.

'You can't...' began Olivia.

'That is the third time you have said that. Run along with the beef, there's a good girl, and then come back here.'

'I...' She caught his eye and did as she was bid, and presently returned.

'On which day do you return to Sylvester Crescent?' he asked her.

'Oh, I have to stay for another day, to tidy up, you know, and leave everything just so.'

'I'm staying with Lady Brennon for a day or two. I'll pick you up and drive you back—I've to be in London myself.'

'Yes, but...'

'But what? Is there some young man waiting for you?'

'A young man? Me? Heavens above! I don't have time to say more than good morning to the milkman—and there aren't any young men around.'

'A pity. Never mind. I'll come for you about ten o'clock in the morning. Are you going away for your holidays?'

'No. I—we—that is, we shall stay with Granny.'

'And what will you do all day?'

She was suddenly cross. 'I don't know—I have not the least idea. I must go.'

'Run along,' said Mr van der Eisler, and carved himself another slice of beef.

Parents were leaving the dining-room and making their way to the assembly hall. Olivia began to clear the plates and glasses and presently went round to the back of the stage to make sure that the choir were all present and looking presentable. The senior girls' play was already in progress and when that was over there would be a brief display of dancing before the choir. She laced up shoes, tied hair-ribbons and stilled childish nerves, and went to peep at the audience through a spyhole in the curtain. Lady Brennon and Mr van der Eisler were sitting in the second row. Lady Brennon was smiling gently; her companion looked as though he might be asleep.

The play over, the dancing done to great applause, the choir was coaxed into a semi-circle, the music mistress struck up a chord, and they were off, speeding the boat over to Skye with tremendous verve.

Olivia, in the wings acting as prompt, thought that if Mr van der Eisler had been dozing, that should have roused him nicely.

They sang a bit of Gilbert and Sullivan next, and then a rather sad song about snow. The choir hadn't liked it but the music mistress had decided that they were to sing it. They got through the first verse well enough, moaning 'Oh, snow' with enthusiasm, but somehow they lost the thread during the second and Olivia had to do some prompting. Several small faces turned to look at her in panic, the music mistress thumped out the last few bars and since no one sang began on them again. Olivia began to sing the words very softly and in a moment a relieved chorus of small voices took over from her. It had been only a slight hitch in an otherwise perfect performance and the applause was deafening.

It was later, as the children began to leave with their parents, that Mr van der Eisler went in search of Olivia. He found her on her hands and knees, grovelling under a schoolroom cupboard.

'I must say,' he remarked pleasantly, 'that you look nice from any angle, Olivia.'

She rose to her splendid height, very red in the face. 'I'm looking for a lost tennis racquet. What do you want?'

'You do not mince your words. To remind you that I shall be waiting for you at ten o'clock on the day after tomorrow.' He smiled and nodded and turned to go. 'You have a pretty singing voice,' he observed as he left the room.

She spent the next day doing whatever she was told to do and then going to the annexe to pack her own things. Her thoughts were muddled. On the one hand she felt a pleasurable excitement at the thought of seeing Mr van der Eisler again, but this was strangely mitigated by her doubts as to whether she should allow herself to be drawn into some kind of friendship with him. Perhaps just this once, she told herself weakly— she wasn't likely to see much of him anyway; he had said that he was taking Nel back to Holland with him and perhaps her mother would bring her back next term. Besides she had a strong suspicion that he and Nel's mother intended to marry.

He was just being kind, she decided. What could be more normal than to offer a lift since they were both going to London on the same day?

The thought of Sylvester Crescent depressed her. It would be lovely to see her mother again but six weeks of living with Granny was daunting.

Just before ten o'clock the next morning she locked her door, took the key along to the school porter, and went outside. The Bentley was there, with Mr van der Eisler, his hands in his pockets, strolling around the flowerbeds bordering the sweep. He saw her at once, took her case from her and put it in the boot, and then opened the car door.

'Good morning,' said Olivia pointedly.

'Don't look so cross. Will you smile if I say good morning to you?'

She laughed. 'Don't be absurd. I'm very grateful for this lift.'

He got in beside her and drove off without any fuss. 'So am I,' he told her. A remark which left her vaguely puzzled.

'I expect Nel is glad to be with her Granny?'

'She is always happy there. I'll take her over to Holland in a week's time when I go back.'

'I'm sorry she was disappointed about her mother, but she soon cheered up, didn't she?'

He grunted non-committally; he had spent a good deal of time trying to smooth over the fact of Nel's mother not coming to the school, and it had been hard work.

The grunt didn't sound very promising. Olivia stayed silent, admiring the scenery to herself and watching his hands on the wheel. They were large, blunt-fingered and beautifully kept.

They had driven for some time in a silence which was strangely companionable when he said, 'How about coffee? I don't know about you, but I was up early; Nel and I took the dogs out.'

'You like dogs?'

'Yes. My own dog, Achilles, is an Alsatian; I've had him since he was a very small puppy. I should like to have a dog here, but I don't have much time to myself when I'm in England. My housekeeper has a cat—you like cats?'

'Yes. We had two, and an Old English Sheepdog. Our cook took the cats and Shep died just before we had to leave.'

After a few moments of silence she ventured. 'Your housekeeper's cat, does it have a name?'

'Bertie.' He laughed suddenly. 'You and I don't need to make small-talk, Olivia. Here's a place where we can have coffee.'

It was a pleasant wayside inn, and they sat outside drinking their coffee in the sun. 'Tell me, what do you intend to do, Olivia?' asked Mr van der Eisler. 'You must have some plans.'

'What is the use of plans? I hope that Miss Cross will keep me on at the school and I can have Mother to stay each term. She isn't happy with Granny, you know. I have thought that I might study for something in my spare time. It would have to be something where I could earn a living and have a home too. Am I too old to be a nurse?'

'No, but that is three years in hospital, and even

when you have trained the chance of your getting a post where you could live outside hospital on your salary wouldn't be too great. I do not wish to bring up the question of Rodney, but there must have been other men in your life, Olivia.'

'Oh, yes. I had a lot of friends, and I suppose if Father hadn't died and left us awkwardly placed I might have married one of them. Although now I'm older I don't think I should have liked that.'

'No, I don't think you would. Wait for the right man, Olivia.'

'Oh, I will,' she assured him.

It was when they were back in the car, she sitting silently beside him, that she realised that there was no need for her to wait for the right man. He was here already, sitting beside her.

Chapter 5

Mr van der Eisler began to talk presently about nothing much, and it served to quieten her jangling nerves. She needed to go somewhere very quiet so that she could think. She mustn't see him again, of course, and she must stop thinking about him, and the sooner the better. Her thoughts were interrupted by his casual, 'Becky will have lunch ready. I hope you will lunch with me, Olivia? I'll take you home afterwards.'

So much for her good resolutions. They flew out of the window and she said happily, 'Oh! Thank you, that would be nice.' Then she added, 'But isn't it interfering with your day?'

'Not in the least. I'm free for the rest of the day.' His voice held just the right note of casualness. He lapsed into silence again and she thought uneasily that he might wonder why she didn't have something to say

for herself. The weather seemed a safe topic, and the
countryside, so she enlarged upon these two items at
some length and he, aware that for some reason she was
feeling awkward with him, allowed her to chatter in a
manner quite unlike her usual self, making suitable re-
plies in his quiet voice so that gradually she regained her
normal composed manner and by the time he stopped
before his house she had herself nicely in hand.

He had told Becky that he was bringing a guest to
lunch and she had the door open as they reached it, a
wide smile on her elderly face while she summed up
Olivia with sharp eyes.

'This is Becky, my housekeeper,' he said, and 'Becky,
this is Miss Olivia Harding. She works at Nel's school.'

'Now isn't that nice,' declared Becky. 'I dare say
Miss Harding would like to tidy herself before lunch.
I'll take her to the cloakroom while you look through
your post, Mr Haso.'

Olivia, recognising the gentle tyranny of the old
family retainer, followed Becky.

Mr van der Eisler was waiting for her in his sitting-
room, standing by the open door leading to a small but
charming garden. It was a pleasant room, furnished
with a nice mixture of antiques and comfortable modern chairs, and wore the air of being well lived-in.
Bertie, Becky's cat, sat washing himself on a small
side-table and gave her a searching glance as she went
in before continuing his toilet, and Mr van der Eisler
put down the letters in his hand and invited her to sit
by the window. 'There's time for a drink before lunch.
Sherry? Or perhaps you would prefer something else?'

'Sherry, please.' She looked around her; the walls
were almost covered by paintings—portraits as far as

she could see. They sat making small-talk for a few minutes until she asked, 'May I look at your paintings? Are they your family?'

'Yes, the English side of it. My grandmother was English and left me this flat and its contents. I came here a good deal as a boy, and later when I was at Cambridge, and I feel very much at home.'

She nodded. 'I'm sure that you must, as you were happy here.' She laughed suddenly. 'And to think that Debbie used to worry about you being lonely in London.'

'A kind-hearted child. Did you worry too, Olivia?'

'No—well, not worry exactly. I did wonder where you lived in London.' She added hastily, 'Just idle curiosity, you know.'

It wasn't too bad, she reflected, once she had gone into the room and seen him standing there. She had spent her few minutes in the cloakroom giving herself good advice and so far she was managing pretty well. True, the wish to fling herself at him and throw her arms round his neck was a strong one, but she prided herself on her good sense. She began to wander round the room, looking at each portrait—elderly gentlemen with side-whiskers, younger men with determined chins resting on snowy stocks, small, fragile-looking ladies, and several miniatures of children's heads. There were one or two portraits of younger women too, with beautiful faces and laughing eyes, and she paused before them and found him beside her. 'My grandmother and my mother. They were so unlike the earlier ladies in the family. As tall and generously built as you, and as beautiful.'

Olivia said, 'Oh,' faintly, and wondered if 'generously built' meant fat. The women in the portraits didn't look fat, just well-covered. She gave her own person a surreptitious glance, and went scarlet when he said blandly, 'No, I don't mean fat, Olivia. You need have no fears about that. You are exactly the right shape for a woman.'

She didn't look at him. Really, the conversation was straying from the coolly friendly path she had intended to tread. She said, politely cool even though her face was still pink, 'You have some charming ancestors.'

'You should see the Dutch side of the family; they must have spent half their lives being painted.'

'Were they doctors too?'

'Almost to a man.'

She faced him then. 'You must have a great deal of wisdom with such a heritage.'

Just for a moment the heavy lids lifted to show the clear blue of his eyes. 'What a very perceptive thing to say, Olivia. I do my best to carry on the family tradition.' He glanced round as the door opened and Becky came in.

'There's that naughty Bertie on your table again, and his dinner waiting for him too. If you've had your drinks, I'll serve the soup, Mr Haso.'

The dining-room was on the other side of the hall. Not a large room, it held a circular mahogany table with ribbon-back chairs around it, a side-table holding some massive silver pieces, and a Regency fireplace with a carriage clock on the mantel above it. The curtains were a rich plum velvet and the floor polished wood. A lovely room in which to have a meal, reflected Olivia, sitting down and accepting the soup Becky had set before her.

It was a good soup—watercress with a swirl of

cream in its centre—and that was followed by lamb cutlets, new potatoes, and peas with baby carrots. The trifle which followed was perfection itself. Olivia, who had a good appetite and never pretended otherwise, ate every morsel.

They went back to the sitting-room for their coffee and this time she took more leisurely stock of her surroundings. The colour scheme wasn't so obvious here—the carpet on the polished wood floor was in muted blues and dull greens and pinks, and the long curtains at the windows at both ends of the room were old rose brocade, while the chairs were upholstered in the same dim colours as the carpet. There was a good deal of yew and apple-wood, and a splendid bow-fronted display cabinet with some intricate marquetry.
'But of course you'll have a study,' observed Olivia, speaking her thoughts out loud.

'Yes, and there is another small room. I don't use it but Becky tells me that my grandmother used it as her own private place, where she could sew and read and so on. It is quite a big flat. Becky has her own flatlet, and there are three bedrooms and bathrooms as well as the kitchen.'

'Did your grandmother like living in Holland?'

'Oh, yes. You see, she and my grandfather were a devoted pair; she would have lived in the middle of the desert if need be, provided she was with him. They came over here a good deal, of course, bringing the children with them, and later their grandchildren too.'

He watched the beautiful face opposite him, alight with interest, and wondered silently why he was telling her all this. Perhaps something of his thoughts showed in his usually impassive face, for Olivia said in a polite visitor's voice, 'How interesting—to have two countries, I mean.' She put her cup down. 'I expect you have things to do—I've enjoyed my lunch, thank you, and it was so kind of you to drive me back. I think I should go.'

He made no demure and after a suitable chat with Becky she followed him out to the car and was driven to Sylvester Crescent. It looked unwelcoming, with all the net curtains covering the windows and the doors tightly shut. Outside her grandmother's flat Olivia said, 'Would you like to come in?' and expected him to say no.

Instead, he said at once, 'I should like to meet your mother again,' and got out to help her out of the car and get her luggage from the boot.

By the time they reached the door her mother had it open, smiling widely. 'Darling, how lovely to see you—it seems such ages.' She kissed Olivia and held out a hand to Mr van der Eisler. 'Do please come in, Mr van der Eisler. You brought Olivia back—how kind. Have you had lunch? Or perhaps coffee?'

'We've had lunch, Mother, at Mr van der Eisler's home...'

'Then tea—it's a little early, but tea is always welcome.'

'I should love a cup,' he said surprisingly, following Mrs Harding into the drawing-room where Mrs Fitzgibbon sat in her uncomfortable chair.

She held out a hand. 'How delightful to see you again,' she said, at her most gracious. 'Do sit down and tell me what you have been doing. I get so little news here, chained as I am to this flat, and only my daughter for company.' She offered an indifferent cheek for Olivia's dutiful kiss. 'You will find it equally dull, Olivia—six weeks' holiday, I understand. I'm sure I don't know what you will do with yourself. Although your mother will be glad of some help around the house, I suppose.' She added, 'Well, now you're here you might make the tea.'

Olivia cooled down in the kitchen. It was a pity that he had chosen to come in; Granny enjoyed belittling her and usually she didn't allow it to rile her too much, but in front of Mr van der Eisler... He had no interest in her as a woman, she was sure of that, but to be held up as a tiresome fool by her grandmother might destroy the mild liking he appeared to have for her. What did it matter? she told herself fiercely, spooning tea into the pot. This was the last time they would see each other. She had heard him tell Nel that her mother would bring her back to school for the autumn term so obviously he had no other plans. Besides, that was weeks away; he would have forgotten all about her by then.

Pouring tea and handing round digestive biscuits, she had to admit that his considerable charm was making a good impression upon Granny, who enlarged upon her distant aristocratic connections at some length, much to her and her mother's discomfort. When he got up to go at last she offered him a hand, thanked him in a cool voice for giving her a lift, and uttered a conventional wish as to his future well-being. All without looking any higher than the middle button of his waistcoat.

'A delightful man,' observed Mrs Fitzgibbon. 'Such a pity that you do not attract him, Olivia. I presume that he intends to marry this small girl's—Nel's—mother? He spoke of her.'

'I've no idea,' said Olivia airily, intent on pulling the wool over her grandparent's sharp eyes. 'I don't know anything about him. He was kind enough to give me a lift, Granny, that is all.'

She caught her mother's eye and that lady, about to say something, obediently didn't.

Life was dull in Sylvester Crescent and, after ten days of Mrs Fitzgibbon's lightly veiled remarks about extra mouths to feed, Olivia went looking for a job. She didn't have to go far. The Coffee-Pot needed part-time help. Four mornings a week, from ten o'clock until the regular waitress came on at one o'clock. The pay was minimal but she could keep her tips. Olivia went back to her grandmother's flat, delivered her news, and listened to a harangue from her grandmother about the humbleness of her new job.

'Honest work for an honest wage,' said Olivia cheerfully.

It wasn't all bad. True, her feet ached, and sometimes the customers were rude, but secretly she sympathised with them, for the coffee was abominable. It gave her something to do, though, and put a little money in her pocket, even after paying over a good deal of it towards her keep.

Since her afternoons were free she took her mother out to the parks or to window-shop, leaving her grandmother to play bridge with her few friends.

'Your granny would be so much happier on her own,' sighed her mother.

Olivia gave her parent's arm a sympathetic squeeze. 'If Miss Cross will take me on permanently next year you shall come and live with me, and you must come and stay next term for just as long as you would like.'

'Your grandmother might need me...'

'Pooh,' said Olivia strongly. 'She was very content

until we went to live with her, and that's all nonsense about her not being able to afford help in the house.'

'You're quite happy, dear?' her mother wanted to know.

'Of course I am, love. Haven't I got everything I want—a job, money in my pocket, a pleasant place in which to work?' The memory of Mr van der Eisler made nonsense of her cheerful reply; she thought about him all day and every day, despite the fact that she wasn't likely to see him again. He would be at Jerome's, she supposed, or back in Holland...

He was in Holland, and very shortly he would return to England bringing with him Nel and her mother. Rita had agreed unwillingly to go over to England and visit her mother-in-law, but only provided that she might leave Nel with her so that she could go to her friends in the South of France. She had found Nel a nuisance, although she had taken advantage of the child being there to see as much of Haso as possible but, although he had been friendly and ready to help in any way, he had evinced no desire to spend his free time with her. Absence makes the heart grow fonder, she told herself; he would be delighted to see her again when she returned.

They were to stay for a couple of days at his flat in London so that Rita could do some shopping, and it was Nel who gave Mr van der Eisler the excuse to go and see Olivia. He had had no intention of going, he told himself, he found her unsettling, and his growing interest in her had been brought about by circumstances and nothing more. All the same, when Nel asked him if they might go and see Olivia, he agreed. 'We might go while your mother is shopping,' he suggested.

But Rita said at once, 'Oh, but I'd love to come too—such a nice girl and so kind to Nel...'

Mrs Harding opened the door to them. 'Do come in.' She shook Rita's hand and smiled at them all. 'Have you come to see Olivia? I'm afraid she's not here. She's got a little job down at the Coffee-Pot...'

'What could be better?' exclaimed Rita. 'We can have our coffee there and talk to her at the same time.'

'Well,' said Mrs Harding doubtfully, 'she will probably be busy.'

'Oh, I'm sure she will be able to find time to have a chat. Nel's so looking forward to seeing her.'

Mr van der Eisler said smoothly, 'I dare say Olivia would rather we didn't call on her while she's working.'

However, Rita persisted. 'We've come all this way, and Nel won't be able to see her now...'

He doubted that her concern was genuine, but undoubtedly Nel was disappointed. He drove them to the Coffee-Pot, parked the car and opened the door.

Olivia had her back to them, serving coffee and buns to four people crowded round one of the little tables. They sat down, the three of them, at the only empty table, and when she turned round she saw them.

She went red and then pale, but she crossed to their table and wished them a composed good morning, smiled at Nel, and asked them if they would like coffee. The look she cast at Mr van der Eisler was reproachful, but it hid delight at seeing him again even if the circumstances were hardly what she would have wished.

'Your mother told us where you were,' he explained easily. 'Nel wanted to see you before she goes to stay with Lady Brennon. You must forgive us for taking you unawares.'

He could see that she wished to go—there were other customers. 'May we have some coffee, and perhaps a milkshake for Nel?'

She went away and Rita said, 'What a poky little place. I dare say the coffee's undrinkable. Still, I suppose if the girl's hard up it's better than nothing.'

She gave him a narrow look as she spoke—there had been something about the way he had looked at Olivia which made her uneasy. She was a beautiful girl, there was no doubt about that, but no sparkle. Rita, who had brought sparkling to a fine art, did so now at Olivia, returning with their coffee, and she could see how easily she could make Mr van der Eisler laugh...

The café emptied momentarily, and Olivia spent a minute or two talking to Nel before more customers arrived and she was kept busy, but when she saw Nel's frantic waving she went back to her.

'We're going now,' said Nel, 'but you will be at school, won't you?'

'Yes, Nel. I'll be there.'

'Such hard work it must be,' said Rita. 'But anything's better than this, I should imagine. And the coffee is vile...' She gave a little laugh. 'I say, do we leave a tip?'

Put in my place, thought Olivia. Between Granny and her, Mr van der Eisler must think me a complete nonentity. She smiled serenely while she seethed. 'Goodbye—I must go. But it was nice seeing Nel again.'

The smile took in the three of them as she turned away to take an order. Mr van der Eisler hadn't said a word. He would very much have liked to utter those which trembled on his tongue, but Olivia's dignity must be preserved at all costs before a room full of strangers, and the words he wished to utter to Rita were harsh indeed, and liable to cause some interest in those sitting around them. In the car he said blandly, 'Why were you rude, Rita, and unkind…?'

'Rude? I didn't mean to be, Haso. Oh, dear, have I upset the poor girl? My silly tongue, I'm so sorry.' She looked over her shoulder at Nel. 'Darling, when you see Olivia next term, do tell her that I didn't mean to upset her. I was joking, but we haven't all got the same sense of humour.'

'Aren't you coming to take me back to school, Mummy?' asked Nel.

'Sweetie, I'll try very hard to come, really I will, but if I'm terribly busy I may not be able to. Granny will take you back and I really will come over at the end of term.'

'Promise?'

'Promise.' She turned a smiling face to Mr van der Eisler's stern profile. 'You'll bring me over, won't you, Haso?'

'That depends on where I am and what I am doing. You can always fly to Bristol and get a car from there.'

Rita pouted charmingly. 'You know I hate travelling alone.'

He said nothing, aware that in a few days' time she would fly—quite alone—down to the South of France to join her friends. He would have liked to tax her with that, but Nel had to be kept happy; she was already getting too bright, too quick not to sense her mother's impatience with her.

He didn't stay long at Lady Brennon's but drove

back to London, wishing that he had Olivia sitting beside him. What on earth had possessed the girl to work as a waitress? Was she so desperately hard-up? Was she to go on taking these dead-end jobs for the rest of her life with little or no opportunity of meeting a suitable young man who would marry her? Heaven knew that she was beautiful enough to attract them. He began to turn over in his mind the various young doctors and surgeons he knew at Jerome's, wondering how to make it possible for her to meet them. A fruitless task which got him nowhere.

He drove straight to the hospital and forgot her, and when he got back to his flat, finally, there were letters to read and answer, phone calls to make and patients' notes to study. He ate a late supper, clucked over by Becky, and went to bed, and during the next few busy days spared her only the most cursory of thoughts.

He had something of a worldwide reputation in his particular field of surgery and an urgent summons took him to Italy, so that when the time came for Nel to return to school he was out of the country and, since Rita was still in the South of France, Nel was taken back to school by her grandmother.

Olivia, detailed to collect the children as they arrived, was confronted by a tearful Nel. 'Mummy didn't come and Uncle Haso sent me a postcard with a lot of blue sky and mountains on it. I expect they forgot...' Her small lip trembled and Lady Brennon said quickly, 'I'm sure they wouldn't forget, darling. Perhaps there wasn't a seat for them on the plane—perhaps they'll come as soon as they can. It's holiday-time, and everyone wants to travel...'

'The planes get so full,' added Olivia, anxious to avert tears.

Nel gave her the clear look that only a child could give. 'Uncle Haso has his own plane,' she said.

Olivia and Lady Brennon exchanged glances. 'Well, in that case,' said Olivia briskly, 'he may even now be on his way here. Will you say goodbye to your granny, poppet? Then I'll take you up to your dormitory—most of your best friends are in it this term.'

Nel brightened a little. 'Oh, good, and may I come and see you, Granny, at half-term?'

'Of course, my pet, but I'll be over before then to watch your sports day.'

It wasn't until Olivia was in bed that night that she had the leisure to think her own thoughts. The day had been busy—the children's trunks to unpack, tuck to be labelled and put away, the homesick to be comforted, mislaid things to be found. She was glad that she had been too busy to think, she reflected, curled up in her bed at last. Now, tired though she was, she had to go over every word Nel and Lady Brennon had uttered about Mr van der Eisler. It was only too apparent that he was with Rita. And why should that upset her, she asked herself angrily, when she had made up her mind to forget him, never think of him again? What business was it of hers if he was to marry Rita? It would be a good thing for Nel's sake; the child was fond of him, more so than she was of her mother. The only real security she had was with her grandmother...

Olivia nodded off.

She woke in the night and had a nice comforting weep, and felt better for it. She couldn't change the way things were so she had better accept them with a good grace and make the best of what she had—a job, a frail security, and a roof over her head. Who knew? She might, any day now, meet some man who would want to marry her. But would she want to marry him?

School routine took over once more. The days followed each other with ordered speed; they got chillier too, and as the evenings darkened she had the task of overseeing the smaller children's leisure before their bedtime. There was a good deal of activity in the gym too, where those who were taking part practised for sports day. Olivia, Jill of all trades and master of none, played the piano for the rhythmic exercises, untangled the formation gymnastics when they got too involved, and soothed bruises and bumps.

It had turned quite cold by now and half-term would follow on after sports day. Her mother was coming to spend two weeks with her and since she would be free for the first week she had planned a trip to Bath—they would lunch out and have tea in the Assembly Rooms and, since she had had no reason to spend much money, they might do a little shopping. Christmas was still some way off and she dreaded spending it with her grandmother, but perhaps she and her mother would be able to spend a day out somewhere.

Parents were to arrive directly after lunch and, after the various displays, be given tea before going home again. The morning was spent on last-minute preparations and the solving of small crises as they occurred, but by one o'clock the whole school was ready—the rows of chairs in place, the trestle tables in the assembly hall covered with white cloths and piled with cups and saucers and plates.

'You will help with the tea,' said Miss Cross, paus-

ing by Olivia as she counted sugar bowls, 'and do whatever Miss Ross wants, and be prepared to give Matron
a hand if there are any mishaps.'

She went on her way and Olivia started counting
the sugar bowls once more.

The children were permitted to greet their parents
when they arrived so that the hall was packed with
excited little girls all talking at once. Olivia, having
counted heads and found them correct, took herself off
to the pantry to make sure that everything was as ready
as possible for tea. The occasion must go off smoothly,
Miss Cross had said. As soon as the last item was over
the parents would be ushered into the assembly hall
and the tea-urns, plates of sandwiches and cakes were
to be ready and waiting for them.

The tide of parents ebbed and flowed, and almost
at the last moment Mr van der Eisler's car drew up
before the entrance. Nel, lingering in the hall almost
in tears, rushed to meet him as he got out, opened the
door to help Lady Brennon out and then bent to swing
her in the air.

'You came, you came!' cried Nel. 'And Granny too.
Olivia said you would.' She looked around her. 'I suppose Mummy's working...'

'Yes, love, she is. Will we do instead? We're looking forward to seeing you do whatever it is...'

Nel laughed and hugged her grandmother. 'I'm in
a gym display.' She looked suddenly anxious. 'It's almost time to start.'

'Then let us go at once and sit down,' said Lady
Brennon. 'Where is your nice Olivia?'

'She's got to see to the tea as well as us. I expect

she's in one of the pantries.' She caught them both by the hand. 'Come along—you will watch me, won't you?'

'I shan't take my eyes off you,' promised Mr van der Eisler.

They found seats at the end of a row, halfway towards the back of the hall and, since there were still some ten minutes before the first event was to take place, he settled Lady Brennon in her seat and got up. 'I'll be back,' he assured her, and disappeared through the nearby door.

In the hall he encountered the porter, enquired where the pantries might be, and with a brisk nod set off to find them.

Olivia, spooning tea into bowls ready for the urns, turned round to his quiet, 'Hello, Olivia.'

She felt the colour leave her cheeks and then rush back in a bright surge. She wished with all her heart that she could say something amusing and casual but all she managed was a breathless 'Oh,' and then added peevishly, 'You startled me.' She put the bowl down with a shaking hand. 'Shouldn't you be in the gym? I am glad you came.' She frowned in case she gave him the wrong impression. 'What I mean is that I'm glad you came for Nel's sake. She was so afraid no one would turn up. Is—are her grandmother and mother here too? I do hope so. She's in a rhythmic gym display, you know.' She paused for breath, aware that she was babbling.

He came into the pantry. 'And are you glad to see me again, Olivia?'

'Glad? Why should I be glad? I hadn't thought about it. You must go.'

He took no notice at all. 'I was sorry I wasn't in England to give you a lift back at the beginning of term.'

'There is an excellent train service,' she told him frostily. 'Nel told me that you were abroad.'

'Ah, yes, I sent her a postcard.'

'I hope you had a pleasant holiday...'

He smiled. 'Holiday? Ah, yes, of course. It seems a long time ago. Are you coming to watch this entertainment?'

'Of course not. I shall be helping behind the scenes and then giving a hand with the teas.' She picked up the bowl again for something to do. 'I hope you enjoy the display; please remember me to Lady Brennon. Goodbye, Mr van der Eisler.' He took his dismissal with a good grace, although he didn't return her goodbye.

As he slipped into his seat beside Lady Brennon, a few moments before the first item on the programme, she whispered, 'Did you find her?'

'Yes, but I fancy I've lost her again for the moment, although I'm not sure why.' He turned his attention to the first of the gym displays.

The afternoon went well—the gymnasts were faultless and the younger ones performed with aplomb, knowing that their mothers and fathers were sitting there admiring their efforts. Miss Cross brought the afternoon to a close with a suitable speech and everyone surged out, bent on getting a cup of tea.

Olivia, entrenched behind an urn, did her best not to look at Mr van der Eisler, poised precariously on a small wooden chair, bowing his vast person to listen to Nel's happy chatter. Her best wasn't good enough; Matron's tart voice brought her back to reality.

'Olivia? Do you not hear what I say? Sophie

Greenslade feels sick. Get her upstairs before she is, and stay with her until I come with her mother. We don't want a fuss…'

With one last lingering glance at Mr van der Eisler, Olivia led the unhappy Sophie up to her dormitory, held the bowl, cleaned the little girl up and tucked her under a blanket on her bed, looking pale but smelling sweet, so that by the time Matron and Mrs Greenslade arrived Matron was able to reassure the anxious mother that little Sophie wasn't suffering from some serious illness.

'Thank you, Olivia, you may go,' said Matron graciously.

Olivia went, as fast as her long legs could carry her. She reached the hall in time to see Lady Brennon, with Mr van der Eisler looming beside her, disappearing through the entrance.

She stood there, filled with bitter disappointment; never mind that she had decided to forget him, one more glimpse would have been nice before she began that difficult task. She looked with longing at his massive shoulders disappearing through the door. This really was the very last time she would see him…

He turned his head and saw her and came back to stand before her. 'Were you hiding?' he asked without preamble.

'Me? No. Sophie was being sick!'

'Ah.' He smiled at her and her heart turned over. 'We shall meet again,' he told her, and went away again.

A remark which made nonsense of her good resolutions, although during the course of a wakeful night she kept to her decision not to see him again. 'Not even to think of him,' she told herself. 'He was just being kind.'

He had said that they would meet again. Did he

mean that he would be coming to fetch Nel at the end of term? If so, she would take care not to be anywhere near him. If necessary, she would feel ill and be excused from her duties. A headache or, better still, a sprained ankle. On this ridiculous thought she fell into a restless doze, to wake the next morning heavy-eyed and pale, so that Matron asked her sharply if she was feeling poorly.

'It will be most inconvenient if you are,' said that lady, 'I shall want you to help me with hair-washing this evening.'

So Olivia washed one small head after the other, an occupation which allowed her to dream a great deal of nonsense. Even though it was nonsense it was comforting imagining what life would be like if Mr van der Eisler were to fall in love with her. She might not be going to see him again but there was no harm in a little daydreaming.

Chapter 6

Mrs Harding came the next day and as the school was empty, save for the cook, the porter and the two daily maids, Olivia and her mother had the pleasant illusion that the whole place was theirs. It was cold but fine weather and they took advantage of the peace and quiet to go for long walks, finding a village pub for lunch and getting back to the annexe in time to cook their supper and spent the evening together catching up on gossip. It was apparent to Olivia that her mother wasn't happy at Sylvester Crescent. She had few friends there, indeed, mere acquaintances, who came to play bridge and rarely asked her back to their homes. Mrs Fitzgibbon was demanding too, so that Mrs Harding felt restricted. It was no good telling her to assert herself, thought Olivia, for her mother was a gentle soul, always determined to expect the best from everyone.

Next year, thought Olivia, we'll make a home here. Mother can come back with me when term starts—at least she will be free to do what she likes with her days.

They sat making their plans, doing sums on scraps of paper, discussing the small things they would buy in order to make the little place like home, and Olivia, despite her secret heartache, was glad to see her mother so happy.

They went to Bath on the last day of the half-term, looking at the shops and having a splendid lunch before visiting the Abbey and then treating themselves to tea. It was a pity that once the school started again Olivia wouldn't be free for more than an hour or so each day, but Mrs Harding declared herself quite happy to potter around on her own. Indeed, she looked so much better that Olivia persuaded her to stay for another week and took it upon herself to phone her grandmother and tell her.

Mrs Fitzgibbon, naturally enough, was annoyed, complaining that she was unable to manage without her daughter's help.

'Doesn't that nice woman—Mrs Lark—come in each day and cook and clean?' asked Olivia.

'Well, of course she does,' snapped her grand-mother. 'You really don't suppose that I would wish to do those things myself, do you?'

'No, Granny. So you're being well looked-after. Good. Mother's very happy here and it's doing her good—she never liked London, you know.'

'You are an impertinent girl.'

Olivia said, 'Yes, Granny,' and then rang off.

School began again and now there was excitement

in the air. Christmas was near enough for the all-important question of presents to be the main topic and there would be the school play at the end of term and a concert by those who were learning some musical instrument or other.

There were the new pupils too, nicely settled in by now but still ignorant of the festivities ahead and anxious to join in everything.

Olivia, not a skilled needlewoman, none the less sewed pantomime costumes and, under the guidance of the art mistress, painted scenery, and when there was no one else available she heard the various parts. There were a great many, for the parents would have been upset if their own particular small daughter had had no part. Those who were hopeless at learning their lines were taught a dance. It had nothing to do with the plot, but what did that matter as long as every child took part?

Nel was one of the Christmas fairies and had a speaking part—well, she had to say, 'And here is Father Christmas' before waving her wand and rejoining the other fairies.

'Mummy will be proud of me,' she assured Olivia. 'She's coming to see me—she promised.'

She sounded so doubtful that Olivia hastened to reassure her.

'You're certain?' asked Nel as Olivia, on dormitory duty, went round tucking the children up for the night. Matron didn't approve of the tucking-up, but Olivia, remembering how cosy it had been to be tucked in at bedtime, took no notice of that.

'If your Mummy promised, then she'll come,' said Olivia firmly. 'Now go to sleep like a good girl.'

'All right. Olivia…?'

She turned back. 'Yes, dear?'

'I'm going to Holland for the holidays. I hope I'll like it. Mummy has a lot of friends and I don't like the lady who looks after me when she's away.'

'Perhaps it will be another lady this time.'

'I do hope so. I wish you were coming too. We could explore together. Where would you like to go most in Amsterdam?'

'Look, love, you must settle down.' And then, seeing that the child waited for an answer, she said, 'Oh, a seat opposite that big picture in the Rijksmuseum so that I could look at it really properly.' She dropped a kiss on the small forehead. 'Goodnight.'

The end of term prize-giving and the play were to be in the very early afternoon, and this time there was to be no lunch, only coffee and sherry beforehand, and tea afterwards while the children got ready to leave with their parents. Olivia, doing two things at once and at everyone's beck and call, longed for the day to be over. She wouldn't be leaving until the following day and she wasn't really looking forward to another Christmas at her grandmother's flat but she had the New Year to look forward to, and a good deal of the holiday would be taken up with getting her mother organised to come back with her. Obedient to Miss Ross's urgent voice, she began attaching the wings to the fairies' small shoulders.

It was a cold and gloomy day and the parents crowded in, intent on coffee and drinks before finding seats in the assembly hall. Olivia, counting fairy heads, found one missing. Nel—perhaps her mother had taken her aside for a moment. Olivia darted away, intent on getting her into her right place before the curtain went up.

Nel was in the hall and Mr van der Eisler was crouching beside her, holding her close in his great arms, crumpling her wings while she sobbed into his shoulder.

'She hasn't come?' hissed Olivia, in a whisper. 'Why didn't you make her? How could you let her not come? You knew that Nel…'

Nel gave a great sniff and paused in her sobs. 'She hasn't come—promised me, she promised me—you heard her, Uncle Haso. I won't go to Holland…'

He took out a very large white handkerchief and wiped her face. 'Must I go back all alone? I was counting on your company.'

She peered up at him. 'Would you be lonely without me?'

'I certainly would. Look, Olivia's here. I expect she wants you to join the other fairies.'

Olivia spoke. 'Nel has a speaking part; she's very important to the story.'

'Then she must do her best. What is it they say? "The show must go on". Actresses with broken hearts always forget their sorrow and act brilliantly, don't they, Olivia?'

'Always.' She didn't look at him but bore Nel away, just in time to join the rest of the troupe before the curtain was jerked open with a certain amount of in-expertise.

The play was loudly applauded, Nel said her line without mishap, and everyone dispersed for tea and biscuits while the children changed back into their school clothes, anxious to be gone now that they had collected their prizes. All the same it took some time to get the chattering, excited children ready and sent down to where their parents were waiting. Olivia, rounding up the last of them, was accosted by a parent.

'A most enjoyable afternoon.' She was a pleasant little lady with a kind face. 'You must be tired and you are so good with the children. I'm sure we shall all be sorry to see you go, but I suppose if the Board of Governors want someone with qualifications there is no choice.' She held out her hand. 'Anyway, I do wish you the best of luck. I'm sure Miss Cross will be very sorry to lose you.'

Olivia shook the hand offered her, smiled, and heard herself saying something which must have been sensible because the little lady smiled and nodded before she went away with her small daughter.

It can't be true, thought Olivia, bustling the rest of the girls downstairs. Miss Cross would have told me. She followed more slowly, her thoughts in a turmoil, glad to see that almost everyone had gone.

Not everyone. Nel and Mr van der Eisler were standing by the door. 'Nel wants to say goodbye,' he said smoothly, and then with an abrupt change of tone, 'Olivia, what is the matter? Are you ill?'

She managed a smile. 'No, no—just a bit tired—it's been a long day but everything was very successful, wasn't it? Nel looked well as a fairy, didn't she...?' And when he didn't speak, she added, 'Are you going back to Holland straight away? I didn't see Lady Brennon.'

'She has had flu—over the worst now, but this would have tired her out. We're going there now and crossing in a day or so.'

'Mummy will be waiting for me,' said Nel. 'Uncle Haso says so.'

'Splendid. You'll have a gorgeous Christmas, I expect.'

The child nodded. 'Mummy's got a new dress for me to wear; I'm to go to some parties.' She peered up at Olivia. 'You look sad…'

'Not a bit of it,' said Olivia in a bright and brittle voice. 'Just a bit tired.' She took care not to look at Mr van der Eisler; she could feel his eyes on her. 'I must be off, there is heaps of clearing up to do.'

'If Mummy invited you, would you come and stay with me, Olivia?'

'What a lovely idea, poppet, but I really must go home. You see, I've a mother and a granny, just like you.'

'Next to Granny and Uncle Haso I like you, Olivia,' said Nel, and lifted her face for a kiss.

'And I like you…'

'And Uncle Haso?'

'And Uncle Haso.' She still didn't look at him. It was really quite difficult to bottle up the torrent of words she wished to utter. To tell him that she was to be given the sack, that she was desolate at the idea of not seeing him again, that she loved him…

She held out a prim hand. 'Goodbye, Mr van der Eisler.' She addressed his chin to be on the safe side. If she looked at him, really looked, she might burst into tears.

His handshake was brief, as was his 'Goodbye, Olivia' and a few moments later he had driven away with Nel beside him.

She stayed where she was for a while, wondering what she should do. Very soon it would be supper-time and the staff would forgather for the end-of-term glass of sherry before the meal. That mother could have been mistaken, she reflected, she might be panicking about nothing at all. The sensible thing to do was to behave as though it was a mistake. She went and joined the others, exchanged comments about the play and the prize-giving, listened to plans for Christmas and ate her supper sitting between Miss Ross, whom she liked, and Matron, who as usual was laying down the law about the correct method of making beds.

It was when the meal was over and they were going their separate ways that Miss Cross asked her to join her in her study. She wasn't there long; it didn't take long to give someone the sack, even if it was done with regret and kindness.

Olivia went to the annexe and began to collect up her things. There was no hurry; she was to stay for another day to help in the general tidying up, label mislaid articles of clothing, make a list of any minor damage to bedlinen, towels and tablecloths. Only then could she get on the bus to take her to her train and so to her home.

She had some money saved and Miss Cross had given her a splendid reference, and had even suggested that she should advertise for a similar post. 'A smaller school,' she had advised. 'There are any number of good private schools around the country. Several of

them do without a qualified Matron, and you would do
very well in such a position where qualifications are
not necessary. You have had experience here. But you
should start looking at once. It is probably too late for
the spring term, but there is always the possibility of
starting at half-term. I'm sure that you have no need
to worry, Olivia.'

She worried none the less, most of the night and all
the next day. She slept that night though, from sheer
exhaustion. Since she had said goodbye to Miss Cross,
and only the domestic staff were left now, she caught
her bus and her train and, since every penny mattered
now, another bus to Sylvester Crescent.

Despite the fact that Christmas was only days away,
there wasn't a single Christmas tree to be seen in any
of the windows shrouded in their net curtains; the only
cheerful sight was Mr Patel's corner shop, bright with
coloured lights and a tree ablaze with coloured ornaments and tinsel, and a counter stacked with sweets
and biscuits. Bless the man, thought Olivia, as the bus
crawled past. I'll go and see him tomorrow.

The air was hardly festive in Mrs Fitzgibbon's flat.
True, there was a display of Christmas cards on the
mantelpiece, but her granny evinced none of the Christmas spirit expected of everyone during the festive season. Olivia hugged her mother and went to kiss her
grandmother's cheek.

'Back again?' asked that lady unnecessarily. 'In my
day school holidays were short; education was considered important.' She studied Olivia's face. 'You look
your age, Olivia.'

Olivia bit back the obvious retort, winked at her

mother to show her that she didn't mind, and took her cases into her bedroom. After a minute or two her mother joined her. 'You don't look a day older, darling,' she said earnestly, 'but you do look tired, love, and I think you've got thinner.'

'The end of the term is always a wild scramble, Mother. But great fun. Has Granny any plans for Christmas?'

'Well, some friends are coming for bridge on Christmas Eve…'

'Good, you and I will go to the midnight service. Any plans for Christmas dinner?'

'I think your granny is ordering a chicken.' She added, 'I bought a pudding from Marks and Spencer…'

'Good. We'll go to Mr Patel's tomorrow and get a bottle of wine and a box of crackers.' She added recklessly, 'And after Christmas you and I will have a day out at the sales.'

It was nice to see her mother's eyes sparkle with pleasure. There was no need to tell her that she had left the school just yet; she would do it after Christmas, when she had put an advert in the papers Miss Cross had recommended.

They went, she and her mother, to Mr Patel's shop the next morning and bought the wine, the crackers, and some festive-looking biscuits, and Olivia added potato crisps, a variety of cheeses and some nuts. Her grandmother would deplore the extravagance but, as Mr Patel had pointed out, it was Christmas and a time of good cheer and goodwill, and to emphasise his point he added a small bottle of lemonade for free.

They returned to the flat in good spirits, to have

them dampened by the old lady's disapproval. They were treated to a homily on the prudent spending of money which showed no sign of ending, so it was with relief that Olivia went to answer the doorbell.

Mr van der Eisler and Nel stood there, the little girl almost hidden under an arrangement of flowers in a basket.

Mr van der Eisler eyed Olivia keenly although his greeting was pleasantly casual. 'Nel wants to give you a Christmas present,' he explained, 'and since we're leaving in the morning we thought we should come today.'

'How very kind.' Olivia stood back to allow them to come in and added, 'What a lovely surprise.' She caught his eye and added quickly, 'The flowers, I mean.' She led the way to the sitting-room and ushered them inside. 'Would you like a cup of coffee? I was just going to get ours, and I'm sure Nel would like some lemonade.'

'Fizzy?' asked Nel.

'Very fizzy.' Mr Patel didn't sell any other kind. She handed their guests over to her mother and went to the kitchen. It was absurd how excited she felt just at the sight of him; it was a good thing he was going away tomorrow. There was no need to tell him that she wouldn't be going back to school after Christmas. 'Out of sight, out of mind,' said Olivia, and dropped the cup she was holding when Mr van der Eisler said, an inch or so from her ear, 'A very misleading statement, I have always thought.'

'Now look what you've done.' She rounded on him and found him smiling down on her so that she mumbled, 'Well, you startled me.'

'Understandably.' He was picking up the broken cup. 'Not one of your grandmother's best, I hope?'

'Well, yes, it is, but I'll tell her later...'

'Could we not throw the pieces into the dustbin and say nothing?'

She shook her head. 'Granny counts everything from time to time. She'd notice at once.'

She fetched another cup and set it on its saucer, wondering what to say next.

'Why did you look like that the other day?' he asked. 'And why are you so sad now? And don't, I beg of you, say that you don't know what I'm talking about.'

Something in his voice made her say at once, 'I'm not to go back to the school; the governors want someone with proper qualifications... It was a bit of a shock. I had hoped that I could stay on, and Mother was going to come and live there with me.'

He went to the stove and took the milk saucepan off just in time.

'My poor girl.' And when she turned her back so that he shouldn't see her threatening tears he busied himself making the coffee, and then opened cupboards until he found a packet of biscuits and arranged them on a plate. 'You haven't told your mother?'

She had turned round again, the tears swallowed. 'No, I thought I'd wait and try and find a job after Christmas.'

'Very sensible, but then you're a sensible girl, aren't you, Olivia?'

'Thank you for making the coffee.' She smiled a little. 'You don't look as though you could—what I mean is, I don't suppose you have to do it very often in your own home.'

'My housekeeper only allows me in the kitchen under her watchful eye, and you've met Becky—a tyrant if ever there was one!'

'A very kind-hearted one...'

He carried the tray into the sitting-room and sat down beside Mrs Fitzgibbon, charming her into good humour while Nel told Olivia and her mother just what a marvellous time she would have when she got to Amsterdam.

'I've a new dress,' she told them breathlessly, 'and of course it's Christmas, so Mummy won't go to her office. I expect we'll have a simply wonderful time.' She looked around her. 'You haven't got a Christmas tree— Uncle Haso has. It's in the window and people in the street can see it lighted up.'

Mrs Harding replied suitably and Olivia went away to get more coffee. The visit lasted some time but Mr van der Eisler had nothing more to say to her other than a polite goodbye and good wishes. Whether they were for Christmas or for her uncertain future she had no idea.

It was early evening and dark when she answered the doorbell again. Mr Patel stood on the doorstep with a large basket filled with tastefully arranged fruit, a large box of chocolates, and a charming floral arrangement of Christmas roses, miniature daffodils, hyacinths and jasmine.

'A surprise for you, miss,' he said cheerfully. 'I myself arranged the basket and went to the market to buy the flowers which the gentleman wished you to have. You are pleased?'

'Oh, Mr Patel, it's magnificent—how beautifully you've arranged it. It must have taken you ages.'

'Yes, indeed, but the gentleman was generous. It was a very splendid order. You will enjoy your Christmas now, miss, and may I remind you that my shop will be open until late on Christmas Eve in case you find yourself without essential food?'

'I'll remember that, Mr Patel—I expect my mother will be along to do some more shopping in the morning.'

'Always welcome and goodnight, miss.'

The cheerful little man went away and Olivia carried the basket into the sitting-room and put it on the table.

'A gift for me?' asked her grandmother.

'Well, no, Granny—it's for me,' Olivia was reading the card tucked behind the pineapple. Mr van der Eisler wished her the compliments of the season in handwriting which was barely readable. He had signed it H v d E. The card had bright red roses in one corner, but she didn't think that they signified anything.

'How very kind,' observed Mrs Harding, and looked pleased; the fruit would enliven their festive table very nicely but that wasn't why she looked pleased. She had a beautiful daughter who deserved an admirer as handsome and delightful as Mr van der Eisler. Of course there was nothing in it—there was Nel's mother, a very pretty woman and charming she had thought, although Nel had said one or two things… Of course, children did exaggerate.

Christmas came; they exchanged small gifts, cooked the chicken, ate the fruit and made up the second bridge table unwillingly on Boxing Day, when Mrs Fitzgibbon's friends came for the afternoon and evening. Olivia, who was as bad at bridge as her mother, sighed with relief as the last of them went home and she could clear the cups and glasses and plates. Their guests had eaten everything offered to them and Olivia was hungry. She did the glasses, filled a bowl with water to do the washing-up, and went to cut herself a slice of bread with a hunk of cheese on top. Her mother and grandmother had gone to bed and she didn't hurry, there was nothing planned for the following day; she would pen an advert ready to post at the first opportunity.

She finished her chores, took a chocolate from the box which her grandmother had offered round with a generous hand, and went to bed.

She was making the early morning tea when the phone rang... It was still dark and very cold and the phone was in the hall. She pulled her dressing-gown tightly round her and padded along to see who it was. A wrong number, she supposed, and her hello was abrupt.

'Have I got you out of bed,' enquired Mr van der Eisler.

'No. I'm getting the tea, and this is a fine time to phone, I must say.'

'Only because I need your help, Olivia. Nel ran away from her home—I found her and she's with me, but I must be at the hospital all day and every day for some time. She wants to go back to Lady Brennon but that has to be arranged. Bronger, who looks after my home, will fly over this morning and fetch you back here. He'll have tickets and money—have you a passport? Yes, good. He'll be with you by midday. Will you do this for me, Olivia? And for Nel? She asks for you continually.'

'Yes, of course I will. What do I bring with me? Enough for a few days?'

'Ten days—something warm. Thank you, Olivia.'

She padded back to the kitchen. The kettle was boiling merrily and she made the tea and sat down to drink hers. She was, of course, out of her mind; he had only to ask her to do something quite preposterous and she agreed without even thinking about it. Her head needed examining. All the same, she would go. She reviewed her wardrobe mentally, thought about money, and took a cup of tea to her mother.

'I heard the phone,' said that lady, with just the hint of a question in her voice.

Olivia explained. 'Do you think I'm mad?' she asked.

'Certainly not, dear. I don't imagine that Mr van der Eisler is a man to waste time on phone calls at seven o'clock in the morning unless he has good reason to do so. You do quite right to go. Poor child…!'

Olivia settled on the end of the bed. 'Only, I'm so sorry to leave you, Mother. We'd planned so much…'

'Yes, I know, love, but you won't be gone all that time, and I'll come and stay with you again.'

'Yes, of course.' Olivia picked at the cotton bedspread. 'Mother, I can't not go. You see, I'm in love with him.'

'Yes, dear.' Her mother sounded unsurprised.

Olivia pulled at a loose thread and watched it unravel. 'It's silly, really. I think he'll marry Rita—Nel's mother—it would be so suitable; she's his dead friend's widow and Nel is devoted to him. Besides, she's pretty and charming and amusing.'

'None the less you love him, Olivia. You must do whatever your heart tells you to do.'

Olivia smiled. 'Granny won't like it.'

'Granny has nothing to do with it, darling. Go and get dressed and pack a bag. I'll get breakfast. Take your Granny a cup of tea first, and don't say a word.'

So Olivia was dressed, her bag packed, her passport found, money in her purse and her winter coat laid out on the bed ready to put on by the time her grandmother came out of her room.

She looked at Olivia's neatly turned-out person. 'Why are you wearing that good skirt?' she wanted to know. 'There's no money to buy you new clothes, you know.'

Olivia handed her a cup of coffee and gave one to her mother.

'I'm going over to Holland, Granny. I've been asked to look after Nel for a week or two.'

'And where's the money coming from to pay for your fare?'

'I'm being fetched.'

As if on cue the door-knocker was thumped, and she went to answer it. A short, stout man stood on the step, very spruce as to dress, with iron-grey hair and very blue eyes.

'Miss Harding. I am Bronger, houseman to Mr van der Eisler; I am to take you to his house in Amsterdam.' He held out a hand and crushed hers with it.

'Do please come in, we're just having coffee. Do we need to go at once or have you time for a cup?'

'That would be good, miss.' His English was fluent but strongly accented. 'If we leave in half an hour, but no later.'

She helped him off with his short, thick jacket. 'How do we go?'

'A car will come here for us, all is arranged. We fly to Schiphol and from there we drive to Amsterdam. I have left the car there.'

'Well, do come in and meet my mother and grandmother.'

He shook hands and bowed slightly, took a chair and drank his coffee, answering Mrs Fitzgibbon's questions with politeness and telling her, in effect, nothing at all. A very discreet man, thought Olivia, liking him.

The car came and they were borne away. 'You have no need to trouble about the journey,' said Bronger. 'All is arranged.'

'In such a short time, too,' said Olivia. 'I can't think how you did it in just a few hours.'

He smiled and said nothing and presently she asked, 'May I ask you a little about Nel? She is with Mr van der Eisler, isn't she? Is there no chance that she might go home?' She paused. 'Perhaps I shouldn't ask you…'

'Mr van der Eisler has confided in me, miss. Nel refuses to go to her home; I do not know exactly why. She left a note when she left home and most fortunately she was found within a few hours. She wishes for you and she is most upset; this is the best plan Mr van der Eisler could make in the short time he had. It is unfortunate that he has a very busy schedule at several hospitals during the next few days which he cannot change. It is good of you to come at so short a notice, miss.'

'Well, I hope I'll be able to help. Mr van der Eisler said on the phone that Nel would go back to her grandmother as soon as he could arrange that.'

Bronger nodded his grey head. 'Nel is happy with her. She is like her father was.'

They had reached the airport and the next half-hour was taken up with being processed to the plane, and once on board they didn't talk. Olivia had a great deal to think about and Bronger closed his eyes and drifted into a light doze. He must have been up very early, thought Olivia.

At Schiphol he escorted her to the main entrance, bade her wait and went away, to return within minutes driving a beautifully kept Jaguar. He got out, stowed her case, and opened the car door.

Olivia hesitated. 'May I sit with you?' she asked. 'I'd much rather.'

He looked pleased. 'A pleasure, miss.' He gave her a rare smile. 'It is a short drive to Amsterdam.'

Once in the heart of the city, Olivia looked about her eagerly. Away from the busy main streets the old houses by the canals looked as though nothing in them had altered for centuries, and when Bronger stopped before Mr van der Eisler's house she got out and stood on the narrow pavement, looking up at it.

She wasn't allowed to loiter. He mounted the double steps, opened the door and ushered her inside. At the same moment a small figure came flying down the stairs and flung herself at Olivia.

'I knew you'd come. Uncle Haso said you would. Oh, Olivia, you'll stay with me, won't you? I won't go back, I won't...'

'Now, now, poppet,' said Olivia, and hugged the child. 'Of course I'll stay, and I'm sure your uncle won't make you do anything which makes you unhappy.'

'She was horrid—she had a wart on her chin and she slapped me and told my Mummy I was disobedient and Mummy just laughed and said I'd have to change my ways… Olivia…'

Bronger took charge. 'Now, Nel, will you let miss go to her room and tidy herself? Presently you'll have your lunch with her; Ofke will have it all ready.'

A door at the end of the hall opened then, and a tall, bony woman joined them. She offered a hand to Olivia and smiled, and Bronger said, 'My wife, Ofke. She housekeeps and cooks. She speaks no English but I will help, and Nel understands Dutch—some at least.'

He said something to his wife, who nodded and led the way up the staircase. The landing was square, with doors on either side and a wide corridor running towards the back of the house. She led the way down this and opened one of the doors, beckoning Olivia to go in.

The room was square and lofty and its one large window overlooked a narrow strip of garden at the back of the house. It was furnished with a canopied bed, a rosewood table with a triple mirror on it, a tall-boy in the same wood, a couple of small armchairs and a bedside table with a lovely porcelain lamp on it. The carpet and the curtains matched the soft pink of the bedspread and it was deliciously warm.

Nel ran past her. 'There's a bathroom—' she opened a door '—and a clothes closet.' She flung open another door. 'Uncle Haso let me choose.' She perched on the bed while Olivia took off her coat and hat. 'I'll tell you about how I ran away, shall I?'

'Yes, darling, I do want to know what happened. But shall we wait until we are downstairs, perhaps over lunch?'

There was no sign of Mr van der Eisler when they went downstairs and presently they had their lunch in a small, cosy room behind the vast drawing-room Olivia had glimpsed, and Nel poured out her story. It was rather garbled and Olivia had difficulty following it. The woman with the wart featured heavily in it and, so, regrettably, did Nel's mother who, it seemed, had hardly ever been at home during Christmas. She let the child talk because she could see that it was what she needed to do—perhaps later Mr van der Eisler would find the time to tell her exactly what had happened.

Nel was a little too bright-eyed, she thought, so after lunch she suggested that they went and sat by the fire in the magnificence of the drawing-room. 'And you can tell me some more,' she suggested. The chairs were large and comfortable. Nel climbed into her lap, had a little weep, and closed her eyes and presently slept. So did Olivia, worn out from the suddenness of it all.

Chapter 7

Mr van der Eisler, coming quietly into his house, paused in the drawing-room doorway, put a cautionary hand on Achilles' great head, and looked his fill at the sleeping occupants of the chair. Olivia's bright hair had come a little loose from its pins and her mouth was just a little open. All the same, she looked very beautiful, sitting there, clutching Nel to her, her chin resting on the child's fair head.

He trod across the room, making no sound on the carpet, and stooped to kiss Nel's cheek and then Olivia's. Neither of them stirred as he went to sit down in his armchair on the opposite side of the great hearth. Achilles arranged himself beside his master's chair and presently sank his head on his paws and dozed. His master, tired though he was after a long list in Theatre, stayed awake, his eyes on the sleeping pair.

Olivia opened her eyes first, suddenly wide awake, staring at him over Nel's head. She whispered, 'We went to sleep—have you been here long? Why didn't you wake us up?'

He smiled and shook his head. 'I wanted to keep my dreams,' he said, and she frowned, wondering what he meant. But there was no chance to ask, for Nel woke up then and scrambled off her lap and on to her uncle's.

'May I stay forever?' she asked him. 'I'll go to school if I must, because then I can see Granny, but I'll come back here and live with you and Olivia.'

'We'll have to think about that, Nel. I'm not sure if it would work. You see, I have to work each day and Olivia must go back to England in a little while.' He looked down at the suddenly unhappy face. 'But you shall certainly stay with Granny as often as you want to, and in two days' time I'll drive you and Olivia up to Friesland for a little holiday.'

'You won't send me back to that horrid lady? Mummy won't mind if I'm not there—I heard her tell that lady that I was an encum…a long word I can't quite remember, but I think it means that she doesn't want me.'

'I think that perhaps we can alter that, *liefje*, but we'll have to wait until I have the time to arrange things differently.'

'I don't suppose you'd like to get married?'

He laughed then. 'Well, I have been giving it serious thought just lately.'

Which would make everyone happy, reflected Olivia, excepting herself, of course. She looked up and found his eyes on her.

'I expect you would like to phone your mother, Olivia. Use the phone in my study—the last door on the opposite side of the hall. And you, my pet, must go and find Ofke and have your supper...'

'You won't go away? And Olivia? Will she put me to bed?'

'Of course,' said Olivia, and got to her feet. 'You go and have your supper while I phone home, and we'll go upstairs together.'

She was glad to get out of the room. Seeing Mr van der Eisler sitting there in his home, planning a convenient future so calmly, was turning her good sense upside-down.

By the time she had finished talking to her mother, Nel had had her supper and the next half-hour or so was taken up by getting her to bed. A long-drawn-out business which Olivia made no attempt to hasten—to spend the rest of the evening with Mr van der Eisler would be heaven but on the other hand living up to his idea of a sensible young woman was going to be difficult—but finally she could prolong the bedtime story no longer. She tucked the little girl in, kissed her and went downstairs.

Mr van der Eisler was sitting in his chair reading, with Achilles still snoozing at his feet. They both got up as she went in. 'Do sit down,' he begged her. 'Nel is a dear child, but quite exhausting. Would you like sherry?'

She accepted the crystal glass he offered her and set it down carefully on the table beside her, hoping that he hadn't seen her trembling hand. Which of course he had. She said, 'She *is* a dear little girl. Perhaps her mother could find another person to look after her? I'm sure that's her real reason for running away. The lady had a wart...' She saw his smile. 'No, I'm serious—warts and witches, you know!—and perhaps being made to eat something she didn't like... Such silly little things which need not have happened if...'

She stopped then, just in time, but he finished the sentence for her. 'If her mother had been there. You're quite right. But Rita has an excellent job at which she excels; she also meets a number of interesting people, goes to various meetings and travels—all of which are important to her.'

Not more important than looking after your small daughter, thought Olivia, although she didn't say so. 'So what do you intend to do?' she asked.

'I shall be free tomorrow afternoon. We will go and see Rita, who has agreed to be at home then. Perhaps Nel will agree to stay with her, if so all the better, but if there is still difficulty I will bring her back here for another night and the following day we will drive up to Friesland—that will be in the late afternoon, so I must ask you to look after her until then.'

'Very well. I shan't be needed in Friesland?'

'Indeed you will. My mother is more than willing to have Nel but she doesn't feel able to cope with the child. My young brother will be at home but I doubt if he will want to spend his time with Nel.'

Olivia thought of several things to say but uttered none of them. No doubt Mr van der Eisler had enough on his mind without her asking what to his mind would be foolish questions. She had almost no money, very few clothes with her, and any chances of getting a job

had been knocked on the head for the time being. Such
trivial matters, she reflected sourly, would mean little
to him. He had arranged everything efficiently and to
suit himself. If she hadn't loved him she might have
flatly refused to be rushed into anything...

Bronger came in and requested that they should dine,
and over a delicious meal in the charming dining-room
she became reconciled to his plans. Due, no doubt, to
his placid conversation, the superb roast pheasant and
the vintage claret. They had their coffee in the drawing-
room and presently he excused himself on the pretext
of having telephone calls to make, and left her to sit by
the fire, leafing through magazines and trying to think
sensibly about her future.

Since it seemed that he didn't intend to return to the
drawing-room she took herself off to bed, escorted to
the stairs by Bronger with the assurance that she would
be called in the morning with tea.

'China or Indian, miss?' he asked, and bade her a
kindly goodnight.

She slept soundly and was wakened by Nel creeping
into her bed and demanding a story, only brought to its
conclusion by the arrival of the morning tea, shared by
the two of them. Later, dressed, they went downstairs
together to find that Mr van der Eisler had already left
home for the hospital, leaving a message that they were
to amuse themselves that morning and be sure to be
ready for him when he got back around two o'clock.

'So, what shall we do?' asked Olivia.

Nel looked surprised. 'You know already,' she said
accusingly. 'We're going to look at the picture in the
Rijksmuseum—you said so...'

'So I did. Stupid of me to have forgotten. I'll ask Bronger how to get there.'

'I will drive you there, miss. The professor wouldn't allow anything else.'

'Oh, wouldn't he? Professor? Is Mr van der Eisler a professor?'

'Yes, miss. Very highly thought of, too. When would you like to go, miss?'

He drove them in the dark blue Jaguar, sleek and gleaming, and set them down at the museum's entrance, handed Olivia a couple of notes with the observation that the professor had told him to deal with expenses, and told her that he would be exactly on that spot at twelve o'clock. 'There is a pleasant café inside,' he suggested. 'I wish you an enjoyable morning.'

Which it certainly was. They prowled round looking at portraits and landscapes and Olivia, who had feared that Nel might get bored, found that she was as interested as she herself was. They had their elevenses and made their way to the Nightwatch, and sat down before it. It was an enormous painting; it took them some time to pick out the many figures in it and, once they had done that, Nel insisted on making up stories about each of them—even the little dog. They sat absorbed, side by side, their heads close together while they whispered.

When Mr van der Eisler slid his vast person on to the bench beside Olivia she gave a gasp. 'Oh, heavens, have we forgotten the time?' She looked at her watch, bending her head to hide the sudden flood of colour in her face.

'No, no—the last operation had to be cancelled so I have been able to leave early. Have you been here long?'

Nel leaned across Olivia. 'Ages and ages,' she said with satisfaction. 'Olivia's been telling me stories about the man in the picture. Will you take us home? Bronger said he'd come for us at twelve o'clock.'

'Will I do instead? I told Bronger I'd fetch you on my way back.'

'Well, of course you will, Uncle Haso. I like Bronger but I like you a lot better—so does Olivia, don't you Olivia?'

Olivia said rather coldly, 'I haven't given the matter much thought.'

'Bronger's married to Ofke,' observed Nel, 'so you can only like him a little otherwise she might mind, but Oom Haso…'

Olivia avoided Mr van der Eisler's eye and said hastily, 'Yes, yes, of course, shouldn't we be going?'

'You haven't told me about that man in the corner of the painting.'

'I think it would be nice to save him for the next time,' said Olivia briskly. 'I'm sure your uncle wants his lunch.'

Mr van der Eisler, who was quite happy where he was, saw that it might be better to agree with Olivia, who looked a little flushed and put out.

'By all means let us go home to our lunch. I dare say we shall have tea with your mother, Nel.' And at the child's quick frown he added, 'and you will have your supper in Friesland.'

A red herring which he trailed successfully all the

way back to his house with Nel perched beside him, happy again.

Nel's high spirits disappeared as they got into the car again to go to her mother's flat. Her small mouth was set in a mutinous tight line and Olivia's coaxing was to no avail. As they stopped outside the block of flats Nel said in a small voice, 'You promise not to leave me here, Uncle Haso?'

'I promise, *liefje*. Your mother wants to see you and make sure that you are happy; she won't stop you going to Friesland with Olivia and when you have had a holiday there perhaps you will change your mind and go back to her. You ought to go back to school in a week or so, but I've arranged that—you won't need to go back until we have things sorted out here.'

'Then will you and Mummy take me back?'

'Very likely, for we need to talk to your granny. She must be told of the plans we have for the future.'

Of course they are going to marry, thought Olivia miserably, and had the thought substantiated by the manner in which Rita greeted Mr van der Eisler. Arms around his neck and looking up at him from under long, curling—and false—eyelashes. He remained placid, but then he wasn't a man to show his feelings, decided Olivia, and urged Nel forward to greet her mother.

Rita enfolded her child in a close embrace, kissed her a great deal and murmured in a loving voice. Olivia wasn't taken in one bit and she didn't think Nel was either, but what Mr van der Eisler thought was being hidden behind a passive countenance.

'Darling,' cooed Rita, 'what a lot of trouble you have given Mummy—I'm almost out of my mind… Now, I want you to run along and play while your uncle and I have a talk. Juffrouw Schalk is in your bedroom, packing some clothes for you. Take...' She paused and smiled prettily at Olivia. 'I've forgotten your name—so stupid...'

'Olivia.'

'Of course, take Olivia with you, darling. I'm sure Juffrouw Schalk will be able to give her some useful tips.'

She flipped a hand in dismissal and turned to Mr van der Eisler as Nel led Olivia from the room. 'Don't go away,' begged the child as they crossed the hall and went into a room on the far side.

Juffrouw Schalk was there, sitting in a comfortable chair by a closed stove, and she was exactly as Olivia had pictured her—dark eyes, small and sly, a long nose, a high forehead from which dark hair was drawn back and a mean mouth, beside which was the wart. Probably she was a good and efficient woman, but Olivia could understand at once why Nel didn't like her.

Juffrouw Schalk spoke sharply in Dutch to Nel, who answered her and added in English, 'Juffrouw Schalk speaks English, Olivia.'

'Good afternoon,' said Olivia politely, and was told to sit down.

'This silly child,' said Juffrouw Schalk in thickly accented English, 'is spoilt by her English grandmother. She should go to one of our schools and learn instead of doing as she likes.'

Olivia wondered if the child had had the chance to do anything she liked while she was with her mother.

'She is a good pupil at her school and happy with her grandmother.'

'An old lady,' shrugged Juffrouw Schalk. 'Who does not punish her, I think.'

'She's not old,' shouted Nel, 'and I don't need to be punished. I'm a good girl, excepting when I'm with you. I hate you.'

'Hush, Nel,' said Olivia. 'Juffrouw Schalk doesn't mean to be unkind; she is merely expressing her opinions.'

She looked at that lady, who was red in the face and about to burst into indignant speech. 'Perhaps Nel might go to the kitchen and get a drink of milk?' she suggested, and didn't wait for an answer but sent her on the errand, aware that Juffrouw Schalk was on the point of exploding.

'You are a fool,' said that lady. 'Mrs Brennon tells me this, that you come to look after the child so that you may entice the professor. But you waste your time, miss, for they will marry soon and you will be sent packing.'

Olivia gave her a thoughtful look. 'What makes you think that I am in the least interested in Mr van der Eisler? I hardly know him. I am merely helping him out in a difficult situation—which never need have arisen if you had treated Nel with kindness.' She drew a steadying breath. 'I must say that I agree with Nel; I find you unkind and far too strict. In fact, I don't like you, Juffrouw Schalk.'

She smiled at the outraged face and walked out of the room, found her way to the kitchen and accepted

a cup of tea from a comfortable woman who was ply-
ing Nel with milk and biscuits.

She was enjoying a second cup and a three-sided
conversation with Nel and the comfortable woman
when the door opened and Rita came in.

'What's this I hear from Juffrouw Schalk?' she demanded. 'That you have questioned her treatment of
Nel—the insolence...'

'No, no, I was quite polite to her,' said Olivia calmly,
'and what I said was true. I'm sure you must have seen
that for yourself, Mrs Brennon.' She added, 'Although
if you aren't at home much you would have noticed
nothing.'

Nel had skipped away, to find her uncle no doubt,
and Olivia watched Rita's face grow ugly with rage.
Might as well be hung for a sheep as for a lamb, she
thought. Mr van der Eisler, appealed to, would send
her packing in the nicest possible way and Rita would
weep prettily on his shoulder and tell him that she had
had no idea that Juffrouw Schalk had been making her
darling Nel unhappy.

'If I had the time to arrange things differently for
Nel, I would do so. Unfortunately I have a most important appointment very shortly, and a dinner party
this evening.' She glared at Olivia. 'But be sure that I
shall not forget this. I shall speak to Mr van der Eisler
and ask him to rearrange his plans for Nel.'

'I'll wait here, shall I? While you talk to him.'

Rita spoke pettishly. 'Don't be absurd. Haven't I
just said that I have no time now? You'll have to go
with Nel and stay with her until I can find the time to

discuss this. Am I never to be allowed to live my life as I want? All this stupid fuss—Nel's only a child…'

Olivia bit back the words she longed to utter and instead thanked the comfortable woman for the tea and held the door open for Rita, who swept past her across the hall and into the room where Nel and Mr van der Eisler were standing at the window, watching the traffic in the street.

Olivia could do nothing but admire the speed with which Rita transformed herself into an ill-done-by and wistful woman.

She said in a wispy voice, 'Oh, Haso, tell me that I'm doing the right thing—I have so looked forward to these weeks with Nel and everything has gone wrong.'

Her eyes had filled with tears and Olivia wondered how she managed to do that. Crocodile tears, she decided. Rita, she suspected, was only too glad to see Nel's small back disappear through the door. It was a perfect performance; she watched Mr van der Eisler's face and wished that just once in a while he would allow his feelings to show. Certainly his voice was kind and patient.

'I am sure that when Nel has had a holiday with my mother, away from all of us, she will feel quite differently. We must talk about it later, of course, but I think that it might be best for her to return to school in a week or so, and perhaps you can arrange to be free for the Easter holidays.'

Rita pouted prettily. 'But I've already arranged…' She glanced at Olivia. 'I don't wish to discuss this before a servant.'

'If you refer to Olivia, I must point out that she is

not a servant; she is looking after Nel at my request and for your convenience.'

Something in his quiet voice made Rita say reluctantly, 'I'm sorry—I'm so upset.' She wasn't too upset to look at her watch and add, 'I simply have to go— an important meeting.' She kissed Nel and then went to him and tucked a hand through his arm. 'Don't be angry with me, Haso, we'll meet and talk. You know that I depend on you utterly.'

Olivia looked away as she kissed his cheek and whispered something with a little trill of laughter. Nel, she noticed, had turned her back and was watching the street outside again. She gave her mother a dutiful kiss when bidden to do so, pressed herself close to Olivia when Juffrouw Schalk came in with her case, and hopped into the car the moment the door was opened. Nobody spoke as Mr van der Eisler drove back to his house. Only once they were inside its warm comfort did he observe, 'A cup of tea before we go, I think. Do go into the drawing-room and Bronger will bring it—I must do some phoning. I'll join you presently.'

They had almost finished when he came back, accepted a cup of tea, made a few non-committal remarks about nothing much and suggested that they should leave in ten minutes or so.

He's angry, thought Olivia, escorting Nel upstairs to fetch a forgotten teddy bear and to collect her own case. It was taken from her by a hovering Bronger, Nel and Achilles were settled on the back seat of the car, and Mr van der Eisler invited her to sit beside him.

An opportunity not to be missed; she would see precious little of him once this small upheaval had been settled. A week, she reflected, or with luck ten days before Nel would be sent back to England—and she with her, no doubt. She would see nothing of him during that time, but just being in the same country was a small comfort.

The afternoon had darkened and she had no doubt that outside the big car's comfortable warmth it was very cold.

'We shall have snow,' said Mr van der Eisler, 'probably before we reach Tierjum.'

'Just where is that?'

'A few miles east of Leeuwarden, a small village close to one of the lakes.' He didn't enlarge upon that, and she supposed that he was vexed with her for upsetting Rita. She sat very still and quiet, watching what she could see in the gathering gloom of the countryside.

They were travelling north and sure enough, as they reached the Afsluitdijk, it began to snow. Soft, feathery flakes at first, and then a whirling mass blown hither and thither by the wind.

'You're not nervous?'

She glanced at his calm profile. 'No. If I were driving, though, I should be terrified.'

'Once we're off the *dijk* the wind won't be so fierce, and we shall be at Tierjum in half an hour or so. Is Nel asleep?'

She turned her head to look. 'Yes, and so is Achilles.'

'He's devoted to her. I must do my best to come up and see her before she goes back and bring him with me.'

It seemed endless, the drive across the *dijk*—the sea *dijk* was too high for her to see the sea, but on the other side of the road it was lower, and she could see the grey waters of the Ijsselmeer roughed up by the wind; they looked cold and forbidding.

The *dijk* ended at last and although the snow was still falling relentlessly there was less wind. 'Franeker,' said Mr van der Eisler, sweeping through a small town with lighted shop windows before taking the main road to Leeuwarden. It was a motorway, she supposed, for although she could see lights from time to time there was nothing close to the road. At Leeuwarden he circumvented the town, leaving its lighted streets for the highway again, but only for a short distance, soon turning off on to a narrow brick road. Although she looked hard she could see nothing on either side of them. 'Fields,' said Mr van der Eisler briefly. 'This is a country road.'

He appeared to know it well, which was a good thing, she considered, for there were no signposts visible at the few crossings. It might be near Leeuwarden but it seemed like a distant and isolated spot. Through the snow she glimpsed lights at last, and he slowed the car to enter a village—a handful of small houses, a lighted shop, the dim outline of a church—and then another lane, to sweep the car between brick pillars and high wrought-iron gates and stop before a house whose windows blazed light. The dark evening and the snow prevented her from seeing the house clearly but she had the impression of a flat, solid front before she was urged up double steps and in through an arched doorway. Achilles loped beside her; Mr van der Eisler, with Nel in his arms, was close on her heels.

A tall, bony man with white hair opened the inner door as they reached it and Mr van der Eisler put Nel down and clapped the older man on the shoulder, talking what to Olivia sounded utter nonsense. Dutch was bad enough, although she had begun to pick out a word here and there, but this was something different. Mr van der Eisler suddenly switched to English.

'This is Tober, Olivia. He has been with the family forever—before I was born—he is part of our lives.'

She held out a hand and said, 'How do you do?' and was a little surprised when Tober told her that he did very well in quite tolerable English. He was embraced by Nel then, before taking their coats and leading the way across the wide hall to the double doors on one side. Nel was hanging on to his hand and Achilles was trotting sedately beside him.

Very much at home, thought Olivia, and as though she had voiced her thought Mr van der Eisler said, 'Nel comes to pay us a visit each time she comes to Holland and, as for Achilles, he regards it as his second home—as indeed it is.'

They had reached the doors and Tober had opened them to reveal a large, lofty room with tall, narrow windows at one end, almost concealed by thick brocade curtains of tawny silk. The walls were hung with the same silk panels, separated by white-painted columns. The floor was polished wood and covered with silky carpets and there were massive bow-fronted display cabinets against the walls and an enormous fireplace with a stone hood. A museum, thought Olivia, and then as her eye took in the comfortable chairs, the tables with their pretty table-lamps, the pile of books on the sofa-table, the jumble of knitting cast down on a low stool and the tabby cat curled up in one of the chairs, A museum perhaps, but a lived-in one, warm and very welcoming.

Nel had darted forward to where a lady was sitting by the fire, and Olivia, propelled gently by a large hand between her shoulders, perforce followed her. The lady got to her feet, stooped to kiss Nel, and then advanced a few steps to meet them.

'Haso—how delightful to see you, my dear.' She lifted her face to receive his kiss. 'And this is Olivia. Welcome, my dear, I am so delighted to have guests.'

She held out a hand, smiling at Olivia. She was of the same height and still a beautiful woman, with bright blue eyes, iron-grey hair, brushed severely back from her forehead, and an upright figure. 'You had a good drive here? The weather can be most unpleasant at this time of year. You must have a cup of coffee before you go upstairs, and you, Nel, shall have warm milk and some of those little biscuits you like so much.'

The coffee was brought and Olivia, sitting beside her hostess before a blazing fire, felt that life just for the moment was perfect. Mr van der Eisler sat in a great wing chair with Nel on a stool beside him and Achilles already dozing at his feet; she smiled at him and his answering smile was kind. It was also impersonal.

Presently she was taken upstairs by Tober's wife, Anke, a short, stout little person, dressed severely in black and bearing all the hallmarks of an old family retainer. It was extraordinary, reflected Olivia as she followed her up the wide, curving staircase, that in this modern world Mr van der Eisler's family appeared to have no shortage of help. He was well served in his London home, and equally well here. Perhaps this house belonged to his mother—perhaps she could discover that while she was here...

She and Nel had adjoining rooms and shared a bathroom. Both were charmingly furnished in soft pastel colours and rosewood. Olivia, running a hand over the patina of the sofa-table, which did duty as a dressing-table, reflected that the house was perfect. She could hardly wait for the morning to examine it from the outside. Nel, tugging at her hand, brought her back to reality, and she tidied the pair of them and they went downstairs again. Nel, she noted, was a changed child, laughing and skipping around—a contrast to the unhappy child she had seen in Amsterdam. Perhaps when Mr van der Eisler and Rita married he would alter things.

He and his mother broke off their conversation as they went in and he said easily, 'We shall dine early as I must get back. Come and sit down and have a drink, Olivia—Nel, Anke has made some of that lemonade you like so much, and I think that you might stay up for dinner just this once.'

He was rewarded with a hug and a great many kisses. 'You really are a super uncle,' said Nel. 'It would be nice if I could live here with you and live with Granny in England.'

His mother said gently, 'But you would miss your mother, *liefje*.'

'I wouldn't, because she's never home with me, only that awful Juffrouw Schalk. She has a wart...'

'I dare say your mother will be able to find someone else without a wart...'

Nel shook her head.

'I'll talk to Mummy,' promised Mr van der Eisler, 'and see if she can find someone you'd like to be with when she's not there.'

'Olivia,' Nel cried happily. 'You wouldn't would you? Oh, do say yes.'

Mr van der Eisler spoke in a smooth voice. 'Olivia has to go back home to her mother and grandmother, Nel.'

Olivia watched the small face pucker; any moment now there would be a storm of tears. 'I dare say,' she said loudly, 'that you could come and see me some-times—you have lots of holidays.'

Mevrouw van der Eisler agreed enthusiastically to this. 'What a splendid idea. We must talk about it while you're here. But Tober is here to tell us that dinner is on the table—I'm sure that you must be hungry.'

They dined in the splendour of a room at the back of the house, with high windows looking out over what Olivia supposed was the garden. The furniture was massive and old, and its walls were hung with rather dark portraits of handsome ancestors, staring down at the celery soup, the roast duck and the elaborate iced confection offered in Nel's honour.

Conversation flowed easily but they didn't linger at the table. Nel was sleepy by now, and Olivia suggested that she should take her up to bed.

'Of course,' agreed Mevrouw van der Eisler, 'but come down as soon as you can and have your coffee.'

So Olivia went upstairs with Nel, ran her bath while she undressed, sponged her briskly, towelled her dry and popped her into bed, already almost asleep. Even when she was free to go back downstairs she hesitated—mother and son might wish to talk together, and she had no idea how long he was staying; he had said nothing to Nel when she had kissed him good-night. She pottered round her room, putting on more lipstick and taking it off again, and finally went slowly down the staircase.

Mr van der Eisler was in the hall, shrugging himself into his overcoat.

'There you are,' he said cheerfully, 'just in time to say goodbye.'

His words fell like so many stones. She summoned a steady voice. 'I hope you have an easy trip back,' she said brightly. 'Has it stopped snowing?'

'No, and isn't likely to for a few days, but you'll be cosy enough here. As soon as Rita and I have had a chance to talk I'll let you know what has been decided.' He came towards her and took her hand. 'I'm grateful to you, Olivia, but I won't keep you longer than is absolutely necessary. This is a sorry business, but Nel's happiness is important. At the same time one must admit that her mother has every right to her own life, but I think I can solve that for her.'

Well, of course he could, thought Olivia pettishly; he had only to marry the woman and everyone, except herself of course, would be happy.

She said in a cool, sedate voice, 'I'll take good care of Nel, Mr van der Eisler,' then edged away from him, relieved to see his mother coming from the drawing-room.

'You'll phone me, Haso?' said that lady. 'I shall be glad to see a satisfactory end to this—a suitable end too.' She added, 'I know Rob was your greatest friend…'

Olivia slipped away into the drawing-room, empty except for the cat, for Achilles was returning with his master. Tober came in with fresh coffee, smiling and nodding, and she smiled and nodded back, her ears stretched to hear the heavy front door close. If she saw Mr van der Eisler again it would be briefly, to discuss her and Nel's return to England. She might as well begin forgetting him from that moment.

The door opened and he crossed the room with rapid strides, swung her round, kissed her hard and quickly and, without a single word, went away again. She heard the door close with a dull thud and a moment later his mother came back to join her.

So much for forgetting him, reflected Olivia foggily. Now I'll have to start all over again.

Chapter 8

Mevrouw van der Eisler glanced at Olivia as she sat down. 'Oh, good, Tober brought fresh coffee. We'll have a cup and talk about Nel. I love having her here but I am grateful for someone to look after her. We've always got on well—she's a dear child, isn't she? But just with me she might get bored. Luckily Haso's young brother will be home for a few days—he's in his last year at Leiden. I've two daughters also—perhaps Haso didn't tell you?—both married, one in Canada and the other in Limburg. Dirk is twenty-four, determined to be as successful as Haso. He'll be company for you too. You haven't brothers or sisters?'

Olivia found herself being put through a gentle catechism regarding her own life. The questions were put so kindly and the answers listened to with so much sympathy that she discovered that she didn't mind.

All the same, she skirted lightly round her lack of a job and the fact that living with Granny wasn't ideal, and was glad when her hostess began to talk about the house.

'It's very old,' she observed. 'There was a house before this one—one of my husband's ancestors was a merchant with the East India Company. He made a fortune and pulled the old house down and built this one about two hundred years ago, but the grounds are very much as they were before he did that. Of course, the house belongs to Haso, but he has to spend a great deal of his time either in Amsterdam or travelling. When he marries I shall move to a smaller town-house we own in Leeuwarden.'

Three homes, thought Olivia wistfully, and said brightly, 'He must have his work cut out keeping an eye on three houses.'

'Yes. Of course he has Becky in London, who is a most capable woman, and Bronger and Ofke in Amsterdam have run the house for his father before him. Tober and Anke have been here all their lives, and I see to the business side of this place when he isn't here.'

'He's very fortunate to have such faithful people working for him.'

'Indeed, they would cheerfully die for him,' said Mevrouw van der Eisler in a matter-of-fact voice. 'As they would have done for his father.'

In bed later, Olivia remembered that. Did Rita, she wondered, realise what a splendid man he was to marry? And would she be good to him? Olivia thumped her pillows and turned over with unnecessary energy. Of course she wouldn't.

It was still snowing the next morning. Olivia,

wrapped up in one of Mevrouw van der Eisler's hooded padded coats and wearing borrowed wellies, went into the gardens with Nel to make a snowman. It gave her the chance to inspect the house from the outside. It had a solid front, crowned with a wide gable, with neat rows of windows on either side of a vast front door and smaller windows higher up across its face. Round the back there were two narrow wings, almost enclosing what she thought might be a lawn once the snow cleared, and at one end a large conservatory. There were outbuildings too, and a brick wall, the same faded colour as the house, running away into the distance. The fields around were hardly visible, for the snow was falling steadily and was already deep underfoot. The snowman made to Nel's satisfaction, they went back indoors, through a side entrance, where they took off their outdoor things and were led by a tolerant Tober to the hall. They hurried upstairs, tidied themselves, and went down again. Olivia, for one, not sure where to go.

'In here,' called Mevrouw van der Eisler from a half-open door at the back of the hall. 'Did you have a good game? Come and sit by the fire. This is the small sitting-room—I spend a good deal of my time here and you must use it as much as you like. There is a cupboard over there—Nel knows it, don't you, my dear?— full of games. We'll have coffee and then I must go and talk to Anke. Do make yourself at home, Olivia—go anywhere you wish. Perhaps this afternoon I will show you the rest of the house, if you would like that.'

'I'd love it,' said Olivia. 'You must wish that Mr van der Eisler stays single so that you can live here forever.' She blushed to the roots of her hair. 'I beg your pardon, that was very rude of me.'

'Not a bit of it, my dear. It is to be hoped that his wife won't object to my paying a visit from time to time.' She smiled. 'Besides, he—and his wife—won't live here all the time. It might be too lonely for someone used to big cities.'

'But you're not lonely—I wouldn't be either…' Olivia went red again. 'Sorry, I just meant that I like the country. Some people do, some don't.'

Mevrouw van der Eisler didn't appear to notice her embarrassment.

'One need never be lonely,' she observed, 'it's a state of mind, isn't it? Now, my dear, when this snow has stopped do you suppose you would both enjoy a trip to Leeuwarden? Tober shall drive us there once the roads are clear. Do you skate, Olivia? No? A pity, but Dirk will be here tomorrow and he'll enjoy teaching you. He taught Nel last winter. We could all go…'

So the day passed pleasantly, with the promised tour of the house after lunch, tea round the fire and then card-games with Nel while Mevrouw van der Eisler sat with her embroidery. The leisurely wander round the house had been a delight to Olivia. It might be severely plain from the outside but inside it was a pleasant mixture of dignified high-ceilinged rooms, beautifully furnished with antiques but still having the air of homeliness, and smaller rooms, dark-panelled, reached by narrow passages, steps up or steps down, with small latticed windows, and all of them in use. The kitchen was vast, with a great Aga along one wall, an old-fashioned dresser facing it, laden with plates and dishes, and a long table with wooden chairs round it. Anke was there, and another woman, cutting up vegetables at the sink.

They both beamed at Olivia and shook hands before she was swept on to look at pantries, dairy and a larder.

'Of course we don't really need these rooms now that we have a refrigerator,' said Mevrouw van der Eisler, 'but the grandchildren love to play hide-and-seek down here. That door leads to the garden and that staircase in the wall leads to the attics. We don't use those either—only the children love to go there.'

Dirk arrived the next morning, shortly after breakfast. He was very like Haso—just as tall, but not as heavily built, and he laughed a lot more. He shook Olivia's hand, swung Nel in the air and declared that he would stay for several days. 'I've just taken some more exams,' he explained, 'so I'm entitled to a holiday. This snow will stop by tonight so we will get out in the car.' He smiled at Olivia. 'You're not nervous?'

'No, although as I've never been driven by you I can't be quite sure, can I?'

He gave a shout of laughter. 'I say, we're going to get on, you and I—trust old Haso to find someone as pretty as you.'

They were sitting at the table in the small sitting-room, playing Snakes and Ladders with Nel. It seemed to Olivia that they had known each other for years. He was younger than she and she felt like a big sister towards him, and he made her laugh. She threw the dice and they all laughed when she had to take her counter all the way down a snake and start again.

'I like you, Dirk,' said Nel. 'I like Uncle Haso best, of course, but you're very nice.'

He gave a mock-sigh. 'It's always the same. I wear myself out being charming and amusing, and Haso doesn't do anything at all and everyone falls about trying to catch his attention. What did you do to catch his critical eye, Olivia?'

He had asked jokingly but when he glanced up and saw her face he said quickly, 'But of course you are so beautiful that you do not need to catch anyone's attention, is that not so, Nel?' He made a great show of throwing the dice. 'I expect Olivia has some glamorous job waiting for her—we shall see her on the front page of the ladies' magazines, all gloss and pearls.'

They all laughed and the awkward little moment was over, but much later that day, when Dirk and his mother were sitting together having a talk before going to their beds, he said, 'Mama, does Haso like Olivia?'

'Why, yes, dear.' She looked at him without surprise at his question.

'Well, I said something today—oh, teasing—and it seemed to me that Olivia…'

'Yes, dear, she is, I feel sure, and she would be so right for Haso, but he has never allowed his feelings to show, has he? And now we have this upset with Nel and Rita. To an outsider the solution is so plain—let him marry Rita, who I suspect would like that very much, and make Nel a happy child again. You see, he and Rob were such friends; Haso may feel that he should do this—that it is his duty.'

Dirk got up and prowled around the room. 'They were friends, so would Rob have wanted Haso to be unhappy for the rest of his life? He could manage Rita because he loved her, but I doubt if Haso loves her.' He kicked a footstool out of his way. 'Olivia doesn't say much about her life. Is it a happy one?'

'From what Haso has told me, and he knows very little, I believe, she lives with her mother and a rather terrible grandmother, who gave them a home when her father died and never ceases to remind them of the fact. He told me that he had been to her home once or twice and it was obvious that her grandmother dislikes Olivia. Her mother is a small, dainty woman, very gentle and quiet, and Olivia hasn't taken after her. That has annoyed the old lady. And of course Olivia has had no training for a career of any sort.'

'I'm surprised that she isn't married.'

'She was engaged, I believe, although Haso told me nothing more than that.'

'How long is Nel to stay here?'

'Until Haso and Rita have solved the problem. Nel is quite happy to go back to school and stay with her grandmother in England, she's devoted to her, but each time she comes here to stay with her mother she becomes most unhappy. It is not my place to criticise Rita but it is a pity that she has to leave the child with someone whom Nel doesn't like. It was quick thinking on Haso's part to persuade Olivia to come here to look after Nel.'

'Is she being paid?'

His mother looked surprised. 'I have no idea. Why do you ask?'

'Her clothes are hardly this year's fashion, are they? Good, but well-worn.'

'You're right, of course. I noticed that her things were useful rather than fashionable; I thought she had brought suitable clothes for the job and the time of year.'

'I'm surprised Haso hasn't noticed…'

Haso had noticed. Indeed, he was so conscious of every aspect of Olivia that he knew to the last button what she was wearing and that it was well cared-for, out of date and had been chosen with an eye to hard-wearing qualities rather than fashion. Beyond a wish to see her dressed in the kind of clothes her beauty merited, he would have found her just as enchanting in a potato sack. He thought about her a great deal while he saw his patients, operated and did his ward-rounds, and he thought about her when he was at Rita's flat, doing his best to persuade her to give up her job and make a home for Nel.

'But the child's quite happy at that school, and what would I do while she's away?'

'Find somewhere to live in England. You don't need the money, Rita.'

'I would be bored to death—of course, if I lived in a town and had a social life…' She paused and smiled at him, and met a blank mask which told her nothing. 'Well, I have no intention of giving up my job,' she said pettishly. 'It's fun, I meet lots of interesting people and I go out a lot—I must have some fun, Haso, I'm young still and I've been told I'm pretty. You can't expect me to spend the rest of my life being a housewife, just with Nel for company.'

'You will remarry, Rita.'

She said at once, 'If that's a proposal, Haso, I will accept at once.'

He remained unperturbed. 'It wasn't. I shall be going to Tierjum this weekend. Would you like to come with me? You could spend some time with Nel.'

'Darling Haso, I'm flying to Paris to spend the weekend with friends. I can't possibly put it off at such short notice. Give Nel my love, won't you, and tell her I'll come and see her soon. Shouldn't she go back to school?'

'When you decide what is to be done, yes. Have you dismissed that woman with the wart?'

'Juffrouw Schalk? Of course not. She's a splendid housekeeper and I'd be lost without her. Nel must learn to like her. The child's spoilt.'

'Would you object if Nel were to live permanently with her grandmother in England? You could, of course, visit whenever you wished?'

'It might be a good idea. I'll think about it. Now, can we stop this disagreeable talk and go somewhere and have a drink? It's barely nine o'clock...'

'I have to go back to hospital. I'm operating to-morrow, going to Rotterdam on the following day and then to Friesland. Let me know if you change your mind, Rita.'

She reached up to kiss his cheek. 'Darling Haso, we would make a lovely pair, you know.' She spoke laughingly, watching him closely. His small, indifferent smile infuriated her.

Mr van der Eisler left directly after breakfast on the Saturday morning and drove himself through the snowy landscape to Tierjum, Achilles sitting beside him. The snow had ceased and the sky for the moment was a cold blue and pale sunlight gave an illusion of warmth. He wondered what Olivia was doing, and then dismissed her from his mind while he reflected on Nel's future. He was no nearer a solution by the time he turned the Bentley into the drive and saw the house ahead of him. He stopped on the sweep and got out, smiling at the sounds of laughter from somewhere behind it. With a warning to Achilles not to bark he walked to the side of the house, making no sound in the thick snow, and went unhurriedly along the shrub-lined path until he reached the vast lawn at the back. Covered now with snow, of course. Nel and Olivia and Dirk were there, building a snowman and making a good deal of noise about it, stopping to throw snowballs at each other. Mr van der Eisler stood for a moment, watching them, a hand on Achilles' great head, and as he watched Nel flung a snowball at Olivia, who ducked, slipped, and would have fallen if Dirk hadn't put out an arm and caught her. They stood for a moment, his arm around her shoulders, completely at ease with one and other. It wasn't until Nel caught sight of Haso that they turned to see him.

Achilles bounded forward, barking happily, and Nel rushed to hug her uncle. Dirk started forward too, shouting a welcome. Only Olivia hung back. The glorious surprise at seeing him again had left her with a thumping heart and no breath.

Dirk said over one shoulder, 'Look who's here, Olivia—come and say hello.'

She went over to him then, and said, 'Hello, Mr van der Eisler,' but anything else she might have said died on her tongue. His, 'Hello, Olivia,' was pleasant, but he looked at her with eyes like blue ice. What had she done? she wondered in panic, searching his bland face for some sign. But it showed nothing. Only his eyes betrayed the fact that he was angry.

Five minutes later she decided that she had imagined it; he was throwing snowballs like a schoolboy, with Nel capering around him and Achilles barking his head off. It was Dirk who called to her, 'Olivia, be an angel and tell Mama that Haso's here—we'll be in presently for coffee.'

She nodded and sped away, glad to be gone. Was

'Haso here for the weekend? she wondered. And had anything been decided about Nel?

She found Mevrouw van der Eisler sitting placidly in her sitting-room, writing letters. She got up from her writing-desk, beaming.

'I wasn't expecting him—he usually phones. How delightful. Anke must get the coffee at once. Where is he?'

'In the garden snowballing.'

'Then fetch him in, my dear, if you will, and tell him to see that Achilles' paws are wiped.'

They were still racing around; she went and stood in the middle, ducking the snow. Her face glowed with the exercise, her bright hair almost hidden in the hood of one of Mevrouw van der Eisler's all-enveloping gardening coats. Mr van der Eisler thought that she had never looked so beautiful. It was inevitable that Dirk should fall for her; he was a young man her own age... And she had looked so happy when she had turned round, Dirk's arm around her shoulders.

They all went indoors, and when they had had coffee Olivia took Nel off on the pretext of choosing what frock she should wear that evening, since she was to be allowed to sit up for dinner for a treat.

'Such a tactful girl,' said Mevrouw van der Eisler. 'Nice, quiet manners and so kind and thoughtful. I am so surprised that she is not married.'

Haso stirred his coffee. 'She had a fiancé. He married another girl—we went to his wedding.'

'You did?' Dirk gave a chuckle. 'The pair of you? Not top hat and morning coat?'

'Indeed, yes.' Haso spoke lightly. 'We drove there in the Bentley and Olivia had a charming hat...'

'But why...?' asked his mother.

'Oh, keeping one's end up—showing the flag.' He smiled. 'I enjoyed it.' He put down his cup. 'I've seen Rita several times. She is unwilling to give up her job, in fact she refuses, and she also refuses to get rid of Juffrouw Schalk. If possible I'll bring her up here next weekend, when I think she must decide what she wants.'

'Does she plan to marry again?' asked his mother.

Dirk said quickly, 'Of course she does—she wants to marry you, Haso.'

'Yes.' Mr van der Eisler spoke calmly. 'But I have no intention of marrying her.'

His mother kept an admirable silence and flashed a warning glance at Dirk. 'Well,' she said presently, 'I'm glad to know that, Haso, for Rita is very much a career-woman. Indeed, I have wondered if Rob could have coped with her if he were still alive.'

'She seems very successful,' said Haso, noncommittally, 'It is a question as to whether Nel is more important to her than her career. We shall have to see if she and Nel can compromise.'

Nel came in then with Olivia, and he got up out of his chair. 'I must do some phoning. Let me know if I am upsetting any plans for the afternoon.'

'We haven't made any,' said Dirk when he had gone out of the room. 'But since he's here with that great car of his how about all of us piling in and doing some sightseeing?'

'In this weather?' asked his mother.

'It's just the weather to see Friesland, and Olivia may not get another chance. We could drive to Sneek and see the lakes and then go north up to the Wadden Zee. Would you like that, Nel?'

Of course Nel would like it, and so would Olivia,

only she restrained her enthusiasm, merely remarking that it sounded very interesting.

'We'll take Achilles,' said Dirk, 'he can sit between us. Nel and Olivia must sit with Haso so that he can point out all the interesting sights.'

Olivia opened her mouth to protest but he stopped her. 'Haso knows every stick and stone in these parts, and you won't get another chance.'

'Perhaps another time?' suggested Olivia, anxious not to look too eager.

'No hope of that. He's bringing Rita with him next weekend and she hates Friesland—too cold and empty.'

He didn't say any more for Nel, who had gone to the other end of the room to play with Achilles, had joined them again.

Haso came back presently and they sat around, carrying on a desultory conversation over their sherry, and presently they went to lunch.

Over that meal, Dirk broached his plans for the afternoon. 'I'll drive,' he offered, 'if you're tired.'

'On the contrary, driving relaxes me. I think it is a very good idea. When do we go?'

Olivia, nervous at the idea of being with Mr van der Eisler for hours on end and at the same time overjoyed at the prospect, settled beside him in the car with a cautious air which secretly amused him. She need not have worried; the outing was a tremendous success. He took the road to Sneek, going south until they reached the little town, and then driving along narrow country roads, still covered by snow, so that she might see the lakes, frozen now, although not yet safe for skating. He joined a main road presently and, when they were almost back in Leeuwarden, turned north.

'Dokkum, I think,' he observed. 'A nice old town—we might stop there and have coffee and then take a quick look at Lauwers Meer.' He glanced at Olivia. 'You're comfortable?'

'Yes, oh, yes, thank you. It's beautiful, isn't it? So still and everything covered by snow. Is it always like this in the winter?'

'Not always, but usually we have snow during the winter.' He looked over his shoulder at Dirk. 'When did we last go skating for more than a few days?'

'Two years ago—last year the ice didn't hold. We might get a day in before these two go back. Do you skate, Olivia?'

'No—at least, roller-skating, but I don't think that's the same, is it?'

'But you can balance—it should be easy. Here's Dokkum. We'll have coffee at de Posthoorn.'

Olivia was enchanted by the little town, with its canal running through its centre and the old houses leaning against each other on either side of it. The hotel was very old and shabby, in a nice way, and when she asked for tea instead of coffee she was served a glass of hot water and a tea-bag. Nel, drinking hot chocolate, thought it was very funny, chattering away happily, the very picture of a contented small girl.

It was cold outside and there was no one much about; Nel walked between the two men, skipping and jumping over the snow, and Mr van der Eisler drew Olivia close and tucked her hand under his arm.

There wasn't much to see and it was too cold to stand about so they went briskly back to the car, stopping on the way to buy four pokes of *potat frites* with generous dollops of pickles on top, which they sat and ate in the car.

Mr van der Eisler, offering Achilles the last of the chips, said, 'It must be years since I ate these. I'd forgotten how delicious they are.'

Olivia poised the last of the pickle on a chip and took a bite. 'Why don't we do this in England?' she wanted to know, and glanced at Nel with a warm smile. The child was so happy—it was a pity she had to go away from all this kindness and fun. It was a pity, too, she reflected, that she had to go as well.

She wasn't going to let such thoughts sadden her, though. Dirk was fun but Haso was a perfect companion; she could have sat for hours on end beside him while he drove. It was strange, she thought, that she felt so at ease with him when by rights she should have been feeling awkward, spending hours in the company of a man she loved but who treated her with kindly indifference and at the same time, she had to admit, made sure of her comfort. He would do that anyway, she reminded herself, for his manners were impeccable. She had a fleeting uneasy memory of the icy stare he had given her when he had arrived that morning. She had taken care not to meet his eyes since then and she wondered if they were still as cold.

They were still going north, this time to the coast. The villages were few and far between but the road was clear of snow, although the fields on either side were white as far as her eye could see.

'What do people do here?' she asked.

'Shrimp-fishing and a big fish auction at Zoutkamp. We're going round the Wadden Meer—Zoutkamp is on the farther side. Actually we are on the border of

Groningen and Friesland, but we turn to the west presently and then we are back in Friesland again. We'll take the road through Engwierum and pick up the E10 at Buitenpost.'

It was almost dark by the time they got back, to be welcomed by Mevrouw van der Eisler with piping-hot coffee in the lovely drawing-room. Nel was tired and a little excited, and wanted to stay up for dinner again, but Haso said no in the nicest possible way, which gave Olivia the chance to suggest that supper in bed might be quite fun.

'If you'll stay with me,' demanded Nel.

'If you promise to eat every scrap and go to sleep afterwards.'

'We are all going to church in the morning,' said Mr van der Eisler cheerfully, 'and after lunch we might take Achilles for a walk. You'd like that?'

The next day's plans having been made, Olivia bore Nel upstairs and, presently bathed, and, by then quite sleepy, the child sat up in her pretty room, her supper on a tray before her. A very tasty supper too—little pastry tarts filled with creamed chicken, a few *potat frites*, the merest suggestion of carrot purée and to follow this a little dish of *poffertjes*—tiny, crisp pancakes, smothered in fine sugar. The glass of warm milk which accompanied these dainties was drunk almost unnoticed and without any persuasion on Olivia's part. It only remained for her to take away the tray and tuck the little girl in, kiss her goodnight and turn on the little nightlight—a small comfort which it seemed Juffrouw Schalk had vetoed.

In her room Olivia showered and got into the one dress she had brought with her. It was a pretty shade of blue, plainly made of good material, and hopelessly out of date. 'Not that it matters,' she muttered, bundling up her hair in a ruthless fashion.

A discreet tap on the door surprised her. It was Tober with the request that she should join the professor in his study at her convenience.

'I'll come now,' said Olivia. Of course he was going to tell her when she was to go back to England with Nel—or without the child? Hadn't he said that Rita was to accompany him when he came the following weekend? So they hadn't decided about Nel yet. She slowed her steps—or they had decided, and Nel was to stay with her mother and he and she were to marry.

Her head full of muddled thoughts, she knocked on the study door.

Mr van der Eisler was sitting behind his desk with the faithful Achilles beside him. He got up as she went in.

'Come and sit here, nearer the fire,' he invited. 'You must find it colder here than in London.'

'Well, yes, but it's a nice cold, isn't it? Dry and bright.'

She sat down, her hands still in her lap, and waited for him to speak. He sat back in his chair, watching her. He thought she looked beautiful in the dull blue dress. 'You're happy here, Olivia?'

'Yes, thank you.'

'So is Nel, but of course matters cannot remain as they are, you realise that?'

'Yes.'

'Do you have any plans as to your future? A job in mind?'

She shook her head. 'No, but of course as soon as I

get home I'll find something to do. Miss Cross promised me a good reference—for a similar post, you know.'

'But it is too late for such a job until the summer term, surely?'

She had hoped he wouldn't think of that. 'Well, yes, but it would be nice to be at home with my mother for a little while.'

He smiled. 'My dear girl, do you take me for a fool? I have met your grandmother and am only too aware that living with her is by no means ideal for you or for your mother.'

She said coldly, 'You have no need to bother with my affairs, Mr van der Eisler.' She met his gaze. 'I am quite able to manage my own life.'

His smile widened. 'You wouldn't consider working over here in Holland?'

She was too surprised to speak for a moment. 'Here, in Holland? What as? I haven't any skills.'

'There is plenty of work for someone like yourself.' But she only shook her head, and after a moment he said, 'I shall be bringing Nel's mother here next weekend— her future must be settled before any other matter can be considered. Once that is decided you and I can talk.'

'What about?' asked Olivia.

'Why, you and I, Olivia.' He got up. 'Shall we join the others for a drink before dinner?'

As they walked across the hall he asked idly, 'You get on well with Dirk?'

A straightforward remark she could answer. 'Oh, yes, he's a dear, isn't he? If I'd had a brother I would have liked him to be just like Dirk. He's very young still, isn't he? All those girlfriends.'

'Something all men experience when they are young.'

She stood still for a moment. 'You too?'

'Certainly. It smooths the rough edges, as it were, while waiting for the one woman in the world…'

'She might not come.'

'Oh, but she does. Make no mistake about that.'

He was looking at her very intently and she looked away. He was thinking of Rita, no doubt.

They all went to church in the morning, standing in a row in the family pew, Olivia with one arm round Nel, her other shoulder wedged against Haso's vast person. The hymns were familiar, even though the words meant nothing to her, and the *dominee* thundered his sermon from the pulpit in what she considered a very severe manner, but when she was introduced to him as they left she found him to be a mild man with a splendid knowledge of English and a friendly manner.

They ate their lunch and then got back into their outdoor things and took Nel for a walk, with Achilles racing to and fro. Haso and Dirk talked comfortably of the village and the country round them and never mentioned Rita once.

Mr van der Eisler was to leave after tea. They all went into the hall to see him off but Olivia slipped back into the drawing-room when she thought no one was looking—after all, she wasn't one of the family.

Of course Haso had seen her; he made his good-byes, kissed and hugged Nel, and went back into the drawing-room.

'Are you not going to wish me goodbye?' he wanted to know.

She had retreated to the window overlooking the

garden. 'I hope you have a good drive back,' she told him soberly, 'and a successful week.'

'Certainly it will be a busy one.' He crossed the room to stand close by her. 'When I come again everything should be settled. Until then you do understand, do you not, that there is nothing I can say.'

About working in Holland? she wondered, and raised a puzzled face to his. He stared down at her for a long moment.

'And so much for my good resolutions,' said Mr van der Eisler in a goaded voice, and swept her into his arms and kissed her soundly.

Even if she had intended to demur she had no chance. He had gone before she had got her breath back.

Chapter 9

Olivia stood where he had left her, her heart galloping along at a great rate. As well as surprise, happiness was welling up and threatening to choke her. Why had he kissed her, and in such a manner? And what had he meant about good resolutions?

She allowed her thoughts to become daydreams, standing there in the centre of the room until the others, returning, shook them free.

'The house always seems so empty when Haso isn't here,' said Dirk. 'A pity I shan't be here next week to see him—and Rita.'

'You will stay for another day or two?' asked his mother.

'Oh, yes. I need to be back in Leiden on Wednesday—I'm starting that new course then.'

'But you are qualified?' asked Olivia, glad of something to talk about.

'Oh, yes, but by no means finished. I can't hope to be as brilliant as Haso, but I shall do my best to uphold the family name.'

'Surgery or medicine?'

'Oh, surgery, it's in the blood, you know, generations of us.' He saw Nel's downcast face. 'Who's for a game of Ludo?'

Two days later she saw him drive away with real regret. He had been an amusing companion and delightful with Nel, and he had made her laugh, something she rarely did at her grandmother's home. She was honest enough to admit to herself that even if he had done none of these things she would have liked him because he was Haso's brother, and anything or anyone close to Haso was close to her too.

There were several days before Haso would come again and there was Nel to keep happy. Because she thought it would please him, she did her best to persuade Nel to live with her mother during her holidays. She didn't have much success, but she persevered.

The snow had ceased several days ago although it still lay thick on the ground. The sky was a cold blue and the sun shone, albeit just as cold as the sky. They wrapped themselves up and went walking, and one day Mevrouw van der Eisler took them to Leeuwarden, with Tober driving.

They had lunch at a large restaurant—Onder de Luifel—and then they went to the shops and Olivia, with woefully few coins in her purse, bought two small vases in the local pottery, wishing that she had had the money to buy some of the silverware—delicate spoons, small bon-bon dishes and silver wire brooches. Her companion admired the vases and wished that Haso had done something about paying Olivia. After all, the poor girl had been whisked over to Holland at a moment's notice, with no chance to go to a bank. Perhaps, thought Mevrouw van der Eisler, she hadn't got a bank. Haso would be vexed when he knew about it. Having more than enough money himself, he nevertheless was thoughtful of the needs of other people. Too generous, she reflected, remembering the money Rita had borrowed from him from time to time and never repaid. Even with the money Rob had left her, and her well-paid job, she never had enough to pay for all the expensive clothes she loved.

Olivia viewed the approaching weekend with some anxiety; so did his mother. True, Haso had said that he had no intention of marrying Rita, but she was a clever young woman—pretty and amusing, and charming when she wished to be. Olivia longed to see Haso again but she doubted if they would be together at all—and how was she to behave? As though he hadn't kissed her? As though she had found it an amusing episode and dismissed it as such? And would he tell her when she was to return to England? Whatever was decided, surely Nel would have to go back to school as soon as possible? And, worst of all, had Rita coerced him into marrying her?

She lay wakeful, wondering about that. If, she reflected, I had been someone like Rita, would he have fallen in love with me and married me? She thought that he might. Given the right clothes and background she would have competed with Rita quite happily and probably won. She shook up the big square pillows and closed her eyes. Negative thinking, she told herself sternly, gets you nowhere, my girl.

She took Nel down to the village to buy sweets on Saturday morning because to wait in the house for Haso and Rita was too nerve-racking. Far better for them to return after they had arrived when any awkwardness would be glossed over in the bustle of greetings. Mevrouw van der Eisler, when consulted, had agreed. 'The child's on edge. I do hope that Rita has agreed to Haso's proposal and that everything is arranged satisfactorily.'

Proposal, thought Olivia unhappily, but she went off with Nel and spent a long time in the village shop buying toffee. When they got back the Bentley was in front of the house and at the sight of it Nel's small fingers curled tightly around Olivia's hand.

'We'll go and say hello quickly,' said Olivia, 'and then go and tidy ourselves. It will soon be time for lunch.'

'It will be nice to see Uncle Haso again,' said Nel in a very small voice.

'And Mummy. I'm sure she's excited at seeing you again.'

Nel gave her an old-fashioned look. 'Don't be silly,' she said.

They went round the house to one of the side doors and got out of their wellies and outdoor things. Olivia was of two minds as to whether to creep up the back stairs and do something to their ruffled persons before going to the drawing-room, but Anke had seen them and swept them along, lecturing them sternly in her own tongue and flinging the drawing-room door wide.

They stood on the threshold and the persons gathered there turned to look at them.

Mevrouw van der Eisler and her son spoke at the same time. 'Good, here you are, my dears,' and 'You've been to the village to buy toffee,' said Mr van der Eisler, and tossed a delighted Nel into the air and gave Olivia the briefest of smiles.

Rita didn't get up from her chair but held out her arms. 'Nel, how very untidy you are. I don't think Olivia can be a very good nanny. Come here and give me a kiss.'

And when the child went reluctantly she put her arms around her. 'Have you missed me?'

'Olivia is a very good nanny,' said Nel in a shaky voice, 'and she's not a nanny, she's a person. Like you or Granny or Mevrouw van der Eisler.'

Her mother said impatiently, 'Yes, yes, of course she is. Now go away and have your hair brushed and your hands washed. Why is there a bulge in your cheek? What are you eating?'

'Toffee. The village shop…'

'Yes, yes, never mind that now. It's almost time for lunch and then Uncle Haso is going to talk to you.'

All this time she had ignored Olivia who, in response to Mevrouw van der Eisler's beckoning finger, had gone to sit by her. Mr van der Eisler, in his chair again with Achilles beside him, took no part in the conversation. What his thoughts were could be anybody's guess.

Well, we will know soon enough, thought Olivia, and I for one can't get back home soon enough. She was aware that this idea had no vestige of truth in it; to go back to England never seeing Haso again wasn't to be borne and, worse, the thought of his marrying Rita made her feel sick.

The woman looked so right against the background of the lovely old house—casual tweeds, costing the earth, boots of leather as supple as silk, a cashmere jumper, hair with not a single strand out of place, perfect make-up...

She and Nel went upstairs and the child dawdled around, reluctant to go downstairs again. Olivia, ruthlessly tugging tangles out of her own hair, knew exactly how she was feeling. Mr van der Eisler's aloof air boded ill for their future.

'Uncle Haso won't make me go back to that horrid lady, will he?' Nel whispered.

Olivia put a comforting arm round her. 'Your Uncle Haso loves you; he won't let you be unhappy. Whatever he decides will be right, my pet.'

'But you'll go away...'

'Yes, and you'll go back to school, and I'll come and see you, I promise.'

'Are you sad?'

The question was unexpected. 'Sad? Me? No, dear, why should I be sad?'

'Your face looks sad.'

'I dare say that's because I'm hungry.' She would have to remember to look cheerful... 'Let's go down.'

Lunch was eaten without haste and the conversation was of the general kind so that everyone took part in it. Olivia, aware of Mr van der Eisler's sharp gaze, smiled when she wasn't actually eating. It must have looked pretty foolish but at least she didn't look sad. She replied politely when Rita spoke to her, agreed with her host that the weather had been quite pleasant during the week and tried to ignore Rita's snappy

asides to Nel, whose table manners weren't quite perfect—hardly to be expected at her age.

Rita wasn't snappy with Haso. On the contrary, she
was amusing and attentive to his every word, looking at him with a sweet smile which Olivia longed to
wipe off her face. A man—any man—would be flattered by her obvious interest in him and the inviting
looks she gave him.

Mr van der Eisler, of course, wasn't any man. He was
the perfect host—attentive, carrying the talk effortlessly
from one topic to another—and all the time he was aware
of Olivia, sitting there saying little, avoiding his eyes,
outwardly serene, inwardly, he had no doubt, seething.

'Shall we have coffee in the drawing-room? Perhaps
Nel would like to go and see what Anke is doing in the
kitchen? Cakes for tea, no doubt…'

Nel escaped willingly enough but when Olivia
started to go with her she was asked if she would be
good enough to go to the drawing-room too.

'For this concerns you, Olivia,' he told her.

Mevrouw van der Eisler was pouring the coffee
when the phone on the table by his chair rang. He
listened without speaking and even when he did, at
some length, Olivia was none the wiser, for he spoke
in Dutch, but she could see by the concern on his mother's face that it wasn't good news.

He put the phone down presently. 'This is most unfortunate; I have to return to Amsterdam at once. Even
if I should operate this afternoon I shan't be able to
leave my patient until tomorrow morning at the earliest. We must delay our talk until then.'

Rita pouted, but his mother said placidly, 'We quite
understand, dear. I hope you will be in time.'

He was already on his feet. 'They'll keep me informed—the phone's in the car. I'll let you know how things are as soon as possible.'

He kissed his mother, said briefly, 'You'll stay, Rita?' And to Olivia, 'Don't worry, leave everything to me. Kiss Nel for me.'

'What a lot can happen in five minutes,' said Olivia.

Mevrouw van der Eisler smiled at her. 'Yes, my dear. Being married to someone in the medical profession isn't easy but you get used to it.'

'There's no need for it,' said Rita. 'If Haso *will* work for all these hospitals instead of just keeping his private patients—heaven knows, he's famous enough to do what he likes.'

'I don't think it has anything to do with fame,' said Olivia, forgetting to whom she was talking. 'It's something he does because he wants to do it. I don't suppose he notices if it's a VIP or someone without a farthing to their name; they're patients and he knows how to help them...'

'What sentimental nonsense,' said Rita. 'Though if I heard aright this patient is a V.I.P.'

'Yes,' agreed Mevrouw van der Eisler, 'but if it had been a beggar off the street Haso would have gone just the same.'

'Oh, I'm sorry,' cried Rita. 'You must think me a heartless creature. I know how good Haso is—better than most people, I believe, for he has taken such care of me.' She smiled sweetly, 'And now we cannot tell you our plans until he returns.'

She became all at once a changed person, listening with interest to what her hostess had to say, talking about Nel's school, asking Olivia if she had enjoyed working there. Olivia didn't trust her an inch.

Nel came in presently. 'Tober says that you are going to the church to do the flowers, Mevrouw. May I go with you? Please? I'll be very good, and Tober said perhaps you'll let me sit in front with him.'

'The flowers—I had quite forgotten.' Mevrouw van der Eisler looked at Rita. 'Perhaps you would like to come with us? It will pass the time.'

'If I may,' gushed Rita, 'I'll stay here. If I might use your desk? I have so many letters to write; this is a chance to do them in peace.'

'And you, Olivia?'

'I shall need to sort out Nel's clothes before we go back—I'd be glad of an hour or two to do that.'

'Run along, then, darling.' Rita was the loving mother. 'I'm sure Olivia will help you with your things…'

'Why not, since we are both going upstairs,' observed Olivia airily.

She sent Nel downstairs again presently, suitably dressed, and followed after a minute or two to stand at the door and wave goodbye as Tober drove away with Nel, as pleased as Punch, sitting beside him.

She went back to Nel's room, for there was little point in joining Rita, who wouldn't expect it anyway. She had just finished making neat little piles of clothes and putting them on the bed ready to pack when she looked up to see Rita at the door.

'Olivia, I must talk to you.' She came into the room and sat down on the chair by the bed.

She looked serious, even worried, and Olivia asked, 'Is something the matter? Don't you feel well?'

Rita had her hands clenched in her lap. 'I know you

don't like me.' She gave a rueful smile. 'Well, I suppose I don't like you, but all the same I can't see you humiliated…'

Olivia folded a small nightgown. 'Why should I feel humiliated?' she wanted to know. 'If it's something to do with going back to England, I knew I'd be going as soon as everything was settled between you and Mr van der Eisler.'

Rita said slowly, 'We are to be married—quite soon—before Nel has her Easter holidays. But you must have guessed that. It's something… I'm not sure how to tell you, and probably you won't believe me, but I beg you to take my word.'

Olivia sat down on the bed. 'I'm quite in the dark. Could you explain?' She was pleased to hear how steady her voice was, and although her insides were turning somersaults she looked, she hoped, normal.

'You're in love with Haso, aren't you?' Rita spoke quietly. 'He didn't realise that at first. He thinks you are a very nice young woman and so reliable, and you have been such a help to him—to both of us. Now he is anxious to spare your feelings, he intended to say goodbye to you and give you your tickets so that you could leave as soon as you wished.' She paused. 'I don't expect you believe me, but I should like to help.'

'Why?'

'Because I am happy and you are not, and to meet Haso again, knowing that he pities you… He would never throw your love back in your face, he is too kind, but you will see the pity…'

Olivia studied Rita's face and had to admit that she looked and sounded sincere. 'And how would you help me?'

'Haso won't be here until tomorrow morning at the earliest—he is always near his patient after that special operation he does, until he feels that he can leave him or her to his registrar. Would you like to go back today? He has your ticket, unfortunately, but I have money with me. You could get the boat train to the Hoek and get the night ferry.' She paused. 'No, perhaps you would rather stay and see him before you go; you will want to say goodbye.'

Olivia didn't see the sly look. And look up into that loved face and see the pity and concern there? Olivia shuddered at the thought. 'I'd like to go today. I can pack in a few minutes and if you will lend me the money I'll go home. What am I to say to Mevrouw van der Eisler?'

Rita frowned in thought. 'You could say that you weren't well—no, that would sound very silly.' She sat up in her chair. 'Of course—could you not say that you have had a phone call from home? That you are needed there? Someone is ill, perhaps?' She frowned. 'And Nel—she will be unhappy, but of course if she thought you were going home to look after someone...'

Olivia was suddenly weary of the whole thing. 'Yes, all right. How am I to get to the train?'

'Mevrouw van der Eisler will send you to Leeuwarden in the car and, when Haso does come, she will explain. If you would like it, I will ask him to write to you.'

'No, no, thank you.' Olivia got up. 'I'll just finish seeing to Nel's things—is she to go back to school?'

'We shall take her in a few days and go to see Lady Brennon.'

Olivia nodded. 'I'll pack my things,' she said, and Rita got up and went to the door.

'I'll get the money,' she said, and added soberly, 'I am so sorry, Olivia.'

When she had gone Olivia sat down on the bed again. After all it was only what she had expected. Well, not quite, she thought. She hadn't expected Haso to discuss her with Rita, although that would be natural enough since they were to marry. At least Nel would have a loving stepfather and perhaps Rita would turn into a loving mother. Perhaps she had misjudged her. She swallowed the threatening tears and began to pack Nel's clothes and, that done, she packed her own. When Rita came back presently she took the money she was offered, thanked her politely, and asked her where she should send it once she was in England.

'Well, Haso had your ticket, and money for expenses, so you don't owe anyone anything. Does he owe you any wages?'

'They haven't been mentioned. So, no, he doesn't.'

'You have been here for several weeks. You can't work for nothing. Poor dear, he has so much on his mind—I'll remind him. I'm sure he'll send you whatever is owing.'

'No,' said Olivia, 'I don't want any money. I would prefer not to...' She smiled. 'A clean break is the expression.'

When Mevrouw van der Eisler came home she had her story ready and, looking at her stony face, that lady believed her, and so did Nel, although she was tearful at the idea of Olivia going away so suddenly.

After that it was easy—Tober was warned to have the car ready, there was tea to be drunk, farewells to be said to the staff, and finally all the right things to be said to her hostess. 'I've written to Mr van der Eisler,' said Olivia, 'and put it in his study.'

She shook hands with Rita, kissed and hugged Nel, and got into the car beside Tober. She didn't look back as he drove out of the grounds and into the narrow road.

'That was very unexpected,' observed Mevrouw van der Eisler. 'I had no idea Olivia's mother was ill. She did have a phone call?'

'Oh, yes. She was here with me, asking me about Nel's clothes, when she took the message. It was a shock for her. I believe she is very fond of her mother.'

'You will, of course, stay here until Haso comes?'

'Oh, yes, of course. Nel must go back to school as soon as possible now that we have everything settled.'

Mevrouw van der Eisler didn't ask what had been settled. She picked up her embroidery and stitched in silence.

Everyone was in bed and the house was quiet when Rita stole downstairs and took Olivia's letter from Haso's desk. Later she would read it. For the moment it was safe enough in her handbag.

Mevrouw van der Eisler was at breakfast when Haso walked in. He was his usual elegant self but his face was grey with fatigue. As he bent to kiss her cheek in reply to her delighted greeting he observed, 'Coffee—good,' and sat down opposite her.

'Where is everyone?' he wanted to know.

'Nel's in the kitchen, helping Anke make vol-au-vents for lunch. Rita is in bed—she prefers her breakfast there.'

'And Olivia?'

His mother buttered a piece of toast. 'At her home in London, dear.'

Mr van der Eisler, about to take a drink of coffee, put the cup down again. His face was as impassive as usual but his eyes were suddenly bright and alert. 'Oh? This is sudden. What has happened?'

'I phoned you at the hospital, Haso, but you were in Theatre and I decided that a message might distract you.'

'As indeed it would have done,' he agreed, although they both knew that nothing distracted him from his work—even the sudden departure of the girl he loved. 'There was a reason?'

'She had a phone call while Nel and I were down at the church. Someone—I don't quite know who—was ill and she was needed at home. When we got home she was already packed, for Rita had advised her that she would be able to get the boat train from Leeuwarden and cross over with the night ferry from the Hoek. I suggested that she phone home again to find out just what was wrong and then tell you, for you could have arranged everything for her, but she had made up her mind.'

'Was she upset?' He spoke very quietly.

'Not crying, just stony-faced and very anxious to be gone.' She poured more coffee. 'She told me that she had left a letter for you in your study.'

'Ah…' He went off at once to fetch it, and came back empty-handed.

'You're sure of that, my dear?'

'Positive. Rita was there, she must have heard her telling me.'

Mr van der Eisler buttered a roll and took a bite. He

was no longer hungry, but performing small, everyday acts would help damp down his rising rage.

He glanced at his watch. 'She won't be home for another two hours at least. I believe that Rita and I must have a talk.'

His mother said regretfully, 'I'm sorry I couldn't stop her, Haso.'

His smile was kind. 'Dearest Mama, I'm sure you did your best. I had already arranged to take Nel back tomorrow and stay in England for a couple of days...'

'With Rita?'

He smiled slowly. 'With Olivia,' he corrected her. He might have said more but Rita came into the room, showing all the signs of having dressed hurriedly. She tripped across the room, wreathed in smiles.

'Haso, what a lovely surprise—we didn't expect you so soon. I got up and dressed the moment I heard you were here.'

He had got to his feet, and something in his face stopped her halfway across the room. She said quickly, 'Isn't it a shame that Olivia had to go home so suddenly? I did all I could to help her...'

'Perhaps you will tell me exactly what happened,' suggested Haso softly.

His mother, taking a look at his face and seeing the bottled-up rage behind its blandness, said quickly, 'I'd better go and see Anke about lunch,' and went quickly from the room. She had no doubt that Rita had been at the bottom of Olivia's departure and her vague dislike of her became something stronger. All the same, she had it in her heart to be sorry for Rita—Haso in a cold fury was hard to face.

Rita sat down. She said chattily, 'So fortunate that

I was here—Olivia had no money, you know. I gave her enough to get home.'

He ignored this. 'You were here when she had the message?'

She opened her eyes wide. 'Yes, she was so shocked. She had no idea how to get herself back to England—so lucky that I was here to advise her. By the time your mother was back everything was seen to.'

Mr van der Eisler, impassive in his chair, spoke pleasantly. 'You have a letter of Olivia's, addressed to me, have you not? Give it to me, please.'

Rita went red and then white. 'A letter? I don't know what you're talking about—and why should I take it? I haven't got it.'

He got up and went to the table by her chair, where she had put her handbag. He picked it up, opened it, and turned it upside-down so that its contents rolled from the table to the floor. The letter he took, and walked over to the window to read it, taking no notice of her indignant cries. 'My lipsticks, my powder compact—it's smashed—and my money's spilled over the floor.'

He gave her a look of utter contempt and opened the envelope.

Olivia hadn't written much and her usually neat handwriting showed signs of the writer's strong feelings. He read it quickly and then a second time, before folding it and putting it in a pocket.

He sat down again and Achilles settled beside him. 'And now, if you please, you will tell me exactly what you have said to Olivia. There was no phone message. That was a tale to tell my mother, presumably.'

Rita said sulkily, 'What are you going to do?' She squeezed out a tear.

'Drive you back to Amsterdam as soon as you have packed. You have decided to let Nel stay at school in England and spend her holidays with her grandmother so that you may lead your own life. That decision rests. Why did you do this, Rita?' He sighed. 'And let us have the truth this time.'

'That great girl,' said Rita nastily, 'and such a fool too. I only had to tell her that you found it tiresome that she was in love with you for her to agree to leave at once. Didn't want to spoil your happiness.' She laughed. 'It was such a chance to get rid of her. Such a pity you had to find out. I'd rather set my heart on marrying you, Haso.'

She shrugged her shoulders. 'Well, there are plenty of fish in the sea—you see, what I want is a rich husband, you understand, who won't interfere with my career.'

'What did you tell Olivia?'

'Why, that we were going to be married, of course, that you loved me and found her an embarrassment.' She glanced at him. 'Don't look at me like that, Haso. You can't blame me for trying.'

He said very evenly, 'Go and pack your things, Rita, we will leave in half an hour.'

When she had gone he took Olivia's letter from his pocket and read it again, and this time he was smiling.

The following day, with Nel beside him, he drove over to England.

Sylvester Crescent looked unwelcoming. It was drizzling with rain, the ferry had got in late, and so of course the boat train up to London was late too. Olivia was tired and hungry and unhappy, and the sight of the prim, net-curtained houses depressed her still further. She got off the bus at the corner, carried her case to her grandmother's flat and knocked on its door.

Her mother opened it. 'Darling, what a lovely surprise. And how sudden.' She looked at Olivia's tired face. 'Come on in. We'll have a cup of tea and then you shall go and have a nap. You can tell me all about it later.'

'Granny?'

'She has gone to that old Mrs Field for lunch. We'll have something in the kitchen. Sit down while I make the tea, then you can have a hot bath while I get something to eat.'

The best part of an hour later, sitting at the kitchen table with her mother, supping soup, and warm from her bath, Olivia felt decidedly better. It wasn't the end of the world. She would find another job and start again. Forgetting Haso wasn't going to be easy, but nothing had been easy for the last year or two.

Her mother hadn't asked any questions while they ate, but over another pot of tea Olivia told her what had happened. She told it without trimmings and in a steady voice, and when she had finished her mother said, 'I'm sorry, my dear. But you have nothing to reproach yourself with. You've done the right thing, although I think that Rita should have left it for Mr van der Eisler to say goodbye to you. I said before that he was a good, kind man, and I still think that. He wouldn't knowingly hurt you or anyone else.'

'It's better this way, Mother. I feel such a fool—Rita made me feel like a silly, lovesick teenager. I'm sure she didn't mean it like that, but that's how it sounded to me.'

Mrs Harding kept her thoughts to herself. 'Well, love, you're home now. Go to bed for an hour or two and I'll break the news to Granny when she gets back.'

'Poor Granny—lumbered with me again. But I'll get a job just as soon as I can.'

Sooner than she expected! Going to Mr Patel's shop for extra groceries, which her grandmother had pro-claimed would be necessary now that there was another mouth to feed, her ears still ringing with the old lady's pithy comments about great healthy girls idling their time away at home, she found Mr Patel darting around his shop in an agitated manner, muttering to himself and wringing his hands.

'What's the trouble?' she asked sympathetically.

'Miss, my wife is ill in bed and my daughter is by the side of her husband, whose mother is being buried today. I have no help—I am in a state...'

'Will I do?' asked Olivia. 'I don't suppose I can serve, but I can fetch and carry and arrange things on the shelves.'

His gentle brown eyes widened. 'You would do that, miss? Help me in the shop? It will be only for a day or two—perhaps for one day only. I shall pay you.'

'Just let me take this stuff to my grandmother's and I'll be back.'

He lent her an apron, showed her how the till worked, and handed her a broom. 'I have no time,' he said apologetically, 'and I cannot keep the customers waiting.'

She swept the floor round the feet of the custom-ers, smiling at the astonished faces of the ladies who lived near enough to her grandmother's to know her by sight. That done, she stacked tins of food, pots of jam, packets of biscuits and then, since there were any number of customers now, went behind the counter and did her best. She was quite worn out by the end of the day and thankfully too tired to think. She sat at supper with her mother and grandmother, listening to the latter lady's comments on suitable work for young ladies and not hearing a word of it. After supper she went back again to the shop, to help Mr Patel arrange his stock for the morning. By the time she got into bed nothing was important any more, only going to sleep as quickly as possible. Which she did.

Mr Patel opened his shop at eight o'clock. It was a chilly, dark morning and spitting with rain, but he was his cheerful self again. His daughter had phoned—she would be back in the evening—his wife was feeling better and he had willing help. Together they handed over bottles of milk, bags of crisps and Mars bars to the steady flow of customers on their way to work. There was just time for a cup of coffee before the housewives came and the day's work really got going.

There was no closing for lunch at Mr Patel's; they took it in turns to eat a sandwich and drink more coffee in the little cubbyhole at the back of the shop before facing more housewives and presently the children, coming home from school wanting their tins of Coke and crisps.

Olivia, pausing for a cup of tea, reflected that Mr Patel would be a millionaire before he was fifty, if he didn't die of exhaustion first. There was a lull from the shoppers; she went outside and began to pile oranges from a crate on to the bench where the fruit and vegetables were displayed. Since it was the end of the day she hardly looked her best—her bright hair coming loose from its pins, an elderly cardigan over the out-size pinny Mr Patel had been kind enough to lend her.

Mr van der Eisler, driving fast round the corner in the Bentley, let out a great sigh when he saw her, swept the car across the road and stopped in the shop's small forecourt.

The passing traffic had masked any sound he might have made; he was inches from her when he spoke.

At the sound of her name Olivia shot round, dropping oranges in all directions. She said, 'Oh, it's you,' in a hollow voice and backed away. Not far, though, for he put out an arm and drew her gently towards him.

'My darling love…'

'No, I'm not,' said Olivia, and blinked back her tears.

'None of it was true,' he told her gently. 'Not a single word. When we came on Sunday, Rita and I, it was to tell you that she had decided to go on with her career, that Nel was to go back to school and stay with Lady Brennon and that I would drive you and Nel back here. I was going to ask you to marry me too…'

'Then why didn't you?' snapped Olivia crossly. 'You never said a word…'

'My darling, I was afraid that you would turn me down…'

'Turn you down? But I love you….'

He smiled. 'Yes, I know that now.' He put his other arm around her. 'Tell me, why are you here, tossing oranges about?'

'I'm helping Mr Patel until this evening—his wife's ill and his daughter is away for the day.' She gave a wriggle without much success. 'You can't park the car here…'

She felt his great chest shake with laughter. 'Dear heart, stop being cross and keep quiet while I propose to you. This is hardly the place I should have chosen for such a romantic occasion, but it is a matter which needs to be dealt with at once. Will you marry me, Olivia? I find that my life has no meaning without you. I suppose that I have been in love with you since we first met and now I cannot endure being without you.'

'Oh, yes, I will,' said Olivia, 'but I must know about Rita and Nel, and what—'

'Time enough for that,' said Mr van der Eisler, and bent his head to kiss her, an unhurried exercise which held Mr Patel's admiration from where he stood in the shop doorway watching them. It was a good thing that there were no customers, for Mr van der Eisler was obviously intent on making the most of the opportunity. Mr Patel, a sentimental man, watched with ready tears in his eyes as Mr van der Eisler reached up and took the pins from Olivia's hair and it tumbled down in a tawny cloud.

'Love,' said Mr Patel, and started to pick up the oranges.

* * * * *

A WINTER LOVE STORY

Chapter 1

Claudia leaned up, took another armful of books from the shelves lining the little room, put them on the table beside her and sneezed as a cloud of mummified dust rose from them. What had possessed her, she wondered, to take on the task of dusting her great-uncle William's library when she could have been enjoying these few weeks at home doing as she pleased?

She picked up her duster, sneezed again, and bent to her task, a tall, slim but shapely girl with a lovely face and shining copper hair, which was piled untidily on top of her head and half covered by another duster, secured by a piece of string. Her shapely person was shrouded in a large print pinny several sizes too big, her face had a dusty smear on one cheek and her nose shone. Nevertheless she looked beautiful, and the man

watching her from the half-open door smiled his ap-
preciation before giving a little cough.

Claudia looked over her shoulder at him. There was
nothing about him to make her feel uneasy—indeed,
he was the epitome of understated elegance, with an
air of assurance which was in itself reassuring. He was
a big man, very tall and powerfully built, not so very
young but with the kind of good looks which could
only improve with age. His hair was pepper and salt,
cut short. He might be in his late thirties. Claudia wondered who he was.

'Have you come to see Great-Uncle William or my
mother? You came in through the wrong door—but of
course you weren't to know that.' She smiled at him
kindly, not wishing him to feel awkward.

He showed no signs of discomfort. 'Colonel Ramsay.' His commanding nose twisted at the dust. 'Should
you not open a window? The dust…'

'Oh, they don't open. They're frightfully old—the
original ones from when the house was built. Why do
you want to see Colonel Ramsay?'

He looked at her before he answered. 'He asked
me to call.'

'None of my business?' She clapped two aged tomes
together and sent another cloud of dust across the room.
'Go back the way you came,' she told him, 'out of the side
door and ring the front doorbell. Tombs will admit you.'

She gave him a nod and turned back to the shelves.
Probably someone from Great-Uncle William's solicitor.

'I don't think I like him much,' said Claudia to the
silent room. All the same she had to admit that she
would have liked to know more about him.

She saw him again, not half an hour later, when, the duster removed from her head and her hands washed, she went along to the kitchen for coffee.

The house was large and rambling, and now, on the edge of winter, with an antiquated heating system, several of its rooms were decidedly chilly. Only the kitchen was cosy, with the Aga warming it, and since there were only her mother, Mrs Pratt the housekeeper, Jennie the maid and, of course, Tombs, who seemed to Claudia to be as old as the house, if not older, it was here that they had their morning coffee.

If there were visitors Mrs Ramsay sat in chilly state in the drawing room and dispensed coffee from a Sèvres coffee pot arranged on a silver tray, but in the kitchen they all had their individual mugs. However, despite this democratic behaviour, no one would have dreamt of sitting down or drinking their coffee until Mrs Ramsay had taken her place at the head of the table and lifted her own special mug to her lips.

Claudia breezed into the kitchen with Rob the Labrador at her heels. Her mother was already there, and sitting beside her, looking as though it was something he had been doing all his life, was the strange man. He got to his feet as she went in, and so did Tombs, and Claudia stopped halfway to the table.

She didn't speak for a moment, but raised eloquent eyebrows at her mother. Mrs Ramsay said comfortably, 'Yes, I know, dear, we ought to be in the drawing room. But there's been a fall of soot so the fire can't be lighted. And Dr Tait-Bullen likes kitchens.'

She smiled round the table, gathering murmured agreements while the doctor looked amused.

'Come and drink your coffee, Claudia,' went on Mrs Ramsay. 'This is Dr Tait-Bullen, who came to see Uncle William. My daughter, Claudia.'

Claudia inclined her head, and said, 'How do you do?' in a rather frosty manner. He could have told her, she thought, instead of just walking away as he had done. 'Uncle William isn't ill?' she asked.

The doctor glanced at her mother before replying. 'Colonel Ramsay has a heart condition which I believe may benefit from surgery.'

'He's ill? But Dr Willis saw him last week—he didn't say anything. Are you sure?'

Dr Tait-Bullen, a surgeon of some fame within his profession, assured her gravely that he was sure. 'Dr Willis very wisely said nothing until he had a second opinion.'

'Then why isn't he here now?' demanded Claudia. 'You could be wrong, whatever you say.'

'Of course. Dr Willis was to have met me here this morning, but I understand that a last-minute emergency prevented him. I have been called in as consultant, but the decision concerning the Colonel's further treatment rests with his doctor and himself.' He added gently, 'I was asked my opinion, nothing more.'

Mrs Ramsay cast a look at Claudia. Sometimes a daughter with red hair could be a problem. She said carefully, 'You may depend upon Dr Willis getting the very best advice, darling.'

Claudia stared across the table at him, and he met her look with an impassive face. If he was annoyed he showed no sign of it.

'What do you advise?' she asked him.

'Dr Willis will come presently. I think we should wait until he is here. He and I will need to talk.'

'But is Great-Uncle William ill? I mean, really ill?'

Her mother interrupted. 'Claudia, we mustn't badger Dr Tait-Bullen.' She looked round the table. 'More coffee for anyone?'

Claudia pushed back her chair. 'No, thank you, Mother. I'll go and get on with the books. Tombs knows where I am if I'm wanted.'

She smiled at the butler and whisked herself out of the room, allowing the smile to embrace everyone there.

Back in the library, she set about clearing the shelves, banging books together in clouds of dust, wielding her duster with quite unnecessary vigour. She had behaved very badly and she was sorry about it—and a bit puzzled, too, for she liked him. What had possessed her to be so rude? She had behaved like a self-conscious teenager. She ought to apologise. Tombs, she knew, would come and tell her what was happening from time to time, so when the doctor was about to leave she would say something polite...

She spent a few minutes making up suitable speeches—a dignified apology, brief and matter-of-fact. She tried out several versions, anxious to get it right. She was halfway through her final choice when she was interrupted.

'If those gracious words were meant for me,' said Dr Tait-Bullen, 'I am flattered.'

He was leaning against the door behind her, smiling at her, and she smiled back without meaning to. 'Well, they were. I was rude. I was going to apologise to you before you left.'

'Quite unnecessary, Miss Ramsay. One must make allowances for red hair and unpleasant news.'

'Now you're being rude,' she muttered, but went on anxiously. 'You really meant that? Great-Uncle William is seriously ill? I can see no reason why I shouldn't be told. I'm not a child.'

He studied her briefly. 'No, you are not a child, but Dr Willis and I must talk first.' He came into the room, moved a pile of books and sat down on the table. 'This is a delightful house, but surely rather large for the three of you?'

He spoke idly and she answered him readily. 'Well, yes, but it's been in the family for a long time. Most of the rooms are shut up, so it's easy enough to run. Tombs has been here forever, and Mrs Pratt and Jennie have been here for years and years. The gardens have got a bit out of hand, but old Stokes from the village comes up to help me.'

'You have a job?'

'I did have. Path Lab assistant—not trained, of course, just general dogsbody. But London's too far off. I've applied for several jobs which aren't so far away so that I can come home often.'

He said casually, 'Ah, yes, of course. Salisbury, Southampton, Exeter—they are all within reasonable distance.'

'And there are several private hospitals, too. I didn't much like London.' She added chattily, 'Do you live there?'

'Most of my work is done there.'

She supposed that he hadn't added to that because Tombs had joined them.

'Dr Willis has arrived, sir.' He looked at Claudia. 'Mrs Ramsay is in the morning room, Miss Claudia. Jennie has lighted the fire there for the convenience of the doctors.'

'Thank you, Tombs.' She glanced at the doctor. 'You'll want to go with Tombs. I'll come presently—I must just tidy myself.'

Left to herself, she took off her pinny, dragged a comb through her hair and went in search of her mother.

Mrs Ramsay was with the two men, making small talk before they began their discussion of their patient's condition. She was still a strikingly beautiful woman, wearing her fifty years lightly. Her hair, once as bright as her daughter's, was streaked with silver, but she was still slim and graceful. She was listening to something Dr Willis was saying, smiling up at him, her hand on his coat sleeve. They were old friends; he had treated her husband before his death several years ago, and since he was a widower, living in a rather gloomy house in the village with an equally gloomy elderly housekeeper, he was a frequent visitor at the Ramsays' house.

He looked up as Claudia joined them.

'My dear, there you are. Come to keep your mother company for a while? Are we to stay here, or would you prefer us to go to the study?'

'No, no, stay here. There's a fire specially lighted for you. Claudia and I will go and see to lunch.' She paused at the door. 'You will tell us exactly what is wrong?'

'Of course.'

In the dining room, helping her mother to set the

lunch, Claudia asked, 'Is Great-Uncle William really very ill, Mother?'

'Well, dear, I'm afraid so. He hasn't really been very well for some time, but we couldn't persuade him to have a second opinion. This Dr Tait-Bullen seems a nice man.'

'Nice?' Claudia hesitated. 'Yes, I'm sure he is.' *Nice,* she reflected, hardly described him; it was far too anaemic a word. Beneath the professional polite detachment she suspected there was a man she would very much like to know.

They were standing idly at the windows, looking out into the wintry garden, when Tombs came to tell them that the doctors had come downstairs from seeing their patient.

Dr Willis went straight to Mrs Ramsay and took her hand. He was a tall, thin man, with a craggy face softened by a comforting smile as he looked at her. He didn't say anything. Claudia saw her mother return his look and swallowed a sudden surprised breath. The look had been one of trust and affection. Don't beat about the bush, Claudia admonished herself silently. They're in love.

There was no chance to think about it; Dr Tait-Bullen was speaking. Great-Uncle William needed a triple bypass, and without undue loss of time. The one difficulty, he pointed out, was that the patient had no intention of agreeing to an operation.

Claudia asked quickly, 'Would that cure him? Would he be able to lead a normal life—be up and about again?'

'The Colonel is an old man, but he should be able to live the life of a man of his age.'

'Yes, but…'

'Claudia, let Dr Tait-Bullen finish…'

'Sorry.'

She flushed and he watched the colour creep into her cheeks before he said, 'I quite understand your anxiety. If Dr Willis wishes, I will come again very shortly and do my best to change the Colonel's mind. I feel sure that if anyone can do that it will be he, for they have known each other for a long time. I can but advise.'

He glanced at the other man. 'We have discussed what is best to be done—there are certain drugs which will help, diet, suitable physiotherapy…'

'I'm sure you have done everything within your power, Doctor,' said Mrs Ramsay. 'We will do our best to persuade Uncle William, and if you would keep an eye on him?' She looked at Dr Willis. 'That is, if you don't mind, George?'

'I am only too glad of expert advice.'

'Oh, good. You'll stay for lunch, Dr Tait-Bullen? In half an hour or so…'

'I must return to London, Mrs Ramsay. You will forgive me if I refuse your kind invitation.'

He shook hands with her, and then with Dr Willis. 'We will be in touch.'

'Claudia, take Dr Tait-Bullen to his car, will you, dear?'

They walked through the house together, out of the door and across the neglected sweep of gravel to where a dark grey Rolls-Royce stood. Claudia stared at it reflectively.

'Are you just a doctor?' She wanted to know. 'Or someone more important?' She glanced at his quiet face. 'Mother called you Doctor, so I thought you were. You're not, are you?'

'Indeed, I am a doctor. I am also a surgeon...'

'So you're *Mr* Tait-Bullen. You're not a professor or anything like that, are you?'

'I'm afraid so...'

'You might have said so.'

'Quite unnecessary. Besides, being called a professor makes me feel old.'

'You're not old.'

He answered her without rancour. 'Thirty-nine. And you?'

She had asked for that. Anyway, what did it matter? 'I'm very nearly twenty-seven,' she told him.

He said smoothly, 'I am surprised that you are not yet married, Miss Ramsay.'

'Well, I'm not,' she snapped. 'I've not met anyone I've wanted to marry.' She added pettishly, 'I have had several proposals.'

'That does not surprise me.' He smiled down at her, thinking how unusual it was to see grey eyes allied with such very red hair. He sounded suddenly brisk. 'You will do your best to persuade the Colonel to agree to surgery, will you?'

When she nodded, he got into his car and drove away. His handshake had been firm and cool and brief.

Claudia went back to the morning room and found her mother and Dr Willis deep in talk. They smiled at her as she went in, and her mother said, 'He's gone? Such a pleasant man, and not a bit stiff or pompous. Dr

Willis has been telling me that he's quite an important surgeon—perhaps I shouldn't have given him coffee in the kitchen.' She frowned. 'Do you suppose Uncle will take his advice?'

'Most unlikely, Mother. I'll take his lunch up presently, and see if he'll talk about it.'

Great-Uncle William had no intention of talking to anyone on the subject. When Claudia made an attempt to broach the matter, she was told to hold her tongue and mind her own business. Advice which she took in good part, for she was used to the old man's irascible temper and had a strong affection for him.

He had been very good to her mother and to her when her father died, giving them a home, educating her, while at the same time making no bones about the fact that he would have been happier living in the house by himself, with his housekeeper and Tombs to look after him. All the same, she suspected that he had some affection for them both, and was grateful for that.

It was a pity that on his death the house would pass to a distant cousin whom she had never met. That Great-Uncle William had made provision for her mother and herself was another reason for gratitude, for Mrs Ramsay had only a small income, and after years of living in comfort it would have been hard for her to move to some small house and count every penny.

They would miss the old house, with its large rooms and elegant shabbiness, and they would miss Tombs and Mrs Pratt and Jennie, too, but Claudia supposed that she would have a job somewhere or other and make a life for herself. Somewhere she could get home easily from time to time. Her mother would miss her friends.

Especially she would miss Dr Willis, always there to cope with any small crisis.

The days went unhurriedly by. Claudia finished turning out the library and turned her attention to the rather battered greenhouse at the bottom of the large garden. The mornings were frosty, and old Stokes, who came up from the village to see to the garden, tidied the beds and dug the ground in the kitchen garden, leaving her free to look after the contents of the glasshouse.

It contained a medley of pots and containers, filled with seedlings and cuttings, and she spent happy hours grubbing around, hopefully sowing seed trays and nursing along the hyacinths and tulips she intended for Christmas.

And every day she spent an hour or so with her great-uncle, reading him dry-as-dust articles from the *Times* or listening to him reminiscing about his military career. He still refused to speak of his illness. It seemed to her anxious eyes that he was weaker, short of breath, easily tired and with an alarming lack of appetite.

Dr Willis came to see him frequently, and it was at the end of a week in which he could detect no improvement in his patient that he told Mrs Ramsay that he had asked Mr Tait-Bullen to come again.

He came on a dreary November morning, misty and damp and cold, and Claudia, busy with her seedlings, an old sack wrapped around her topped by a jacket colourless with age, knew nothing of his arrival. True, she had been told that he was to come again, but no day had been fixed; he was an exceedingly busy man, she'd been told, and his out of town visits had to be fitted in whenever possible.

He had spent some time with the Colonel, and even longer with Dr Willis, before talking to Mrs Ramsay, and when that lady observed that she would send Tombs to fetch Claudia to join them, volunteered to fetch her himself.

Studying the sack and the old jacket as he entered the greenhouse, he wondered if he was ever to have the pleasure of seeing Claudia looking like the other young women of his acquaintance—fashionably clad, hair immaculate, expertly made-up—and decided that she looked very nice as she was. The thought made him smile.

She had looked round as he opened the door and her smile was welcoming.

'Hello—does Mother know you're here?' And then, 'Great-Uncle isn't worse?'

'I've seen the Colonel and talked to your mother and Dr Willis. I've been here for some time. Your mother would like you to join us at the house.'

She put down the tray of seedlings slowly. 'Great-Uncle William won't let you operate—I tried to talk him into it but he wouldn't listen...'

He said gently, 'I'm afraid so. And the delay has made an operation questionable.'

'You mean it's too late? But it's only a little more than a week since you saw him.'

'If I could have operated immediately he would have had a fair chance of recovering and leading a normal, quiet life.'

'And now he has no chance at all?'

He said gravely, 'We shall continue to do all that we can.'

She nodded. 'Yes, I know that you will. I'll come. Is Mother upset? Does she know?'

'Yes.' He watched while she took off the deplorable jacket and untied the sack and went to wash her hands at the stone sink.

The water was icy and her hands were grimy. She saw his look. 'You can't handle seedlings in gloves,' she told him. 'They are too small and delicate.'

'You prefer them to dusting books?' he asked as they started for the house.

'Yes, though books are something I couldn't possibly manage without. I'd rather buy a book than a hat.'

He reflected that it would be a pity to hide that glorious hair under a hat, however becoming, but he didn't say so.

Her mother and Dr Willis were in the morning room again, and Mrs Ramsay said in a relieved voice, 'Oh, there you are, dear. I expect Mr Tait-Bullen has explained…'

'Yes, Mother. Do you want me to go and sit with Great-Uncle?'

'He told us all to go away, so I expect you'd better wait a while. Mr Tait-Bullen is going to see him again presently, but he doesn't want anyone else there.' She turned as Tombs came in with the coffee tray. 'But you'll have coffee first, won't you?'

They drank their coffee while the two men sustained the kind of small talk which needed very little reply, and presently Mr Tait-Bullen went back upstairs.

He was gone for some time and Claudia, getting impatient, got up and prowled round the room. 'I don't suppose he'll come again,' she said at length.

'There is no need for him to do so, but the Colonel has taken quite a fancy to him. Mr Tait-Bullen calls a spade a spade when necessary, but in the nicest possible way. What is more, his patients aren't just patients. They are men and women with feelings and wishes which he respects. Your great-uncle knows that.'

Mr Tait-Bullen, driving along the narrow roads which would take him from the village of Little Planting to the M3 and thence to London, allowed his thoughts to wander. He and the Colonel had talked about many things, none of which had anything to do with his condition. The Colonel had made it clear that he intended to die in his own bed, and, while conceding that Mr Tait-Bullen was undoubtedly a splendid surgeon and cardiologist, he wished to have no truck with surgery, which he considered, at his time of life, to be quite worthless.

Mr Tait-Bullen had made no effort to change his mind for him. True, he could have prolonged his patient's life and allowed him to live for a period at least in moderate health, but he considered that if he had overridden the Colonel's wishes, the old man would have died of frustration at having his wishes ignored. They had parted good friends, and on the mutual understanding that if and when Mr Tait-Bullen had a few hours of leisure he would pay another visit as a friend.

Something he intended to do, for he wanted to see Claudia again.

He went straight to the hospital when he reached London; he had an afternoon clinic which lasted longer than usual. He had no lunch, merely swallowed a cup of tea between patients. It was with a sigh of relief that he stopped the car outside his front door in a small tree-lined street tucked away behind Harley Street, where he had his consulting rooms.

It was a narrow Regency house in a row of similar houses, three storeys high with bow windows and a beautiful front door with a handsome pediment, reached by three steps bordered by delicate iron railings. He let himself in quietly and was met in the hall by a middle-aged man with a craggy face and a fringe of hair. He looked like a dignified church warden, and ran Mr Tait-Bullen's house to perfection. He greeted him now with a touch of severity.

'There's that Miss Thompson on the phone, reminding you that she expects to see you this evening. I told her that you were still at the hospital and there was no knowing when you'd be home.' Cork lowered his eyes deferentially. 'I trust I did right, sir.'

Mr Tait-Bullen was looking through the post on the hall table. 'You did exactly right, Cork. I don't know what I would do without you.' He glanced up. 'Did I say I would take her somewhere this evening? It has quite slipped my mind.'

Cork drew a deep breath through pinched nostrils. In anyone less dignified it would have been a sniff. 'You were invited to attend the new play. The opening night, I believe.'

'Did I say I'd go? I can't remember writing it down in my diary.'

'You prevaricated, sir. Said if you were free you'd be glad to accept.'

Mr Tait-Bullen picked up his case and opened his study door. 'I'm not free, Cork, and I'm famished!'

'Dinner will be served in fifteen minutes, sir. The young lady's phone number is on your desk.'

Mr Tait-Bullen sat down at his desk and picked up the receiver. Honor Thompson's rather shrill voice, sounding peevish, answered.

'And about time, too. Why are you never at home? It's so late. I'll go on to the theatre and meet you there. The Pickerings are picking me up in ten minutes.'

Mr Tait-Bullen said smoothly, 'Honor, I'm so sorry, but there is absolutely no chance of me getting away until late this evening. I did tell you that I might not be free. Will you make my excuses to the Pickerings?'

They talked for a few minutes, until she said, 'Oh, well, you're not much use as an escort, are you, Thomas?' She gave a little laugh. 'I might as well give you up.'

'There must be any number of men queueing up to take you out. I'm not reliable, Honor.'

'You'll end up a crusty old bachelor, Thomas, unless you take time off to fall in love.'

'I'll have to think about that.'

'Well, let me know when you've made up your mind.' She rang off, and he put the phone down and forgot all about her. He had a teaching round the next morning and he needed to prepare a few notes for that.

He ate the dinner Cork set before him and went back to his study to work. He was going to his bed when he had a sudden memory of Claudia, her fiery hair in a mess, enveloped in that old jacket and a sack. He found himself smiling, thinking of her.

The first few days of November, with their frosty mornings and chilly pale skies, had turned dull and damp, and as they faded towards winter Great-Uncle William faded with them. But although he was physically weaker there was nothing weak about his mental state. He was as peppery as he always had been, defying anyone to show sympathy towards him, demanding that Claudia should read the *Times* to him each morning, never mind that he dozed off every now and then.

His faithful housekeeper's endless efforts to prepare tasty morsels for his meals met with no success at all. And no amount of coaxing would persuade him to allow a nurse to attend to his wants. Between them, Claudia, her mother and Tombs did as much as he would allow them to. Dr Willis, inured to his patient's caustic tongue, came daily, but it was less than a week after Mr Tait-Bullen's visit when Great-Uncle William, glaring at him from his bed, observed in an echo of his former commanding tones, 'I shall die within the next day or so. Tell Tait-Bullen to come and see me.'

'He's a busy man...'

'I know that. I'm not a fool.' The Colonel looked suddenly exhausted. 'He said that he would come.' He turned his head to look at Claudia, standing at the window, lingering after she had brought Dr Willis upstairs.

'You—Claudia, go and telephone him. Now, girl!'

She glanced at Dr Willis, and at his nod went down to the hall and dialled Mr Tait-Bullen's number. Cork's dignified voice regretted that Mr Tait-Bullen was not at home.

'It's urgent. Do you know where I can get him?' She added, so as to make things clear, 'I'm not a friend or anything. My great-uncle is a patient of Mr Tait-Bullen's and he wants to see him. He's very ill.'

'In that case, miss, I will give you the number of his consulting rooms.'

She thanked him and dialled again, and this time Mrs Truelove, Mr Tait-Bullen's receptionist, answered.

'Colonel Ramsay? You are his niece? Mr Tait-Bullen has mentioned him. He's with a patient at the moment. Ring off, my dear. I'll call you the moment he's free.'

Claudia waited, wondering if Mr Tait-Bullen would have time to visit Great-Uncle William or even to phone him. She supposed that he was a very busy man; he could hardly be blamed if he hadn't the time to leave London and his patients to obey the whim of an old man who had refused his services. Then the phone rang, and she picked it up.

'Yes,' said a voice in her ear. 'Tait-Bullen speaking.'

This was no time for polite chit-chat. 'Great-Uncle William wants to see you. He says he's going to die in a day or two. He told me to phone you, so I am, because he asked me to, but you don't have to.'

She wasn't sure if she had made herself clear, but apparently she had. Mr Tait-Bullen disentangled the muddle with a twitching lip and answered her with exactly the right amount of impersonal friendliness.

'It is very possible that your great-uncle is quite right. I'm free this evening. I will be with you at about seven o'clock.'

He heard her relieved sigh.

'Thank you very much. I'm sorry if I've disturbed your work.'

'I'm glad you phoned me.'

She could hear the faint impatience in his voice.

'Goodbye, then.' She rang off smartly, and then wondered if she'd been rather too abrupt.

He arrived punctually, unfussed and unhurried. No one looking at his immaculate person would have guessed that he had been up since six o'clock, had missed his lunch and stopped only for the tea and bun his faithful Mrs Truelove had pressed upon him. Dr Willis was waiting for him, and they spent a few minutes talking together before they went up to the Colonel's room. Dr Willis came down presently. 'They're discussing the merits of pyrenaicum aureum as opposed to tenuifolium pumilum…'

Mrs Ramsay looked puzzled. 'Is that some new symptom? It sounds alarming. Poor Uncle William.'

'Lilies,' said Claudia. 'Two varieties of lily, Mother.'

Dr Willis patted her mother's arm. 'Don't alarm yourself, my dear. Your uncle is enjoying his little chat. It was good of Mr Tait-Bullen to come.'

'But he's not doing anything to help Uncle…'

But that was exactly what he *was* doing, reflected Claudia, although she didn't say so. Instead she asked, 'Do you suppose he will stay for supper? Mrs Pratt can grill a couple more chops.'

But when he joined them presently, he declined Mrs Ramsay's offer of supper, saying that he must return to London.

'I hope we haven't spoilt your evening for you—caused you to cancel a date?'

Claudia noticed that he didn't answer that, merely thanked her mother for her invitation. 'If I might have a word with Dr Willis?'

They left the two men, returning when they heard them in the hall.

Mrs Ramsay shook hands. 'We're so grateful to you. Uncle did so wish to see you again—although I'm sure you are a very busy man.'

He said gravely, 'The Colonel is going to die very soon now, Mrs Ramsay. He is content, and in no pain, and in Dr Willis's good hands.'

He turned to Claudia. 'I was bidden to tell you to read the editorial in the *Times* before he has his supper.' His hand was firm and cool and comforting. 'He's fond of you, you know.'

He left then, getting into his car and driving back to his house to eat the meal Cork had ready for him and then go to his study and concentrate on the notes of the patients upon whom he would be operating in the morning. Before that, he paused to think about the Colonel. A courageous old man hidden behind that crusty manner. He hoped that he would die quietly in his sleep.

Great-Uncle William died while Claudia was still reading the editorial. So quietly and peacefully that it wasn't until she had finished it that she realised.

She said softly, 'You had a happy talk about lilies, didn't you, Great-Uncle William? I'm glad he came.'

She bent to kiss the craggy old face and went downstairs to tell her mother.

Chapter 2

The Colonel had been respected in the village; he had had no use for a social life or mere acquaintances, although he had lifelong friends.

Claudia had very little time to grieve. Her mother saw the callers when they came, arranged things with the undertaker and planned the flowers and the gathering of friends and family after the funeral, but it was left to Claudia to carry out her wishes, answer the telephone and make a tidy pile of the letters which would have to be answered later.

Dr Willis was a tower of strength, of course, but he was more concerned with her mother than anything else, and Mrs Ramsay leaned on him heavily for comfort and support. She needed both when, on the day before the funeral, the cousin who was to inherit the house arrived.

He was a middle-aged man, with austere good looks and cold eyes. He treated them with cool courtesy, expressed a token regret at the death of the Colonel and went away to see the Colonel's solicitor. When he returned he requested that Mrs Ramsay and Claudia should join him in the morning room.

He stood with his back to the fire and begged them to sit down. Already master of the house, thought Claudia, and wondered what was coming.

He spoke loudly, as though he thought that they were deaf. 'Everything seems to be in order. The will is not yet read, of course, but I gather that there are no surprises in it. I must return to York after the funeral, but I intend to return within two or three days. Monica—my wife—will accompany me and we will take up residence then. My house there is already on the market. You will, of course, wish to leave here as soon as possible.'

Claudia heard her mother's quick breath. 'Are you interested as to where we are going?'

'It is hardly my concern.' He eyed Claudia coldly. 'You must have been aware for some time that the house would become my property and have some plans of your own.'

'Well,' said Claudia slowly, 'whatever plans we may have had didn't include being thrown out lock, stock and barrel at a moment's notice.' When he started to speak, she added, 'No, let me finish. Let us know when you and your wife will arrive and we will be gone in good time. What about Tombs and Mrs Pratt and Jennie? I understand that they have been remembered in Great-Uncle William's will.'

'I shall, of course, give them a month's wages.' He considered the matter for a moment. 'It might be convenient if Mrs Pratt remained, and the girl. It will save Monica a good deal of trouble if the servants remain.'

'And Tombs?'

'Oh! He's past an honest day's work. He will have his state pension.'

'Have you any children?'

He looked surprised. 'No. Why do you ask?'

She didn't answer that, merely said in a matter-of-fact voice, 'Well, that's a blessing, isn't it?' Then she added, 'I'm glad you're only a distant cousin.'

He said loftily, 'I cannot understand you...'

'Well, of course you can't. But never mind that. Is that all? We'll see you at dinner presently.'

She saw him go red in the face as she got up and urged her mother out of the room.

In the hall, her mother said, 'Darling, you were awfully rude.'

'Mother, he's going to throw Tombs out, not to mention us. He's the most awful man I've ever met. And I'm sure Mrs Pratt and Jennie won't want to stay. I'm going to see them now.'

She gave her mother a reassuring pat on the shoulder. 'Why don't you go and phone Dr Willis and see what he says?'

Over a mug of powerfully brewed tea, she told Tombs and Mrs Pratt and Jennie what her cousin had said. They listened in growing unrest.

'You'll not catch me staying with the likes of him,' said Mrs Pratt. She looked at Jennie. 'And what about you, Jennie, girl?'

'Me neither.' They both looked at Tombs.

Claudia hadn't repeated all her cousin had said about Tombs, but he had read between the lines.

'I'll never get another place at my age,' he told them. 'But I wouldn't stay for all the tea in China.'

He turned a worried old face towards Claudia. 'Where will you and madam go, Miss Claudia? It's a scandal, turning you out of house and home.'

'We'll think of something, Tombs. We've several days to plan something.'

'And Rob?'

'He'll come with us. I don't know about Stokes...'

'I'll see that he gives in his notice,' said Tombs. 'What a mercy that the Colonel isn't here. He would never have allowed these goings-on.'

'No, but you see this cousin of his has every right to do what he likes. If you intend to leave when we do, have you somewhere to go? Mother's on the phone to Dr Willis, who may be able to help. If not then we will all put up at the Duck and Thistle in the village.'

'I could go home,' ventured Jennie. 'Me mum'll give me a bed for a bit.' She sounded doubtful.

Claudia said, 'Well, perhaps Dr Willis will know of someone local who needs help in the house. I think we'd all better start packing our things as soon as the funeral is over.'

She found her mother in the morning room. It was cold there, for the fire hadn't been lighted, and Mrs Ramsay was walking up and down in a flurried way.

'Mother, it's too cold for you here, and you're upset.'

'No, dear, there's nothing wrong—in fact, quite the reverse. Only I'm not sure how to talk to you about it.'

Claudia sat her parent down on the sofa and settled beside her.

'You talked to Dr Willis? He had some suggestions? Some advice?'

'Well, yes…'

'Mother, dear, does he want to marry you? I know you're fond of each other…'

'Oh, yes, we are, love, but how can I possibly marry him and leave you and the others in the lurch? At least…'

'Yes?' Claudia had taken her mother's hand. 'Do tell. I'm sure it's something helpful. He's such a dear. I'll love having him for a stepfather.'

Mrs Ramsay gave a shaky little laugh. 'Oh, darling, will you really? But I haven't said I'd marry him.'

'But you will. Now, what else does he suggest?'

'Well, it's coincidental, but his housekeeper has given him notice—wants to go back to her family somewhere in Lancashire—so Mrs Pratt could take over if she would like the job. And he knows everyone here, doesn't he? He says it should be easy to find a place for Jennie.'

'And Tombs?'

'George said he's always wanted a butler. His house is quite small, but there would be plenty for Tombs to do. And he'd love to have Rob… Only there's you, darling.'

'But, Mother dear, I'll be getting a job. I've already applied for several, you know, and none of them are too far from here. I can come for holidays and weekends, if George will have me.'

'You're not just saying that to make it easy for the rest of us?'

'Of course not. You know that was the plan, wasn't it? That I should come here for a week or two while I looked for something nearer than London?'

She didn't mention that she had had two answers that morning from her applications, and both posts had been filled. There was still another one to come…

'Well, Claudia, if you think that's the right thing to do. We shall go and tell Tombs and the others.'

'Yes, but no one had better say a word to Mr Ramsay. When do you see Dr Willis—no, I shall call him George if he doesn't mind?'

'After the funeral. He thought it best not to come here.'

'Quite right, too. We don't want Cousin Ramsay smelling a rat. Mother, you go to the kitchen. I'll hang around the house in case he comes looking for us.'

Later at dinner, Mr Ramsay made no mention of their plans; he had a good deal to say about the various alterations he intended making in the house. Monica, he told them, was a woman of excellent taste. She would have the shabby upholstery covered and the thick velvet curtains in the drawing room and dining room torn down and replaced by something more up-to-date.

'The curtains were chosen by Uncle William's mother,' observed Mrs Ramsay, 'when she came here as a bride.'

'Then it's high time that they were removed. They are probably full of dust and germs.'

'Most unlikely,' said Claudia quickly. 'Everything in the house has been beautifully cared for.'

He gave her an annoyed look. He didn't like this girl, with the fiery hair and the too-ready tongue. He

decided not to answer her, but instead addressed Mrs
Ramsay with some query about the following day.

It was after the last of the Colonel's friends and acquaintances had taken their leave, after returning to
the house for tea and Mrs Pratt's delicious sandwiches
and cakes, that Mr Potter, the Colonel's solicitor, led
the way across the hall to the morning room. He had
been a friend of the family for years, and his feelings
had been hurt when Mr Ramsay had told him that he
would no longer require his services.

His father and his father before him had looked after
the Ramsays' modest estate, but he was old himself and
he supposed that Mr Ramsay's own lawyer would be
perfectly capable. He said now, 'If someone would ask
Tombs and Mrs Pratt and Jennie to come in here.' He
beamed across at Dr Willis. 'I had already asked you
to be present, George.'

He took no notice of Mr Ramsay's frown, but waited
patiently until everyone was there.

The will was simple and short. The house and estate
were to go to Cousin Ramsay, and afterwards to his
heirs. Mrs Ramsay was to receive shares in a company,
sufficient to maintain her lifestyle, and Claudia was
to receive the same amount, but neither of them could
use the capital. Tombs received five thousand pounds,
Mrs Pratt the same amount and Jennie one thousand
pounds. Claudia heard Cousin Ramsay draw in a disapproving breath at that.

Mr Potter put the will back in his briefcase and said,
suddenly grave, 'If I might have a word with you, Mrs
Ramsay, and Claudia, and you, Mr Ramsay?'

When the others had gone, he said, 'I am afraid that I have bad news for you. The company in which the shares were invested and destined for you, Mrs Ramsay, and you, Claudia, has gone bankrupt. I ascertained this the day before the Colonel died, and I intended to visit him on that very day. There is nothing to be done about the terms of the will, but perhaps you, Mr Ramsay, will wish to make some adjustment so that Mrs Ramsay and Claudia are not left penniless.'

He saw no sign of encouragement in Mr Ramsay's stern features. Nevertheless he persisted. 'Their incomes would have been small, but adequate. I can advise you as to the amount they would have been. One wouldn't expect you to make good the full amount, but I'm sure that a small allowance for each of them...' His voice faded away under Mr Ramsay's icy stare.

Claudia saw the painful colour in her mother's face. 'That is very thoughtful of you, Mr Potter, but I think that neither Mother nor I would wish to accept anything from Mr Ramsay.'

Mr Ramsay looked above their heads and cleared his throat. 'I have many commitments,' he observed. 'Any such arrangement would be quite beyond my means.'

Mr Potter opened his mouth to protest, but Claudia caught his eye and shook her head. And, although the old man looked bewildered, he closed it again.

It was Mrs Ramsay who said, in a voice which gave away none of her feelings, 'You'll stay for supper, Mr Potter? I remember Uncle William promised you that little painting on the stairs, which you always admired. Will you fetch it, Claudia?'

She smiled at Mr Ramsay. 'It is of no value, and one must keep one's promises, must one not?'

Mr Potter refused supper and, clutching the picture, was escorted to his car by Claudia. 'It is all most unsatisfactory,' he told her. 'Your great-uncle would never have allowed it to happen. How will you manage? Surely even a small allowance—'

Claudia popped him into the car and kissed his cheek. 'I'll tell you a secret. Mother is going to marry Dr Willis and I've my eye on a good job. We haven't told Mr Ramsay and we don't intend to. And Tombs and Mrs Pratt and Jennie are all fixed up. So don't worry about us.'

He cheered up then. 'In that case I feel very relieved. You will keep in touch?'

'Of course.'

She waved and smiled as he drove off, then went back into the house. Despite her cheerful words she would hate leaving the old house, although she told herself sensibly that she would have hated staying on there with Mr Ramsay and his wife, who would doubtless alter the whole place so much that she would never recognise it again.

Later, in her mother's bedroom, she said, 'You'll have to marry George now, because I told Mr Potter you were going to.'

'But, Claudia, there's nothing arranged...'

'Then arrange it, Mother dear, as quickly as you can. There's something called a special licence, and the vicar's an old friend. Now, what's to happen when we leave? Is George giving us beds, or shall we go to the Duck and Thistle?'

'George wants me to go and see him tomorrow morning. I think he has something planned. Will you stay here, in case Mr Ramsay wants to talk to us about something?'

'Not likely. But I'll be here. Take Rob with you, Mother. *He* doesn't like dogs.'

Mr Ramsay spent the next morning going from room to room, taking careful note of his new possessions. The kitchen and its occupants he ignored; they could be dealt with when he was satisfied with his arrangements. He kept Claudia busy answering his questions about the furniture and pictures, all of which he valued.

'We shall sell a good deal,' he told her loftily. 'There are several pieces which I think may be of real value. But these...' He waved an arm at a pair of Regency terrestrial and celestial globes in one corner of the morning room. 'I doubt if they'd fetch more than a few pounds in a junk shop.'

Claudia, who happened to know that they were worth in the region of twenty thousand pounds and had been in the family for well over a hundred years, agreed politely.

'And this clock—Monica has no liking for such old-fashioned stuff—that can go.' He pointed to a William the Fourth bracket clock, very plain and worth at least two thousand pounds.

He brushed aside a stool. 'And there are all these around. I have never seen such a collection of out-of-date furniture.'

The stool was early Victorian, covered with petit point tapestry. Claudia didn't mention its value, instead she said politely, 'There is a very good firm at Ringwood, I believe—a branch of one of the London antiques dealers. But I expect that you would prefer to go to someone you know in York.'

'Certainly not. I am more likely to get good prices from a firm which has some knowledge of this area.'

Claudia cast down her eyes and murmured. If and when he sold Great-Uncle William's family treasures, and she could find out who had bought them, she might be able to buy one or two of them back. She had no idea how she would do this, but that was something she would worry about later.

She knew the elder son of the antiques dealer at Ringwood; he might let her buy things back with instalments. Which reminded her of the letter she had stuffed in her pocket that morning. The postmark was Southampton, and it was the last reply from the batch of applications she had sent. Perhaps she would be lucky…

She was roused from her thoughts by Mr Ramsay's sharp, 'Where is your mother?'

She looked at him for a moment before replying. She wondered if she dared to tell him to mind his own business, but decided against it.

'Well, she will have gone upstairs to check the linen cupboard with Mrs Pratt—a long job—then she told me that she would be taking Rob for his walk and doing some necessary shopping in the village. She should be back by lunchtime. I don't know what she will be doing this afternoon.'

He gave her a suspicious glance. 'I wish to inform her of my final plans for moving here.'

'Well, I am going to the kitchen now to see about lunch.'

But first she went into the hall and out of the side door at its end, taking an old coat off a hook as she went and making for the glasshouse.

The letter was a reply to her application for the post of general helper at a geriatric hospital on the outskirts of Southampton. She had applied for it for the simple reason that there had been nothing else advertised, and she hadn't expected a reply.

Providing that her references were satisfactory, the job was hers. Her duties were vague, and the money was less than she had hoped for, but on the other hand she could start as soon as her references had been checked. It would solve the problem of her immediate future, set her mother's mind at rest and put a little money into her pocket.

She didn't see her mother until the three of them were sitting down to lunch, but she deduced from the faintly smug look on that lady's face that her talk with Dr Willis had been entirely satisfactory. It wasn't until they left the house together to take Rob for another walk that they were able to talk.

'When's the wedding?' asked Claudia as soon as they had left the house.

Her mother laughed. 'Darling, I'm not sure. I won't marry George until you're settled...'

'Then he'd better get a licence as soon as he can. I've got a job—in Southampton at one of the hospitals. I had the letter this morning.'

Mrs Ramsay beamed at her. 'Oh, Claudia, really? I

mean, it's something you want to do, not just any old job you're taking to make things easy for us?'

To tell a lie was sometimes necessary, reflected Claudia, if it was to a good purpose, and surely this was. 'It's exactly what I'm looking for—quite good money and I can come back here for weekends and holidays, if George will have me?'

'Of course we'll have you.' Her mother squeezed her arm. 'Isn't it strange how everything is coming right despite Uncle William's horrid cousin? And George has found a place for Jennie—they were looking for someone up at the Manor, so she will still keep her friends in the village and see Mrs Pratt and Tombs if she wants to.'

'Good. Now, when will you marry?'

'Well, as soon as George can get a licence.'

'You'll stay with him, of course?'

'Mrs Pratt and Tombs will be with me.'

'Mr Ramsay wants to talk to you about his plans. He didn't say anything at lunch…'

'Perhaps this evening.'

He was waiting for them when they got back. 'Be good enough to come to my study?' he asked Mrs Ramsay. 'I dare say Claudia has things to do.'

Dismissed, she went to her room; there were clothes to pack and small, treasured ornaments she had been given since childhood to be wrapped and stowed in boxes. As soon as Mr Ramsay went back to York, Dr Willis would come and load up his car and stow everything they didn't want in his attics.

She hoped that the new owner of the house would stay away for several days, for they all intended to be gone, the house empty of people, by the time he and his wife arrived. He had said nothing to Tombs or Mrs Pratt, nor to Jennie; perhaps he expected them to stay on until he saw fit to discharge Tombs. He was arrogant enough to suppose that Mrs Pratt and Jennie would be only too thankful to remain in his service.

Since it was teatime, she went downstairs and found her mother in the morning room. There was no sign of Mr Ramsay, and at her questioning look Mrs Ramsay said, 'He's gone to see the vicar. He's going to York tomorrow afternoon and returning with Monica in two days' time. I am to tell Mrs Pratt and Jennie that they are to stay on in his employment—he hasn't bothered to ask them if they want to—and I'm to dismiss Tombs.'

'Why doesn't he do his own dirty work?' demanded Claudia. 'What else?'

'He avoided asking me where you and I were going. He made some remark about us having friends and he was sure we had sufficient funds to tide us over until we had settled somewhere.'

'Mother, he's despicable. Does he know about you and George?'

'No, I'm sure he doesn't, for he made a great thing of offering to send on our belongings once we had left.'

'Have you had a chance to tell Tombs?'

'No, I'd better go now. If he comes back, come and let me know.'

Not a word was said about their departure during dinner, and the following day Mr Ramsay got into his car and drove himself back to York.

'You may, of course, remain until the day following our return,' he told Mrs Ramsay. 'Monica will wish to be shown round the house.' He looked over her head, avoiding her eyes. 'Kindly see that Tombs has gone by the time we return.'

He turned back at the door. 'It will probably be late afternoon by the time we get here. Tell Mrs Pratt to have a meal ready and see that the maid has the rooms warm.'

Mrs Ramsay lowered her eyes and said, 'Yes,' meekly. She looked very like her daughter. 'I'm sure that if you think of anything else you will phone as soon as you get home.'

They waited a prudent hour before starting on their packing up. He was, observed Claudia, the kind of man who would sneak back to make sure that they weren't making off with the spoons. They collected their belongings, taking only what was theirs, and presently, when Dr Willis drove up, loaded his car. Mr Ramsay had said two days before he returned, but to be on the safe side they had decided to move out on the following day.

Dr Willis would have taken them all to his house for supper, but they refused and, while Mrs Pratt got a meal for them, began on the business of leaving the house in perfect condition. Tombs was set to polish the silver, Jennie saw to the bedrooms and Claudia and her mother hoovered and dusted downstairs. After supper, tired but happy, they all went to bed.

They were up early in the morning, making sure that there was nothing with which the new owner could find fault, and as soon as the morning surgery was over Dr Willis came to fetch them to his house. He had to make two journeys, and Claudia left last of all, wheeling her bike and leading Rob on his lead. Mr Ramsay had a key—he had taken care to have all of the keys in his possession—but she had a key to the garden door which she had kept. She wasn't sure why and she didn't intend to tell anyone.

Dr Willis's housekeeper had already left, and Mrs Pratt slipped into the kitchen as though she had been there all her life, taking Tombs and Jennie with her.

'There are an awful lot of us,' worried Mrs Ramsay as they ate the lunch the unflappable Mrs Pratt had produced.

'The house is large enough, my dear, and Jennie goes to her new job tomorrow.'

'And I go to mine in a day or two,' said Claudia.

'You're quite happy about it?' he asked her kindly. 'There's no hurry, you know.'

'It sounds just what I'm looking for. When will you marry? I'd like to come to the wedding.'

'Darling, we wouldn't dream of getting married unless you were there.'

'Within the week, I hope,' said George. 'Very quiet, of course, just us and a few friends here at the church. I've put a notice in the *Telegraph*.'

Everyone in the village knew by now that there was a new owner at Colonel Ramsay's house. Those that had met him didn't like him overmuch. The postman, who had been spoken to sharply by Mr Ramsay because he whistled too loudly as he delivered the letters and had been discovered drinking tea in the kitchen, had promised that any letters would be delivered to the doctor's house. The village considered Mr Ramsay an outsider, for he had made no effort to be pleasant. Even the vicar, a mild and godly man, pursed his lips when his name was mentioned.

There was a letter for Claudia the next morning. Her references had been accepted for the post of general assistant and she should present herself without delay to take up her duties. The list enclosed was vague about these, but the off duty seemed fair enough. She was to have two days a week free and the money was adequate. There was accommodation for her within the hospital.

She wrote back at once, accepting the post and saying that she would present herself for duty in the early evening of the following day. Feeling pleased that things were turning out so well, she went away to unpack and repack what she would need to take with her.

Dr Willis drove her to Southampton after lunch the following day, and that same afternoon, as dusk was gathering, Mr Ramsay came back to take possession of his new home. An arrogant man, and insensitive to other people's feelings, he had taken it for granted that he would be received suitably—the house lighted and warm, a meal waiting to be put on the table, Mrs Ramsay there to show his wife round, Jennie to see to the luggage. He got out of the car and surveyed the dark, silent house with a frown before unlocking the door.

It was obvious that there was no one there. Monica pushed past him, switched on the lights and looked around her. She saw the letter on the side table and opened it. Mrs Ramsay wrote politely that as Mr Ramsay had requested they had left the house. And, since neither Mrs Pratt nor Jennie wished to work for him, they had also left. There was food in the fridge, the fires were laid ready to light and the beds were aired and made up.

Monica laughed. 'You told them you wanted them out, and they've gone. I wonder where they went?'

'It's of no consequence. We can get help from the village easily enough, and I had nothing in common with either Mrs Ramsay or that daughter of hers.'

'A pity about the servants…'

'Easily come by in a small place like this—they'll be only too glad to have the work.'

'There was a butler, you said.'

'Oh, he was too old to work. I dare say he has found himself a room or gone to live with someone. He'd have his pension.'

His wife gave him a long look. 'You're a heartless man, aren't you? You'd better bring in the luggage while I find the kitchen and see what there is to eat.'

Dr Willis left Claudia at the door of the hospital with some reluctance. The place looked gloomy and down at heel, and he was sorry that he hadn't found out about it before. True, geriatric hospitals were usually the last ones to get facelifts—probably inside it was bright and cheerful enough, and she had wished him goodbye very happily, with the promise that she would be at the wedding. She poked her head through the open window of the car.

'I know that you and Mother will be happy. You really are a very nice man, George.'

She picked up her case and went into the hospital.

She knew she wasn't going to like it before she had gone ten yards from the door, but she ignored that. A tired-looking porter asked her what she wanted, told her to leave her case and follow him and led her down a long passage. He knocked on the door at the end of it. The label on the door said Hospital Manager, and when the porter opened the door in answer to the voice inside, she went past him into a small austere room.

It was furnished sparsely, with a desk and chair, two other chairs along one wall and a great many shelves stuffed with paper files. The woman behind the desk had a narrow, pale face, a straight haircut in an unbecoming bob and small dark eyes. She looked up as Claudia went in, pursing her mouth and frowning a little.

'Miss Ramsay? It's too late for you to do much for the rest of the day. I'll get someone to show you your room and take you to where you will be working. But if you will draw up a chair I will explain your schedule to you.'

Not a very good start, reflected Claudia, but perhaps the poor soul was tired.

Her duties were many and varied and rather vague. She would work from seven o'clock until three in the afternoon three days a week, and her free day would follow that duty, and for the other three days the hours would be three o'clock in the afternoon until ten o'clock at night.

'The off duty is arranged so that you are free from three o'clock before your day off, and not on duty until three o'clock on the day following.'

Two nights at home, thought Claudia, and felt cheered by the thought.

She asked politely, 'Am I to call you Matron?'

'Miss Norton,' she was told, in a manner which implied that she should have known that without being told. She was dismissed into the care of a small woman with a kind face and a bright smile, who told her that her name was Nurse Symes.

'You're on duty in the morning,' she told her. 'Ward B—that's on the other wing. First floor, thirty beds. Sister Clark is in charge there.'

She paused, and Claudia said encouragingly, 'And...?'

'She's terribly overworked, you know—we can't get the staff. She doesn't mean half she says.'

'Tell me, what exactly do I do? General assistant covers a lot of ground, and Miss Norton was a bit vague.'

'Well, dear, there aren't many trained nurses, so you do anything that's needed.'

They got into the lift at the back of the hall and stepped out on the top floor, went through a door with Private on it and started down another corridor lined with doors.

'Here we are,' said Nurse Symes. 'Quite a nice room, and the bathrooms are at the end. There's a little kitchen, too, if you want to make tea.'

The room was small, with a bed, a small easy chair, a bedside table and a clothes cupboard. It was very clean and there was a view of chimney pots from its window. There was a washbasin on one corner, and a small mirror over the wide shelf which served as a dressing table. A few cushions and photos and a vase of flowers, thought Claudia with resolute cheerfulness, and it would be quite pretty.

'We'll go to the linen room and get you some

dresses. You'll get three, but of course you'll wear a plastic apron when you're on duty.'

The dresses—a useful mud-brown—duly chosen and taken to her room, they began a tour of the hospital. It was surprisingly large, with old-fashioned wards with beds on either side and tables with pot plants down the centre. The wards were full, and most of the patients were sitting in chairs by their beds, watching television if they were near enough to the two sets at either end of the wards.

Most of them appeared to be asleep; one or two had visitors. Claudia could see only one or two nurses, but there were several young women shrouded in plastic pinnies, carrying trays, mops and buckets and helping those patients who chose to trundle around with their walking aids.

It wasn't quite what she had expected, but it was too early to have an opinion, and first impressions weren't always the right ones.

It was Cork who folded the *Telegraph* at the appropriate page and silently pointed out the notice of the forthcoming marriage between George Willis and Doreen Ramsay to Professor Tait-Bullen as he ate his breakfast.

He read it in an absent-minded fashion, and then read it again.

'Interesting,' he observed, and then, 'I wonder what will happen to the daughter? Staying on at the Colonel's house, I suppose.'

He thought no more about it until that evening when, urged by some niggling doubt at the back of his mind, he phoned Dr Willis. His congratulations were sincere. 'You will be marrying shortly?'

'In four days' time. Mrs Ramsay is here with me, so are Mrs Pratt and Tombs. Jennie, their maid, went to the Manor to a new job this morning.' George added drily, 'They were turned out by the new owner.'

The Professor asked sharply, 'And the daughter—Claudia?'

'Fortunately she found a job at Southampton, in a hospital there—geriatrics. Didn't like the look of the place, but they wanted someone at once.'

'You mean to tell me that this man turned them all out? Is he no relation?'

'A cousin of sorts.'

'Extraordinary.' The Professor had a fleeting memory of a lovely girl with red hair and decided that he wanted to know more. 'I'm going to Bristol in a couple of days. May I call in and wish you both well?'

'We'd be delighted. And if you can come to the wedding we should very much like that.'

Mr Tait-Bullen put down the receiver and sat back in his chair. With a little careful planning there was no reason why he shouldn't go to the wedding.

Chapter 3

By the end of her first day at the hospital Claudia knew exactly what a general assistant was: a maker of beds, a carrier of trays, bedpans and bags of bed linen. And when she wasn't doing this she was getting the old and infirm in and out of bed, finding slippers, spectacles, dentures, feeding those who were no longer able to help themselves and trotting the more spry of the ladies to the loo.

It was non-stop work, and, going off duty soon after three o'clock, she was thankful that she was free until seven o'clock the next morning and that by some miracle she would have her day off on the day following that. The whole day, she thought joyfully, and not on duty until the afternoon after that. She got into her outdoor clothes and hurried out to the nearest phone box.

Her mother and George were to be married in three

days' time; she would be able to go to the wedding, although she would have to leave Little Planting directly after the ceremony. The bus service between Romsey and Southampton was frequent; it was just a question of getting from Romsey to Little Planting and back again.

She would be met, declared her mother; any of their friends in the village would be glad to collect her. 'Phone me tomorrow and let me know what time the bus gets to Romsey. And don't worry about getting back to Southampton, there'll be someone to give you a lift. You're happy there, Claudia?'

'Yes,' said Claudia, 'I'm sure I shall be happy.' She was so convincing that her mother observed happily to George that Claudia sounded perfectly content, and wasn't it lucky that she should be free for the wedding?

Claudia went back to the hospital and had a cup of tea with some of the other girls, then went to her room, kicked off her shoes and curled up on the bed. Her feet ached and she was tired. It had been a hard day's work, but it wasn't only that; she felt sad and lonely and uncertain of the future. She was prepared to stay in this job for as long as it took to save enough money for her to train in something which would allow her more freedom. Enough money for her to have nice clothes, and a holiday. A career girl.

It would have to be something to do with computers, shorthand and typing and a knowledge of the business world. A receptionist, mused Claudia, a nine-to-five job with free weekends so that she could go and stay with her mother and George from time to time. And, of course, a nicely furnished flat, and friends to enter-

tain and to be entertained by. She might even meet a
man who would fall in love with her and marry her...

Mr Tait-Bullen's handsome features imposed themselves upon her wishful thinking, but she brushed them
away. One didn't cry for the moon, and she was never
likely to meet him again. Even if she did, she wasn't
sure if he had noticed her as a woman. She wondered
what he was really like behind that impersonal, impassive face. Probably quite nice...

A thump on the door brought her back to reality,
and when she called, 'Come in,' a girl opened the door.
One of those on the afternoon shift.

'Oh, good, you're here. The other two are out and
Sister sent me. Mrs Legge—who's the one with the
Zimmer walker—fell over and she's broken a leg and
an arm. She'll have to go to the City General with a
nurse, and that only leaves Sister and me and we're up
to our eyes. Could you come back on duty for an hour
or two, just until someone can be found to take over?'

Claudia crammed her feet back into her shoes. It
would be, after all, a way of passing the empty evening.

She stayed on the ward for more than two hours,
and was sent off at last with the promise of extra time
off when it was convenient. She ate supper with several of the other girls, watched television for half an
hour and then went to bed. She was too tired to think
much. Someone had to look after those old ladies...
She would be an old lady herself one day, but hopefully loved and cherished by a husband. Someone like
Mr Tait-Bullen, she decided, half asleep.

By the end of the following day she had realised
that—never mind what Miss Norton had told her—

the off duty was very much in the hands of the ward sister. It was possible, one of the other assistants told her, to have five days in a row of seven o'clock duty, or several days of afternoon shift with no more than an hour or two's notice.

So she wasn't altogether surprised when she was told that she would have an afternoon shift before her day off. That meant she wouldn't be able to go home until the following morning. Still, that would give her all the day before the wedding, and she had already told her mother that she would have to leave directly after the ceremony. She caught the first bus in the morning, after phoning her mother, and found Tombs waiting for her at Romsey. He was driving the doctor's car—a battered old Ford, long ago pensioned off in one corner of the garage, but used in emergencies. It wasn't a long drive, and Tombs filled it with gossip about Mrs Ramsay, the wedding and how well they had settled in at the doctor's house. Indeed, he seemed to have shed several years. Claudia hadn't seen him as happy for some time, and she was glad of that; she had known him all her life and he was part of it. They talked about the wedding at some length, and he said, 'It is a great pity that you have to return so soon, Miss Claudia. Mrs Ramsay tells me that you have a very good job.'

She enlarged upon that, drawing upon her imagination rather more than was truthful, and was rewarded by his satisfied, 'We all want you to be happy, Miss Claudia.'

At the doctor's house she was greeted by her mother and borne away to inspect the wedding hat, give her opinion of the outfit to go with it and listen while her parent told her of the plans for the wedding.

'Very quiet, of course, but that's how we want it. George can't get away for a week or two, but then we're going down to Cornwall. He has a cottage at St Anthony—that's a bit farther on from Falmouth. But we'll be back for Christmas, of course. Will you be able to come home?'

'I don't know, Mother. The off duty is made out a week or two at a time, and it has to be altered from time to time. I'll certainly do my best.'

Christmas was still five weeks or more away; anything could happen...

The wedding was to be at eleven o'clock in the morning. A fellow doctor had come over from a neighbouring village to keep an eye on the practice until the evening, and Mrs Pratt had arranged luncheon for the few friends who had been invited. Tombs, to his tremendous delight, was to give the bride away, and Miss Tremble, who had played the organ for more years than anyone could remember, had insisted on playing for the service.

Claudia, in the grey suit she had had for rather longer than she would have wished, perched a velvet beret on her bright hair and took herself off to the church, leaving her mother and Tombs to follow in George's car.

The handful of friends who had been invited were completely swallowed up by the villagers, who had turned out to a man and woman to see the doctor they respected and liked marry Mrs Ramsay. Claudia, sitting in the front pew greeting those she knew, turned round, craning her neck to see who was there. Almost everyone, except of course Mr and Mrs Ramsay, but they wouldn't have been welcome anyway. She turned round again and looked at George's upright elderly back, and then turned her head once more, this time with everyone else, to watch her mother coming down the aisle, her hand on Tombs's arm.

It was a short, simple service, but what it lacked in grandeur it made up for in warmth and friendliness as the congregation surged down the aisle after the happy pair. Claudia, hemmed in by well-wishers and friends she hadn't seen for some time, looked around her as she waited patiently to leave the church.

At the back of the church Mr Tait-Bullen, towering over those around him, was looking at her. He wasn't smiling, but that didn't prevent her from feeling pleasure at the sight of him. She made her way towards him and held out a hand.

'Hello, how nice to see you here. Did George invite you?'

He took her hand, shook it briskly and gave it back to her. 'I invited myself. I saw the notice in the *Telegraph* and, since I am on my way to Bristol, George kindly suggested that I might like to come to the church.'

They were outside now, everyone getting into cars or walking back to the doctor's house.

'You're coming to the house?'

'Yes.' Without asking her, he opened the car door and popped her in. 'Are you still at the Colonel's house? George said something about you leaving...'

He didn't sound very interested, so all she said was, 'Yes, we have all left.'

'And you?'

'Oh, I've got a job at Southampton. I'm going back this afternoon.'

They had reached the doctor's house, and Mr Tait-Bullen parked the car, opened her door and followed her inside. They were separated almost at once by other guests, and, feeling let down that he had evinced so little interest in her, Claudia wormed her way to where her mother and George were standing.

She kissed them both. 'I know you're going to be happy,' she told them. 'And this is a lovely wedding. Everyone here wants you to be happy, too.'

Her mother beamed at her. 'Darling, it's such a wonderful day. Must you go back so soon?'

'I'm afraid so. I'm on duty at three o'clock. I must get to Romsey in time to catch the bus, it goes at a quarter past the hour. Could Tombs take me?'

'Of course he can. And if he can't there are plenty of people here who wouldn't mind running you over to Romsey.' Her mother frowned. 'I meant to have fixed something up, but there was so much to do and think about…'

'Don't worry, Mother. And it will be a pity to take Tombs away. He's being so useful here. I'll get Tom Hicks from the garage to run me over.'

It was ten minutes or so later when she went back to the buffet with the plate of canapés she had been handing round, that she found Mr Tait-Bullen beside her. He took the plate from her, put it back on the table and handed her a glass of champagne. He said pleasantly, 'I'll drive you to Southampton. When do you want to leave?'

'But you're not going to Southampton. You're going to Bristol. You said so.'

'Indeed I am, but I have ample time to take you back on my way. At what time do you need to leave here?'

'I'm on duty at three o'clock. I was going to catch a bus from Romsey. There's really no need—it's very kind of you, but you'll miss the rest of the reception.'

Looking at him, she could see that he was taking no notice of what she was saying. He said now, 'If we leave at half past one that should give us ample time. Presumably you will need time to get ready for whatever job you are in.'

'I'm a general assistant at a geriatric hospital. It's near the docks.'

She spoke defiantly, as though she expected him to argue with her, but all he said was, 'You'll have to guide me. Do you like your work?'

'Yes. I've only been there for a short while. It's—it's very interesting.'

The vicar joined them then, and presently she excused herself and went to talk to Mr Potter, who asked her worriedly if she was managing.

'I hear you have work at Southampton. Providential, my dear, providential. I have been worried about you and your mother, and can only be thankful that things have turned out so well for you both.'

'Oh, everything is splendid,' said Claudia. 'And Dr Willis has been so kind and thoughtful to all of us.'

'You have not seen Mr and Mrs Ramsay since they returned to the house?'

'No, and I don't want to.' She patted his arm. 'We don't need to worry about them anymore, Mr Potter. We hated leaving the house, but we couldn't have stayed even if he had suggested it.'

She wandered round the room then, talking to other guests, most of them old friends who had known her for years. But she kept her eye on the clock, and when she saw that it had just struck one, she went in search of her mother and George, wished them goodbye, assured them that Mr Tait-Bullen was driving her back and promised to come again just as soon as she had a free day.

Then she got her case and went into the hall. Tombs was there, talking to Mr Tait-Bullen as he shrugged himself into his coat.

'Ah, there you are, Miss Claudia. I was just saying you'd be here dead on time, and so you are.'

'Tombs, it's been a lovely wedding, and I'm sure you did a great deal to make it so. I'll be back when I get a day off. Take care of yourself, won't you? I've seen Mrs Pratt and Jennie.'

'Bless you, miss,' said Tombs, and opened the door for them. 'A safe journey.'

Claudia settled herself in the comfortable seat. 'Do you know how to get onto the Romsey road? Through the village and keep straight on, then turn left at the crossroads. Then it's a right-hand fork. The roads are narrow.'

He said thank you so meekly that she was emboldened to say chattily, 'We're so glad that George gave Tombs a job. He'd been with my great-uncle for years and years. I don't suppose there are many like him…'

Mr Tait-Bullen, not a man for small talk, gave a grunt. And, since he had nothing to say, Claudia observed, 'Are you one of those people who don't like to talk while they are driving? I dare say it takes quite a lot of concentration, especially in a car like this one.'

Mr Tait-Bullen, whose work demanded powers of concentration well beyond the average, gave another grunt.

Claudia, not one to give up easily, took a look at his profile. It looked severe. 'Oh, well, if you don't want to talk…' She turned her head to look out of the window. 'Probably you're tired.'

'No, I am not in the least tired. Claudia, tell me your off duty for next week…'

'Whatever for?' When he didn't answer, she said, 'Oh, well…' and told him. 'But it gets changed at the last minute very often. There don't seem to be enough staff…'

'It is not, I believe, the most popular form of nursing.'

'Oh, I can quite see that, and I'm not even a nurse.'

'You say that you will be free at three o'clock on Friday? I shall call for you shortly after that and we will spend the rest of the day together.'

'Oh, will we? Have I been asked?'

'Ah, forgive me. I presumed that you would like to see me again, just as I would like to see you.'

'Well!' exclaimed Claudia. 'Whatever next…?'

'Just so. That is what I wish to find out.'

A remark which needed to be thought about and still remained puzzling.

'Well, thank you,' said Claudia, deciding to ignore

his remark for the moment. 'But don't be annoyed if my off duty's been changed.'

'I don't think you need worry about that.'

They were threading their way through the outskirts of Southampton. 'Tell me where I should turn off?' he said.

It was half past two when he stopped before the hospital entrance. He got out to open her door and walked with her into the entrance hall. He handed her case over, and when she put out a hand, shook it briefly.

'Thank you for the lift.' She smiled up at him and he smiled in return, a slow, gentle smile so that he looked quite different from the rather silent, reserved man she had thought him to be. And the smile warmed her loneliness, making the future full of unexpected hope. It wasn't until then that she realised how much she needed a friend.

When she had gone, Mr Tait-Bullen strolled over to the old-fashioned porter's lodge. He was there for several minutes, until its elderly occupant led him away down a long, dreary corridor, knocked on a door and ushered him inside.

Claudia didn't exactly forget him for the rest of the day; he was there at the back of her mind, almost smothered in her non-stop chores. The old ladies were such a cruel contrast to the pleasures of the morning she could have wept with pity for them. Not that weeping would have helped in any way. Cups of tea, endless trundles to the loo, mopping up after the inevitable accidents, making beds and the back-breaking task of getting elderly frail bodies back into bed... By ten o'clock, when she went off duty, her mother's wedding seemed part of a dream.

She fell into bed and was instantly asleep. In the morning, after a quick shower, she got into the brown dress and went down to her breakfast, her spirits fully restored. And they stayed that way all day, despite the hundred and one setbacks and Sister's sharp tongue. Claudia forgave her that, for coping with forty old ladies, keeping them clean and tidy and well fed, was no easy task. Claudia, putting clean sheets on a bed for the umpteenth time, considered Sister a splendid woman, even if she had no time to waste on being friendly.

All the same, it was difficult not to feel hard done by when that lady told her that her Friday off duty would be altered; she was to go on the afternoon shift instead of the morning. She wouldn't be able to go out with Mr Tait-Bullen after all, and there was no way of letting him know. She hoped that he wouldn't be too annoyed about it; not to annoy him was suddenly important. Not that it mattered anymore. He would go away and not bother to see her again. That thought left her feeling sad.

She was going off duty the next day when Sister called her into the office.

'You'll take your original off duty on Friday.' She sounded cross. 'There will be an extra nurse here for a couple of days, so there will be no need for you to change.'

'I shall be free at three o'clock on Friday?' asked Claudia, just to make sure.

'I've just said so, haven't I? You young girls are all alike, never listening to a word that is said to them.'

Claudia begged her pardon in a suitably humble voice, and once out of the office did a few dance steps along the corridor. Maybe the future wasn't going to be so bad, after all.

Friday dawned wet and cold. Claudia, deep in her morning chores, found the time to look out of the windows in the hope that the weather would improve. It did no such thing. Indeed a nasty wind had sprung up. It would have to be the grey suit and a raincoat— both suitable for the conditions out of doors, but hardly likely to inspire Mr Tait-Bullen to take her anywhere fashionable for tea.

She thought that three o'clock would never come, and even if it did, would she get off duty punctually? She did, hurrying through the hospital to her room, in a panic that she would be called back at the last moment.

Once there, she didn't waste a second—tearing out of the brown uniform, racing to the shower room before someone else got there, dressing with the speed of light. He had said shortly after three o'clock, but if she didn't show up within fifteen minutes of that time she hardly hoped that he would wait much longer. It was already five minutes over time as she gained the entrance hall, out of breath, and with her hair bundled up underneath the velvet beret. There had been no time to do more than powder her nose and put on some lipstick. She didn't look her best, she worried. He would take one look at her and decide that he was wasting his time...

Mr Tait-Bullen, leaning his length against a marble bust of a bewhiskered Victorian dignitary, entertained no such thought. He watched her slither to a dignified walk as she crossed the hall and reflected that she was the most beautiful girl that he had ever set eyes on. Even in the unbecoming garment in which she was swathed. But then she would look mouth-watering in a tablecloth with a hole cut for her head.

None of these interesting thoughts showed on his face as he went to meet her.

'Hello,' said Claudia, her smile so enchanting that he had difficulty in keeping his hands to himself. 'I haven't kept you waiting? I was so afraid that you might think I wasn't coming.' She plucked a bright lock of hair which had escaped her brush and tucked it behind an ear. 'I haven't done my hair properly.' She searched his calm face. 'I'm not dressed up either. You don't mind?'

'No, I don't mind. You look very nice.'

A tepid compliment which satisfied her; he had smiled at her when he had made it, which gave her a comfortable feeling that he had meant exactly what he had said.

'Shall we have tea first? I thought we might drive into the country for dinner later.'

'That would be lovely. Nowhere grand—I'm not dressed for it. I mean, I didn't know if we would be going out this evening—I was in a hurry so's not to miss you...' She paused, aware that she was babbling.

He said gently, 'There's a nice quiet hotel at Wickham. But tea first.'

He drove into the heart of Southampton and took her to a small quiet tea room tucked away in a side road where he was able to park the car. The place was half full, warm and pleasantly lighted, and they sat down at a table in the window curtained against the gathering dark of the late afternoon.

They ate hot buttered teacakes, and Claudia, urged to do so, sampled the creamy confections the waitress brought, and all the while Mr Tait-Bullen kept up an undemanding flow of small talk, calculated to put her at her ease so that presently, warm and nicely full, she answered his carefully put questions with less caution than she might have done.

Yes, it was hard work, she admitted, but the other girls were friendly and most of the old ladies were dears. 'Although there are one or two who are a bit difficult...'

'In what way?'

'Oh, they don't mean to be. They get cross, but I'd get cross if I had to sit in a chair because I couldn't do anything for myself. You see, they don't seem to have anyone to look after them—if they had daughters or someone, or sons or husbands who could look after them...'

'That might be difficult in a household with children, or where everyone goes out to work.'

'Yes, I know. Only it would be nice.'

Her hand was lying on the table, and he saw that it was rough and rather red. He said lightly, 'I dare say you have a lot of mopping up to do.'

'Oh, yes. All the time.' She smiled suddenly. 'It's not the cool hand on the brow kind of work—more like a charwoman—plastic pinnies and mops and buckets.'

'You intend to stay there?'

'When I've saved up enough money I shall train for something...' She saw his raised eyebrows. 'Well,

I don't know what yet.' She paused. 'I'm talking too much. Will you tell me about you?'

'I live and work in London. I have a house there, and Cork, who has been with me for a long time, looks after me. I have patients in several hospitals and hold clinics in each of them. I have a private practice, and I operate twice a week—sometimes three times. I travel round the country from time to time if I'm wanted for a consultation or to operate.'

'You have lots of friends?'

'I have a few old friends and acquaintances, yes. I'm not married, Claudia.'

She went pink. 'I should have asked you that ages ago, shouldn't I? I did want to, but I—well, I don't know you well enough…'

'We must do something about that. At what time do you have to be back?' And when she told him, he said, 'Good, we'll drive to Evershot for dinner. It's a pleasant drive, even in the dark, and we have no need to hurry.'

At her uncertain look, he added, 'Don't worry, it's a quite small hotel. At this time of the year it will be half empty, and it isn't somewhere where one needs to dress up.'

They went back to the car then, and he drove through the heavy evening traffic until they had left the city behind, taking the secondary roads through the New Forest. Mr Tait-Bullen drove slowly, stopping from time to time to allow the ponies to cross the road ahead of him, and a badger to amble along, refusing to be hurried. He drove for the most part in silence, an easy, undemanding silence in which there was no need to talk for the sake of uttering.

Claudia sat cocooned in warmth and comfort and watched the road unwind ahead of them in the car's headlights. She hadn't felt so quietly happy for a long time.

Evershot was a sizeable village, and even on a dark, wintry night looked charming. The hotel was charming, too—not large, but delightfully furnished, warm and welcoming. They went to the bar and sat over drinks, then dined on crab ravioli with ginger, breast of duck with potato straws and tiny Brussels sprouts, and pear tatin with cinnamon ice cream. Claudia ate it all with a splendid appetite, sharpened by the wholesome, rather stodgy fare offered at the hospital.

She sat back, savouring the last mouthful of ice cream. 'That was lovely—and do you know it was just luck that I was free this afternoon? Sister changed my duty to the afternoon shift, and then she changed her mind. It was a miracle...'

Mr Tait-Bullen, who had engineered the miracle, agreed that indeed it was.

They sat over their coffee and Claudia, gently encouraged by her companion, talked. There was not much time to talk at the hospital—really talk. On duty conversations were confined to cheerful chat with those of the patients who welcomed it, and only that when there were a few minutes to spare. And off duty, although she got on well with the other girls, the inclination was either to go out or to sit in front of the television. But now she allowed her tongue full rein, vaguely aware that later on she would regret it, but happy now, saying whatever came into her head. She paused briefly.

'Am I boring you?'

'No. I do not think that you will ever bore me, Claudia. I have to go away for a couple of days. When I return I should like to take you out again.'

'Oh, would you? I'd like that, too.' She beamed at him. 'We get on well together, don't we? I didn't think I would like you when we met, but I've changed my mind.'

'I hoped that you would. As you say, we get on well together.'

He drove her back presently, saw her into the hospital and, under the porter's interested eye, bent to kiss her cheek. It wasn't until she was in her room that she realised that he hadn't said anything more about seeing her again.

Claudia, brushing her fiery locks, stopped to stare into the small mirror above the little dressing table.

'You're a fool,' she told her reflection. 'Whatever he said, he must have been bored out of his mind. I must have sounded like a garrulous old maid. No wonder he didn't say when he would want to see me again.' She put down the brush and got into bed, suddenly sad; she liked him and felt at ease in his company. If only she hadn't behaved like an idiot. Living in London, obviously a successful man in his profession, and presumably comfortably off, she thought gloomily, he would have his pick of elegant women who had a fund of witty and amusing talk and knew when to hold their tongues...

Two days later she was on the afternoon shift. It was drizzling outside, with a mean wind, and the thought of a morning doing nothing by the gas fire in the recreation room was tempting. Then Claudia thought of the long hours on the ward until the late evening, buttoned herself into her mac, tied a scarf over her hair, found her gloves and sensible shoes and made her way to the side door the hospital staff used. A brisk walk would do her good...

She was crossing the back of the hall when the porter called after her.

'I've been ringing round for you,' he grumbled. 'You're to go to the visitors' room.'

'Me? Why?'

'How should I know? That's the message I got and I'm telling it to you.'

'Yes—well, thank you!'

She turned round and went the other way along the wide corridor from which the boardroom, the manager's office and the consultants' room opened.

'Mother,' she said, suddenly afraid of bad news, and opened the door.

The room didn't encourage visitors. It was a dark brown, with shiny lino on the floor and a hideous glass lantern housing a stark white bulb glaring down onto the solid table beneath it. Chairs were arranged stiffly around the walls, and, half lost in the massive fireplace, there was a very small gas fire. Watching her from the other side of the table was Mr Tait-Bullen.

Claudia slithered to a halt. 'Oh, it's you.' And then, aware that perhaps that had sounded rude, added, 'What I meant is, I didn't expect you.' He smiled then, and she smiled back. 'I was just going out for a walk.'

When he didn't speak, she asked, 'Are you on your way somewhere or are you on holiday?'

'I'm on my way back to London.'

'Well, what luck I'm on afternoon duty.' She flushed. 'What I mean is, you could have called in and I would have been working.' She hurried on, because it sounded as though she expected him to take her out. 'I expect you're anxious to get back home…'

'In which case I should have driven straight back to London…'

'But you didn't know if I was free…'

'Yes, I did. I phoned up first to find out. I have to go away again for a couple of days, and I wanted to see you before I go.'

'Me? Why? Mother's not ill, or George? Did they ask you to come?'

'No, they are both, as far as I know, in the best of middle-aged health.'

He smiled at her, a slow, warm smile. 'Claudia, before I say anything more, will you answer me truthfully? Are you happy here? Are you content to be, eventually, a career girl and, if not, will you tell me what you really wish for?'

'Why do you want to know?' she asked, and, when he didn't answer, went on, 'Well, all right—no, I'm not happy here. I'm truly sorry for the old ladies, but I miss the garden and the village and being out of doors. We're well looked after, you know, but I feel trapped.' She had lost herself in her own thoughts. 'And I suppose I wish for what every woman wants—a home and a husband and children.'

'Not love?'

'That, too, but I think that isn't granted to everyone—I mean, the kind of love that doesn't mind being poor or neglected or kept hidden, and will love and cherish despite that.' She stopped suddenly. 'Why did you make me say all that?'

He didn't answer her at once, but stared at her across the table, seeing a rather untidy figure, her bright hair escaping from the scarf, enveloped in her sensible mac.

'Will you marry me, Claudia?' he asked quietly.

At her astonished look, he said, 'No, don't say anything for a moment or two. You see, I think we might have a successful and happy marriage. I need a wife and you long for freedom. We could help each other in many ways. I have no doubt that you will be an excellent housewife and hostess, and a companion I shall always enjoy, and you could be free to spread your wings in whichever direction you wish to fly.

'I haven't said that I love you, nor do I expect you to tell me that. There's time enough for us to get to know each other. And I shan't hurry you. But it seems to me that to marry as soon as possible would be the sensible thing to do. You will need to give a week's notice at the hospital, but there is no reason why we shouldn't marry before Christmas.'

Claudia opened her mouth to speak, and shut it again, reflecting on what he had said. It all sounded so sensible, so calmly thought out. And he didn't love her. On the other hand he must like her, if he intended to marry her, and she would enjoy having a household of her own—meeting people, making friends, being there when he wanted a companion. And she liked him; she liked him very much.

Mr Tait-Bullen asked quietly, 'You would like to think about it? I shall quite understand if you dislike the idea, but I shall be disappointed. You see, Claudia, I have been honest with you. I have not promised love and endless devotion, but I have offered you what I hope will be a happy and contented life together. We like the same things, don't we? And laugh at the same jokes. We would be good companions and friends. That, I think, is more important than a sudden and uncertain infatuation.'

He was right, of course. It was, she told herself, a sensible and sincere offer of marriage made by one of the handsomest men she had ever met, and a man she liked wholeheartedly. She didn't know much about him, but, as he had said, getting to know each other was something they could do in their own good time. She would be a good wife, just as she was instinctively aware that he would be a good husband.

She looked across the table at him, standing there with no sign of impatience.

'Yes, thank you, I should like to marry you.' She laughed suddenly. 'I don't know your name...'

He came round the table and put gentle hands on her shoulders. 'Thomas,' he said, and bent to kiss her. 'Thank you, Claudia.'

Chapter 4

Claudia looked up into his quiet face. 'What do we do next?'

Mr Tait-Bullen suppressed a smile. A girl after his own heart; no coy smiles and fluttering of the eyelashes, no girlish whispers. Claudia obviously liked to meet a situation, when she encountered it, head-on.

'If you will give in your notice today? Phone me this evening—I'll be in Edinburgh. I'll give you my number—let me know the soonest you can leave and I'll fetch you.'

'Where will I go?'

'To George Willis. We'll marry there if you would like that. I'll get a special licence—remind me to ask you for some particulars when you phone. Your mother?'

'I'll phone her.'

'A pity that I have to go back to town this morning.

I could have called in at Little Planting. I'll telephone her this evening.'

He was holding her hands in his. 'This must be the most unlikely place in the world in which to receive a proposal of marriage.'

'I don't think that matters at all. I mean, moonlight and roses wouldn't have been suitable, would they? Not for us.'

He frowned a little. 'You will be happy, Claudia? I am a good deal older than you...'

'I like you just as you are, Thomas. Please don't change any of you. We shall be happy together.'

'I must go. Forgive me, there isn't even time to give you a cup of coffee.'

She went with him to the hospital entrance and he kissed her again, a light kiss which meant nothing, although she hadn't expected it to, got into his car and drove away.

It was a few moments before she moved—back into the hospital, intent on doing what Thomas had suggested, not noticing the porter's interested stare. She must compose a suitable letter and then take it to Miss Norton, and she must do it at once, so that when Thomas phoned that evening she could tell him when she could leave. And she must phone her mother...

She wrote her letter of resignation and presented herself at Miss Norton's office, inwardly quaking; could she be prevented from leaving? She hadn't signed a contract, and she was paid weekly, all the same she wasn't absolutely sure...

Fifteen minutes later she closed the office door behind her with a sigh of relief. Miss Norton hadn't been very pleased. Indeed, she had read Claudia a lecture on young women who were irresponsible and said she hoped that she had given marriage serious thought, but she hadn't refused to let Claudia go. She was, she had pointed out, scrupulously fair in such matters; if a girl wasn't happy in her work then she was entitled to leave. Normally, said Miss Norton severely, after a reasonable period. Claudia had hardly given herself time to settle down, but in the circumstances she could, of course, leave.

Claudia had thanked her and asked if she could leave two days earlier, since she would have her week's days off due. Miss Norton had looked affronted but she had agreed.

Claudia got into her mac again and went to telephone her mother; there was a phone in the hospital, but it was in a passage and in constant use; to discuss anything other than the weather was impossible.

Her mother was delighted, surprised, as well. 'Darling, I didn't know that you and Mr Tait-Bullen—Thomas—were so close. I'm delighted, and I'm sure George will be, too, when I tell him. What are your plans?'

Claudia inserted all the money she had, and explained. 'And we want to have a very quiet wedding, Mother. Thomas is getting a special licence and we'd like to marry at Little Planting. I'm leaving in five days. Thomas will fetch me. May I stay with you and George until the wedding? It'll only be for a day or two.'

'Of course, darling. And we must do something about clothes...'

Claudia, with an inward eye on her scanty ward-robe, agreed.

The rest of the day passed in a dream. Since she was happy, she wanted everyone else to be happy, too, coaxing smiles from even the most cantankerous of the old ladies, clearing up unmentionable messes, changing sheets, trundling round the ward with the tea trolley, the supper trolley, and at the end of the day having to listen to a lecture from Sister, who, apprised of her leaving, took it as a personal affront.

It was after ten o'clock by the time she left the ward—too late to go to the phone box at the end of the road. Besides, the passage where the hospital phone was was empty so late in the evening. She rang the number Thomas had given her and waited, half afraid that he wouldn't answer.

His voice sounded strangely businesslike.

'It's me,' said Claudia, heedless of grammar. And she added quite unnecessarily, 'You told me to ring you up, but I haven't kept you up, have I?'

Mr Tait-Bullen, studying the notes of a patient he was to operate on the next day, assured her that she hadn't.

'You saw Miss Norton?'

'Yes, I may leave in five days' time—actually, it's four days now. That's a Friday.'

'In the morning? You're actually free to leave after duty on Thursday?'

'Yes, but I must pack my things and give my uniform back…'

'I'll come for you at nine o'clock on Friday morning, Claudia.'

'Thank you, but don't you have to work?'

He said gently, 'Oh, yes, but not until the afternoon. I'll drop you off at Little Planting on my way back. Now, tell me—where were you born, how old are you, have you any other names besides Claudia and are you British by birth?'

She told him in a matter-of-fact voice, sensing that he hadn't time to waste on idle talk. She hesitated before she said, 'My other name is Eliza…' and waited for him to laugh.

But he didn't. All he said was, 'That's a nice old-fashioned name. You must be tired, my dear. Get to bed and sleep well. I'll see you on Friday.'

'Goodnight, then,' Claudia said, and hung up. It would have been nice if he had said something like 'I miss you,' or 'I'm looking forward to seeing you.' But he wouldn't pretend to feelings he didn't feel; she quite understood that. Theirs would be a sensible marriage, she reflected, undressing and falling into bed, there would be no false sentiment.

The following afternoon she took herself off to the shops; she hadn't much money, but it was essential that she had something suitable in which to be married. Luck was on her side; she found a small dress shop going out of business and selling up at half price. Claudia thrust aside a wish to wear white chiffon and a gauzy veil and tried on a plainly cut dress and jacket in fine wool. It was in a misty blue, with a grey velvet collar and cuffs, and fastened with a row of velvet buttons. And when the saleslady found a charming hat in matching velvet, Claudia decided that she need look no further.

'It's for a special occasion?' enquired the saleslady.

'Well, yes—my wedding.'

Which prompted the saleslady, who had a sentimental heart under her smart black dress, to make a special price. And that meant that there was enough money left to buy gloves and shoes—and some essential underpinnings from Marks and Spencer.

Well pleased with her purchases, Claudia went back to the hospital—too late for tea and too early for supper, but that didn't matter. She tried everything on once more and spent a long time trying out various new hairstyles, none of which pleased her. Perhaps once she was married she would be able to go to a good London hairdresser and have it expertly cut.

The days dragged; Friday was never coming, and she had ample time to wonder if she was about to make the mistake of a lifetime. A letter or a phone call from Thomas would have cleared up her uncertainty, but there was nothing. He had told her that he would see her on Friday and with that she had to be content. She had phoned her mother again, and that lady, agog with maternal delight, had told her that she was to go with her to Salisbury and get a few clothes. 'Our wedding present to you, darling. Have you bought anything yet?'

Claudia described the dress and jacket.

'They sound just right. Aren't you excited? And will you have a honeymoon?'

'No. Thomas can only take a day off—we'll go later.'

On the Thursday she bade the old ladies goodbye, leaving a vase filled with chrysanthemums on one of the tables, wishing she could have done more to brighten the ward. Sister wished her goodbye in an ill-humoured way, and then surprised her by saying, 'A pity you are leaving. The old ladies liked you.'

And the other girls were friendly—laughing and joking and asking her to send photos of the wedding.

'Well, it's not that kind of wedding,' she explained. 'Just us and a few family and no one else…'

'Who'd want anyone else but him, anyway?' declared one of the girls, who had seen Mr Tait-Bullen leaving the hospital. Everyone laughed and Claudia got out a bottle of sherry and a packet of biscuits. It seemed the right moment for a farewell party.

She was ready and waiting long before nine o'clock the next morning. Supposing Thomas had changed his mind? Had a breakdown, an accident, been called away to an emergency? She sat, as still as a mouse, wrapped in the mac, since it was raining again, her hair glowing in the gloomy entrance hall.

Mr Tait-Bullen knew exactly how she felt the moment he set eyes on her.

He nodded to the porter and reached her before she could get to her feet, his eyes searching her face. What he saw there reassured him, and he smiled.

'I can see that I am marrying a treasure. Do you know that the one virtue a medical man longs for in a wife is punctuality? You see, he is never punctual himself…'

'I was a bit early. I wasn't sure—that is, I thought that perhaps…' She met his steady gaze. 'No, that's not quite true—I knew you'd come.'

'Of course. Do you have to see anyone? You've said your goodbyes?'

And, when she nodded, he picked up her case and together they left the hospital.

They were clear of Southampton, driving through a dripping countryside, before he said, 'If you will agree, we can be married on Monday. I'll come down to Little Planting on Sunday evening, and we can marry in the morning and drive back in the afternoon.'

He had a list on Tuesday, but there would be Monday evening in which to show Claudia her new home. Cork had confided plans for a splendid supper, and Mr Tait-Bullen had left his devoted servant icing a cake for tea. It wasn't the kind of wedding that Cork would have liked for his master, but he was determined to make it as bridal an occasion as possible.

And that reminded him of something. He brought the car to a gentle halt and fished around in a pocket.

'Ours must be one of the briefest engagements ever known,' he observed, and opened the little velvet box in his hand. The ring it contained was a sapphire, a rich, sparkling blue surrounded by diamonds and mounted in gold. He picked up Claudia's left hand, resting in her lap, took off her glove and slipped the ring on her finger.

'Oh, it's beautiful—and it fits.' Claudia's sigh was one of pure delight. 'Thank you, Thomas.' She stared at it, incongruous on her roughened hand with its short, clipped nails. She would have to do something about that before the wedding.

She looked at him and saw that he was studying her hand. She said quite awkwardly, 'We did wear gloves whenever we could, but sometimes it just wasn't possible.'

His smile was kind. 'It was my grandmother's engagement ring. She left it to me with the wish that I would give it to the girl I married.'

'She was fond of you?'

'Indeed, she was. We were the best of friends.'

'You miss her?'

'Yes, we all do—my mother and father, my two sisters and younger brother. You will meet them all at Christmas...'

Claudia said faintly, 'Oh, shall I? Do they all live in London?'

'No, Mother and Father live in Cumbria, a small village called Finsthwaite, at the southern end of Lake Windermere. It is rather remote but very beautiful, close to the heart of Grizedale Forest but not too far from Kendal. My sisters are married. Ann—she's the elder—lives in York. Her husband's a solicitor. Amy and her husband live near Melton Mowbray. He's a farmer. James is at Birmingham Children's Hospital— a junior registrar.'

'They won't be coming to our wedding?'

'Mother and Father—the rest of the family you'll meet at Christmas. We shall spend it at Finsthwaite.' He added casually, 'They'll be delighted to welcome you into the family.'

'They don't know me. They might not like me...'

'You will be my wife,' said Thomas.

A fact which she could not dispute.

Tombs, beaming widely, opened the door to them when they reached George's house. He shook Claudia by the hand, and then Mr Tait-Bullen, wished them happy and led them across the hall to the sitting room.

Her mother was there and embraced Claudia warmly before offering a cheek for her future son-in-law.

'Such a surprise,' she told them. 'We're all so excited. George is in his surgery but Tombs has gone to fetch him. We had no idea…'

Nor had I, thought Claudia, but she didn't say so. 'We thought we'd be married on Monday…'

'Darling—but you haven't any clothes, and I must have a new hat at least, and who is to be invited? Such short notice…'

'Thomas would like his parents to come, Mother.' Claudia looked at him and felt a touch of peevishness at the sight of him standing there, looking faintly amused.

'May they do that, Mrs Willis? We both want a quiet wedding, and I can't spare more than a day. We would like to marry in the morning, then drive back to London, which would give us the rest of the day together.'

'Of course, you poor dears—scarcely more than a few hours to be together.'

'We shall make up for that later on,' said Mr Tait-Bullen soothingly.

He turned as George came into the room. 'We do hope we haven't spoilt any plans you and Mrs Willis may have made…'

Dr Willis kissed Claudia and shook hands with him. 'We don't go away until the end of next week, and even if we had plans we would be delighted to upset them for such a happy occasion. Staying for lunch, I hope?'

Tombs had brought in the coffee tray, and Mrs Willis poured while Claudia, glad of something to do, handed around cups and saucers and biscuits.

'I must get back. I've a clinic this afternoon and patients to see this evening.'

Claudia, sitting beside her mother, watched Thomas, perfectly at ease, everything arranged as he had wished, calm and self-assured, listening to George explaining the difficulties of being a GP's wife. He made no attempt to mention his own work; she guessed that it was just as time-consuming and demanding.

She went out with him to his car presently, and he stood for a minute, looking down at her. 'I'll see you on Sunday evening. My mother and father will be with me in their own car. We'll put up at the Duck and Thistle.'

He took her two hands in his. 'Quite sure, Claudia?'

She said steadily, 'Yes, Thomas. It's a bit unusual, isn't it? Getting married like this. But if we're sure, and it's what we want, there's no point in mulling it over for months, is there? And I don't suppose that if we were engaged for a long time we'd see much of each other—I mean, get to know each other better—for you would be working and I'd be bogged down in plans for the wedding.'

'What a sensible girl you are, Claudia.' He bent and kissed her, a brief, friendly kiss, before getting into his car and driving away.

Back in the sitting room, her mother said, 'Darling, we're all so happy for you. He's just right for you and so handsome. You'll have a delightful life together. I can hardly believe it—there we were a few weeks ago, with not a penny piece between us and no roof over our heads, and look at us now. I'm here with George, and so very happy, and you'll be happy, too, with Thomas.'

She paused to look at Claudia. 'Clothes—you must have some new things…'

'I've told you about the dress and jacket, and the hat, and I've bought one or two other things. Enough to go on with. I expect I'll get some new clothes when we're in London. There hasn't been time, and Thomas knows that.' She added carefully, 'You see, there didn't seem much point in waiting—my job in the hospital wasn't quite what I thought it would be, and Thomas wanted me to leave as soon as possible.' She smiled suddenly. 'So did I.'

Mrs Willis started to say something, and then stopped. Instead she observed, 'I expect Thomas fell in love with you the first time you met…'

'It happens all the time,' said Claudia. 'Look at you and George.'

'Well, dear, for George, yes. But it took me a long time to discover that I loved him. And I dare say if it hadn't been for that awful Ramsay cousin, and us being turned out of the house, I might never have discovered how I felt.'

'What a good thing it happened that way, then. Though it was horrid, wasn't it? Do you hear or see anything of him and his wife?'

'No, dear. They keep themselves very much to themselves, and the village isn't friendly towards them.' Mrs Willis sighed happily. 'How nice that we don't have to think about them anymore. Now, on Monday I thought that we would have a buffet lunch. Mrs Pratt is longing to prepare a feast for you. A pity that it is to be such a quiet wedding.' She glanced at Claudia. 'You don't mind?'

'No, Mother, I'm happy to do whatever Thomas wants. If we had decided to marry later on, we wouldn't have seen much of each other—he's busy all day most days. At least I shall see him when he comes home in the evenings.'

A remark which satisfied her mother, just as Claudia had meant it to.

Claudia woke early on Monday morning. It was still dark outside as she got out of bed, wrapped herself in her dressing gown and crept downstairs. The light was on in the kitchen and Mrs Pratt was there, carefully lifting tiny vol-au-vents from a baking sheet onto one of Dr Willis's best china dishes. Tombs was there, too, sitting by the Aga, polishing wine glasses.

'No, no. Don't move,' said Claudia as he started to get up. 'I thought I'd make a cup of tea.'

Mrs Pratt beamed at her. 'You should still be in your bed, Miss Claudia. I dare say you're excited. It isn't every day a girl marries. The kettle's boiling, if you'd like to make tea…'

'We'll all have a cup. You're both coming to the church, aren't you?'

'Wouldn't miss it for all the tea in China, Miss Claudia,' said Tombs. 'Me and Mrs Pratt are that pleased. Took to the doctor the moment we set eyes on him, didn't we?'

Mrs Pratt, whipping something delicious in a bowl, agreed. 'A handsome pair you'll be—though it's to be hoped you won't let him see that old dressing gown, Miss Claudia. Warm and cosy it may have been at one time, but it's past its best…'

Claudia warmed the teapot and had a sudden moment of doubt. Surely Thomas would have realised that she had had no time to buy a lot of clothes? And would he mind anyway? She had gained the impression that her appearance wasn't something he found important. True, he had told her that she looked nice...

'I shall go shopping in London.' She turned to smile at Mrs Pratt. 'I'll leave this dressing gown behind!'

The three of them drank their tea in a friendly silence, and Rob, rousing from sleep in his basket, came to join them.

'I'll let him out and take the tea up as I go,' said Claudia.

'Begging your pardon, Miss Claudia,' said Tombs, at his most stately. 'You will do no such thing. That is a morning task for myself.'

'Oh, Tombs,' cried Claudia. 'I'm going to miss you and Mrs Pratt.'

She finished her tea and went to the garden door with Rob, who lumbered out into the garden. She stood watching him and looked at the sky, beginning to lighten. It had been a frosty night, and her breath drifted away in soft swirls. It was going to be a lovely winter's day. A good omen? She hoped so.

Rob came in then, making for the warmth of the Aga, and she went back to her room.

It was growing lighter by the minute. She went to the window, opened it wide and leaned out, breathing the cold air. At the other end of the village Thomas was sleeping—his parents, too. They had come at tea-time—Thomas in his Rolls-Royce, his father driving a Daimler. She had seen them arrive from her bedroom

window and hurried downstairs, her hair very tidy for
once, wearing a dark green jersey dress which she had
had for so long it had become quite fashionable again.

It was essential to make a good impression; Thomas's
parents might live miles away, but they were bound to
meet occasionally. She hadn't allowed herself to specu-
late about them, she'd only hoped that they would like
her.

Thomas's mother had come in first, pausing to smile
at Tombs, but before she reached Claudia, Thomas had
been there, bending to kiss her cheek, putting an arm
round her shoulder.

'This is Claudia, Mother—Father.' And they had
both shaken her hand and kissed her warmly, so that
her vague doubts had vanished.

Thomas's father was an elderly edition of his son,
still very upright, grey-haired and handsome. His
mother was almost as tall as Claudia, and still a beautiful woman, with a beauty she had allowed to age gradually, without excess make-up or tinted hair. Her face
wrinkled in all the right places, and her hair was grey
and simply dressed. But her eyes were still young—
vivid blue and smiling. She was well dressed, too, in
an understated and slightly old-fashioned way. Claudia
had liked her at once.

It had been easy after that first meeting. Her mother
and George had joined them, and the evening had been
pleasant. Neither of the Tait-Bullens had badgered her
with questions; they had talked about the wedding in a
soothing manner, remarked upon the charm of the village and told her something—but not much—of their
own home. And she had had no chance to talk for more

than a few moments to Thomas. Only as they had been leaving to go to the Duck and Thistle had he asked her kindly, 'Cold feet, Claudia?'

'Certainly not,' she had answered him indignantly, and then, looking into his face, seeing the casual friendliness in it, had added softly, 'No, I promise you, Thomas.'

Someone was coming down the lane from the village. She withdrew her head and then poked it out again; in the dim light of dawn Thomas was coming through the open gate and up the short drive. He stopped under her window.

'Come for a walk?' he invited.

How could he have known that that was the very thing she most wanted to do?

'Five minutes,' said Claudia, and closed the window.

There were trousers and an old sweater in the cupboard; she put them on over her nightie, tied back her hair, cleaned her teeth and went down to the kitchen; her wellies were there, with socks stuffed inside them. Under Tombs's and Mrs Pratt's astonished gaze, she put them on, bundled on one of the coats hanging behind the kitchen door, blew them a kiss and went out into the garden round the house to where Thomas was waiting.

He took her arm and walked her briskly along the lane, away from the village. 'No gloves?' he asked, and took his own off and put them onto her cold hands. 'This isn't quite the usual behaviour of the bride and groom on their wedding day...'

'But it isn't a usual kind of wedding, is it?'

The lane petered out into a rough track, its rutted surface frost-bound, and as they walked Thomas began to talk—a nicely calculated jumble of odds and ends about his work, and information about his home, his friends… 'I hope you will like them—most of them are married…'

'Have you had any girlfriends? I'm not being nosy, but if I were to meet them I'd have to know who they are, wouldn't I?'

Mr Tait-Bullen didn't pause in his stride. He said briskly, 'Naturally I have been out and about with several woman acquaintances, but they have never been more than that, Claudia.'

'Have I annoyed you by asking? I don't expect to know about your life, but I don't want to be taken unawares. Anyway, I don't suppose you've had much time to fall in love.'

'I'm not sure if time is needed when one falls in love. I imagine it happens in the blink of an eye. I can promise you that I have had neither the inclination nor the time. I have always been too busy. But I shall enjoy being married to you. We shall be good friends and companions and above all we like each other. Liking the person you marry is as important as loving them.'

'I'm sure you're right,' said Claudia, 'although we can't be quite certain, can we? I mean, you'd have to be married to someone you loved and didn't like…'

They had been walking uphill; now they paused to watch the first rays of a wintry sun creep over the countryside. They stood and watched for a moment, and Claudia said, 'Nice, isn't it?' She added slowly, 'That's the only thing. I expect I'll miss this for a bit.'

'Yes, I can understand that. I thought we might look

around for a small house not too far from here, where we can spend weekends. It's an easy run up to town.'

He had flung an arm round her, and she turned within its comfort so that she could see his face. 'Oh, Thomas, that would be lovely. But would you like that, too?'

'Very much. We will wait till after Christmas and then go house-hunting. There are plenty of villages between here and the M3.'

The sun was above the horizon now, and Claudia said reluctantly, 'We'd better go back. We're not dressed for the wedding, are we?'

Mr Tait-Bullen took a good look at her. 'No. I like the hair, but you look all the wrong shape...'

'Well, I didn't stop to dress—only an old sweater and trousers over my nightie. And I don't know whose coat this is—I took it from the back door.'

'And you still contrive to look beautiful,' he told her, and then turned her round smartly and marched her back.

He left her at the kitchen door, bending to kiss her quickly. 'Don't be late,' he said, and walked away as she opened the door.

'Your ma is in a fine state,' said Mrs Pratt. 'Miss Claudia, whatever possessed you to go gallivanting off like that? Looking like a scarecrow, too.'

Claudia flung her arms round her old friend's neck. 'It was lovely—a kind of ending and a beginning, if you see what I mean.' She skipped to the door and flew upstairs to shower, then put on her dressing gown again and went down to breakfast.

Mrs Willis submitted to her hug. 'Darling, you

shouldn't have gone off like that—you and Thomas aren't supposed to see each other until you meet in church, and Mrs Pratt says you looked like a bag lady...'

Claudia helped herself to toast. 'It was lovely. We watched the sun come up. Mother, I'm so happy!'

And Mrs Willis, happy herself, leaned across the table and patted her daughter's arm. 'Oh, love, I do understand. So does George. He was called out just before you came downstairs—old Mrs Parson's grandson cut his arm on a bottle.'

'George will be back in time for the wedding?'

'Don't worry, dear, he will. It's only a matter of a few stitches.'

Claudia, casting a critical eye over her reflection, wished for a brief moment that it was white chiffon and yards of veiling and not the blue outfit she was looking at. She had dressed with care, taken pains with her face and her hair, and arranged the hat at the most becoming angle. She supposed that for a quiet wedding she looked all right.

Supposing it didn't work out well? Thomas was so sure that it would, and so was she, but that hadn't prevented last-minute doubts creeping in. Did all brides feel as she did? she wondered. Wondering if they were making the biggest mistake of their lives? Or was that because she was marrying Thomas after such a short time in which to know him?

She turned away from the mirror and went to look out of the window; she couldn't even see the Duck and Thistle from it, but it was only a few minutes' walk away. Was Thomas standing at his window as full of doubts as she was, perhaps wishing that he had never set eyes on her?

Her mother, coming into the room, broke into her thoughts. 'Darling, just look at this—Thomas doesn't know what you're wearing, so the flowers are white—isn't it gorgeous?'

The bouquet she was offering Claudia was truly bridal; white roses very faintly tinged with pink, lilies of the valley, hyacinth pips, orange blossom, little white tulips and miniature white narcissi nestling in a circle of green leaves. It made up for the lack of white chiffon; just looking at it made her feel like a bride.

A very quiet wedding, Thomas had said, but that hadn't prevented everyone in the village who could get to the church from going to see Claudia married. But they understood, sitting at the back of the church quietly so that Claudia and Thomas were unaware of them, knowing that they wanted a quiet wedding. Only as they left the church did she become aware of smiling faces and voices wishing them luck and happiness.

Back at George's house, they drank the champagne which Mr Tait-Bullen had thoughtfully provided, and presently sat down to an early lunch, waited upon by Tombs at his most majestic. Mrs Pratt, refusing to be discouraged by the brief notice she had had of the wedding, had sat up late and got up early in order to provide a feast worthy of the occasion.

Cheese soufflés, each in their own small ramekin, followed by salmon en croûte, watercress salad and potato straws, and, following that, Tombs carried in the wedding cake. Not quite in the traditional manner, perhaps—Mrs Pratt hadn't had time for that—but she had iced a fruit cake and ornamented it with silver leaves, searched for at length in the village shop, and arranged it on one of George's much prized Coalport plates, which he kept under lock and key.

'Nothing but the best for Miss Claudia,' Mrs Pratt had told him, standing over him while he took the plate from the glass cabinet where it was displayed.

It was a pleasant meal. No one made a speech, although they did drink to the bride and groom's health, with Tombs and Mrs Pratt summoned from the kitchen, well pleased with their efforts, beaming at them from the door.

It was Thomas, refilling their glasses, who said, 'My wife and I thank you both for giving us such a delightful lunch. It has made our happy day even happier.'

They had coffee in the drawing room, and presently Thomas said, 'I think we should be going, Claudia.' He looked at George. 'We both thank you for making our wedding such a happy occasion. Once we are settled in we do hope that you will come and visit us.' He turned to his mother and said, 'And of course you and Father. But we shall be seeing you at Christmas.'

'We look forward to that, Thomas.'

It took quite a while saying goodbye to everyone. Thomas put the luggage in the car and then waited with no sign of impatience while Claudia went from one to the other. Tombs and Mrs Pratt had to be bidden goodbye, messages left for Jennie and Rob hugged. But finally there were no more goodbyes to be said, and she went out to the car with Thomas and got in beside him.

It wasn't until they had driven for a mile or two that she said in a small voice, 'It has all been so sudden…'

He touched her hand briefly. 'Don't worry, Claudia, I shan't hurry you. Think of us as being engaged, if that makes you feel happier…'

'Well, I dare say it would, but I won't. We're married, aren't we? Once I get used to that everything will be fine.' She added quickly, 'Don't think I'm regretting it. I'm not. I'm very happy—only a bit out of my depth.'

'You may have all the time in the world to find your feet. I have to work tomorrow, but on Wednesday I shall be home in the morning—time for us to talk.'

He was on the motorway now, driving fast through the already fading light.

'Cork will have tea for us and we shall have this evening together. I enjoyed our wedding, Claudia, and I hope you did, too?'

'Oh, yes, I did. And the flowers—they were glorious. They made me forget that I was wearing an ordinary outfit. I felt as though I was in white chiffon and a veil—a real bride.'

'But you were a real bride, my dear. You looked beautiful…'

A remark which lifted her spirits, so that for the rest of the journey she was utterly happy.

Chapter 5

Thomas's description of his home in London had been vague; Claudia had gathered that he lived near his consulting rooms in a terraced house, and she had pictured a typical London house—solid, mid-Victorian, with rather a lot of red brickwork. And, since she knew very little of London, her visits having been confined to brief shopping expeditions and the occasional visit to a theatre, she'd visualised a busy road, noisy with traffic and not a tree in sight.

When Thomas stopped before his home, got out and opened her door, she got out, too, and stared around her. It was quite dark by now, but the street lighting was shining onto the elegant houses standing back from the tree-lined pavement. He took her arm and led her up the three steps to the door being held open, giving a glimpse of a softly lighted hall.

'Ah, Cork,' said Mr Tait-Bullen. 'Claudia, this is Cork, who looks after me so well and will doubtless do the same for you.' He put a hand on the other man's shoulder. 'My wife, Cork.'

Claudia offered a hand and smiled into the craggy face, and Cork allowed himself a pleased and relieved smile in return. A nice young lady, he saw at once, just right for his master.

'May I wish you both every happiness?' he observed solemnly. 'And I shall hope to give you as much satisfaction, madam, as the master.'

'Very nicely put,' said Mr Tait-Bullen, busy taking Claudia's coat and gloves and tossing them and his own coat onto one of the chairs flanking the side table.

Cork allowed himself another smile. 'Tea will be brought to the drawing room in five minutes, sir.'

He melted away, and Thomas took Claudia's arm and led her through a door—one of three leading from the hall.

The room was large, with its windows overlooking the quiet street. There was an Adam fireplace, with two sofas and a maple and rosewood library table arranged before it, a Regency writing table under the window and a magnificent Chinese lacquer display cabinet facing the window. There were comfortable chairs, too, upholstered in the same burgundy velvet as the curtains draping the window. And small lamp tables here and there, too, piled with books and magazines. A lovely room, restful and lived in.

Claudia felt instantly at home in it—a good augur for the future? she wondered, smiling at Cork, coming in with the tea tray. He didn't return the smile. She appeared to be a nice young lady, at first sight a suitable wife for his master, but time would tell, and he was a man who did nothing hastily. She might want to interfere in his kitchen...

Claudia had seen the prim set of his mouth. If Cork was anything like Tombs then she would need to tread carefully for a while. It had taken her quite a time to win over Tombs, but once she had he had become her firm friend and ally. She sat down in the chair Thomas had offered her and composedly poured their tea, as though she had been doing it for years.

Mr Tait-Bullen, leafing through his post, observed her from under his lids. He had known instinctively that she was the right wife for him: taking things in her stride, accepting each new challenge as it arose, fitting into his life without fuss. And he liked her; he liked her very much.

He considered himself beyond the age of falling in love, and he had no intention of doing so. His work was all-engrossing. The way of life that he had chosen suited him very well; he had no doubt that Claudia would accept that. They had similar tastes. She would be free to make her own friends, and whenever they had the time they would spend a day or so in the country. He must remember to do something about that...

Cork came back presently, removed the tea things and ushered her upstairs. The staircase was narrow, and curved against the end wall of the hall, and Claudia stopped to admire it. She ran a hand over its mahogany banisters, gleaming with polish. 'Lots of elbow grease,' she reflected out loud, and Cork gave her a respectful look.

'Nothing beats it, madam.' He allowed himself the ghost of a smile.

Her room was at the back of the house, overlooking a long, narrow garden. Even in winter it looked charming, with a tracery of leafless trees grouped here and there. Doubtless in the spring there would be crocuses and daffodils around them, and bright flowers in the summer.

She turned from the window and found Cork still standing at the door. 'The bathroom is through the door on the right, madam, and beyond that is the Professor's room. Tomorrow, if you wish, I will conduct you round the house.'

'Oh, please, Cork. And if you will tell me anything that I should know—advise me. You will know exactly how the...the Professor likes things done.'

'I trust so, madam.'

When she was alone she took stock of the room and could find no fault with it. The bed was a satinwood four-poster, curtained and covered with a gossamer-fine ivory silk patterned with forget-me-nots, and the bow-fronted chest was of the same wood. There was a satinwood and mahogany mirror on the mahogany sofa table under the two windows, and a tallboy in exquisite marquetry. On either side of the bed were delicate little side tables, each with a china figure bearing a rose-coloured lamp. There was a wall cupboard, too, she discovered, and beyond the farther door a bathroom to be drooled over. She peeped round the door in the bathroom, too—another bedroom, furnished more plainly, but with the same beautiful old pieces.

It was something she hadn't thought about; that

Thomas had comfortable means had always been apparent, but this house of his was full of treasures. Had he inherited them? she wondered. Or did he collect old and valuable furniture as a hobby?

She went downstairs presently, determined to find out.

Thomas looked up from his letters as she went into the room. 'Is your room all right? Most of the furniture here was left to me by my grandmother, who had it from her husband's family—they had an enormous old house in Berkshire. I loved it when I went to stay with her as a boy, and I still do.'

'So do I, and it's just right for this house, isn't it?'

'I think so, and I'm glad you agree. This place isn't large but the period's right.'

'I was wondering—you know, while I was upstairs—if you collected old furniture or something like that?'

'No, but when we have found the house we like in the country we will spend time finding exactly the right furniture for it. I'm seldom free for any length of time, so it may take months.'

Lying in the four-poster, nicely drowsy, Claudia reviewed her wedding day. They had spent a happy evening together, talking like an old married couple, disagreeing pleasantly from time to time, discovering that they agreed about most things which mattered. Cork had served them with a splendid dinner: watercress soup, roast pheasant with all its trimmings, a dessert of his own devising—a concoction of ground almonds and whipped cream, angelica and crystallised fruit—and finally coffee in a very beautiful silver coffee pot, poured into paper-thin cups. They had drunk champagne, too, with Cork toasting them gravely and wishing them long life and happiness.

She had gone to bed quite happily. Wasn't there a song 'Getting to Know You'? That was what they were doing, wasn't it? Taking their time like two sensible people, but instead of getting engaged for a time before they married, they had married first.

'Let us give ourselves time to get to know and understand each other,' Thomas had said, and she had agreed. Life spread before her, undemanding and rather exciting. Tomorrow, she thought sleepily, she would go over the house with Cork, taking care not to encroach on his orderly life. She would wait for him to make the first suggestions as to what she should or should not do; later on, when he had accepted her, it would be for her to make suggestions...

Breakfast was at half past seven. When Thomas had suggested that she might like hers in bed, or later in the morning, she had told him that, no, she liked getting up early and would breakfast with him. She had seen his faint frown and hastened to add, 'Don't worry, I won't talk!'

In the morning she was as good as her word. Beyond a cheerful good morning she stayed silent, eating the scrambled eggs Cork put before her and following that with toast and marmalade. Thomas left before she had finished, dropping a hand on her shoulder as he went past her chair.

'I may be late home...'

'How late is late? Does Cork have a meal ready for you whatever time it is?'

'Yes. But I'll do my best to be here by eight o'clock. If I'm held up I'll phone, or get someone to do it for me.'

He had gone. She heard him speak to Cork in the hall before he went out to his car. She had finished breakfast when Cork came to clear the table.

'You will wish to see over the house, madam?'

'Yes, please, Cork. When it's convenient to you. I'm sure you have your day organised. I'd like to telephone my mother and write a letter or two, so will you let me know when you are ready? Does someone come in to give you a hand?'

'Mrs Rumbold comes each morning except Saturday and Sunday. A reliable, hardworking person, and entirely trustworthy. If it suits you, I will bring you coffee at ten o'clock, after which I shall be free to take you round the house.'

'Thank you, Cork. Ought I to meet Mrs Rumbold?'

'Certainly, if you wish, madam. I will bring her to you—she comes at nine o'clock.'

Claudia had a long and satisfying conversation with her mother, declaring herself to be entirely happy and promising a full description of the house later. She put the phone down as Cork came in with Mrs Rumbold— a stout lady with small dark eyes in a round face, a great deal of hair, in a most unlikely shade of ebony, and a wide smile.

Claudia got up and shook hands, and murmured suitably, and Mrs Rumbold's vast person quivered with cheerful laughter.

'Lor' bless me, ma'am, it's a great treat to see another female in the house. A bit of a surprise, but Mr Cork tells me as 'ow you and the Professor 'as known each other awhile.'

Claudia smiled and said that, yes, indeed that was so. Cork coughed, a signal for Mrs Rumbold to take her departure, declaring that she'd do her best, same as always, and had never given Mr Cork cause to complain…

'I'm sure you haven't, Mrs Rumbold…'

She had her coffee presently, this time from a small silver coffee pot and a much larger cup, delicately patterned with roses. It looked so fragile that Claudia was in two minds as to whether to drink from it. But she did.

She went for a walk after lunch, finding her way round the quiet streets, lined by similar houses, going to the nearest main road to study the bus timetables. There were no large stores close by, although she did find a row of small shops tucked away behind an elegant row of houses. The kind of shops she was used to, selling wools and knitting needles and high-class green groceries, an antiquarian bookshop, a tiny tea shop—very elegant—and at the end a dusty, rather shabby little place selling small antiques and a variety of odds and ends.

She spent some time looking in its window, and then walked back, thinking about her morning. Cork had been very helpful, but she felt he was still suspicious of her. He had shown her every nook and cranny of the house, every cupboard… The house was bigger than she had thought at first: three storeys high and every room charmingly furnished. Cork had a room and bathroom behind the kitchen in the semi-basement, and she had no doubt that it was comfortably furnished, too.

The kitchen was very much to her own taste—a cheerful red Aga, a vast old-fashioned dresser along one wall, filled with plates and dishes, a square wooden table in the centre of the room, around which were an assortment of comfortable, rather shabby chairs, and pots and saucepans neatly stacked on the shelves on the walls. There were checked curtains at the window and a thick rug before the Aga. It reminded her of Great-Uncle William's kitchen… She reached the front door and rang the bell, reminding herself that she must ask Thomas for a key.

Thomas didn't get home until almost eight o'clock. She saw that he was tired and, beyond answering his queries as to how she had spent her day, she forbore from chattering. They dined in a companionable silence, and, since it was by then getting late in the evening, she said that she was tired and would go to bed if he didn't mind. It had been the right thing to say, but she tried not to mind when she saw the relief on his face.

Still, he bade her goodnight and kissed her cheek, then reminded her that he was free in the morning and they would go shopping. 'I shall open an account for you at Harrods and Harvey Nichols, and arrange for an allowance to be paid into your bank. But tomorrow we will shop together.'

He took her first to Harrods the next morning, accompanying her to the fashion floor, telling her to buy whatever she liked and making himself comfortable in one of the easy chairs scattered around.

'You mean a dress and coat, and things like that?' asked Claudia. 'How much may I spend?'

'One dress will hardly do. Buy several—and certainly a winter coat and anything else you like. Don't look at the price tags, Claudia.' He smiled at her. 'Buy all you need for the next few weeks. We shall be going out a good deal, I have no doubt...'

'Dinner dresses,' breathed Claudia, and her eyes sparkled.

'Certainly, and a couple of dresses for dancing—the hospital ball and so on. And something tweedy for the lakes. I shall take you walking.'

'You don't mind waiting here?'

'Not in the least. Come and show me what you buy from time to time, if you like.'

So Claudia, guided by a majestic saleslady in black crêpe, went shopping in earnest. She had had nothing new for some time, and her present wardrobe was sparse in the extreme, but that didn't prevent her from knowing exactly what she needed to buy.

A beautifully tailored winter coat in dark green, a tweed skirt with a matching soft leather jacket, a twinset in cashmere, peat-brown, a jersey dress in soft blue and another in dove-grey, and, at the saleslady's suggestion, a handful of silk blouses and another cardigan. She had shown most of these to a patient Mr Tait-Bullen, then gone with him to the restaurant for a cup of coffee before embarking on the choosing of a crêpe dress in old gold, and another in a green patterned silk jersey. She would have bought a little black dress, but when she mentioned her intention to Thomas he begged her not to. 'They're not for you,' he told her. 'Get something with a waist and a wide skirt.'

Which wasn't much to go by. Anxious to please him, she spent some time looking for such a garment, and found it at last. Blue again—a smoky blue—with long sleeves and a modest neckline, and a tucked bodice cinched in at the waist by an embroidered belt, the skirt was several layers of chiffon, and it showed off her splendid figure. She paraded before him in it and saw that he approved.

'Would you like me to stop now?' she asked him.

'No. No. Let us by all means get the basics. What else do you need?'

'Well, evening dresses. I won't be long...'

She knew what suited her and she didn't dither, although there was a magnificent black taffeta she longed to own... She chose instead a russet taffeta with a tucked bodice, shoestring shoulder straps and a wide skirt which rustled delightfully as she walked. And a honey-coloured crêpe, very simple in cut.

'I've bought masses of clothes,' she told Thomas finally. 'I do hope...'

'We'll have lunch, and, if you haven't made me bankrupt, we will go to Harvey Nichols.'

'But I've bought masses of stuff.'

'Undies, dressing gowns, shoes, boots, a Burberry—a hat for church on Christmas Day?'

She stared up at him with wide eyes. 'You think of everything.'

'No, my dear, but you forget I have sisters, and I have from time to time accompanied them on shopping expeditions.'

'Oh, well, if you don't mind.'

'No, I don't mind,' said Mr Tait-Bullen, and thought how very pretty she looked.

They lunched at Harvey Nichols, in the basement bar-restaurant because Claudia declared that she was too full of excitement to eat much. All the same, gently urged on by Thomas, she managed grilled salmon and a salad, and apple tart, and, thus fortified, spent the next hour or so adding to her wardrobe. Having approved of the Burberry, boots and shoes, Thomas left her in the undies department.

'I'll look around for presents for the family,' he told her, 'on the ground floor.' He glanced at his watch. 'An hour? I'll be waiting by the main entrance.' He smiled down at her happy face. 'Don't hurry.'

She lost herself in the delights of the lingerie department, but she remembered that he had said an hour. Laden with carrier bags, she went punctually to the ground floor and found him waiting.

He looked at the bags. 'They can be delivered with the other things,' he suggested.

She shook her head. 'I can't bear to part with them,' she told him seriously. 'You have no idea how lovely...'

'Shall we go home for tea?' he asked in a matter-of-fact way, which stopped her short.

They had their tea, and then an hour or so sitting together talking about nothing in particular. There would be more Christmas presents to buy, he warned her. And would she like to go to Little Planting before Christmas?

'I can spare a Sunday, if you would like that. And don't forget the hospital ball next week. You will be bound to get any number of invitations for us both from the people we meet there. I rely on you to deal with them. There is a certain amount of hospital social life, and you will probably be roped in for some charity or other. Don't take on too much...'

They were halfway through dinner when he was called away. He went quickly, warning her that he might be late back.

As he went he dropped a kiss on her cheek. 'I enjoyed our day together,' he told her.

'Me, too. Only I've spent an awful lot of your money.'

'Our money,' he said quietly. 'It was a great pleasure.'

She sat in the drawing room that evening, leafing through magazines, thinking about her delightful day. Thomas had been a splendid companion, too. Patient, and interested in what she had bought. Of course, she quite understood that as the wife of a well-known cardiologist she needed to be well turned out—he wouldn't want her to meet any of his friends and colleagues wearing the shabby tweeds and woollies she had always worn at Little Planting.

She got up and took a look at herself in the Georgian giltwood mirror. Perhaps she should have her hair cut and styled? Go to a beauty parlour and learn how to apply make-up? She tended to forget anything but lipstick; there had seemed no point in it when she lived with Great-Uncle William. On the sparse occasions when she'd gone out to dinner she had dashed powder over her nose, added lipstick and done her best with her hands, so often grubby from gardening. She would remedy this, she promised herself, so that Thomas need never feel ashamed of her.

The longcase clock in the hall had struck eleven, and he still wasn't back. She went to the kitchen and found Cork sitting there, reading the evening paper.

She said quickly, 'No, no. Don't get up, Cork. I think I'll go to bed. Do you wait up or does the Professor let himself in? And does he need anything? A drink? Or sandwiches?'

'I wait up, madam. There is coffee, and there are sandwiches if he should require them. I'm sure he would wish you to take your normal rest.'

'Yes, well… I'll go to bed, then. Thank you, Cork.'

'Thank you, madam, and goodnight.'

He held the door for her and didn't return her smile. She went up to her room, still not sure if he approved of her or not. She must have been a surprise to him, and doubtless he wondered if she was going to interfere. She didn't intend to; perhaps she'd do the flowers, discuss the food with him, and then later on, when he had accepted her, he might allow her into the kitchen.

Thomas was already at breakfast when she went down in the morning. He looked as he always did, immaculate in his sober grey suit and silk tie, but there were lines in his face…

She wished him good morning. 'When did you get home?' she asked.

'Round about one o'clock. I didn't disturb you?'

'No, no. Do you often get called out? I thought specialists and consultants could more or less please themselves.'

Mr Tait-Bullen looked surprised. 'We're just the same as any other medical man. We go when and where we're needed.'

'And you are going to the hospital this morning?'

'No, first to one of the private hospitals. I operated there a couple of days ago, and I must visit my patient there first. Then to the hospital, and a clinic after lunch, and then private patients at my consulting rooms.'

'Will you come home for lunch?'

He shook his head. 'I'm afraid not. I may be back in time for tea, though.' He glanced at her. 'You'll be all right?'

'Yes…'

'I should have warned you that I'm away a good deal.'

He left the house presently, and, since Cork informed her that it was Mrs Rumbold's day for turning out the drawing room, she guessed quite rightly that they would like her out of the house.

'I thought I'd explore a bit,' she told him. 'Hyde Park and perhaps Kensington Gardens…'

'A pleasant walk, madam. Lunch at one o'clock?'

'Yes, please. Something on a tray will do.'

She had put on the tweed skirt and one of the silk shirts, and, since it was drizzling with a chilly wind, she donned the Burberry and the boots. The Burberry had a little matching hat, which she crammed onto her hair with no regard to her appearance, so that copper strands escaped. She took her new shoulder bag, her expensive leather gloves, bade Cork goodbye and left the house.

There weren't many people about as she made her way to Marble Arch. Cork, that paragon of servants, had thoughtfully provided her with a small street map, and it wasn't until she reached Marble Arch that there was much traffic and the first sight of Christmas shoppers.

She crossed the road into the park, following the Serpentine, enjoying the quiet emptiness, for there was scarcely anyone else to be seen. She was halfway to Rennie's Bridge, which would lead her to Kensington Gardens, when she saw a very small dog sitting under the bushes some yards from the path. He didn't bark, nor did he take any notice of her, and she walked on, supposing that its owner was somewhere nearby. But an hour later, as she came back the same way, he was still there.

There was no one in sight; she crossed the grass and bent down to take a closer look.

It was a very small dog indeed—a puppy, pitifully thin and shivering with cold. It made no sound as Claudia touched his matted coat with a gentle hand; it only looked at her with terrified eyes, cringing away from her. He was tied by a thin rope to a thicket behind him, and she could see that the rope was tight around his throat. If he'd tried to run away he would have choked.

She opened her bag, found the small folded scissors she always carried with her and began to saw through the rope. It took time, but the puppy didn't move, and when at last he was free she scooped him up and tucked him into the front of her Burberry, where he shivered and shook but made no effort to escape.

'You poor little scrap,' said Claudia. 'You're coming home with me, and I'll make sure that you're never frightened nor hungry again.'

It was only as she reached the house that she wondered what Thomas would say—or Cork!

He had seen her coming along the street and had the door open before she had a chance to get out her key.

She didn't beat about the bush. 'Cork, I found this tiny dog tied to a tree in Hyde Park. He's starving and cold…'

Cork peered at the small creature. 'The Professor has said on various occasions that he intended to get a dog, madam. Perhaps a box with an old blanket by the Aga?'

'Oh, Cork, may he stay just until he's warm? And I thought a little warm milk… I'll have him as soon as I've got my things off.'

'If I might suggest, madam, you allow him to rest quietly for a period while you have lunch. By then we shall be able to see if he is recovering.'

So the puppy was settled in a cardboard box and covered warmly, and Claudia fed him with warm milk. Although he cringed still, he looked less terrified.

He was asleep when she went to fetch him after lunch.

'Thank you for having him in the kitchen, Cork, I won't let him bother you.'

'I have no doubt that when he is feeling more himself he will be a nice little dog. I'm partial to dogs, madam.'

Claudia beamed at him. 'Oh, are you, Cork? So am I.'

She took the little beast with her to the sitting room beside Thomas's study—a charming little room, where she chose to sit and have her meals when Thomas was away from home—and he fell asleep by the warmth of the fire, twitching and whimpering in his sleep. And when Cork brought her tea tray he handed her a small jug. 'Egg and milk, madam,' he explained. 'Perhaps a few spoonfuls from time to time...'

They inspected the sleeping puppy and decided that he looked a little better.

'As soon as I dare, I'll clean him up a bit,' said Claudia. 'He's stopped shivering...'

She went to her room presently, and changed her blouse and skirt for one of the jersey dresses, not bothering overmuch about her face and hair. She was feeding the puppy, kneeling by the box, rather untidy about the head, when Thomas came quietly to join her.

She scrambled to her feet when she saw him. 'Thomas, I'm so glad you're home. Come and see what I found this morning...' She paused while Cork placed a tea tray on the rent table by the easy chair where Mr Tait-Bullen often sat. 'I'll pour your tea. Have you had a busy day?'

He could see that for the moment his day would have to take second place to whatever it was in the box which had given her eyes such a sparkle and her cheeks such a fine colour.

'And what did you find?' He went over to the box and got down on his hunkers to take a better look.

'Cork says you always wanted a dog...'

Mr Tait-Bullen choked back a laugh. 'Oh, indeed I have.' He put a gentle finger on the skinny little body. 'Lost? Starved? Probably ill-treated. Where did you find him?'

'Sit down and drink your tea and I'll tell you. Then you can examine him, can't you?'

He drank his tea and ate the toast she offered him, and listened without interrupting. 'And Cork has been marvellous. I thought he would mind—I mean, a grubby little dog in this lovely house—'

'Our house,' he interrupted her gently.

'Well, of course it is, but you know what I mean, don't you? Please may we keep him? I don't know what kind of a dog he is, but I dare say he'll be handsome when he's older.'

Mr Tait-Bullen studied the puppy thoughtfully. 'There is always that possibility,' he agreed. 'Let's have a look at him.'

Claudia was surprised to see that the puppy accepted Thomas's gentle hands feeling his poor, bony frame, with no more than the whisper of a whine.

'Starved and kicked around, but I can't feel any broken bones. I'm on nodding terms with the local vet. I'll get him to come round and take a look.'

'May we keep him? You don't mind?'

'No, I don't mind. Cork was right. I have often said that I would like a dog.' He didn't add that the dog he had had in mind was a thoroughbred Labrador.

They dined presently, and tended to the puppy's needs, and later that evening the vet came. He was a youngish, thickset man, with a great deal of black hair and a face one could trust.

'Thomas, what's all this about a dog? Where did you get it?'

'Come and meet my wife. It was she who found the creature.'

The two men crossed the hall to the sitting room, where Claudia had gone to feed the puppy.

The vet shook hands. He had heard about Tait-Bullen's unexpected marriage, and, glancing at Clau-

dia, he considered him to be a lucky fellow. Beautiful
and charming—nice voice, too.

He said out loud, 'I must get Alice—my wife—to
call on you. Now, where's this dog?'

He took his time going over the puppy's small
frame. 'No bones broken. Several swellings, though—
he's been kicked. And just look at these paws—he's
been tied up somewhere and tried to escape. Poor little beast.'

'Any idea what breed?' said Mr Tait-Bullen.

'Take your pick. He'll never be a large dog, nor perhaps a handsome one, but I guarantee he'll be a faithful
companion to you both. I'll give him a couple of jabs
while I'm here. As to food and exercise...'

He outlined suitable treatment. 'And a run in the
garden is all he'll need for several weeks—that and
frequent small meals.' He looked at Claudia. 'You will
be busy, Mrs Tait-Bullen.'

'I've time enough to look after him, and I shall enjoy
it. You'll have a cup of coffee?'

He stayed for a while, idly chatting, and presently
Thomas went with him to the door. 'You've a charming
wife, Thomas. You must come to dinner one evening.'

'We'll be delighted.'

He went back to the sitting room, where Claudia
was kneeling by the puppy's box. She looked up as
he went in. 'Thomas, thank you. Perhaps he's not the
kind of dog you wanted, but he'll be such fun to have.'

Mr Tait-Bullen contemplated the skinny creature,
sitting up now and no longer cowering, knowing that
he was among friends. Under the dirt and mud his coat
was black. His ears were far too large for his small

foxy face, and he had a long, thin tail of which any rat would have been proud.

'I have no doubt that he will grow into the most unusual type,' he observed gravely.

'That's what I thought,' said Claudia happily. 'I like the vet. Are all your friends as nice?'

'I hope you will think so. You will meet a good many of them at the ball.' He went to sit in his chair, stretching his long legs to the fire. 'I'm sure you have a grand gown to wear among your purchases, or would you like to look for something else?'

'I have a gown. It's not grand, but I think it's suitable for your wife, if you see what I mean?'

'I trust your judgement, Claudia. You have excellent taste.'

Claudia went to bed with the pleasant feeling that it had been a happy day; they got on so well together, she reflected, and there was so much to talk about, so much that they intended to do together. Every day, she was discovering, she was finding out something else about Thomas that she liked; she hoped that he felt the same about her. She curled up and closed her eyes. Tomorrow was another day; she wondered what it would bring.

Fortunately for her peace of mind she wasn't to know *who* it would bring!

Chapter 6

The day began well. Thomas had no need to leave the house until nine o'clock, so they had leisure to clean up the puppy, anoint his battered little paws and brush his coat while he lay on Claudia's lap.

'What shall we call him?' she asked. 'A nice English name, since I found him in Hyde Park.'

'Since you found him you must choose his name.'

'Yes, well…' She thought for a moment. 'Harvey—that's easy to say, isn't it?'

Harvey cocked an ungainly ear; he was beginning to look more like a dog every minute.

Mr Tait-Bullen went presently, promising that he would be back for tea unless some emergency turned up.

'Oh, good,' said Claudia, with such transparent pleasure that he turned to look at her. She met his gaze with a look of faint enquiry. 'You look surprised. But teatime is one of the nicest parts of the day, isn't it? You can tell me what you've been doing and I'll listen...'

Mr Tait-Bullen discovered to his surprise that the idea appealed to him.

At four o'clock Cork arranged the tea things on a small table in the drawing room, and, since Mr Tait-Bullen had phoned to say that he would be home shortly after half past four, Claudia carried Harvey in his box from the sitting room and set it near the open fire. She had been out walking again, and was still in the tweed skirt and a blouse, but she had tidied her hair and powdered her nose and put on a pair of elegant kid slippers. She was sitting admiring them when Thomas came in.

He crossed the room and dropped a quick kiss on her cheek. 'How very cosy it is here. Cork's bringing the tea.'

He sat down opposite her. 'You have had a happy day? Harvey is doing well?'

'He's better. Look at him, Thomas. He's almost like a normal puppy.'

Harvey took this as a compliment and waved his tail.

'You don't mind him being in here? I don't think he'll get out of his box.'

'I don't imagine he could do much harm even if he did. He certainly looks more like a dog.' Thomas stretched an arm and tickled Harvey behind one ear. 'I must let John know how he's getting on. I dare say he'll want to see him again.'

Cork brought in the tea then, and buttered muffins in a dish, a fruit cake and a plate of paper-thin sandwiches. He arranged everything just so, and stood back to admire his handiwork.

Claudia said, 'Thank you, Cork, it all looks delicious. I hope you're going to have your own tea now?'

'Thank you, madam, yes. Dinner at the usual hour? You won't be going out again, sir?'

'I hope not, Cork.' And, as Cork slid through the door, Thomas added, 'I've a mass of paperwork to sort out. A quiet evening at home to get that done will be delightful.'

Claudia, pouring tea, agreed placidly. If she had been looking forward to an evening in his company, she didn't utter the thought aloud.

They were inspecting the fruit cake when the front doorbell was rung. And, before either of them had time to speak, Cork opened the door and stood aside to let someone in.

Mr Tait-Bullen got to his feet, his face expressionless, and his pleasant, 'Why, Honor, how nice to see you,' giving nothing away of his feelings.

Claudia stood up, too, recognising in an instant that here was someone she wasn't going to like and who wasn't going to like her. But she smiled, a bright social smile, and then looked enquiringly at Thomas.

'My dear, let me introduce Honor Thompson. Honor, my wife, Claudia.'

Claudia offered a hand. 'Do sit down and have a cup of tea. I'll get Cork to bring a fresh pot...'

Honor sat on the sofa facing the fire, throwing off her coat to reveal a black dress—very short, very smart and undoubtedly very expensive. It showed off her long legs and her very slim body.

No shape at all, thought Claudia, and wondered if Thomas admired women who looked like beanpoles. She was suddenly aware of her own curves, and busied herself with the fresh tea Cork had brought in, listening with half an ear to Honor's rather loud voice complaining that she had had no idea that Thomas was getting married and why hadn't he told her. 'You must have known what a shock it would be to me.'

She glanced at Claudia, who handed her a cup and saucer. 'I expect you and Thomas are very old friends,' Claudia remarked. 'But, you see, we didn't tell anyone except our families. It was a very quiet wedding.'

'Well, I for one shan't forgive you easily, Thomas,' said Honor, and she leaned forward to lay a hand on his arm.

Mr Tait-Bullen got up and put his cup and saucer on the table without answering her, and she flushed angrily.

'Of course, I don't suppose you know much about Thomas. You can't have known each other long.' She gave Claudia a sly look.

'Long enough to know that we wanted to be married,' said Claudia, in a matter-of-fact voice which robbed the question of drama. 'You live in London?'

'Of course. Where else is there?'

'You don't care to travel?' asked Claudia guilelessly. 'I mean, around England? Perhaps all your friends live here?'

'I hate the country. I adore the theatre and dining out and dancing.' She gave a little trill of laughter. 'I can see that Thomas will have to change his ways now that he is a married man.'

'I expect most men do,' said Claudia cheerfully.

'And I don't suppose they mind or they wouldn't marry, would they?' She smiled at Thomas. 'Don't you agree, Thomas?'

'Wholeheartedly. Honor, take a look at our addition to the household.'

He bent and picked up Harvey, tucked him under an arm and went over to where Honor was sitting.

She eyed Harvey with dislike. 'You aren't serious? It's a horrid little stray. He must be filthy, and he's hideously ugly...'

'He's a brave little dog. We call him Harvey—he'll probably grow into something quite splendid. He's still rather grubby, but he's been ill-treated—look at this sore on his shoulder, and under his paws...'

Honor shrank back. 'Don't come any nearer with the nasty little brute...' She stood up. 'I must go. I'm going out this evening.' She turned a cold eye on Claudia. 'Nice meeting you, Claudia. I dare say we shall see each other around—that is, if you go out much socially.'

She didn't shake hands, and she didn't shake hands with Thomas either, since he was still holding Harvey. She reached the door as Cork, summoned by the bell push by the fireplace, opened it and ushered her out.

It wasn't until he had returned and carried away the tea tray that Claudia said, 'I hope you're grateful that I married you. She would have eaten you alive in a couple of years. Are all your girlfriends like that?'

Mr Tait-Bullen had gone back to his chair with Harvey curled up on his knee. He had expected a reproachful comment, or at least coolness and hurt looks, and he was taken aback by Claudia's cheerful question. Taken aback and, he had to admit, amused.

'I only now begin to realise what a treasure I have married. I am indeed grateful that you are my wife—calm, good sense and not a single sulky look. I can assure you that I have never had any intention of marrying Honor, although I suspect that she had the intention of marrying me. And I have had no girlfriends. Oh, I have taken Honor out from time to time, and other women, too, but on a strictly platonic basis. I have not been in love for a very long time. If that were so, I would have told you.'

'Oh, my goodness, I didn't mean to pry. It's none of my business. All the same, I'm glad that it's me you married.'

'And so am I. Now, let us forget the woman and talk about other things which matter. I can be free next Sunday. Shall we go down to Little Planting? Will your mother and George be home?'

'Yes, they only went away for a few days because they want to spend Christmas at home, and Mother enjoys all the preparations, you know—the tree and paper chains and holly and presents. She always managed to make it a lovely time when we lived with Great-Uncle William.'

'Then we will go, and take Harvey with us. Do you want to shop for presents?'

'I could go tomorrow… And what about your family? Should we not buy more presents for them?'

'I can't spare the time. If I give you a list, will you do your best for us both?'

It was the kind of question that required nothing more than a meek answer.

She went shopping the next morning; Thomas had

left the house early, and she found no one when she went down to breakfast, but by her plate was a list of names scrawled in his unreadable writing. A long list, starting with his mother and ending with someone called Maggie, with brackets beside her name requesting warm slippers, size six! His father wasn't mentioned—presumably he bought that present himself. She added Cork's name, and Mrs Rumbold's. Probably Thomas gave them money, but a personal gift was always nice to have…

She found a cashmere stole for her mother-in-law, silk scarves for his sisters and a small leather case containing razor, hairbrush and a variety of small necessities which a man might need when travelling. And then she decided that scarves weren't enough for his sisters; she added a small silver photo frame and a little enamelled box. There were nephews and nieces, too; she spent a happy hour in the toy department of Harrods.

Thomas got home in the early evening, and she saw at once that for the moment at least he had no wish to look at what she had bought. He had greeted her in his usual manner, given her a drink, poured one for himself and gone to sit in his chair. Harvey had climbed out of his box and wriggled his way on to his knee, and Thomas now stroked the small creature gently.

'You have had a pleasant day?' he asked presently.

'Yes, thank you. But you don't want to hear about it for the moment, do you? Do you want to talk about your day? I dare say I won't understand the half of it, but I'll be a pair of ears.'

He laughed then. 'Claudia, you are so understanding. It is as if we had been married for years—you are such a comfortable woman to come home to. And at the end of the day sometimes a pair of ears is what I most want.'

He began to talk: a difficult diagnosis, a long list in Theatre, a post-operative patient who wasn't progressing as well as he should and always a backlog of patients who needed his skill.

Claudia listened to every word. There was quite a bit she didn't understand, but that didn't matter; she was intelligent enough to have a good idea as to his working day.

Presently she asked, 'Do you have a team working with you?'

'Yes, a splendid one. My senior registrar is a most dependable man, and I have two junior registrars and a couple of young surgeons—you'll meet them all at the ball. And a splendid theatre sister, too.'

Claudia felt a faint flicker of something which she didn't recognise as jealousy. All she knew was that she felt regret that *she* couldn't be his theatre sister, working beside him.

Thomas smiled across at her. 'Have I bored you? You must tell me if I do.'

'No, I like to know something of your work. I'm really interested.'

Cork came to tell them then that dinner was on the table, and Thomas said, 'You must tell me what you have bought…'

She spent the next day shopping for her mother and George, and Tombs, Mrs Pratt and Jennie. It was nice having enough money to choose presents without having to bother too much about their price. Thomas had

given her a very generous allowance, and told her care-
lessly not to worry if she spent too much, but she reminded herself that she hadn't married him for his
money. Indeed, she admitted, she would have married
him if he were penniless. The thought surprised her,
and left her feeling disquieted.

The day after that was the hospital ball. Anxious to
present as pleasing a picture as possible, Claudia spent
most of the afternoon doing her nails, washing her hair
and experimenting with make-up. But by teatime she
had decided that her usual dash of powder and lipstick
would do. As for her hair, after a tiring hour pinning it
into a variety of elaborate styles, she decided to twist it
into a chignon—a simple style which suited her lovely
face and which required no fuss. She suspected that
Thomas would dislike it if she were to fidget about
her appearance.

He had expected to be home early, but Cork had
carried away the tea things and there was no sign of
him. They had planned to have a light meal before
going to the ball, and when she heard the clock strike
seven she went along to the kitchen with Harvey trotting beside her.

'Cork, what is best to be done? We are to leave here
by half past eight, and the Professor will want time to
change. Would it be a good idea if you served a meal in
the sitting room? We were going to have grilled soles,
weren't we? Could they be saved for tomorrow? And
could you give us soup and an omelette? Then whatever time he comes in we could eat when he is ready?'

'I have been thinking along those lines, madam. A

plain omelette with a small salad, and I have prepared a sustaining soup with fresh-baked rolls.'

'Cork, that will be simply splendid. I'm going up to dress…'

Thomas came home half an hour later and Claudia, fresh from her bath and ready save for getting into her dress, wrapped her dressing gown round her and went down to meet him.

He looked tired after his long day, but he said cheerfully, 'Hello—did you begin to think I wasn't coming home?'

'Well, we were getting a bit anxious.' He hadn't kissed her, but she told herself that it didn't matter a bit. 'Would you like a meal at once, or do you want to change first?'

'I see that you aren't dressed yet.' He eyed her pretty pink quilted dressing gown. 'Shall we eat now?'

'Cork has a meal ready for us. We're having it in the sitting room. How well he looks after you, Thomas.'

He looked at her sharply. 'And you, too?'

'Heavens, yes! He's a treasure.' She led the way into the sitting room, scooping up Harvey as they went. He was still a somewhat battered little animal, but now that he found himself among friends, he was full of a desire to please.

Cork offered the soup, and presently the omelette, looking gratified when Thomas observed that it was exactly the meal he needed. Cork, having overheard Claudia's praise of him, murmured that it was madam who had suggested it. It was an unusually generous remark on his part, but he was becoming aware that Claudia had no intention of ousting him from his position in the household. In fact, he was beginning to like her.

The meal eaten, they went away to dress and, half an hour later, met again in the drawing room. Claudia, in the cream chiffon, wasn't sure if Thomas would find it grand enough, but she need not have worried.

He watched her cross the room. 'Delightful, Claudia. Exactly right. You look charming.' He took a box from the table beside him. 'Will you wear these?' he asked. 'I think they will go very well with the dress.'

He offered pearls, a double row with a diamond clasp, and to go with them earrings, pearl drops set in a delicate network of diamonds.

'My goodness,' said Claudia, 'they're magnificent, Thomas.' She touched the pearls with a gentle finger. 'I'm almost afraid to wear them.' She smiled at him. 'Thank you very much.'

She stretched up and kissed his cheek, and he took the necklace from her and fastened it round her throat.

'My grandmother left them to me with the advice that they should be given to my wife when I married.'

'She must have loved you,' said Claudia, and swallowed disappointment; they weren't a present from Thomas—not something he had wanted to buy for her, to give her as a present; he was merely carrying out his grandmother's wishes.

She said rather too brightly, 'I'm ready if you want to leave now.'

He gave her a thoughtful look, which she met with an equally bright smile. He looked distinguished in his black tie; the formal suit, cut by a master tailor, emphasised his height and size. He was a handsome man, she reflected, who ignored his good looks and had not an ounce of conceit. He was high-handed at times, perhaps, and capable of a fine rage, she suspected, but, like so many large men, gentle.

Cork, with Harvey tucked under an arm, saw them from the house, and it was only when they were driving through the quiet streets towards the busy heart of the city that Claudia felt the first pangs of nervousness.

'I don't know anyone...'

She felt his large, comforting hand on her knee for a moment. 'Don't worry, my dear, you will soon have more friends and acquaintances than you can imagine.'

'Oh—are you very well known, Thomas?'

'Well, I do visit a number of hospitals, and have done for some years now.'

He turned the car into the hospital forecourt, parked and helped her out.

He nodded to one of the porters standing at the entrance, and one of them got into the car and drove it away as they went in.

After that Claudia found herself in a sort of dream world. Thomas led her from one hospital dignitary to the other, a hand under her elbow guiding her, and when the formalities were over he took her onto the dance floor. He danced well, in an unspectacular way, guiding her effortlessly through the crowded hall, talking casually from time to time, putting her at her ease so that presently she found herself dancing with a variety of partners and enjoying herself.

From time to time she glimpsed him dancing, partnering his colleagues' wives, she supposed, slightly older women, well dressed and self-assured, but once or twice she saw that he was dancing with pretty girls, who laughed up into his face as though they had known him for years...

She was about to take to the floor with a stout, bearded man, whom she vaguely remembered having been introduced to, when Thomas slipped a hand under her elbow.

'The supper dance,' he observed mildly. 'You don't mind, Harry, if I claim my wife?'

The bearded man laughed. 'It wouldn't make a scrap of difference if I did, Thomas, but I shall lie in wait for you, Mrs Tait-Bullen!'

'Who was that?' asked Claudia, accepting a plate of vol-au-vents and a glass of wine. 'I've met him, haven't I?'

'Yes, he's the consultant pathologist and an old friend.' He smiled. 'You're enjoying yourself? I've been showered with compliments about my bride.'

She went pink. 'Oh, have you? People are very kind.'

'I have been told how beautiful you are—and you are, Claudia, that dress is exactly right.'

Somehow that last bit spoilt the compliment.

'You have been dancing with some very pretty girls. Of course, you must know all the nurses.'

He fetched her a little dish of ice cream before he replied.

'Not quite all. You see, I meet only ward sisters and staff nurses, and then our conversation is purely professional, but once a year at this ball the senior staff dance with those of the nursing staff they work with on the wards or in Theatre or the clinics. I don't know who started the idea, but the custom is handed down from one generation of doctors to the next.'

A remark which she found reassuring.

It was well past midnight when they got back home. Cork had left hot chocolate on the Aga, and they sat drinking it while Harvey snoozed in his basket.

'A very pleasant evening,' observed Mr Tait-Bullen, 'and you have won all hearts, Claudia.'

'It's nice of you to say so, but it's only because I'm a nine-days wonder.'

He laughed. 'What a matter-of-fact girl you are.' He took her mug from her. 'And a sleepy one, too. I must leave the house by seven o'clock, so don't get up until you have had your sleep. I should be home for tea.'

'Oh, good.' She yawned, and rubbed her eyes like a child. 'It was a lovely evening, and it was lovely to dance.'

He got up and hauled her gently from her chair. 'Indeed it was.'

He opened the door and gave her a gentle shove. 'Off to bed, and sleep well.'

She hesitated a moment, but he held the door open, smiling a little, so she wished him goodnight and took herself off to bed, feeling vaguely unhappy.

She woke late, and when she went downstairs Cork was waiting for her with Harvey scampering at his heels.

'You slept well, madam? I have set breakfast in the sitting room by the fire. A most inclement day, I'm afraid. I am to tell you from the Professor not to venture too far in this weather.'

Claudia peeped out of the window. Indeed, it looked

horrid outside—dull and grey with an unremitting drizzle.

'It looks awful, Cork, but Harvey must have his run...'

'Perhaps a brisk turn in the garden, madam. There is always the chance that the weather will improve.'

'Well, I hope it does, for we are going to Little Planting on Sunday. We'll take Harvey with us.' She poured her coffee. 'Cork, you do have a day off each week, don't you?'

'I have two half days, madam, and such free time as I can arrange without upset to the running of the house.'

He sounded cagey, and she added hastily, 'I'm sure you have it all worked out, Cork. But I just thought that it would be a chance for you to have a day to yourself while we are out.'

'Thank you, madam. I shall avail myself of your offer...'

'I expect that you have family and friends to visit?'

'Indeed, I have. At what time will you be leaving on Sunday, madam?'

'Quite early, I believe, and we shan't be back here until after tea.'

She finished her breakfast and spent the morning tying up presents, considerably hampered by Harvey. When, after lunch, the drizzle ceased, she got into her mac, tied Harvey into his waterproof jacket and led him out for a quick walk. On the way home she stopped to look in the windows of the little shops she had found. The wool shop had a pretty knitting pattern in the window, with a basket of wools every colour of the rainbow. She already had a present for her mother, but there was no reason why she shouldn't give her another one. She scooped up Harvey, tucked him under her arm and went into the shop.

In the end shop, in amongst the glass and silver bits and pieces, she found a small porcelain model of a dog, the spitting image of Harvey, just right for Thomas's desk. She went home well pleased with her finds, and found Thomas sitting by the drawing room fire reading the papers.

'Oh, how lovely, you're home. No, don't get up. I'll tell Cork I'm back and we'll have tea.'

When she had poured the tea and offered him sandwiches, she asked, 'Have you had a busy day?'

Mr Tait-Bullen bit into a buttered scone. 'Much as usual.' He offered Harvey a bit of scone, and didn't see the disappointment on her face. He seemed to shut her out of his working life sometimes. Perhaps he thought that she was not really interested. He added, 'You have created quite a sensation, you know...'

'Me? Didn't I behave like a consultant's wife? Shouldn't I have danced so much?'

'You behaved beautifully, my dear, and everyone is enchanted by you. I was inundated with invitations. I can see that we have a busy social winter ahead of us.'

'Do you mind that? If you do, I'll make excuses.'

'No, you mustn't do that. I rely on you to organise our leisure, and several of the invitations will be for you alone, I imagine—coffee mornings and tea parties.'

He finished his tea, and, with the remark that he had work to do, went to his study. Harvey went with him and she was left sitting alone. She had declared rather too quickly that she had letters to write, and he had nodded casually with the remark that they would meet at dinner.

He had told her before they married that he wanted a companion. It seemed to her that he had forgotten that—or was it that she bored him? She told herself not to be silly, allowing imagination—and, it must be admitted, a modicum of self-pity—to take over.

But she forgot all that when at dinner he suggested that they leave early on Sunday morning so that they might take a look at some likely villages not too far from Little Planting.

'Is there any particular village you fancy? We might at least look around us, so that after Christmas we can house-hunt in earnest.'

'Would we spend the weekends there?'

'Whenever possible, and any free days that I can manage. Somewhere not too far from a good road back to town.'

'Well, there's a lovely little village—Child Okeford—south of Shaftesbury, close to Blandford, and only a mile or so from the main roads. Years ago I used to go there with Mother, she had an old schoolfriend living there, but she moved away. I dare say it's changed. I must have been nine or ten years old.'

'Then we will have a look at it before we go to Little Planting. If we leave really early we should have plenty of time to look around.'

They left at eight o'clock. It still wasn't full daylight, and the streets were Sunday morning quiet. The presents were packed in the boot, and Harvey, wrapped in an old shawl, slept peacefully on the back seat. Claudia felt her spirits soar as she got into the car. She was wearing the leather jacket over a silk shirt and a tweed skirt, and leather boots which had cost so much that she felt quite faint when she thought about it. But they were worth every penny—as supple as velvet and exactly matching the colour of her jacket.

She would have liked to draw Thomas's attention to them, but he seldom noticed what she wore, although he never failed to tell her that she looked nice. But he didn't *look,* she reflected, not at her, not to see her in detail, as it were. She dismissed the thought as unworthy; he was a kind and thoughtful husband and they got on famously.

They reached Child Okeford an hour and a half later. There was a pale watery sun now, and the village still slept under it. In another hour there would be church, and people setting off in their cars or going for a country walk, but for the moment they had the place to themselves.

'Could we park and look around?' asked Claudia.

They left the car in the centre of the village and, with Harvey on his lead, began to explore.

'It hasn't changed much,' said Claudia. 'The village shop's still there, and the pub.' They paused to admire the church and walked the length of the main street, stopping to explore the narrow side turnings. It was a charming place, its cottages well kept, with one or two bigger houses standing back from the road. They had gone its length when Claudia saw a narrow lane leading away from it, half hidden by high hedges.

'Let's take a look, Thomas...'

The lane curved, and they passed two cottages with their doors opening directly onto the lane, and then round the next curve they saw another cottage, quite large, standing behind hedges. There was a For Sale board beside its old-fashioned wrought iron gate.

It must have been empty for some time, for the windows were uncurtained and the garden was woefully overgrown.

Claudia looked at Thomas, and he opened the gate and they walked up the brick path to the solid door under the thatched porch. There were windows on either side, and small windows above, tucked away under the thatch.

Claudia went to peer through one of the windows. 'The kitchen,' she said. 'There's another window at the side, and two doors. Come and look, Thomas.'

She went round the side of the cottage and found a door, and, at the back, more windows. A quite large room and next to it a room which took up the whole of the other side of the cottage. She bent to peer through the letter box. 'There's a staircase,' she told Thomas, but when she turned round he wasn't there. He was by the gate, writing down the address of the house agents.

'Oh, Thomas, do you like it? I mean, well enough to want to see inside?'

Mr Tait-Bullen put away his notebook and walked up the path to join her.

'Yes, I like it, too. The agent is a local man—Bland-ford—supposing we go and see him? I'll phone him from the car—he might even come here to us.'

'Now? This morning? Oh, Thomas…'

He looked at her, smiling a little. Her cheeks were flushed and her eyes shone with excitement. He had the sudden urge to wrap her in his arms and kiss her.

The thought took him by surprise; it was as though he was seeing her for the first time.

'Now, this morning,' he assured her, and nothing in his level voice showed his feelings.

They went back to the car and he phoned from there. The agent was willing to drive to meet them at the cottage. He would be with them in half an hour, he assured them.

'Shall we phone your mother?' suggested Thomas. 'Tell her that we may be a little later than we intended?'

That done, they went back to the cottage, and while they were waiting poked round the garden. It was quite large, and there was a rough track at the side of it which led to a sizeable barn.

'The garage?' asked Claudia hopefully. 'And, look, there was a greenhouse there and a summer house…' She clutched his arm. 'Oh, Thomas.'

The agent was middle-aged and fatherly, wearing comfortable country tweeds and carrying a bunch of large keys. When Mr Tait-Bullen apologised for disturbing his Sunday, he made light of it. 'Come inside,' he invited. 'It's solid enough, roof was thatched a couple of years ago, brick and cob walls, the usual mod cons. The old lady who lived here went into a nursing home six months ago, but she kept the place in good order.'

He opened the door with a flourish and stood aside to let them in.

The hall was narrow, with a staircase along one wall. There were three doors, and Claudia opened the first one. The room was large, with windows both at the front and the back of the house, an inglenook and open beams. Claudia rotated slowly, seeing the room in her mind's eye just how it would look—an open fire, comfortable chairs, little tables with lamps on them, bookshelves. She crossed the hall, taking Thomas with her. The room on the other side of the hall was smaller, with cupboards on either side of an old-fashioned grate and more open beams.

'The dining room,' she breathed happily, and went into the kitchen. A quite large room, with an old-fashioned dresser and windows on either side of a door to the garden. And upstairs, leading off the small landing, were three rooms, two of them small but the third of an ample size. There was a bathroom, too, rather old-fashioned, but the plumbing, the agent assured them, was up-to-date.

Claudia wandered round on her own while the two men talked quietly in the hall, and presently Thomas went in search of her. She was hanging out of a bedroom window, planning the garden in her mind's eye.

'You like it? I've made an offer. He'll let me know tomorrow when he's contacted the owner.'

Claudia flung her arms round his neck. 'Thomas, oh, Thomas!' And she kissed him. She hadn't kissed him like that before, and she drew back at once, rather red in the face. 'Sorry—I got carried away.'

Mr Tait-Bullen didn't allow the normally calm expression on his face to alter. The kiss had stirred him, but all he said was, 'Let us hope that we are able to buy the place.'

She reminded herself that he was not a man to be easily aroused from his habitual calm. But he liked the little place; she could see that. They would furnish it together and spend happy weekends there and get to know each other.

Chapter 7

Claudia's mother came to meet them as they stopped before George's door.

'Darling, what kept you? You haven't had an accident?' She looked anxiously at Thomas. 'All you said was that you were unexpectedly delayed... But come in, do, there's coffee and mince pies...'

It had been a happy day, reflected Claudia, sitting beside Thomas as he drove back to London in the early evening. Such a lot of cheerful talk, presents to exchange, Tombs and Mrs Pratt to visit, a walk after lunch with Rob and Harvey, and, of course, the cottage to be discussed while the men exchanged views on medical matters.

Claudia, with her mother's enthusiastic help had had the place metaphorically furnished, the curtains hung and the garden dug and in full bloom by the time they got into the car. She'd still been thinking about it as Thomas began the journey home.

'Blue and white checked curtains in the kitchen, and that white china with blue rings round it—you know the kind I mean?'

'I can't say that I do, but I shall leave such matters to you—if and when the cottage is ours.'

She felt a stab of disappointment. Furnishing the little place together would have been fun. She reminded herself that he was a busy man, and that any free time he had he would want to spend in a way to please himself. She said, 'It was a lovely day, Thomas, thank you for bringing me. Harvey enjoyed himself, too.'

They didn't talk much more on the way back. Thomas replied cheerfully enough to her remarks, but she sensed indifference. A polite indifference, but all the same it was there, like an invisible wall between them. It was a relief to get home and find Cork waiting for them in the warm, well-lighted hall.

He led Harvey away to the kitchen for his supper, and Claudia, casting off her jacket, followed him.

'Have you had a pleasant day, Cork?'

'Yes, thank you, madam. I trust that you had an enjoyable trip?'

'Yes, yes, we did.' She would have liked to tell him about the cottage, but perhaps Thomas might not like that.

Cork, spooning Harvey's supper into a dish, said civilly, 'Would supper in half an hour suit you, madam?'

She said that yes, that would be fine, and wandered away out of the kitchen and up to her room to tidy herself. When she went downstairs presently there was no sign of Thomas.

Cork met her in the hall. 'The Professor has been called away—an emergency—he will phone you as soon as he is able. He had no time to say more, madam.'

Claudia stood in the hall looking at him, saying nothing, so he added, 'I'll serve you supper at once— there's no knowing when he will be back, madam.'

'All right, Cork. Let's hope it's nothing that will keep him away for too long.'

She ate her solitary meal and then went to sit in the drawing room, with Harvey for company. The evening was well advanced by now, and there had been no message. She sat there, pretending to read, her ears stretched to hear the sound of his return or a phone call, but there was neither. At midnight she took Harvey to his bed in the kitchen, and bade Cork goodnight after being told that he would wait up. 'The Professor wouldn't want you to lose your sleep, madam,' he said, and was interrupted by the phone.

He answered it, and then handed it to Claudia.

'Go to bed, Claudia. I shall probably be here for most of the night. Sleep well—I'll have a word with Cork.'

She handed the phone to Cork, who listened with an expressionless face. His 'Very well, sir' was uttered in a disapproving voice, and when he rang off he said, 'I am not to wait up, madam. I'll lock up as soon as you are upstairs.'

There was nothing else to do but wish him goodnight, give Harvey a quick cuddle and go to her room.

She had expected to stay awake, waiting for Thomas's return, but she fell asleep almost at once to wake hours later, not knowing why she had wakened. The house was quiet, but all the same she got up, peered at her clock and saw that it was almost four o'clock. She got into her dressing gown and slippers and crept downstairs, and as she reached the hall, the front door opened very quietly and Thomas came in.

He closed the door equally quietly before he spoke. 'Shouldn't you be in bed?'

Disappointment at his terse greeting turned her pleasure at seeing him to peevishness. 'Of course I should,' she snapped. 'I'm not in the habit of wandering round the house at this hour. I woke up—I don't know why...'

She started towards the kitchen. 'I'll get you a drink. You're tired.'

'Nothing to drink, thank you, but I am tired. Go back to bed. I'll go to bed myself as soon as I've put my bag away.'

She felt a childish wish to burst into tears. He was behaving as though he wished she wasn't there. She turned to go upstairs again, and then paused.

'At what time will you want breakfast?'

He was already at his study door. 'The usual time.'

'But it's after four o'clock!'

He didn't answer, but went in and shut the door. Now that there was no one to see, she allowed unhappy tears to trickle down her cheeks as she went upstairs.

As for Mr Tait-Bullen, he sat down at his desk and allowed all kinds of thoughts to fill his head. The sight of Claudia, standing in the hall in her pink gown, her hair in glorious wildness with that look on her face, had disturbed him deeply. When he had envisaged being married to her he hadn't imagined anything like that. She was Claudia, a girl he admired and liked, a perfect companion and a wife whose company he would enjoy without any of the hazards of being in love with her.

Being in love was something he had lost faith in years ago, when he had given his heart to a woman and it had been thrown back to him. Not that his heart had been broken, not even cracked—indeed, he had remained happily heart-whole ever since. But, since then, falling in love had been something in which he didn't believe.

And now, suddenly, he had discovered that that wasn't true.

Claudia, crying her eyes out in the comfort of her bed, fell asleep at last, and woke a few hours later looking much the worse for wear. She still looked beautiful, but her eyelids were pink and so was the tip of her delightful nose; she disguised the pinkness with expensive cream and powder guaranteed to work miracles, happily unaware that they made no difference at all, and went down to breakfast, rehearsing a few polite remarks about the weather as she went, just to let Thomas see that their unfortunate conversation earlier that morning was to be ignored.

He was already at the table, the post scattered around his plate. He got up as she went to the table and wished her good morning in a brisk voice which warned her that he didn't wish to talk, so she discarded the weather and replied even more briskly. Cork, offering coffee, buttered eggs and fresh toast, returned to the kitchen quite worried, for he had allowed himself to approve of his mistress after a doubtful start. She didn't interfere, but at the same time she had made it her business to know exactly how the house was run—without interfering. She was looking unhappy, and he was uneasy.

'If it was anyone else but the Professor,' he told Harvey, 'I'd have said it was a tiff, but he's not one to waste his time on anything as silly. Very polite he is this morning, too—in a rage, no doubt. And she's been crying…'

Harvey looked sympathetic and allowed his ears to droop, so that Cork felt constrained to offer him a couple of nicely crisped bacon rinds.

Mr Tait-Bullen studied Claudia from beneath lowered lids; she had been crying, but it seemed best not to mention that, for she wore a haughty expression which warned him off. It was hardly the moment to tell her that he had fallen in love with her. Claudia, being Claudia, would probably turn on him and tell him not to talk nonsense.

He said mildly, 'I hope to be home for tea today.'

Claudia said, 'Very well, Thomas,' and, since she was anxious to be friends, even though they weren't on the best of terms at the moment, added, 'Is there any shopping you need? Have we all the presents for your family?'

'If you would check the list? Have we remembered Mrs Rumbold?'

'Yes—a cardigan. Would you mind if I added a box of chocolates? A big box tied with ribbon…'

'By all means.' He got to his feet. 'I'll see you later. Enjoy your day.'

It was her last chance to find a present for Thomas. It was a pity that he had everything. She had the little figure of the dog like Harvey, but that wasn't enough. She spent an anxious morning peering into shop windows; a tie wasn't enough, besides, he might not like it—all the same she bought one in a rich silk—dark, glowing colours in a subdued pattern.

Looking at a display of photo frames gave her an idea. She chose a small one in silver and took it back home, found one of the photos which Tombs had taken at their wedding and inserted it. It wasn't a very good photo, but they had both been laughing—perhaps it would remind him that they had declared their intention of making their sensible marriage a success!

She was in the drawing room, bent over a piece of tapestry she had bought, of roses on a creamy background which, when finished, would become a cushion cover, when Thomas came home. She saw with relief that he was his usual calm self, and they had tea together, talking casually—Christmas, his work, Harvey's progress, Christmas again—and later, after dinner, they sat together in the drawing room, she with her tapestry, he with the evening papers and his medical journals. Just like an old married couple, thought Claudia contentedly. She must remember not to bother him when he had had a hard day.

It was almost dark when she took Harvey for his evening trot the next day. It was cold, but dry, and a brisk run in the park would do him good. There were few people about—most were shopping frenziedly for Christmas. She kept to the main paths and decided to keep Harvey on his lead. He was an obedient little beast, but if he were frightened by something he might run off in a panic. She had turned back towards the road when two youths passed her, and then turned and followed her. She didn't dare look round, but she picked up Harvey and quickened her pace. The road wasn't more than a few minutes' walk away, and there would be other people...

Only there weren't—there was no one in sight!

She could feel they were close to her now. Should she run for it, scream, or turn and confront them? She spun round and found them within inches of her.

Mr Tait-Bullen, arriving home earlier than he had expected, found the sitting room and drawing room empty. Cork, coming to meet him in the hall, wished him good evening, adding that Mrs Tait-Bullen had taken Harvey for a run in Hyde Park.

'I did suggest that it was a bit dark, sir, but she said that they both needed a breath of fresh air. She usually goes there from the Bayswater Road.'

'Then I'll go and meet her,' said Mr Tait-Bullen, and got into his overcoat again. 'Explain to her if she gets back first, Cork.'

The streets were almost empty and he walked fast, which was a good thing, for he had no sooner got to the park than he heard Harvey's shrill bark.

It was quite dark now, but he could see Claudia and the two youths. As he reached them she landed a nicely placed kick on one of the youth's shins and he yelped with pain.

'Let's 'ave the dog and break 'is neck for him...'

Thomas didn't waste time in talk. He knocked the pair off their feet, begged them in a terrifyingly quiet voice to be off before he called the police and turned his attention to Claudia.

The youths scrambled to their feet and ran off, and Claudia said in a rather shaky voice, 'Oh, thank you, Thomas. They were going to hurt Harvey.'

Thomas's quiet voice was harsh. 'They were going to hurt you, too. It was foolish of you to come here at this time of day. You have only yourself to blame.'

He had turned her round and was marching her back, out of the park, into the lighted respectable streets with their sedate houses and infrequent passers-by.

She hadn't expected that; she had expected sympathy, kindly concern, enquiries as to whether she had been frightened or hurt. The fact that he had only uttered the truth made no difference. Rage and delayed fright made her shiver. He was an inhuman monster! Scathing remarks she would have liked to make in reply remained unuttered, for they were walking too fast for her to talk; his hand on her arm urged her forward, but it didn't feel friendly.

Mr Tait-Bullen, aware of her thoughts, remained silent. The wish to sweep her into his arms, Harvey and all, was strong, but if he did that, and kissed her, things might get out of hand. Rather, let her dislike him for the moment than be frightened off by a love she hadn't expected or asked for.

Indoors once more, he took Harvey from her, took off her coat and gloves, sat her down in the drawing room and put a glass in her hand.

'Drink this. It will make you feel better.' He sounded like a friendly family doctor.

'What is it?'

'Brandy. You don't like it, but drink it—there's a good girl.'

She tossed it back, caught her breath, whooped, was slapped gently on the back and burst into tears.

'I'm not crying,' said Claudia fiercely. 'It's this beastly brandy.'

He forbore from comment, only smiled a little and went away to take off his own coat. Cork was hovering in the hall. 'Madam isn't hurt? An accident?'

'Thugs. No, she isn't hurt—only frightened and shocked.'

'I'll bring in the tea at once.'

'Splendid, and give Harvey a biscuit or a bone. He's been frightened, too.'

Cork, quite shaken, glided away, to return within a few minutes with the tea tray and Harvey.

He arranged the tea things on a table convenient to Claudia, murmured his regrets at her unpleasant adventure, assured her that the crumpets were freshly toasted and took himself off. His mistress certainly didn't look quite the thing; she was usually as neat as a new pin, but now her hair was decidedly untidy and she was crying. He hoped that the master would comfort her in the proper fashion.

Claudia, in a haze of brandy, took the handkerchief which Thomas offered and mopped her face and blew her nose.

'I'll go and tidy myself,' she muttered, and started to get out of her chair.

'No need. You look very nice as you are.' Thomas's voice was soothing, and at the same time matter-of-fact. 'I'll pour the tea. The brandy will wear off if you eat something.'

He was regretting his harshness in the park; he had been afraid for her when he had first caught sight of her with the youths and fear had made him angry. He must repair the damage as quickly as possible.

He gave her tea, and put a crumpet on a plate and set it on the small table by her chair. He said cheerfully, 'You know, you had me scared for a moment—those boys can be so rough. Will you promise me not to go into the parks—any of them—once it is dusk?'

'All right—you were so angry…'

'Yes, but it was anger which spilled over from those thugs, and I had no right to blame you. Life at Little Planting is free from such unpleasant encounters—you weren't to know…'

It was going to be all right again, thought Claudia. They were back on their friendly footing once more. She bit into her crumpet. 'I should have used my head,' she conceded.

They didn't hurry over their tea; Thomas led the talk round to Christmas, and their journey north. 'There are some splendid walks,' he told her, 'and there is a special beauty in winter. I'm looking forward to showing you something of the countryside.'

'I'll bring my boots…'

'And something warm to wear. Have you had time to tie up all the presents?'

She nodded. 'Yes, and I've put in one or two extra things—some chocolates and a scarf and some scent, just in case we've missed someone, or someone turns up who isn't expected.'

Nothing had changed, reflected Claudia, going to bed after a quiet evening with Thomas. True, he hadn't said much, but just having him there, sitting opposite her, was nice…

They were to drive up to Finsthwaite on Christmas Eve. A long drive but, as Thomas pointed out, they would be on a motorway for almost the whole distance: the M1 as far as Birmingham, then the M6 until they left it, just before Kendal, and took the road to the lower end of Lake Windermere and, a few miles farther on, Finsthwaite—a matter of just under three hundred miles. He would go to the hospital in the morning, and they should be able to leave London by mid-afternoon—a little over four hours' driving; once out of town and on the motorway, it would be a straightforward run.

Claudia packed carefully, made sure that the presents were stowed in the big box Cork found for her and collected Harvey's basket, tins of food and his favourite bone. She would travel in the leather jacket, with a tweed skirt and a cashmere sweater—suitable garments if they were to go walking. She took her winter coat, too, for she was sure they would go to church, and added a little velvet hat, one of the jersey dresses, the green patterned dress, silk shirts and cardigans, sensible shoes—her boots she would wear—and a pair of elegant slippers. She wanted Thomas to be proud of her…

They left at three o'clock. The afternoon was already turning into a raw, cold evening, but the shops were lighted, there were Christmas trees and coloured lights and, as they drove out of the city, pavements packed with last-minute shoppers.

'I love Christmas,' said Claudia happily. 'And people look so happy... I hope Cork will have a good time.'

'I fancy he will. His widowed sister comes for Christmas Day, and on Boxing Day some old friends of his come to lunch and stay until the evening.'

'Oh, good.'

She stayed silent then, while he threaded his way through the streets until they were on the M1.

'We'll stop this side of Birmingham for a cup of tea and allow Harvey a breath of air. There's a service station.'

After that he was mostly silent, but it was a friendly silence, and Claudia had a good deal to think about. His family—she had met his parents, but only briefly at the wedding. Supposing his mother had decided that she didn't like her? And his sisters... She began to compose a series of suitable topics of conversation.

The Rolls swept with silent speed towards Birmingham. There wasn't much traffic going north, and nothing impeded its progress. The service station lights loomed ahead of them and they parked and got out, glad of a few minutes to stretch their legs while Harvey aired his tail and then, tucked under Claudia's arm, went with them to the restaurant.

Thomas found a table, told her to sit down and went away to fetch their tea. Watching him coming back, with a tray of tea things and a plate of buttered teacakes, Claudia thought that Cork would have a fit if he could see his master now.

They didn't waste time, but drank the strong hot

tea, ate the teacakes, and, since there was no one to see for the moment, Claudia gave Harvey a saucer of milk, tucked a paper napkin under his small chin and fed him the last of the teacakes.

'Are we going to stop again?' she asked.

'If necessary. I'd like to get off the motorway before we do, but if you need to stop, say so.'

'I was thinking of Harvey,' said Claudia primly.

Mr Tait-Bullen suppressed a chuckle. 'Of course. But with luck he'll sleep for a few hours.'

They were bypassing Liverpool in just over an hour; in another hour they were off the motorway and through Kendal. There the road was still good, but narrow in places, with long stretches of dark countryside and few villages—Grigghall, Croathwaite, Bowland Bridge, and then nothing until they rounded the end of the lake at Staveley. Now the road had become a narrow lane, running between trees.

Finsthwaite was a small village: farms, a cluster of cottages, a village store and post office, a church and a village school lower down a gentle slope. A short walk away there was Grizedale Forest. It was a little paradise, but now shrouded in darkness, save for a few lighted windows, and then, unexpectedly, a lighted Christmas tree by the church.

Thomas drove through the village, turned into an open gateway and stopped before the house where he had been born; it was a nice old house, built of grey stone, with light streaming from its windows and its solid door flung open before they were out of the car.

Claudia need not have worried about her welcome. She was drawn at once into the family circle, kissed and hugged, helped out of her coat, then carried away by Ann and Amy to warm herself by the log fire in the drawing room and be plied with delicious coffee.

'Just to warm you up,' said Ann. 'Dinner will be in about half an hour. Don't change.' She hesitated. 'Well, perhaps you'd rather. Did you have a good trip here? Thomas is such a good driver. A pity it was dark, but I don't suppose you could come any earlier?'

When Claudia had finished her coffee they took her up the wide staircase at the back of the hall and along the gallery above it. 'You're here, Thomas's dressing room is next to it and there's a bathroom. I expect he'll be up presently. Come down as soon as you can. We've still got to put the presents round the tree.'

They left her then, in the high-ceilinged big room. The furniture was big, too: a vast brass bed, a tallboy and a mighty wardrobe in mahogany, an old-fashioned dressing table with a great many little drawers and a triple mirror standing in the window. Despite the heavy furniture the room was charming, with its sprigged wallpaper, thick cream carpet and chintz curtains and bedcover, and two bedside tables, each with a rose-shaded lamp.

Claudia opened the door in the farther wall and saw the bathroom beyond, and another door on its opposite side which she opened, too. The dressing room.

She went back then, unpacked her case, which some-one had brought to the room, and changed into the pat-terned jersey. She did her hair and her face and then sat down on the bed. She was suddenly nervous of going downstairs. Thomas had no right to leave her alone...

There was a tap on the door and Thomas came in.

He took one look at her and sat down beside her on the bed. 'Feeling a bit overpowered?' he asked, and put an arm round her shoulders. 'Don't—they are all so delighted to see you. Come down. Father's waiting to open the champagne and James wants to kiss you under the mistletoe!'

They went down to the drawing room together, and Claudia stifled a wish that Thomas had been the one who wanted to kiss her. A silly wish, she reflected. He wasn't a demonstrative man… Hadn't he told her that before they married? That he had no interest in being in love, that he had loved once, but never again? And she had accepted that.

Everyone was in the drawing room—a square room with two windows overlooking the front garden. It had panelled walls, and chairs that were roomy and very slightly shabby, but the furniture was solid and beautifully kept, the chairs covered in a dark red damask which matched the curtains, and a vast sofa before the stone fireplace, which housed a roaring log fire. The room was warm—warm with content and happiness and love; there was no doubting the affection Thomas's family had for each other, although it wasn't on display.

They drank their champagne and presently crossed the hall to the dining room. It was panelled, like the drawing room, and had a vast mahogany table surrounded by Victorian balloon back chairs, a William the Fourth pedestal sideboard, which took up almost all of one wall, and a magnificent giltwood side table. There were a number of paintings on the walls—Claudia supposed that they were family portraits—dimly lit by wall sconces.

The table had been decked for Christmas, with a centrepiece of holly and Christmas roses, a white damask cloth and napkins and heavy silverware. When the soup was served Claudia recognised Coalport china.

She was hungry and dinner was excellent: game soup, roast pheasant and a chocolate and almond pudding. She wasn't sure what she was drinking; all she knew was that she was very happy and enjoying herself. And Thomas, sitting beside her, had once or twice put his hand over hers, which gave her a warm glow inside.

They arranged the presents round the tree after dinner.

'We all go to church in the morning,' Amy told her. 'But perhaps you and Thomas would like to go to the midnight service? It's only a short walk to the church and it's a lovely service. We always went, but now we have the children we stay at home. They still wake in the night sometimes, and we like to be there.'

'How many have you?'

'Two, and another one in the spring. Ann has one so far.' She smiled. 'They're such fun, but an awful lot of work.'

Claudia went to sit by her mother-in-law then, until that lady declared that it was time they all went to bed. 'You still have the children's stockings to fill,' she reminded them. 'Breakfast at eight o'clock. Church at half-ten.'

'I'm taking Claudia to the midnight service,' said Thomas quietly, and smiled across the room at her.

'Then we'll leave the side door unlocked. I'll tell Maggie to leave coffee on the Aga, and there are sandwiches in the fridge if you feel hungry.'

There was a leisurely round of goodnights as the

party broke up, leaving Claudia and Thomas sitting by the fire.

'Well?' he asked. 'Are you going to like my family?'

'Yes, very much. I've never had more than Mother— and Father, of course, but he died several years ago. I think it must be wonderful to be one of a large family.'

'Indeed, it is. We don't see a great deal of each other, but we make a point of meeting for important occasions. Amy and Ann are happily married—Jake and Will are sound men—and I suppose James will marry in due course.'

'Your mother and father aren't lonely so far from you all?'

'No. They are happy to be together. Mother has her garden, Father sits on various committees, and they both enjoy walking. Besides, there is quite a social life here, even in the winter.'

He glanced at the walnut longcase clock. 'Would you like to walk to church? It's only a question of five or ten minutes.'

'I'll go and get a coat.'

It would be cold outside. She put on her winter coat and the little velvet hat, found gloves and sensible shoes and went back downstairs to where Thomas was waiting for her in the hall.

He took her to a door beyond the staircase and opened it onto the night. There was a clear sky, alight with stars and a dying moon, and he walked her along a path leading from the side door of the house to a small gate which led onto the lane.

'The church is below the village,' he told her, and took her arm. And round a bend she saw its squat tower close by. There were other people making their way there, too, and when they reached the church she saw that it was already almost full. Thomas made his unhurried way to a pew in the front, stopping to greet people he knew and introduce her, but presently she had time to glance around her. The church was small, rather cold, but scented with the evergreens and holly and Christmas flowers which decorated it. She liked it, and she enjoyed the service, simple and peaceful.

They walked home later, and Claudia said, 'It's Christmas Day...'

Thomas stopped. 'Ah, yes, and we have no need to wait for the mistletoe.' He hugged her close and kissed her, and then let her go rather abruptly. He had very nearly lost his self-control.

Claudia had enjoyed the kiss very much; if she hadn't been taken by surprise she would have kissed him back, but he had released her before she had the chance. Perhaps later...

The house was in darkness as they went quietly through the side door and into the kitchen. It was a thoroughly old-fashioned one, with a huge dresser along one wall, a big scrubbed table with ash and elm Windsor chairs around it and two elbow chairs on either side of the Aga. The floor was of flagstones and there was a rag rug before the Aga. Harvey was fast asleep in his basket, and curled up on one of the chairs was a large tabby cat.

Thomas fetched two mugs and poured their coffee. 'Maggie has been with us for a lifetime,' he told her. 'She's a really marvellous cook. We all love her, and the children can't be kept away from her when they come to stay. She has plenty of help, of course, but both maids have gone home for Christmas Eve. They'll be here in the morning, and go again after lunch. There's an ancient man who does the heavy work in the garden. He should have been pensioned off years ago, but the people round here don't retire.'

'Would you rather live here than in London?'

'This is my home, and I love it, but my work is in London and that is my life. I am fortunate enough to be able to have both.' He glanced at her. 'You like living in London, Claudia?'

'Oh, yes, you have a lovely home, and the parks are close by.'

'I've bought the cottage at Child Okeford. We'll go down to see it in the New Year. It seems pretty sound, but it will need painting and some small alterations.'

'You've bought it? Oh, Thomas, how splendid. Did you forget to tell me?'

'I didn't know myself until this morning, when the agent phoned. You're pleased?'

'Yes. Oh, yes. You're pleased, too?'

'Yes!' He got up and took her mug. 'It's very late. Go to bed, my dear, you have had a long day.'

'And a very happy one.' She leaned up and kissed his cheek. 'This is such a lovely Christmas.'

For a second time that evening Thomas very nearly lost his self-imposed restraint.

Claudia went down to breakfast in the morning to a chorus of greetings and good wishes. The children were there, too. Ann's small son was in a high chair, but Amy's two—little girls—were sitting at the table.

There was a lot of noise and laughing while they ate, and afterwards, before they all went to church.

Claudia could see that Thomas was on excellent terms with his nephew and nieces. He would be a splendid father, only it seemed that he had no desire to be one. Perhaps in a few years' time, when they had grown closer to each other... She shut the thought away; he had married her for companionship and because he wanted a wife to order his household and entertain his friends. Their marriage was a sensible one, based on friendship and compatibility, and a genuine liking for each other.

The church was warmer now, and there were even more people there. She stood between Thomas and his mother and sang the carols, and told herself that she was the luckiest girl on earth.

Chapter 8

Christmas dinner was at midday, so that the children could share it—turkey and Brussels sprouts, roasted potatoes, braised celery, cranberry sauce—nothing had been overlooked. Then the Christmas pudding, set alight with great ceremony, and last of all mince pies. They drank champagne again, and then coffee before going to the drawing room to open their presents. The children first, of course, before they went for their afternoon naps, and for a while the room was awash with coloured paper, ribbon and toys.

Presently it was the grown-ups' turn. Everyone was there, including Maggie, the two maids and the gardener, and they collected their gifts first, drank a glass of sherry and went off to the kitchen to enjoy a splendid high tea.

Mr Tait-Bullen Senior handed out the presents,

and very soon the room was just as untidy as when the children had been there. Claudia, looking round her, thought how delightful the room looked, with the lighted tree and the gaily covered presents, the roaring fire and the soft lamplight. She wished that her mother and George could have been there, too, although when she had phoned her mother that morning that lady had sounded in the best of good spirits. She caught Thomas's eye and smiled—a wobbly smile, for she was on the verge of tears—and he came to sit by her, taking her hand in his large, cool one and giving it a friendly squeeze.

'You haven't opened all your presents...'

'No. There are so many and they're all so lovely.' She picked up a small box and tore away the paper. A jeweller's box, blue velvet and quite small. She looked at the tag then, and said, 'Oh, Thomas, it's from you...' She opened it and looked at the earrings bedded in white satin—sapphires in a network of gold and diamonds.

'Oh, Thomas...'

'Go on, kiss him,' said Amy, who had been watching. 'You're in the family now.' They had all turned to look, smiling and nodding, so she kissed him, very pink in the cheeks, feeling shy.

Thomas didn't kiss her back. She thought he might have done, with everyone watching, but he took the earrings out of the box and fitted the hooks neatly into her ears. She got up then, and went to admire the earrings in the gilt mirror opposite the fireplace, and that gave her time to let the blush die down and regain her composure.

She still had more presents to open, so she went back and sat down again on the massive sofa beside Thomas and started to open them. A gorgeous silk scarf from Harvey, who was sitting at her feet and muttered sleepily when she thanked him. A leather writing case from her in-laws—red leather with her initials. Gloves and scent and a jewel case from Thomas's sisters and brother. She went round thanking everyone, and being thanked, and when she sat down again Thomas was opening his presents. He had a great many, but he saved hers till the last, quietly approving of the tie. When he unwrapped the photo frame he said nothing for a few moments.

'It's a kind of reminder,' said Claudia quickly. Perhaps he didn't like it; perhaps he thought it was a silly, sentimental thing to have done.

'I shall put it on my desk at my consulting room,' he told her quietly, 'so that everyone can see what a beautiful wife I have.'

'That wasn't why I did it,' she told him. 'I thought it would remind you...' She paused to get it right. 'It's difficult to explain...'

'Then don't try, Claudia. I think I understand and I shall treasure it.'

The presents had all been opened by now, and everyone was sitting round, content to do nothing for the moment.

'Shall we go for a quick walk?' Thomas pulled her to her feet.

'Yes, dear, take Claudia towards the forest,' his mother said. 'Tea will be a little later because of the children. Be back by five o'clock.'

So Claudia fetched her coat, tied her new scarf over her head, got into her boots and went down to the hall where Thomas, coated but bareheaded, was waiting.

They went out of the side door again, and along the lane towards the church, and then turned away along a rough track which took them almost at once into the forest. It was a perfect late afternoon, the sky in the west a blaze of red and yellow, the rest of the heavens already darkening, lights from the village and outlying farms twinkling.

'It's been such a lovely day,' said Claudia as they walked along arm in arm. 'I feel happy, don't you, Thomas?'

He didn't answer that, but observed, 'It would be hard to be unhappy here. Some places are meant to be happy in—I think the cottage at Child Okeford will be such a place.' He looked down at her face, rosy with the cold. 'What are we going to call it?'

'Why, Christmas Cottage, of course.' She went on happily. 'We'll have a cat—at least, he'll have to live with us in London and go to and fro like Harvey... Should we have brought Harvey out with us?'

'Harvey is sleeping off a much too large dinner. I'll give him a run after tea.'

'Your parents haven't got a dog? I know Maggie has a cat...'

'Jasper, our Labrador, died a month or so ago. He was old and a devoted friend. In a while, when they are over his death, I've arranged for a puppy—another Labrador—to join the family.'

'Oh, Thomas, how kind. They must miss him terribly.' She stopped to stare into his face in the gathering dusk. 'You think of everything, don't you?'

'I do my best.' He reflected that he hadn't thought of falling in love...

They walked back presently, to eat Christmas cake and drink tea from delicate porcelain teacups round the fire while the children sat at a small table eating an early supper. They had had an exciting day and were inclined to be peevish. Amy and Claudia went to sit with them, coaxing them to eat their peanut butter sandwiches, the little fairy cakes Maggie had made for them, which followed the Marmite toast, and to drink their milk.

When they were borne off to bed there were plaintive requests for Daddy to tuck them up and read them a story. They were taken upstairs then, and presently Amy and Ann came down again. 'Now it's your turn,' Amy told the men, and as they went away she said laughingly to Thomas, 'Just you wait. It'll be your turn next. I don't know why fathers read bedtime stories better than mothers, but be prepared for it!'

Thomas said mildly, 'What do you suggest? That I start rereading Hans Andersen? A bit out of date, I dare say. How about *The Wind in the Willows?* My favourite when I was a small boy.'

The conversation became general then, and Claudia joined in, avoiding Thomas's eye. She supposed that there would be a good many such remarks, but, since they didn't seem to disconcert Thomas, she must learn to treat them in a light-hearted manner.

She had married him so quickly there hadn't been

time to foresee the small pitfalls, but as long as he didn't mind, she wouldn't allow it to bother her.

Everyone went away to dress presently, and when she came downstairs there were guests, invited for a drink—local people who, it seemed, had known Thomas and his family for years. They accepted her as one of the family at once, but the talk inevitably turned to reminiscences, so that she felt an outsider despite everyone's efforts to include her in their talk. But she did her best, and Thomas's hand on her arm reassured her.

When the last guest had gone, they went in to supper. A buffet—the vast sideboard laden with bowls and dishes filled with Maggie's delicious food: smoked salmon, salads of every kind, a ham on the bone, stuffed eggs, chicken pie, miniature hot rolls. Claudia allowed Thomas to fill her plate and found herself sitting by James.

'Pity you have to go back tomorrow. I suppose Thomas can't be away for more than a few days. Time he took a holiday. He doesn't need to work quite so hard, you know.'

'Yes, I do know, but he loves his work, doesn't he? It's important to him.'

'He's good, of course, you know that. You should see him in Theatre...'

'And people like him, I think. He came to see my great-uncle, you know—that's how we met...' She paused, remembering that she hadn't much liked him then. 'They got on awfully well together. People do things for him, too, don't they?'

James chuckled. 'Well, he can be a bit hoity-toity

if he can't get what he wants—in the nicest possible way, mind you. And in no time they are all doing exactly what he wants!'

But it was something Ann said which made her vaguely uneasy.

'You're so right for Thomas. We've all hoped he would marry, but for years and years—ever since he had that miserable love affair with that girl who went off with a tycoon from South America—he's been considered a splendid catch. Not that he's bothered about that. I don't suppose you've met a woman called Honor Thompson? She'll be livid when she hears that he's married...'

'I've met her,' said Claudia in a carefully level voice.

'You have? I expect Thomas told you about her. She's one of the persistent ones. Don't let her worry you, though. He doesn't care tuppence for any of them. He's always known what he wanted from life and now he's got you.'

Was that why Thomas had married her? she wondered. To be a barrier against wishful partners? Someone who wouldn't spoil the even tenor of his life by demanding undying love? Really, it was a sound idea! An undemanding relationship, the tolerance of good friends towards each other, shared pleasures—and they did like the same things. He could have married Honor, or any other of his women acquaintances if he had wished, but he had chosen her. Well, she was quite prepared to be the wife he wanted. And just let Honor try any of her tricks, Claudia thought waspishly.

They didn't leave until after lunch on the following day. In the morning they had gone for another walk, taking one of the paths which led into the heart of the forest. They had talked about Christmas, and plans to come again, perhaps for Easter, or perhaps he could persuade his parents to visit them.

'The cottage should be quite ready by then, and I'm sure they would enjoy it. We will go down there as soon as possible and see what needs doing. I'm sure you have some ideas, and the place will need painting and decorating.'

'And furnishing.' Claudia's eyes sparkled. 'Curtains and things.'

It had been a most satisfactory morning, she reflected, and began a leisurely round of goodbyes. Christmas had been two wonderful days; she liked Thomas's family, and she loved the countryside around his home and the comfortable old house. She hoped that they would come again, but she doubted if Thomas could spare the time to drive up frequently. She got into the car with real regret, made sure that Harvey was comfortable on his blanket on the back seat and turned to give a final wave.

It was still light, although the day was fading. She looked around her at the country as Thomas drove back to join the motorway, and, since he didn't speak other than to ask her if she was comfortable, she stayed silent.

They were approaching the motorway when he said, 'We'll stop for tea just before Birmingham, but do tell me if you want to stop before then.'

Her 'Yes, Thomas' was the epitome of wifely obedience.

It was quite some time before he said, 'You're very quiet.'

'Well, I thought that's what you wanted. I'm sure you have a great deal to think about...'

'For instance?' He sounded amused.

'Your work and your patients, and perhaps you are wishing you were back with your family and that Christmas was just beginning and not over.'

He didn't comment on that. 'You enjoyed your Christmas?'

'Oh, I did. I loved every minute of it, and I like your parents and your sisters and brother.'

'They like you, Claudia.'

They stopped for tea at a service station, took Harvey for a brisk walk around the car park and resumed their journey, speeding along the motorway, talking of this and that. And Claudia had the feeling that even while he talked Thomas's mind was on something else.

'Are you worried about something?' she asked. 'You don't have to talk if you don't want to. I shan't take umbrage.'

He laughed then. 'I'm not worried, Claudia.' He began to talk about plans for Christmas Cottage, and she felt as though she had been snubbed. It had been nicely done, but whatever it was, she wasn't to be told about it.

London was empty of traffic; Boxing Day was a family visiting day and many people were indoors. Later they would return to their own homes, but just now it was quiet.

Cork opened the door and they went in to a welcoming warmth and a faint but delicious smell from the kitchen. He welcomed them with grave pleasure, fetched the cases and then announced that dinner would be in half an hour if that suited them.

'Excellent,' said Thomas. 'I'll take Harvey for a run.' Which left Claudia to go to her room and tidy herself and unpack before going down to the drawing room. Thomas wasn't there, but Harvey was sitting before the fire looking drowsy.

'I gave Harvey his supper, madam,' said Cork, coming silently into the room. 'The master's in his study. He will be joining you presently.'

'Thank you, Cork. Have you had a happy Christmas?'

'Very pleasant, madam. I trust that you enjoyed yourself?'

'Very much. The country was beautiful.'

Cork went away, and she fetched her tapestry and began to stitch. It was a bit of an anticlimax after the cheerful racket that had been such fun. Only yesterday, she thought, and it seems like weeks ago already.

Mr Tait-Bullen, coming into the drawing room some minutes later, paused for a moment in the doorway; Claudia looked delightful, sitting there working away at her embroidery. It seemed to him that she had always been there; it was hard to think of the house without her in it. He wondered what she would say if he were to tell her that he had fallen in love with her, but he thrust the temptation aside. He thought she was happy and content, and he must have patience; in time she might come to love him, but until then they must stay good friends. It was lucky that he had more than enough work to keep him busy.

He sat down opposite her and observed mildly, 'I've

a good deal of work on my hands for the next week or so, but we might go down to Child Okeford next Sunday and take a good look round. You might like to spend an hour or two with your mother.'

'Yes, I would, and I'm longing to see the cottage again. You don't have to go away, do you?'

'In a couple of weeks I have a seminar in Liverpool—two days or so.' He gave her a thoughtful look. 'I'm afraid you will be on your own a good deal, Claudia.'

'Oh, I don't mind that,' she said cheerfully. 'I've all those coffee mornings and tea parties to go to—with people I met at the hospital ball—and plans for the cottage.'

'Ah, yes. You must decide how you want it furnished…'

'Well, you must decide, too, for you'll be living there as well, whenever we get the chance.'

They spent the rest of the evening together. 'Like an old married couple,' said Cork to himself. 'They ought to be out dancing or whatever. It isn't right.'

Such an idea hadn't entered Claudia's head. She was perfectly content, sitting there, making heavy weather of the tapestry while Thomas immersed himself in a pile of medical journals. It was nice, she reflected, that they enjoyed each other's company but made no demands on each other.

Soon after ten o'clock she folded her work, declared that she was tired and took herself off to bed, after giving Harvey a hug and bestowing a friendly goodnight on Thomas as he got up to open the door for her. His manners were beautiful, she reflected as she went upstairs, and he was unfailingly kind. She heaved a sigh, not knowing quite why.

She didn't see a great deal of him for the next few days. He was away early in the mornings and didn't get home until early evening; there was a good deal of flu, he told her, and his registrar was off sick.

'Take care!' said Claudia. 'Are there many off sick at the hospital?'

'Amongst the nursing staff, yes—quite a few of the medical staff, too. And, of course, the wards are all full…'

There was nothing she could do to help, but she took care to see that a meal was ready when he got home, with welcoming warmth and no disturbances if he wanted to work. As for herself, her days were nicely filled. Walks with Harvey, such shopping as Cork allowed her to do, coffee with various of the ladies she had met at the ball and most afternoons spent reading though not always understanding some of the medical books in Thomas's study. But it was necessary that she had some idea of his work, and now was no time to bother him with any questions. If ever he chose to talk to her about work, at least she would have some idea of what he was talking about.

There was also the New Year to look forward to—only a day away—and all being well they were to go out to dinner tonight, and dance the New Year in. Claudia washed her hair, did her nails and massaged in a cream guaranteed to improve the complexion. That she had no need of it was quite beside the point.

She took Harvey for a long walk in the afternoon and returned home, thankful to be out of the damp cold, looking forward to tea round the fire. She let herself in, dried Harvey and took off her outdoor things, then went to sit down in the small sitting room. It was already past the usual teatime, but she supposed that Cork had forgotten the time. After half an hour she went to the kitchen, vaguely uneasy. Cork ran the house like clockwork. Perhaps he had had to go out for some reason...

He was huddled in a chair by the Aga, with a white face and shivering.

'Cork, you're ill.' She put a hand on his forehead and felt its heat. 'You must go to bed at once.' When he protested feebly, she added, 'No, please do as I say.' She saw that the effort to get out of the chair was too much for him, so she heaved him up and helped him to his room, sat him on the bed, took off his shoes and pulled the bedclothes over him. 'Now, lie still, there's a good man. I'm going to get you a drink.'

There was bottled water in the fridge; she filled a jug, found a glass and took them to his room, gave him a drink and tucked the bedclothes round him.

'Your tea, madam,' croaked Cork. He closed his eyes.

'Don't give it a thought. Go to sleep if you can. I'm going to find a warm water bottle for you. As soon as the Professor gets home he'll come and see you. I expect it's the flu.' She cast a worried glance at him. He really looked ill; thank heaven Thomas would be home early.

She went to the kitchen and made a pot of tea. Cork wouldn't have any, although he drank some more of the water, so she went back to the kitchen and drank her own tea. She ate some of the sandwiches on the tray, fed Harvey and, since they wouldn't be going out to spend the evening, peered into the fridge and the cupboards, collecting the makings of a meal.

She was still there when Thomas came home. Harvey ran into the hall to greet him, and as the dog came into the kitchen, with Thomas behind him, she dropped the potato she was peeling and ran to him, quite forgetting to be calm and sensible.

'Thomas, I'm so glad to see you. Cork's ill. I've put him to bed but he's so hot and shivery.' She tugged at his sleeve. 'Do come and see what's wrong.'

Mr Tait-Bullen's features displayed nothing but calm assurance. He said in an unhurried manner, 'This wretched flu, I expect. I'll take a look.' He paused on his way. 'You didn't take his temperature?'

'Well, no. His teeth were chattering so much I was afraid he would break the thermometer.'

He nodded and went out of the kitchen and into Cork's room, and Claudia peeled the last of the potatoes. There was plenty of food in the fridge; she had chosen salmon steaks to go with the potatoes, frozen petit pois and there was a cabbage in the sink to clean and cook. Dull fare for Old Year's Night, but with Cork ill, food didn't seem very important.

'It will have to be cheese and biscuits afterwards,' she told Harvey, 'and I just hope he likes it.'

'He'll like it,' said Thomas, from somewhere behind her. 'Cork has the flu, but he's not too bad. I've given him paracetamol and I'll go back presently and settle him down. We've plenty of orange juice and cold drinks, I presume? That's all he'll need for a while...'

'Poor man. Now, just you sit down and I'll make a

pot of tea. Supper won't be very exciting, but it'll be food...'

Mr Tait-Bullen sat, watching his wife trot to and fro, her glorious hair getting very untidy, her lovely face flushed. She might look a bit disorganised, he reflected, but she was efficient and quick. A pot of tea was placed before him, with the sandwiches, now rather dry, and a dish of the little cakes Cork was so clever at baking.

'If you don't mind waiting for dinner, I'll go and see to Cork.'

'My dear girl, he would rather die. He needs to be undressed and put to bed—washed and so on.'

'Oh, well, I'm quite able to do that, you know.'

'Of course you are. All the same, I think it is better if I see to him while you get our dinner. By all means see to his drinks and any food that may take his fancy.'

He got to his feet. 'I'll check the post and be back very shortly.'

He was as good as his word. 'We'll eat here, shall we?' he asked, taking off his jacket. 'I'll see to the table presently.' He didn't wait for an answer, but went to Cork's room and shut the door.

Claudia drank another cup of cooling tea, offered Harvey a biscuit, because he was being such a good boy, and turned her attention to the salmon. She was a good cook; if she had known that she was to cook the meal that evening she would have thought out a dinner worthy of the occasion, but it would have to be a simple meal. She thought with regret of the pretty dress she had laid out ready to wear this evening, the delicious supper they would have had, the excitement of toasting the New Year. What could they have for a pudding? she wondered, and began to squeeze oranges for poor Cork.

Thomas came back presently, put on his jacket and then started to lay the table. It took some time, since he had to search for everything in drawers and cupboards, but the end result was as elegant as if Cork had done it himself. He took a bowl of hyacinths from the windowsill and put it at the centre of the table, arranged silver and glass just so and went to look in the fridge. Cork, that admirable man, had put a couple of bottles of champagne in it earlier that day. Thomas opened one, filled a glass and took it to Claudia.

'I'm sorry—you must be disappointed that we can't go dining and dancing with the rest of the world,' he told her. 'We'll make up for it later on.'

Claudia took a good drink of champagne. 'I don't mind a bit. I'm so sorry for Cork.' She wrinkled her nose. 'Why does champagne make you feel so uplifted?'

'A good question.' He topped up her glass. 'Something smells good.'

Claudia drained the cabbage, chopped it fine, added nutmeg and a squeeze of lemon and put it on the dish Thomas had got from the dresser. She had creamed the potatoes with plenty of butter and milk and dished up the peas; now she laid the salmon on two warmed plates and took it to the table.

'Not very exciting, I'm afraid,' she said. 'But there's a nice piece of Stilton for pudding!'

Mr Tait-Bullen, who had snatched a sandwich for his lunch, cleared the plate. 'You're a good cook,' he told her. 'What a treasure I have married.'

Claudia went pink. 'Well, I can't cook anything fancy. Great-Uncle William didn't hold with spending a great deal of money on what he called "elaborate food" so I became good at fancying up sausages and things.'

'Tell me more about your great-uncle,' suggested Thomas and filled her glass again.

And Claudia, nothing loath, her tongue nicely loosened by the champagne, told—until she stopped suddenly. 'I'm being boring. It's all the champagne—you should have stopped me...'

Mr Tait-Bullen, enjoying himself, made haste to assure her that he hadn't been in the least bored. 'After all, we know very little about each other even now.'

While she made coffee he went to look at Cork.

'Sleeping like a baby. Now, let us discuss the cottage. As soon as Cork is better, we will spend a day at Child Okeford, see what is to be done and get hold of a builder. We had better find a gardener, too, to get the place into some shape before we can take over. I'll get hold of the estate agent—he may be able to recommend someone. We will try not to alter the place too much, but the barn will need a secure door and a firm run-in for the car. Had you thought of anything you wanted changed or added to?'

Claudia shook her head. 'I loved it as it was. Will it take long, the necessary repairs and the garden?'

'It shouldn't. We can choose carpets and furniture once we have all the measurements. A local firm, I think, don't you? Sherborne or Shaftesbury.'

'Carpets and curtains,' said Claudia happily, 'and

comfortable furniture. Thomas, it will cost an awful lot of money…'

'Probably, but it will be our second home, won't it? We mustn't spoil the ship for ha'porth of tar.'

They washed the dishes together then, and in no time at all, it seemed, it was five minutes to midnight.

Cork was still asleep. Thomas came back into the kitchen, filled their glasses and went to stand by her. As the clock struck midnight they toasted the New Year, and then he took the glass from her hand, put it with his on the table and bent to kiss her. An unhurried, gentle kiss, quite different from his usual rather brisk salute, it stirred something inside Claudia's person, and she stared up into his face, vaguely puzzled.

He was as calm as he always was. 'A Happy New Year, my dear.'

'You, too, Thomas.' She paused. 'You're quite happy, aren't you? I mean, with us being married? We're good friends, aren't we? And I promise I'll not get in your way—with your work, you know. When we married I hadn't thought of all the things which could go wrong.'

He had seen the puzzled look; his Sleeping Beauty was beginning to wake up. He said in a matter-of-fact manner, 'I'm very happy, Claudia. Getting married was something I should have done years ago—to you, of course!'

'Well, you didn't know me, did you? Do you have to go to the hospital tomorrow—no, today?'

'No, unless I'm needed. Supposing we go down to the cottage?'

'But we can't leave Cork.'

He took the phone out of his pocket and dialled.

'A male nurse will be along at eight o'clock. He'll stay with Cork until we get back. He's a good man— kind and trustworthy.'

'But won't he be on duty?'

'No, he has days off, and he'll be glad of the fee.'

'Oh, won't anyone mind?'

He smiled and shook his head, and she said, 'Are you so important that you can do things like that?'

'I must admit to having a certain amount of clout.'

'Well, it would be marvellous. All day? We must take a notebook and pen and a tape measure. But only if Cork feels better...'

'Of course. Now, go to bed, Claudia. If we're to leave early you'll need your beauty sleep.' He added, 'You don't need any beauty sleep, actually. You're already as beautiful as it is possible to be.'

A remark so unlike Thomas that she stopped to stare at him. Then, 'It's all that champagne,' she told him. 'You're looking at me through rose-coloured spectacles.'

Thomas only smiled, and he didn't kiss her as she went past him. She was quite disappointed.

Mr Tait-Bullen saw to Cork, locked up and took himself off to his study. He still had reports to read, patients' notes to examine, his workload to be checked. Harvey went with him, to snooze on his shoes until Thomas went to his bed after a last visit to Cork, who, while still very much under the weather, was prepared to stay alive after all.

Claudia woke soon after six o'clock and went down to the kitchen to make tea. She peeped at Cork, made him another jug of lemonade, laid the table and went back to dress. A day at the cottage meant sensible clothes: the leather jacket, a sensible tweed skirt and a pullover. She made short work of her hair, did almost nothing to her face and went back downstairs. She could hear the murmur of voices from Cork's room as she set about frying bacon and eggs and making toast, and presently Thomas came in with a short, middle-aged man.

He wished her good morning and added, 'This is Sam Peverell, my dear. Sam, my wife. We'll have breakfast as soon as it's ready. You know what to do for Cork, and you can reach me on my mobile, of course, if you need me. We should be back in the early evening.'

Claudia piled plates with bacon and eggs and made more toast. 'I'll put your lunch ready for you, Mr Peverell, and a tray for tea. There are oranges and lemons in the fridge, and milk and yoghurt. So will you help yourself?'

'Certainly, Mrs Tait-Bullen.' He turned to Thomas. 'Phone calls, sir?'

'I'll put on the answering machine. But get hold of someone at the hospital if you're worried.'

'It's very kind of you to come, Mr Peverell,' said Claudia. 'On your day off, too. We're awfully grateful.'

'No problem, Mrs Tait-Bullen. My wife's gone to her mother's, and the girls are spending the day with friends.'

'You have daughters?'

'Two, fourteen and sixteen, and you wouldn't believe what a worry they are...'

Mr Tait-Bullen sat back, listening to Claudia charming Sam—a martinet on the ward, a splendid nurse and reputed not to have much of an opinion of young women. *His* Claudia, he reminded himself, who was a delight to the eye and the ear and whom he loved.

They left well before nine o'clock, and, since the streets were almost empty after the night's celebrations, they were on the motorway in no time at all. They stopped at a service station after more than an hour's driving, had coffee and allowed Harvey a brief stroll before resuming their journey. Claudia felt a little thrill of excitement as Thomas turned the Rolls into the network of small lanes which would lead them to Child Okeford. Supposing they didn't like the cottage now that they had the leisure to look it over?

'Where's the key?' asked Claudia, a bit late in the day.

'I'm to fetch it from the end cottage as we pass.'

The village was quiet, its inhabitants no doubt sleeping off the excesses of the previous night, but when Thomas knocked on the cottage door he was soon given the key; several keys, in fact.

The cottage looked a bit forlorn, for it was a dull morning with the hint of rain, but Claudia, seeing it in her mind's eye with roses round the door, curtains at the open windows, the garden full of flowers, skipped inside the moment Thomas had the door open.

They went slowly from room to room, checking them with the particulars which the estate agent had sent. The cottage was in good heart, its small windows secure and solid, large cupboards, the stairs sound. The kitchen would need cupboards and shelves, and an Aga, and its flagstone floor cleaned, but the vast stone sink was something Claudia wanted to keep.

They went round a second time while Claudia argued the merits of porridge-coloured carpeting against different colours in each room. Thomas listened patiently, told her to have whatever she liked and suggested that they went and looked round the garden. It was larger than they had first thought, and there were apple trees forming a screen between the garden and the open fields beyond.

'We can grow vegetables,' said Claudia, quite carried away, 'and there's space for a little greenhouse, and we could have a small summer house in that corner, so that you could have somewhere quiet to go.'

Thomas agreed gravely, waiting to see if she would suggest a swimming pool, but she didn't. She did suggest a rockery, and a little pool where frogs might live.

They went to the village pub presently, and ate a ploughman's lunch and emptied a pot of coffee between them. The cottage was every bit as delightful as they remembered it—better, even, for now they had explored it from bottom to roof.

'I'll get on to the agent tomorrow,' said Thomas, 'and get things started.'

He glanced at his watch. 'Do you want to see your mother and George as we go back?'

'May I? Is there time? And what about Cork?'

'I'll check when we go back to the cottage. We must lock up properly.'

Claudia beamed at him across the pub table. 'Oh, Thomas, I'm so happy…'

Chapter 9

Claudia's glow of happiness lasted until they were back home. They had called at George's house, had tea with him and her mother and stayed for a while. Claudia and her mother had a lot to say to each other, but, mindful of Cork, she'd got up at once when Thomas suggested mildly that they should go. It wasn't for a while that she'd realised Thomas was rather silent. She'd stopped talking then, sitting quietly beside him, still happy, her thoughts busily occupied with the cottage.

It wasn't until they were home again, and Sam Peverell had given his report, pocketed his fee and gone home, and she had been to see Cork and gone to the kitchen to get a meal, that she realised that Thomas, after seeing Sam Peverell off home and spending a short time with Cork, had gone to his study and shut the door.

It was as if he had erected an invisible barrier between them. She told herself that he was probably tired or had work to do, and that the faint air of reserve would have disappeared by the time their supper was ready.

Lamb chops, sprouts, potatoes and mint sauce. Plain fare indeed, but it was already after seven o'clock and she still had to cook... She rummaged around in the cupboards, found what she wanted, made an apple pie and popped it in the oven and then made an egg custard for Cork. He was feeling more himself, assuring her that he would be on his feet in another day or so, adding, with a touch of suspicion, that he hoped she could find everything she wanted in the kitchen.

'Oh, indeed I could, Cork, and I've been careful to put everything back where it belongs.' She gave him a motherly smile. 'We do miss your lovely cooking.'

Cork, still pale and poorly, nevertheless looked smug at that.

The first few days of January went swiftly by; Claudia enjoyed them, for she was kept busy shopping and cooking, and although Mrs Rumbold came each day there was always something to be done: the flowers to arrange, the phone to answer, the bills to pay. She was careful to ask Cork's advice about most things, and in a few days, when he was feeling better, he sat by the Aga, warmly wrapped, and advised her about the best methods to cook their meals.

She found this rather tiresome, since she was a capable cook, but she knew that he meant it kindly and nothing would have induced her to snub him. And Cork, for his part, acknowledged the fact that she was an ideal mistress, never encroaching on his preserves while asserting a gentle authority. The master was a lucky man.

The master was a busy man, too, away early in the morning and for the most part not back again until the early evening. He made time, though, to visit Cork, and spent what leisure he had in Claudia's company, although she sensed his reserve towards her. She tried to remember if she had said or done something to annoy him and wondered if she had disappointed him in some way. One day, she promised herself, when he wasn't away from home so much, she would ask him.

Cork, back on his feet once more, took over his normal duties again. He made her a little speech of thanks with the voice and manner of a benevolent person, making it quite clear that, much though he had appreciated her help, he no longer required it. Claudia, thrown back onto her own resources, took long walks with Harvey, drank coffee with various of the wives she had met at the ball and ploughed her way through the books in Thomas's study, not understanding them by half but feeling that by doing so she was bridging the gap which she felt was between them.

It was something of a relief when he told her that he had to go to Liverpool for two or three days, and would she like to visit her mother?

'I can drop you off on my way, and then why not bring your mother back here for a day or so? There's the possibility that I may go on to Leeds and have to spend the night there.'

'I'd like that, Thomas. I'll phone Mother. I'm sure she'd love to come, and we might do some shopping.'

'Yes, well, take her to Harrods or Harvey Nichols and use our account.'

He looked so kind when he said it that she was tempted to ask him if there was anything wrong, but she didn't; he had come home later than usual and he looked tired.

Harvey was to stay with Cork, for she intended to stay only one night at George's house; she and her mother could return by train and they would spend two days together. Her mother hadn't seen Thomas's home, and Claudia was longing to show it to her. They could have a good gossip and shop. She got into the car two days later, on a still dark morning, and Thomas drove out of town, leaving Cork and a protesting Harvey behind.

'I hope Harvey won't pine,' said Claudia, 'and that Cork will take care of himself…all alone,' she added doubtfully.

'I should imagine that he is pleased to see the back of us. He now has the opportunity to take a nap when he feels like it, and rearrange everything around the house to his satisfaction. He will spoil Harvey, bully Mrs Rumbold and probably drink my port.'

She laughed. 'He'd never do that. He's your devoted slave.'

'And yours, I fancy. I'll phone you this evening, but don't worry if you don't hear from me after that. I'll let you know when I'm coming home.'

They didn't talk much, just casual remarks from time to time, and although Thomas was friendly it was as though the real Thomas was hidden behind this pleasant man sitting beside her. She could say something about that now, she supposed, but then changed her mind. He wouldn't want to be bothered when he had the seminar ahead of him to think about.

They reached George's house by mid-morning and, despite her mother's pleas that he should stay for lunch, he was on his way again after a cup of coffee. Claudia went with him to the car and he kissed her lightly as he got in. She poked her head through the window as he was about to drive off.

'Do be careful, Thomas, and I hope everything is successful.'

Her face was very close to his, and he drew back with a jerk, an action which sent a cold shiver down her spine. She stood back, fighting sudden tears. It was as though he couldn't bear her near him. When he got home again they would have to talk...

She enjoyed her day with her mother and George. That they were quietly happy together was evident, and Mrs Pratt and Tombs were, in their own way, just as happy. George drove them over to Child Okeford one evening, and they looked round the cottage. She hadn't got the key, but the builders had already started on the repairs and they peered through the windows and explored the garden. George pronounced it a nice little property, and her mother could find no fault with it.

She bore her mother off to London the next day. Thomas had phoned on the previous evening, expressed the hope that she was enjoying herself and warned her that he might not phone her for a couple of days. He had sounded friendly, but even over the telephone she'd imagined she could hear the constraint in his voice.

Her mother was delighted with the London house. She professed herself overwhelmed with its comfort and luxury, and Cork's perfections. Claudia took her walking in the park with Harvey, and the next day went shopping with her. George had given her money with which to buy herself something she liked, and Claudia, mindful of Thomas's suggestion, persuaded her mother to accept a cashmere twinset, and the wool skirt which went so well with it…

Thomas had told her not to expect to hear from him for a day or so, but all the same she was disappointed that there was no word from him. She had to explain this to her mother, who said roundly, 'The poor man. It's time he slowed down. After all, he's a married man now. His work is important, but so is his married life.'

Claudia said cheerfully, 'He loves his work, Mother, but once the cottage is ready we shall be able to spend weekends there, away from his patients.'

She took her mother to the station the following morning and saw her onto the train. Feeling suddenly lonely, Claudia lingered at the station entrance, trying to decide whether she would join the taxi queue or walk home. She could cross the road and go through Hyde Park—quite a long walk, but it would fill in her morning.

She had left the park, crossed Park Lane and was walking along Brook Street when she came face-to-face with Honor.

She summoned a social smile and a hello, and went on walking, but Honor put out a hand so that she was forced to stop.

'Claudia—it is Claudia, isn't it? How delightful to

meet you again. I've been away. I can't stand London at this time of year. I phoned Thomas at his rooms before I left, and he told me that you were very occupied getting ready for Christmas. Such a bore, having to go all that way to the Lakes just for a couple of days.'

'I enjoyed it,' said Claudia. 'Nice to see you again. I really must get on…'

Honor didn't let go of her arm. 'My dear, you can spare half an hour, surely? Let's have a cup of coffee…?'

Against her will, Claudia agreed. Perhaps Honor really was an old friend of Thomas's, in which case she shouldn't be rude—besides, Honor was making herself pleasant.

Over coffee, after a witty account of her holiday in Italy, Honor began asking questions put so casually it was difficult to ignore them.

'Thomas is away?' she asked. 'Off on one of his jaunts?'

'Well, it's not a jaunt. He's in Liverpool, and probably going on to Leeds.'

'Has he taken Emma with him?' Honor gave Claudia a sly glance. 'His secretary goes everywhere with him. A beautiful creature—very efficient and very sexy. Of course, now he's a married man, I expect he's more discreet.'

'I haven't the least idea what you're talking about.'

Honor said quickly, 'Oh, my dear, I'm sorry. I quite thought you knew. After all, it isn't as if you and Thomas are desperately in love—anyone could see with their eyes that neither of you are…' She paused as Claudia got to her feet.

'You're talking rubbish, and spiteful rubbish at that,' said Claudia. 'If making mischief is all you know how to do, I pity you.'

'You're upset,' said Honor. 'Naturally. You don't have to believe me, but if you ring Thomas's rooms I'm quite sure that Emma won't be there.'

'I'll do no such thing,' said Claudia. 'Goodbye, Honor, I hope we don't need to meet again.'

Honor had a parting shot. 'You wouldn't dare find out for yourself.' She laughed. 'But I shouldn't be surprised to hear that Thomas won't be home for a few more days.'

Claudia didn't answer that, but walked out of the elegant café where they had been sitting and then walked all the way home.

This gave her time to remember every word Honor had said, and to assure herself over and over again that nothing would induce her to phone his rooms—a nasty, low-down action not to be contemplated.

She hardly touched the lunch Cork had ready for her; she took Harvey for his afternoon walk, and the moment she got back picked up the phone.

Mrs Truelove answered. After an exchange of pleasantries, she said that, no, Emma wasn't there. 'She doesn't come in when the Professor is on one of his trips. A most efficient girl,' enthused Mrs Truelove, 'quite indispensable.'

Claudia chatted for a few minutes before putting down the phone. Mrs Truelove hadn't asked her why she had rung, and she hoped that she wouldn't wonder about it later. She felt mean and wicked and disloyal, but no more so than Thomas...

'I hate him,' said Claudia to Harvey, and burst into tears. She didn't hate him, she loved him, and what a time to discover it.

Before she'd made that shattering discovery it wouldn't have mattered about Emma—after all, he had never said that he loved her or was likely to do so. Theirs was to be a sensible marriage, wasn't it? So he was free to do what he liked, wasn't he? She knew that he would never be unkind to her, would always be a friend, even be a little fond of her and share at least some of her life, but now, with the discovery that she loved him, that wouldn't do.

This was something they would have to talk about. She would never tell him that she had fallen in love with him, but she would make sure that he wasn't having second thoughts about their marriage. And he would be home the next day.

She had pecked at her dinner and was poking her needle in and out of her tapestry when Thomas phoned. He would be delayed for another day, perhaps two, he told her. 'I'm in Leeds. I'll come home as soon as possible.'

She said, 'Yes, Thomas. Goodnight,' and hung up on him. If she had said more she would have burst into tears.

The next day seemed endless. She filled it with walks and arranging the flowers and trying to eat the delicious little meals Cork had set before her, but by the evening she was restless, and at ten o'clock she decided to go to bed. The day had been long enough, and there was all tomorrow to get through before Thomas got home.

'Bed,' she told Harvey, and started towards the kitchen with him, but in the hall he stopped and rushed to the door, barking furiously, and a moment later Thomas came in.

He closed the door gently behind him, bent to fondle Harvey and looked at Claudia, standing speechless. She had rehearsed all the things she was going to say to him but she couldn't remember a word of them. She said, 'Hello,' and then, 'You said you'd be home tomorrow.'

'I'm home today because something's wrong, isn't it? You were upset when I phoned last night.'

He was taking off his coat as he spoke, and Cork, coming into the hall, greeted him with grave pleasure, took the coat, enquired if he would like a meal or drinks and then went away, taking Harvey with him.

'Cut the air with a knife, I could,' Cork told the little dog. 'What's up, I'd like to know. Well, we'll have to leave them to it, won't we? And hope it comes out in the wash.'

Harvey, accepting a biscuit, wagged his ridiculous tail.

Claudia found her voice. 'Would you like a meal, or something to drink?'

Thomas smiled briefly. 'Cork just asked me. You couldn't have been listening. And, no, I don't need anything. What I do need is to know why you sounded as you did last evening?'

Claudia, playing for time, asked, 'How did I sound?'

'Don't waste time, Claudia. You were upset, angry— too angry to speak to me. Why?'

He took her by the arm, marched her into the drawing room and shut the door. 'Let us sit down...'

He sounded friendly, and reassuringly calm, and she longed to fling herself at him, feel his arms around her, but first she must know about this secretary of his. She wouldn't mention Honor, for he might dismiss her as a malicious gossip bent on making mischief, and perhaps she was, but Mrs Truelove was quite another kettle of fish.

'Where do you go when you aren't at a hospital? I mean, do you have friends or stay at a hotel—in the evenings when you're free.'

If she had been looking at him she would have seen the sudden stern set of his mouth and his cool stare, but she wasn't, so she plunged on, getting muddled and resenting his calm silence. 'Don't you meet people you know? Or—or have a meal out, or something?'

She did look up then, and sat up straight at the sight of his cold anger.

He said in a quiet, icy voice, 'Are you accusing me of something, Claudia? Perhaps you should be more explicit.'

She had gone too far now to stop. Besides, she had to know... She steeled herself to look at his expressionless face. 'Your secretary, Emma—she wasn't at your rooms. Mrs Truelove said that she was never there when you were away...'

Mr Tait-Bullen crossed one long leg over the other. He said mildly, 'You wish to know where she was for some reason?'

'Yes, well, I think you should have been honest about it. I know it doesn't matter, because we...we don't love each other, but I am your wife.'

'Let me get this quite clear. You have been told by

someone that when I go away Emma goes with me, so when I'm not working we can—er—live it up together.'

He spoke quietly, but Claudia flinched at the contempt in his voice. 'And who told you this?' He smiled thinly. 'I'll give you credit for not imagining it for yourself.'

'Of course I didn't imagine it,' said Claudia hotly. 'It never entered my head. I met Honor…'

'And you believed her?'

She peeped at his face. He was in a splendid rage, but he was controlling it with an iron will. She said recklessly now, knowing that she had cooked her goose with a vengeance, 'Not quite. I tried not to think about what she had said, but she told me Emma wasn't at your rooms—she laughed and said I didn't dare to find out for myself… So I did. I phoned Mrs Truelove and she told me that Emma wasn't there.'

'I see.' He got to his feet. 'Our marriage may not be quite as other marriages, Claudia, but I thought that we shared a mutual trust, and I hoped that our liking might have turned into something deeper in time. It seems as if I was wrong. This is something which must be put right as soon as possible. If you are unhappy, and I think you are, you must make up your mind what you want to do. Take your time, and we'll talk again later.'

He walked to the door. 'And now I must do some work. Goodnight, Claudia.'

She said in a squeaky voice, 'Thomas, are you very angry?'

He smiled then. 'Yes, my dear.' It was a bitter smile. She heard him whistle to Harvey and then shut his study door, and she went up to her room, reflecting that he still hadn't told her if Emma had been with him.

The night seemed endless, and by the end of it she hadn't had a single sensible thought. She would never be able to tell Thomas that she loved him now. Not that she would have done, she contradicted herself, but they would have made something of their marriage, because loving him, even secretly, would have made it worthwhile. Something would have to be done, but she had no idea what.

She went down to breakfast, her pale face carefully made-up. It didn't conceal her puffy eyelids or her pinkened nose, and Thomas, bidding her good morning in his usual voice, had difficulty in restraining himself from picking her out of her chair and carrying her off somewhere quiet, where he could tell her how much he loved her. But of course that wasn't possible; she had demonstrated only too clearly last night that her feeling for him wasn't strong enough to overcome her doubts.

He said in his usual calm way, 'I shall be away all day. Could dinner be a little later? I've a meeting at the hospital, and I'm not sure how long it may last.'

He finished his breakfast, wished her a pleasant day and went away, leaving her to feed Harvey with her neglected toast.

She was trying to decide what to do when the phone rang, and she went to answer it.

'Mrs Tait-Bullen? This is Emma, the Professor's secretary. Mrs Truelove told me that you had asked for me. I'm sorry I wasn't here. When the Professor goes away he allows me to go home—I live in Norfolk—at least, my parents do. I'm getting married in the summer, and there's such a lot of planning to do. Was there something I could do for you?'

Claudia, astonished at herself, heard her own voice saying the first thing which came into her head. 'Emma, how nice of you to phone. I just wondered if you had any ideas about a wedding present? I've seen some lovely china… The Professor says I should make it a surprise, but perhaps there's something you would like to choose? A dinner set, or something for the house? Will you think about it and let me know?'

She rang off presently, Emma's thanks ringing in her ears. But she forgot that immediately. What a fool she had been; with her stupid outburst yesterday evening she had destroyed any chance of Thomas ever falling in love with her. He must despise her. They would have to go on living together, outwardly friendly, while she ate her heart out for him, and he would treat her with a distant courtesy which would chill her to the bone.

She suddenly couldn't bear it any longer. Thomas would be at his consulting rooms until ten o'clock; she picked up the phone and dialled.

Mrs Truelove answered her. The Professor had just seen a patient. If Mrs Tait-Bullen would wait a second, she would get him to come to the phone before she ushered in the next one. She came back to the phone very quickly.

'I'm so sorry, the Professor asked me to say that he is unable to talk to you at the moment. I was also to tell you that he would be late home this evening and that you weren't to wait up for him.'

The dear soul sounded worried, and Claudia hastened to say that it wasn't important and that she had expected him not to be home early. 'It was nothing important,' she added, 'really, it wasn't.' As though repeating it would convince her, as well as Mrs Truelove.

Her normal common sense had been taken over by a kind of recklessness. To stay quietly at home waiting for his return and then probably be met by his cold stare and refusal to talk was impossible. She swept upstairs, changed into a tweed skirt, a sweater and the leather jacket, pulled on boots, found scarf, gloves and a handbag and went in search of Cork.

'I'd like to go for a drive in the Mini,' she told him. 'Would you fetch it round from the garage for me, Cork, while I take Harvey for a quick walk?'

Cork put down the silver he was polishing. The Mini lived in the garage in the mews behind the house, for his use and as a second car if it was needed. It was kept in good order, ready for the road at a moment's notice, and there was no reason why Claudia shouldn't drive it. All the same, he felt doubtful.

'I could drive you, madam. The traffic's very heavy...'

'I've been driving for years,' Claudia told him, which wasn't true; she had used Great-Uncle William's old car from time to time, driving him to friends, before he took to his bed, and her mother to the nearest supermarket, but now fright and rage and bitter unhappiness had made her pot valiant. 'I won't take Harvey. I've had a message to say that the Professor won't be back until very late this evening, so something on a tray will suit me. I'll be out to lunch.'

She fastened Harvey's lead, gave Cork a reassuring smile and went for a brisk walk, going over in her mind the route she must take to get her onto the motorway. It was still early, and the morning rush was at its height, but it was coming into the city; traffic going out of it would be much lighter.

When she got back Cork had the Mini at the door. He was still uneasy, but he received Harvey, begged her to take care as she drove away and went indoors. He wasn't a man to say much, but he voiced his doubts to Mrs Rumbold.

'Don't you worry, Mr Cork,' said that lady comfortably. 'You just said she'd had a message about him not being home early. Like as not she told him where she was going.'

Cork took comfort from that. At least Claudia had looked confident as she had driven away.

She might have looked confident, but several times during the next hour she wished herself anywhere but behind the wheel of the Mini. She was a good driver, but London traffic was something she hadn't had to deal with, and it was daunting. Only the despairing urge to get away from Thomas as far as possible kept her going.

She followed the route Thomas had taken, driving steadily, thankful at last to turn into the country roads from the motorway. It was after midday when she turned the little car from Child Okeford's main street and down the lane to Christmas Cottage.

The dry morning had clouded over, and it was drizzling. The cottage looked forlorn, although she could hear voices from within. She got out of the car and opened the front door.

There were several men working there and she

stood, forgetful of her worries for a moment, marvelling at the amount of work which had been done. The walls were plastered and the woodwork painted, and two men were laying an oak floor in the sitting room.

She wished them good afternoon, told them who she was and asked if she would be in the way if she looked round.

No one minded, and one of the men led her from room to room, pointing out what had been done and what was still needed.

The plumbing was done, he pointed out, but none of the bathroom fitments had arrived yet. 'Nor yet the stuff your husband ordered for the kitchen.'

'You've been so quick...'

'Well, seeing as how there's not much work around at this time of year, and us being paid on the nail, we got started right away. Staying in the village, are you, missus?'

She crossed her fingers and fibbed. 'No, I just came down to have a look on the way to visit my mother. I expect my husband and I will be coming down at the weekend if he's free.'

'Busy man, isn't he? The house agent told us he is a famous doctor.'

'Yes, he is.' She couldn't bear to think of Thomas. 'Look, I'm going to the pub for lunch, and then I want to look round the village. What time do you go?'

'We'll pack up as soon as the flooring's down— can't do much outside with this rain. About three o'clock, I should say.'

'Well, if I'm not back before you go, thank you for letting me see round. I've a key, but you'll lock up, won't you? The car won't be in the way if I leave it there? I'd like to have a walk.'

'Right you are, missus.'

They parted the best of friends, and Claudia went back to the village main street and went into the pub. It was almost two o'clock, but the landlord found coffee and sandwiches for her and, when she told him who she was, came and sat at the table while she ate, giving her a friendly insight into the village and the people who lived there. By the time she had finished her leisurely meal it was already dusk, and almost three o'clock.

She made her way back to the cottage and found the men loading their van, ready to leave. It was obvious they expected her to leave, too, so she got into the Mini, reversed it into the lane so that the van could pass and waved them on. She stayed where she was, though, until they had been gone for a few minutes, then drove back and parked the car at the side of the cottage, found the key and went in.

The electricity had been turned on, but there was only one naked bulb in the kitchen. Someone had left an old wooden chair there and she sat down. Her sudden spurt of recklessness had worn itself out. She had been a fool to come, but she had wanted to see the place where she had hoped that they were going to be happy. She hadn't thought beyond that. 'I'll sit here for a bit,' she said out loud, 'and presently I'll drive back. Perhaps Thomas will let me explain.'

Mr Tait-Bullen saw the last of his private patients out, got into his car and went to the hospital, where he had a clinic and ward round waiting for him. He would be finished by teatime, and then he would go home and he and Claudia could talk. There was a great deal to be talked about. Their sensible marriage wasn't working out; after only a few short weeks she had let him see that she didn't trust him. All the same, he was going to tell her that he loved her...

The ward round went smoothly, and the clinic wasn't quite as busy as usual. He saw his new patients, giving them his meticulous attention, and then, waiting for the first of his old patients, he phoned Cork.

'Is Mrs Tait-Bullen home, Cork?'

'Sir—a good thing you called. I was getting that worried. She took the Mini early this morning, and said she wouldn't be back for lunch. Didn't say where she was going.'

'Took the Mini? Did she seem upset, Cork?'

'Worked up, as it were, sir. Left Harvey with me, said you wouldn't be home until late, and that she'd have something on a tray.'

'I see, Cork. I'll be home as soon as I can. She may have decided to go and see her mother. Phone Mrs Willis, will you, and find out? Don't ring me here as I shall leave as soon as I can.'

He put the phone down, deliberately dismissing Claudia from his mind while he looked through the patients' notes to see if there was anyone whom he should see. There wasn't; he could safely leave them to the registrar.

It was too early for the evening rush hour, and he took shortcuts.

Cork was hovering in the hall when he went in, and

said at once, 'She's not at Mrs Willis's. I shouldn't have let her go.'

Thomas gave him a reassuring pat on the shoulder. 'Nonsense, Cork. You weren't to know that she would be gone for so long. Besides, I think I know where she is.'

Cork brightened. 'You do, sir? I'll get your tea...'

'Later, Cork. I'll bring her back in the car. The Mini can be fetched later.'

Mr Tait-Bullen drove out of London a good deal faster than Claudia had done, and once on the motorway put his large, well-shod foot down, sliding past traffic, a sleek, dark shadow, there one minute, miles away the next. He had taken time to go to Claudia's room before he left the house, and had seen with satisfaction that she had taken no clothes with her. Indeed, all the usual things a girl would put carefully into her handbag before a day out were strewn on the dressing table. Her driving licence was there, too. He had smiled when he saw it. His Claudia had left the house without her usual common sense.

He was forced to slow down once he left the motorway; all the same he made the journey in record time. He slid the car slowly up the lane and its lights showed him the Mini. He turned off his own lights and got out of the car, and saw the faint glow of light from the kitchen. He had brought Harvey with him; now he tucked the little beast under one arm, one hand over his muzzle to muffle his bark, and went into the house.

Claudia was still on the wooden chair. She was sitting very untidily and she was fast asleep, her head at an awkward angle. She would be stiff and cramped when she woke.

He stood looking at her, loving her very much, and Harvey, suddenly realising who it was sitting there, gave a small, pleased yelp. Claudia opened her eyes.

She stared up at Thomas for a few moments, eased her stiff neck away from the chair and said in a wondering voice, 'Thomas, dear Thomas. I thought I'd never see you again.'

He put Harvey down then, and stooped and swept her into his arms. He was tired, and he had been very worried, but now that didn't matter. He said slowly, 'You said "dear Thomas"…'

'Well, you are. Only I didn't know, and now it's all such an awful muddle…'

'No, it's not, my darling. You see, I love you. I've loved you for quite a while now. Just when I have despaired of you ever loving me, you called me dear Thomas.'

'Oh, you are, you are. I must have been blind or something. I think I've loved you for a long time, too, only we both thought the other one didn't, didn't we?'

Mr Tait-Bullen listened to this muddled speech with delight. 'Dear love, you couldn't have put it more clearly.'

He bent and kissed her in a way which proved how right she was. 'Were you running away?' he asked, and bent to kiss her again. 'Because if you try to do so again, remember to take your driving licence with you.'

'I'll never do it again, Thomas. Thomas, you do love me? Really love me?'

'My dearest love, I would not wish to live without you.'

Claudia kissed him. 'We have the rest of our lives together,' she said, 'and we'll come here whenever we can, won't we? And be happy together—with Harvey, of course.'

'And a handful of sons and daughters, my darling. Harvey will need young company...'

'He has us.'

'Yes, and I have you, too, Claudia.'

She peered up into his face. The bland calm wasn't there anymore; she saw the man she loved, the man who had been there all the time.

'We're going home now,' said Mr Tait-Bullen.

* * * * *

SPECIAL EXCERPT FROM

HARLEQUIN®

SPECIAL EDITION

Stricken with temporary amnesia, Maddie Wolfe can't remember a single thing about her life...or her husband, Sawyer. But even with electricity crackling between them, it turns out their fairy tale was careening toward disaster. Will a little Christmas spirit help Maddie find her memories—and the Wolfes find the spark again?

Read on for a sneak preview of
A Wyoming Christmas to Remember
by Melissa Senate,
the next book in the Wyoming Multiples miniseries.

"Three weeks?" she repeated. "I might not remember anything about myself for three weeks?"

Dr. Addison gave her a reassuring smile. "Could be sooner. But we'll run some tests, and based on how well you're doing now, I don't see any reason why you can't be discharged later today."

Discharged where? Where did she live?

With your husband, she reminded herself.

She bolted upright again, her gaze moving to Sawyer, who pocketed his phone and came back over, sitting down and taking her hand in both of his. "Do I—do we—have children?" she asked him. She couldn't forget her own children. She couldn't.

"No," he said, glancing away for a moment. "Your parents and Jenna will be here in fifteen minutes," he said. "They're ecstatic you're awake. I let them know you might not remember them straightaway."

"Jenna?" she asked.

"Your twin sister. You're very close. To your parents, too. Your family is incredible—very warm and loving."

That was good.

She took a deep breath and looked at her hand in his. Her left hand. She wasn't wearing a wedding ring. He wore one, though—a gold band. So where was hers?

"Why aren't I wearing a wedding ring?" she asked.

His expression changed on a dime. He looked at her, then down at his feet. Dark brown cowboy boots.

Uh-oh, she thought. *He doesn't want to tell me. What is that about?*

Two orderlies came in just then, and Dr. Addison let Maddie know it was time for her CT scan, and that by the time she was done, her family would probably be here.

"I'll be waiting right here," Sawyer said, gently cupping his hand to her cheek.

As the orderlies wheeled her toward the door, she realized she missed Sawyer—looking at him, talking to him, her hand in his, his hand on her face. That had to be a good sign, right?

Even if she wasn't wearing her ring.

Don't miss
A Wyoming Christmas to Remember
by Melissa Senate,
available November 2019 wherever
Harlequin® *Special Edition books and ebooks are sold.*

www.Harlequin.com

Christmastime brings a single mom and her baby back home, but reconnecting with her high school sweetheart, now a wounded veteran, puts her darkest secret at risk.

Read on for a sneak preview of
The Secret Christmas Child *by Lee Tobin McClain, the first book in her new Rescue Haven miniseries.*

He reached out a hand, meaning to shake hers, but she grasped his and held it. Looked into his eyes. "Reese, I'm sorry about what happened before."

He narrowed his eyes and frowned at her. "You mean…after I went into the service?"

She nodded and swallowed hard. "Something happened, and I couldn't…I couldn't keep the promise I made."

That something being another guy, Izzy's father. He drew in a breath. Was he going to hold on to his grudge, or his hurt feelings, about what had happened?

Looking into her eyes, he breathed out the last of his anger. Like Corbin had said, everyone was a sinner. "It's understood."

"Thank you," she said simply. She held his gaze for another moment and then looked down and away.

She was still holding on to his hand, and slowly, he twisted and opened his hand until their palms were flat together. Pressed between them as close as he'd like to be pressed to Gabby.

The only light in the room came from the kitchen and

the dying fire. Outside the windows, snow had started to fall, blanketing the little house in solitude.

This night with her family had been one of the best he'd had in a long time. Made him realize how much he missed having a family.

Gabby's hand against his felt small and delicate, but he knew better. He slipped his own hand to the side and captured hers, tracing his thumb along the calluses.

He heard her breath hitch and looked quickly at her face. Her eyes were wide, her lips parted and moist.

Without looking away, acting on impulse, he slowly lifted her hand to his lips and kissed each fingertip.

Her breath hitched and came faster, and his sense of himself as a man, a man who could have an effect on a woman, swelled, almost making him giddy.

This was Gabby, and the truth burst inside him: he'd never gotten over her, never stopped wishing they could be together, that they could make that family they'd dreamed of as kids. That was why he'd gotten so angry when she'd strayed: because the dream she'd shattered had been so big, so bright and shining.

In the back of his mind, a voice of caution scolded and warned. She'd gone out with his cousin. She'd had a child with another man. What had been so major in his emotional life hadn't been so big in hers.

He shouldn't trust her. And he definitely shouldn't kiss her.

But when had he ever done what he should?

Don't miss
The Secret Christmas Child *by Lee Tobin McClain,*
available December 2019 wherever
Love Inspired® books and ebooks are sold.

Love Harlequin romance?

DISCOVER.

Be the first to find out about promotions, news and exclusive content!

Facebook.com/HarlequinBooks

Twitter.com/HarlequinBooks

Instagram.com/HarlequinBooks

Pinterest.com/HarlequinBooks

ReaderService.com

EXPLORE.

Sign up for the Harlequin e-newsletter and download a free book from any series at **TryHarlequin.com.**

CONNECT.

Join our Harlequin community to share your thoughts and connect with other romance readers!
Facebook.com/groups/HarlequinConnection

ROMANCE WHEN YOU NEED IT

HSOCIAL2018